KT McCaffrey

is a native of Clara, County Offaly, Ireland. Apart from being an author, he is also a highly respected graphic designer. He set up his own studio in 1982 and has since become a major freelance artist specialising in website design and computer graphics. By 1989 he was illustrating children's books based on Irish folklore, which sparked his interest in writing.

KT McCaffrey's three previous crime mysteries – also featuring investigative journalist, Emma Boylan – were only published in Ireland, but established him as a major voice in contemporary crime fiction.

End of the Line

a novel by

KT McCaffrey

First Published in Great Britain in 2003 by
The Do-Not Press Limited
16 The Woodlands
London SE13 6TY
www.thedonotpress.co.uk
email: EOTL@thedonotpress.co.uk

B-format paperback: ISBN 1 904 316 19 0
Casebound edition: ISBN 1 904 316 16 6

British Library Cataloguing in Publication Data. A catalogue
record for this book is available from the British Library.

1 3 5 7 9 10 8 6 4 2

For Ethel and Alex Pinkerton

24th February, 1943

35 Girls Die In School Fire

35 girls from the Industrial School and orphanage in Cavan town were burnt to death after a fire swept through their dormitories. One adult also died in the blaze. The school was attached to the convent of the Poor Claires.

Author's Note

I have long been interested in the incident described above, wondering how such an appalling tragedy could have been allowed to happen. I have spoken to a number of direct descendants of the children involved and have drawn inspiration from their legacy while recreating an analogous fictional account of the events. In my scenario, the contents of a diary written by one of the fire's survivors is the catalyst for the compelling tale of crime, passion and betrayal that follows. For *End of the Line*, I have brought forward the timeline by nineteen years and woven the event into the diary of Nelly Joyce.

Yet each man kills the thing he loves,
By each let this be heard,
Some do it with a bitter look,
Some with a flattering word,
The coward does it with a kiss,
The brave man with a sword!

Oscar Wilde
The Ballad of Reading Gaol

Chapter 1

Freed from the dual slip-leash, two hounds bound forward. With amazing acceleration they reach maximum speed by their third stride. Ahead of them, a hare bobs up and down, its buff coat, white belly and under-tail scurrying above the uneven grassland. Running for its life, the terrified animal must outwit the greyhounds if it hopes to reach the escape zone at the top end of the open field.

It's an uneven contest.

Soaring in leaps and bounds, moving at 40 miles per hour, the hounds will close in on the hare before it makes the final quarter of the coursing field.

Ted Harris sits atop a chestnut stallion, watching proceedings. Away from the comforts of his bank manager's office, he appears little bothered by the February chill. A devotee to wildlife sport and coursing in particular, he will decide which greyhound advances to the next round. As judge, he is looking for the hound with the greater ability to negotiate sharp turns, the hound capable of forcing the hare to change direction most frequently. Donned in hunting livery, Harris seldom moves faster than a trot. He is aware that it has been a bad morning for the organisers of the meeting.

With just two stakes completed, each consisting of sixteen dogs, two hares have already failed to reach the safety zone. Others will meet a similar fate before the day is through. Dead hares spell trouble. A situation guaranteed to enrage the noisy band of animal-rights activists present. They have come to protest. For the moment they remain corralled by the security stewards at the entrance to the grounds, but previous experience has taught him just how volatile a lot they are. Concern shows on his face. He wants to ignore their threat, to focus instead on the contest.

Carnival Princess, a brindled bitch, wearing a red collar, leads the chase. With a superior burst of speed to that of her rival, Little Mac, she is first to close in on their furry quarry.

A hissing sound from the crowd urges the animals forward.

Punters, with betting slips in hand, seem unconcerned for the smaller animal's fate; their concentration resolutely focused on the dogs' progress.

'Come on the red collar,' they shout.

'Come on the white.'

Carnival Princess snaps at the fleeing hind legs. The hare swerves at an acute angle, escapes, but then veers into the path of the white-collared Little Mac. It must now negotiate another lightning-fast swerve. The retreating hare feels Little Mac's hot breath, but manages narrowly to avoid the lethal fangs.

Carnival Princess overshoots the duel after missing its chance on the first turn.

The crowd gasp. They think the dog has lost sight of the hare. They are wrong. Carnival Princess is experienced in the art of coursing. She knows the hare is about to swerve into her path.

Unwittingly, the hare obliges.

Carnival Princess snaps her incisors, vice-like on the back of the hare's neck. In an instant, Little Mac, now up with the action, sinks his fangs into the doomed animal's hindquarters. A deadly tug-of-war ensues. The dogs pull in opposite directions, their blood-splattered teeth clamping down hard until the hare's puny bones are crushed between their jaws. In a frenzy of triumph, the dogs toss their heads back and forth, pulling, tearing, wrenching flesh from the screaming animal, ripping it asunder, limb from limb. Ear-piercing wails of terror split the air.

Ted Harris observes the action from his vantage point. He signals to the course stewards to prise the dogs away from the kill.

The crowd is momentarily silenced.

To divert attention, Harris flags the red-collar dog, Carnival Princess, as the winner. But spectators have become agitated by the prolonged death struggle. Voices cry out to the stewards:

'Hurry! Hurry! For Christ's sake, hurry!'

'Get the dogs off! Quickly!'

'Kill the hare.'

'Stop it screaming!'

A man with a camcorder breaks from the crowd, dashes on to the field. Ted Harris spots the activity. His worst fears realised. A blood-sports protester to contend with. He tugs at the reins, urges his mount towards the interloper. Before the cameraman can get close enough to film the hare's death struggle, he is struck a glancing blow by the stallion. Thrown to the ground, his camcorder soars into the air. The crowd gasp as they watch the incident unfold, their eyes following the camcorder's acute trajectory as it comes crashing back to earth.

In response to frantic signals from Harris, a steward rushes to where the sprawled man lies, picks up the camcorder and removes the cassette. He smiles triumphantly as he tosses the camera back to the ground. The stricken man has a bloodied face but appears not to have suffered unduly. His vocal chords are certainly not affected. 'Bastards, killers, cruel bastards, the lot of you,' he shouts angrily. 'I'll have you for assault.'

While this action unfolds, several stewards manage clumsily to put the hare out of its misery and bring the dogs under control.

The crowd applauds.

The stewards now surround the protester. Efficiently, they lift him to his feet, thrust the camcorder into his hands and drag him forcibly from the field.

More applause and jeers come from the crowd.

Judge Ted Harris's face is flushed, crimson as his hunting coat. He is angry that the incident should have happened but pleased with how it has been handled. He tugs on the reins to encourage his mount to canter away from the spot of conflict and signals that the coursing can continue.

A murmur of approval from the crowd greets the decision.

Punters who have backed Carnival Princess push their way to the on-course bookies to collect their winnings. Ten minutes later, two fresh dogs struggle to break free. Another hare scurries on to the field.

Talk in the hospitality tent centres around the outcome of the different chases. The merits and demerits of every dog is discussed, dissected, and argued over. Less vocal are the mutterings about the number of hares killed or the effectiveness of the animal-rights activists' protest. Lonsdale's bank manager-cum-judge-for-the-day is praised for his handling of events. One young man, with a glass of lager in his hand, stands on his own by the makeshift bar counter unobtrusively inspecting those around him. Every so often he tosses back strands of toffee-coloured hair from his eyes with a jerk of his head. He pretends to sip his drink. Three people sitting at the table nearest to him are of particular interest. They are the ones he has come to the coursing meeting to observe. He already knows quite a lot about them but this is his first time to encounter them at such close proximity.

The one in clerical garb is parish priest, Fr Jack O'Gorman, owner of Carnival Princess. He is deep in conversation with the dog's trainer, Thelma Duggan. He compliments her for having done such a fine job with the dog. In response, she makes a series of little pouting expressions with her lips, giving the impression that a little too much drink has been consumed.

From research carried out, the observer knows that Fr O'Gorman is fifty-seven years of age. Yet, to him, the priest looks a decade younger. The full head of corn-coloured hair helps. The priest's face has weathered the ageing process particularly well. It retains some of that pink, scrubbed quality one associates with infants.

Sitting next to the cleric and his trainer, Tom Moran is busy studying a coursing card. Moran is a handsome, dapper man in his mid-fifties, employed by Fr O'Gorman as sacristan in St John the Baptist Church. Today, Moran acts as the priest's driver, a necessity that's come about because the law saw fit to revoke O'Gorman's driving licence six months earlier. The priest had been caught driving while under the influence of alcohol. Moran enjoys his role of chauffeur and treats it as a welcome diversion from the work at the church.

Thelma Duggan, the third person under the gaze of the observer, lolls back on a seat between the two men, glass of brandy in hand. Pushing perilously close to the big 5-0 age bracket, she wears a sheepskin jacket, leather slacks and boots; obligatory apparel for trainers it would appear, given that most of the other owners and trainers are attired in similar fashion. The woman has a good face, large expressive eyes, stylish auburn hair and a body that has all but lost its battle with the bulge.

The young man decides to make his presence felt. He places his glass on the counter and pushes into the seat beside the three subjects he's been scrutinising. 'There'll be trouble over that fellow who was knocked to the ground by the geezer on the horse,' he says, looking at them for reaction. Fr O'Gorman ignores him, his face a mask of stony impassivity. Thelma Duggan's body language suggests a similar disposition. But Tom Moran nods at him. 'You could be right there, son,' he admits.

'Damn right, I'm right,' the man insists.

Moran nods. 'T'was unfortunate.'

'Unfortunate? No, it was deliberate.'

'Ted Harris could be in trouble right enough,' Moran replies with little enthusiasm, sorry now to have embarked on the conversation. Out of habit, the chauffeur-for-the-day looks to his boss. 'What d'you think, Father?'

'Harris was right,' the priest replies, annoyed at being dragged into the discourse. 'If the man who ran on to the field is dumb enough to bring charges against Harris, he'll be sent packing quick enough.'

'Oh? You think so? You're right of course,' Moran replies, attempting to get back on-side with his employer. The parish priest glares at him.

Thelma Duggan comes to Moran's rescue. 'Ted Harris is respected as Lonsdale's bank manager; he will say that the man with the camera spooked his horse and got accidentally knocked down by the startled animal.'

The young man tosses back unruly blond hair from his eyes and stares wildly at Thelma. 'But that's not what happened... you saw it.'

'That, my friend, is exactly what happened,' Fr O'Gorman proclaims, 'and there'll be—'

'No, what happened was—' the man tries to cut in.

'—and,' Fr O'Gorman continues, dismissing the interruption with a wrist flick, 'there'll be a few hundred witnesses willing and eager to swear, on the Bible if necessary, that Harris's account of events is accurate.'

Hostility blazes in the man's eyes. 'You're bloody hypocrites, all of you. You're nothing but a bunch of sanctimonious charlatans,' he says, getting to his feet and moving back to his spot by the counter.

He picks up his lager again, smiles to himself and watches as the priest and his companions head for the tent's exit. Punters around him, engrossed in highly animated affability, greedily guzzling booze, pay scant attention to him or to what's just happened. He thinks about the three people who have vacated the tent and the verbal exchange he's just had with them. That they should hold the animal-rights activist in such low regard does not surprise him. Neither does it come as any great shock to discover that the welfare of the unfortunate hares matters so little to them. This thought makes him wonder what store, if any, they hold for human life? Same as the animals? Less? More? Should be interesting to find out. He has plans set in motion to ensure they face such a prospect. Soon, very soon, he'll have his answer. He is not like them. He is different. He's incapable of killing a harmless, defenceless animal. But he has no qualms about having humans put down, especially ones who watch the destruction and death of small animals and remain unmoved by the sickening spectacle.

Before handing over Carnival Princess for the third and penultimate round, Thelma Duggan quaffed a mouthful of brandy from her pocket flask. The mellow nectar allowed her thoughts to jump ahead to events planned for two days' time: the marriage of her daughter, Yvonne.

For the past two months it had been the main topic of conversation in the house. All appropriate arrangements were in place, every last detail accounted for, and yet there had been a family row that very morning. George, her husband, joined Yvonne, in ganging up on her. They didn't want her to attend the coursing today, accusing her of putting her dogs ahead of them, giving the coursing priority over the wedding. After exhaustive argument, the nub of the problem became evident. It wasn't so much the greyhounds that her husband and daughter resented; it was all to do with her involvement with Fr Jack O'Gorman.

Chapter 2

vinner in the category – *Best Press Investigative*
the Year – goes to…'

ant hush stills the audience.

gan, TV news reporter, pauses for a second while
envelope. His fingers move with the dexterity of a
he extracts a gilt-edged card. Adjusting his reading
ams his practised television smile for the benefit of

again…

er is… *Post* reporter, Ms Emma Boylan.'

applause greets the announcement. Heads in the
ain to catch sight of the recipient. They watch her
es, hugs and congratulations of those beside her –
her mother and father – before approaching the
cknowledges the good wishes with a radiant smile.
lently, she makes her way up the three steps to the
pts her award – a hand-cut crystal ink jar and silver
move in for close-up shots as she stands at the
nounce the customary words of thanks.

lare of television lights, her tan-coloured trouser suit
wn hair absorbs the unforgiving illumination, trans-
tures of her face to an almost translucent delicacy. As
on television programmes, Emma knows the devas-
dio lights can inflict on anyone foolish enough to
make-up or clothes in front of the cameras.

the darkened auditorium, she picks out the spot
and Vinny Bailey sits. Her words are pitched to
the award, with far more reverence than it
oices her appreciation to the sponsors and the
he award ceremony before allowing her more
s to dictate what she is saying.

'People are talking about the two of you,' Yvonne said,
'always in each other's company, going to coursing meetings
together, seen at the track week in, week out.'

'Nonsense. Your father and I have been friends with Fr Jack
since before you were born,' she told Yvonne. 'If the people have
nothing better to do than gossip and snigger about how decent
folk lead their lives, then they can go hump off with themselves.'

Too much to hope for support from George. As usual, he
sided with Yvonne. 'Damn-it-to-hell, Thelma, people *are* talking,
spreading rumours. I mean, shit, Thelma, you know what people
are like. Only natural they'll make assumptions.'

'So what?'

'Jesus, Thelma, how do you think it looks to them when, two
days before your daughter's wedding, you shag off to a coursing?'

The starter's whistle brought her thoughts back to the present.
Another chase had begun.

A hare bound forward, moving swiftly up the field. It had travelled about two hundred yards when the dogs were released.
Carnival Princess charged ahead like a dog possessed. Three-
quarters of the way up the course she closed in on her prey. Twice,
in quick succession, the hare was forced to execute acute turns in
order to escape. However, it soon became evident that the smaller
animal had the measure of its pursuers. Time after time, as the
dogs moved in for the kill, the hare managed to swerve and weave
its way out of danger. Thelma could tell that the hare would make
good its escape, but in doing so it would exhaust the two hounds.

After a gruelling encounter, Judge Ted Harris awarded the
round to Carnival Princess but one look at the dog let Thelma
know their coursing was over for the day. Examination of the
dog's feet revealed cuts and peeled pads. Withdrawing from
competing was upsetting but that was how things went sometimes in coursing.

The coursing was well and truly over by the time Fr O'Gorman
and Tom Moran made their way out of the hospitality tent.
Outside, it had become dark and cold, the temperature hovering
just above the freezing mark. Leaving only a handful of revellers
behind, they braced themselves against the chill and headed to

where they had parked the car that morning. Apart from the yelping of a few greyhounds awaiting the return of their owners, the evening was quiet. Above them, a ghostly moon rode pale and remote through scudding clouds. A few dozen cars, temporarily marooned by their drivers, brooded silently in the semi-darkness.

Strapping himself into the passenger's seat, O'Gorman closed his eyes, gave vent to the turmoil clogging up his mind. Tom Moran gently nudged his arm with his elbow. 'Going to take the scenic route back through the city suburbs,' he said. 'Less traffic at night, no cops, no breathalysers. We'd be rightly had if both of us got disqualified.'

O'Gorman made no reply. He was asleep.

Moran had driven less than two miles along a narrow stretch of road when two red lights and a bulky shape seemed to materialise out of nowhere on the road ahead of him. He applied the brakes, slowed down, and peered through the windscreen. Had to be careful on minor roads, especially at night. He'd travelled this road before some years earlier during daylight hours and remembered crossing a one-lane viaduct. Everything looked a lot different at night. The tail-lights ahead of him, glowing like two red eyes in the netherworld of darkness, grew larger and more distinct as he closed in on them. It was now possible to recognise the bulky shape as that of a low-loader truck with bulldozer on board. He flashed his main beams to alert the driver of his presence, an act that failed to elicit any kind of response. He would not be able to pass the heavy load until it cleared the viaduct on the other side.

As Moran prepared to shift to a lower gear, a blast of bright light came from behind him. The glare in his rear-view mirror forced him to squint. A mountainous shape was bearing down on him like an advancing avalanche. What the hell was it? A truck? A bus? Couldn't be sure. His senses went on alert. Something was wrong. The low-loader stalled halfway across the arches, forcing him to brake. In the passenger's seat, Fr O'Gorman felt the abrupt halt, awoke from his snooze and glanced around him. 'What's up, Tom, icy patch or what?'

'It's not ice… blasted low-loader has broken down. I think—'

Moran never finished the se[ntence]
watched the truck plough int[o]
lifted the car off the road an[d]
low-loader. His screams were
Propelled broadside, the car c
Coca-Cola can. In the blink
watched as the windscreen
spider's web before complete
glass spearheads scarred thei[r]
lacerations. Through bloodie
space where the passenger wi
mouth gaped in a silent screa
for an instant in the hellish c
engine screeched to a deafen
thundered once more into th

Fr Jack O'Gorman was a
through the viaduct's railin
somersaulted twice before e
fifty feet below.

…And the
Journalist o[f]
An expe[ct]
Jim Finn
opening the
magician as
glasses, he b
the camera.
He speak
'The win
Prolonge
auditorium s
enjoy the kis
her husband,
stage. Emma
Striding conf
stage and acc
pen. Camera
podium to pr
Under the
and golden-br
forming the fe
a frequent gues
tating effect st
wear the wron
Peering int
where her hus
him. Clutchi
deserved, she
organisers of
personal feelin

'—and it is especially gratifying to receive this award in view of the difficulties and sad times my husband, my family and I have experienced in the past year.' This reference, as most of the media personnel in the audience already know, refers to her recent miscarriage, an event precipitated by her pursuance of a particularly difficult case she had been investigating at the time. 'Without the love and understanding of my husband and my family I could not have returned to the world of investigative journalism.'

Spontaneous applause greets this sentiment.

'With them in mind; my wonderful editor at the *Post*, Bob Crosby, and of course my readers, I am proud to accept this beautiful trophy.'

Prolonged applause.

Emma, touched by the warmth of the appreciation, fights back tears, determined not to do an Oscar number like Gwyneth Paltrow or Halle Berry, as she makes her stage exit.

One hour later, away from the television studio, Emma, along with Vinny and her parents, sat down to a meal. Her father, Arthur Boylan, anticipating the good news had reserved a table in Restaurant on the Green, one of Dublin's most fashionable dining establishments. The trophy now took pride of place in the centre of the table, replacing a vase of flowers that had been there on their arrival. The restaurant's maitre d', aware of Emma's success, had complimentary drinks brought to the table to toast the occasion. Diners, seated at nearby tables, joined in with the excitement and offered Emma their congratulations.

It was only when the waiters arrived to serve their dishes that any degree of intimacy descended. Hazel Boylan, Emma's mother, a handsome woman who could pass as an older sister, chided Vinny for not bringing his father along. 'Having Ciarán here would make the family complete,' she enthused, 'not to mention the bit of fun and devilment he would provide.'

'You mean *bedlam*, I think' Vinny offered, not unkindly.

'Acceptable bedlam,' Hazel corrected.

'Actually, he had intended to be with us tonight but he's not feeling the best at the moment.'

'I'm sorry to hear that. What's the matter with him?'

'He's been under a bit of pressure to finish restoration work on two huge canvases for the National Gallery.'

'At his age?' Hazel exclaimed.

'Yeah I know, but he refuses to slow down, forgets he's almost seventy. Anyway, he managed to make the deadline by the skin of his teeth but it took its toll on him.'

The conversation at the table continued with each contribution unconsciously resurrecting anecdotes that extolled Ciarán's colourful, if somewhat dubious, escapades. Quality food and fine wine, served in good measure, ensured that repartee flowed freely for the duration of the meal. It was not until their dessert plates had been removed that a change of mood occurred. Arthur's mobile phone bleeped. 'Damn it,' he said. 'I thought I'd switched it off.' Like the others, he'd seen the sign requesting all patrons to switch off their phones. The maitre d', who'd been so accommodating earlier, cast a look of disdain in their direction. Arthur shrugged his shoulders, his expression mirroring the look one might expect to find on the boy caught smoking behind the school shed. Awkwardly, he extracted the offending object from his inside jacket pocket and glanced at the small screen to examine the incoming call number. 'Sorry about this,' he said, 'I'd better answer it.'

Vinny watched with amusement as Emma and Hazel played at carrying on with their conversation while busily eavesdropping on the call. If curiosity killed the cat then his wife and mother-in-law were in immediate mortal danger. But even Vinny could tell from Arthur's raised eyebrows that the exchange had an element of shock value to it. When Arthur finished the call, three pairs of eyes looked to him expectantly.

'Trouble? Hazel asked.

For a moment Arthur said nothing. He looked a little stunned. 'That was George Duggan, a client of mine,' he said, dispatching the mobile back to his pocket. 'He's just told me about a bad accident: The parish priest from Lonsdale was killed in a car accident earlier this evening.'

'Where did it happen?' Emma asked.

'The viaduct on the Dallard Road.'

'The viaduct on Dallard Road?' Emma repeated. 'Isn't that the old road that links Blanchardstown to Lonsdale?'

'Yes, badly lit, hardly anyone uses it since they opened the new roads there. Can't think what he was doing on it in the first place.'

'And he's dead. How terrible,' Hazel said, making a quick sign of the cross against her breast. 'How did it happen?'

Arthur shook his head. 'Too soon to say. Seems his car skidded on ice, shot off the road, exploded into flames.'

'What's the priest's name? Was he on his own?' Hazel asked.

'O'Gorman, I think. Yeah, Fr O'Gorman. He had a driver with him.'

'Is he dead too?' Hazel asked.

'No, still alive but not expected to make it.'

'God, that's terrible,' Emma said, 'but why would George Duggan phone you to tell you this?'

'There speaks the news hound,' Arthur said, 'always ready with the questions.'

'Sorry Dad, I know what you're going to say: your client, none of my business.'

'Right, Emma. As it happens, George Duggan was ringing me about a different matter entirely. He had just heard the news about the crash and was a bit upset. His family were good friends with the priest and his wife trains greyhounds for him so they're all a bit shocked.'

Emma wanted to push further but her father held both his palms up, a signal to her that he'd said all he was going to say on the subject. Emma nodded her compliance and received a thankful smile in return. When a waiter appeared at their table, Arthur insisted, in spite of dissenting noises from Emma and Hazel, on ordering one last round of drinks. 'I'd like this evening to end on a high note,' he said. 'I want to congratulate Emma again on her achievement as a journalist. I know I speak for the rest of the family when I say how very proud of her we all are.'

Sergeant Ken McGettigan glanced disparagingly at the mounting pile of paper and files that lay scattered on his desktop. He inhaled smoke into the inner depths of his lungs, flicked ash from his cigarette, and attempted to sort out the conflicting theories doing the rounds of his brain. On the face of it, the death of Fr Jack O'Gorman could be attributed to a freak accident. Weather charts for that day showed heavy frost and icy patches but the sergeant doubted whether these conditions had any bearing on what happened. Something about the incident didn't quite gel. Putting his finger on what that something might be had eluded him so far.

Earlier in the day, he had attended a press briefing to update the media on what was known about Fr O'Gorman's final moments of life on this earth. Questions had come fast and furious, everyone wanting to know more about the circumstances surrounding the fatality. He assured them that the causes that led to the crash were being fully investigated. He'd extended his sympathies to the priest's friends and relatives. This done, he returned to his desk and attempted to put some sort of construction on what happened. Phones rang continually, the media hungry for any titbit of information. He could give them little.

In the aftermath of the crash, the sergeant and his team had been kept busy examining the scene, seeking witnesses and overseeing the operation to recover the twisted scraps of metal from the dry riverbed beneath the viaduct. Because of industrial development in the area and the preponderance of heavy-moving equipment and lorries, it was impossible to deduce any telling facts from the multiple tyre tracks on the road's surface. Railings torn from the side of the viaduct structure proved especially puzzling. It was difficult to envisage how such damage could be wrought by the impact of a car... unless that car had been travelling at very high speed. Blood samples showed Moran's alcohol level above the legal limit. Given this fact, McGettigan's normal inclination would be to blame driver error, but in this instance, he wasn't so sure.

As things stood, everything depended on what the technical experts discovered on their examination of the wreckage. If someone or something had pushed the car off the road, McGettigan would have a full-blown murder investigation on his hands. If that happened he would be forced to hand over the files to the serious crime squad in the Phoenix Park. Having the 'suits' invade his patch was a situation he did not want to contemplate.

Keeping law and order in the small city suburb of Lonsdale had been his responsibility for almost a decade and he was satisfied that he had done a reasonable job. The threat of having his extra-curricular activities exposed to outside scrutiny was something he desperately wanted to avoid. He had worked hard to gain the few fringe benefits he now enjoyed and saw them as no more than a just reward for his services to the community. During his stint as Lonsdale's guardian of the peace he had watched neighbouring suburbs like Mulhuddart and Blanchardstown develop out of all recognition. So far, Lonsdale had, to a large extent, escaped this fate. Even so, the crime rate had risen steadily in recent months – petty crime, mostly to do with drugs, joyriding, break-ins and minor misdemeanours. There had been some serious incidents too: drug-related stabbings and the death of some elderly residents, beaten up for their pension money. But until now, never an investigation into what could turn out to be a high-profile murder case.

Until hard evidence emerged that the crash was other than an accident, he would try to remain optimistic. If Moran regained consciousness, he could explain how he managed to plunge into thin air. If, on the other hand, Moran did not regain consciousness and no proof of foul play emerged then, given time, life as he knew it would return to normal.

Right now, Tom Moran could tell them nothing; prognoses for his chances of recovery were not encouraging. In the immediate aftermath of the accident, the unpleasant task of giving the bad news to Moran's wife had fallen to him. He'd arranged to have her rushed to the hospital, thinking it likely that her husband's death was imminent. Thankfully, that hadn't happened, but the strong possibility remained that he would never regain consciousness. One thing was certain: Moran would never walk on his own legs again. His escape from the jaws of death had been nothing short of miraculous. Not wearing a safety belt had played to his advantage. He had been thrown from the wreckage before the exploding flames had time to consume him.

McGettigan had been allowed to see the patient in the intensive care unit of St Michael's Hospital. He knew the Moran family and had, on occasion, joined Tom for a jar in the Mill House bar. The Moran family lived less than a mile away from the police station, in one of Lonsdale's better housing estates.

Seeing Tom in the hospital, all broken up like that, had been a chastening experience for the sergeant. Brenda Moran and her daughter Olive had been present at the time, both shocked by what confronted them. He had done what little he could to console them, not an easy task under the circumstances. Olive held her mother's hand, tears streaming down her face.

Even in that moment of great sorrow, McGettigan was conscious of Olive's beauty. Shades of the actress Cameron Diaz — minus all the makeup but with an additional dash of innocence thrown into the mix. Olive had inherited her looks from both parents but seemed unaware of the effect she had on those around her. There wasn't a red-blooded male in Lonsdale who didn't cast hungry leers in her directions, none more so than McGettigan himself. Looking at her in that moment of grief, so vulnerable, so lovely, he had felt a twinge of guilt; his feelings for her running more to lustful longings than those of sympathy. Story of his life. Women never failed to provoke a strong testosterone response in him and he never missed an opportunity to gratify this over-developed masculine characteristic.

He knew he had a way with certain kinds of women – the ones that were profoundly lonely. The vulnerable ones. The ones that yearned for affection, for human kindness. The ones that burned with an unfulfilled desire for carnal intimacy. He could see it in their eyes, pick up the silent signals; it was an art form, a gift he'd honed to perfection. In his younger days he could turn them inside out with his dark blue eyes, have them flutter about him like moths round a candle's flame. They all wanted the same thing: to be appreciated, told they were beautiful, promised undying affection. That presented him with no problem; he could take them on a flight of fancy, fulfil their dreams, ply them with silken endearments, fuel their most basic desires, and then, with their hearts aquiver, crash-land in their thighs.

Now, at forty-seven, the sexual conquests were harder to come by, but he still managed to get enough action to satisfy what he called his 'thirst for lust'. The providers of this pleasure were no longer as young or as pretty as they once were. Lately, his women were a little more desperate, less discerning, but it didn't bother him unduly. He believed in the old adage – one didn't have to look at the mantelpiece while poking the fire. His own looks, he realised, had all but deserted him. Of late, the mirror in his bathroom forced him to accept some rather unpleasant facts. He carried too much weight; his face had become doughy, his jaw line sagged; his mouth had slackened and his hair, once his pride and joy, was hanging on for dear life. Only his eyes retained their ability to reach out and entrap lonely hearts.

Unfortunately for him, Olive Moran did not fall into the lonely hearts category. For one thing, she was twenty years his junior; for another, she had never shown the slightest interest in him. Still, he would remain ever vigilant, alert to any changes in her outlook on life. Maybe, just maybe, some day he'd get lucky. There could be a positive aspect to the death of Fr O'Gorman after all. It just might present him with an opportunity to get to know Olive Moran a little better.

Chapter 3

Behind the wheel of her new 2-litre Hyundai Coupé, Emma Boylan made her exit from the congested traffic lanes of Dublin's quays and headed for the town of Navan. Tourist promotions for the town used the tag line – *Only an hour from Dublin*. Emma was hoping to better that. Leaving the Phoenix Park via the Ashtown Gate, she allowed the car to reach 60mph. It was her first day to try out the car outside the city and she was looking forward to putting the silver machine through its paces. Trading in her old Volvo 360 GLT after many years of faithful service, she'd been seduced by the Hyundai's lines and curves, its leather upholstery and chrome dash. Sitting in the car in the showroom, she'd felt comfortable, at ease with its interior. Vinny, who had insisted on inspecting the car with her – believing himself to be something of an expert on the subject – expressed qualms. Was it not a bit too powerful for a woman driver, he offered.

That clinched it. She bought the car.

And now, on its first proper road test, it had come through with flying colours. According to the clock on the dash, the journey had taken fifty-four minutes exactly. Not bad.

It was rare enough for Emma Boylan to visit the Victorian building that housed her father's law practice. Her father did not encourage the habit, nor was it something she particularly enjoyed herself. But today she had decided to call on him unannounced. Even though he was busy talking on the telephone, he waved to her good-naturedly as she was shown into his office.

She sat in an armchair with springs that threatened to ambush her bottom and waited for him to finish the call. Little had changed in her father's place of work over the years: flock wallpaper from skirting board to stuccoed ceiling, wine-coloured carpet on the floor, framed hunting scenes on the walls.

Décor she considered oppressive. Muted noise from the traffic in the street filtered through windows that were top-heavy with elaborate pelmets. An array of photographs stood on top of a drinks cabinet. Studies of her father – *the family man*, posing with her and her mother at various events throughout their lives; her father – *the business man*, happily smiling in the company of well-known movers and shakers from the world of finance and politics. Emma suspected that the display was more for the benefit of visitors than for the man sitting behind the desk. It never ceased to amuse her to note how accurately her father's office reflected his personality. She could not envisage working in such an environment, not that she would ever share such thoughts with her father.

Arthur Boylan finished his phone call, leaned forward in his swivel chair and smiled broadly. 'Emma, dear girl, what brings you down from the big smoke?'

'Had a little time on my hands... thought I'd drop by.'

'Emma,' he said, arching his head back, peering at her down the length of his finely sculptured aquiline nose, 'you're talking to your father now, remember? I know you never do anything without a reason. So, why are you here? What do you want?'

'Ah, Dad, you're being rotten.'

Her father got up from his chair, walked to a window facing Trimgate Street and stood there for a moment, his back to her. 'Huh, another coach-load of tourists taking pictures of our church,' he said, gesturing with his index finger at St Mary's Church across the street. 'They've discovered that Pierce Brosnan was an altar boy there when he was growing up here in the town. Strange to think of a Navan man playing James Bond, don't you think?' Emma remained silent. He turned to face her, adjusted the handkerchief sprouting over the breast pocket of his navy pinstripe suit. 'Come on, Emma,' he said, doing a passable impression of a barrister admonishing a witness, 'answer me one question: what are you looking for?'

'Oh, all right then, if you're going to be a pain, Dad, I was hoping you could give me a little background information on—'

'—George Duggan,' he cut in.

'You knew?'

'Course I knew. Knew as soon as you showed up. Saw your reaction in the restaurant the other night... when I told you George Duggan was a client... knew you'd follow up on it.'

'I'm that transparent?'

'To me, yes. But then, like I say, I'm your father. You might manage to fool the rest of the world... that's why you're such a good journalist.'

'Huh, fat lot of good trying to pull the wool over your eyes.'

'You got that right.'

'Hmmmm. Actually, I've caught wind of some gossip doing the rounds, tittle-tattle about Fr O'Gorman's death and a supposed relationship he might've had with George Duggan's wife. There's been speculation that the crash might not have been accidental. Could be a load of rubbish, I know, but if there's any truth in it I want to be on the inside track. So, what can you tell me about George Duggan?'

'Nothing!'

'Dad,' Emma moaned with feigned exasperation.

'Can't betray confidences. Unethical.' This accompanied by a fatherly smile. 'I *can*, however, tell you what's in the public domain... on record.'

Emma responded with her best daughterly smile. 'I just need a bit of background colour,' she said, 'if that's not asking too much, Daddy dearest.'

'Hmmm, let me see,' Arthur Boylan said, returning to his customary chair. 'I've handled two cases for George Duggan recently. Both received publicity.'

'Can't say I recall reading about them,' Emma confessed.

'You wouldn't. Barely made the front pages... there were bigger stories hogging the headlines at the time. The first case involved the possession of Clenbuterol.'

'Clenbuterol? The stuff we call Angel Dust?'

'Exactly. It's a banned hormonal growth promoter. It's fed to cattle to artificially increase their bulk. Helps fetch better prices for the animals.'

'George Duggan was giving Angel Dust to his cattle?'

'That was the accusation levelled against him, yes. Someone with a grudge claimed he was doctoring his herd. It was enough to instigate a raid on the farm by the Department of Agriculture. The search revealed a quantity of animal remedies that did not have appropriate veterinary receipts and a number of illegal hormone guns.'

'Guns? What the hell are hormone guns?'

'They're used for inserting hormones into animals. Bit like the old Western six-guns only bigger. Instead of bullets, tubes of hormone substances are inserted into the chamber. When the trigger is pulled, a tube shoots into the animal, usually at the base of the ear. The injected substance slowly seeps into the beast's system.'

Emma shuddered. 'You've just turned me off eating meat for life.'

'A bit extreme, Emma.' Arthur said. 'Most of what's pumped into cattle is quite harmless, openly used in many countries throughout the world.'

'Great, now you've ruined my eating habits worldwide.'

Arthur suppressed a smile and continued. 'However, in this country all use of hormones constitutes an infringement of the law. Because of finding these items on the Duggan farm, the authorities decided to get him on the big one – Angel Dust. They believed he had to be using it on account of finding the other stuff. Turns out they were wrong.'

'He wasn't guilty?'

'Right. I managed to get an out-of-court settlement for Duggan. The original charge of possessing Clenbuterol was dropped. He conceded the lesser charge of having unauthorised antibiotics on his farm and agreed to a fine of eight grand.'

'You said you handled a second case for George Duggan.'

'Ah, yes. This was more recent. Still ongoing, as a matter of fact. It concerns a planning application. George Duggan bought twenty acres of land in Lonsdale. Zoned as prime agricultural land, it abutted the local graveyard. Duggan applied for planning permission to build forty dwellings on the site. He went to great lengths to get the development up and running, levelling the site, getting permission to put in sewerage pipes that would connect to the city's main system. His application for a grant to build a new road adjacent to the land met with no serious opposition.

'Everything appeared to be going smoothly until about six months ago when, out of the blue, an objection was formally lodged against the scheme. The objector described the proposed development as detrimental to the area's visual and environmental amenities. Because of its proximity to Lonsdale's graveyard and because the walls of an ancient church ruin, supposedly dating back to the time of St Brigid, formed part of the development's boundary, the objection was upheld... planning permission refused.'

'Did he appeal?'

'Course he did. Trouble was, each time he re-applied, new objections were added to the original ones.'

'Who was lodging the objections?'

Arthur Boylan thought about this question before deciding what he should tell her. 'The graveyard and part of the land bordering Duggan's site is the property of the Catholic Church. But the person who put the kibosh on George Duggan's plans was none other than the parish priest of St John the Baptist Church, the late Fr Jack O'Gorman.'

'Phew!' Emma hissed, unable to conceal the interest with which she greeted the revelation. 'And all of what you say is documented?'

A smile returned to Arthur Boylan's face. 'I wouldn't have told you otherwise, my dear,' he beamed. 'You want more, you're going to have to do some digging; exercise those investigative skills of yours.'

'Gee, thanks Dad, you're all heart.'

'Don't mention it.'

Caroline Blackman stood in front of the drinks cabinet, deciding which tipple to have. She did not consider herself any great shakes as a drinker but activity in the parochial house since Fr Jack's death had been hectic. A little sustenance was required. She helped herself to a shot of vodka, added a dash of tonic.

Fr Patterson, the young curate, had tried to help during the stressful period but only succeeded in getting in her way instead. He had spent several hours in the parochial house each day since the accident, attempting to look after the church's day-to-day chores, making hard work of co-ordinating funeral arrangements with Bishop Gannon. Younger than herself by a year or so, he was lanky and awkward and had a propensity for bumping into objects. On odd occasions she caught him eyeing up the curvature of her figure whenever the opportunity presented itself.

Earlier this morning she had queried Fr Patterson on the question of who would be appointed to replace Fr O'Gorman. As usual, the curate's answers, like the repertoire of expressions on his face, strayed all over the place. Thinking himself to be unobserved, his eyes scanned her bodily contours with a mixture of boyish glee and queasy lustfulness. She ignored his wanton glances, endeavouring instead to elicit information from him. To that end she had met with considerable success.

He had been appointed acting parish priest, he informed her, a position he would hold until someone took the post permanently.

'I've decided to move back in here,' he announced, showing little enthusiasm, 'back to my old bedroom. It goes without saying that you will stay on in your present capacity.'

'Well, actually, Father, I've been doing some thinking about whether or not I should remain on.'

'What? Of course you'll stay.'

'I don't know, Father, it's something I need to think about.'

'What's there to think about, Caroline?' he asked, surprised that she would even consider such a move. 'I always thought you were happy here... the place just wouldn't be the same without you.'

'Oh, I don't know about that, there's bound to be big changes, a new broom and all that... I think maybe I should be part of that change.'

Alone now, with a drink in her hand, Caroline considered just how she could put that change into effect. Bringing the glass to her mouth, she caught sight of her own reflection in the cabinet's mirrors. 'Cheers to you, girl,' she said, offering herself a toast. The image smiled back. Momentarily, she studied the face. Not bad, not bad at all. Nature had been kind to her. Not exactly a beauty, but a long way from being plain. Facing the prospect of her thirtieth birthday within the year she had no real complaints on that score. With a pleasing cordate face, good eyes, and a rich crop of auburn hair, she knew she was quite presentable.

Time to make a move. Time to kick her life on to another level. She would give serious consideration to the notion of returning to England, from where she had come five years earlier. She had come to one of those crossroads, so pivotal in mapping one's life. Five years earlier, the last occasion she had faced a life-changing set of circumstances, she had come to Ireland. There had been little choice at the time. Her mother was dying. What followed had been harrowing.

Watching cancer claim her mother's life provided the catalyst for the most profound change ever to overtake her. In response to instructions delivered in faltering words by the dying woman, Caroline had opened a cardboard box that lay beneath the bed. The box contained dozens of notebooks, copybooks and ledgers, all of them filled from cover to cover with her mother's neat handwriting. Upon reading a few pages, she realised that what her mother had given her amounted to an elaborate journal, a detailed diary. With extraordinary clarity, the entries traced the day-to-day events of her life, going right back to childhood. In the days and weeks that followed her mother's burial, Caroline discovered revelations about her family's history that shocked her profoundly.

Feeling slightly invigorated by the effect of consumed vodka, she accepted that she had not as yet fully come to terms with the contents of those entries. Reading about the circumstances of her own birth had been a hugely upsetting experience. It had been responsible for bringing her to Lonsdale; it had forced her to come face-to-face with the people who had shaped her mother's life; the same people who in turn had dictated the course of her own life. Being the custodian of such knowledge had thrown her life into chaos.

Chapter 4

The shit had hit the fan… in bucketfuls.

This was Sergeant McGettigan's take on the current situation. His worst fears realised. A fully-fledged murder investigation up and running. Forensic examinations on the car, and the twisted railings of the Dallard Road viaduct, yielded conclusive evidence: the crash had been deliberately engineered.

Lonsdale had made the headlines. And for all the wrong reasons.

He had to hand over his office to Detective Inspector Jim Connolly and a number of 'suits' that had arrived from head-quarters in the Phoenix Park. Their job, to head up the investigation. His job, to assist them in every way, and look happy about it. With the exception of Connolly, the so-called 'suits' didn't actually wear suits, designer casual being the order of the day. With arrogant swagger, they examined the crash site and inspected what remained of the car. In a thinly veiled attack on investigative methods employed prior to his arrival, Connolly lamented the fact that the crime scene had been compromised and subjected to incorrect procedures.

McGettigan cited mitigating circumstances: he'd no reason to suspect murder at the time. Sounded like a whine, even to McGettigan's own ears. Connolly's nodded response and imperceptible grimace spoke volumes.

McGettigan resented Connolly. A smart arse, if ever he saw one. Wearing a three-piece, hand-tailored suit that had probably cost as much as a month's salary from the sergeant's annual pay pack. Difficult not to feel resentment. Being roughly the same age, late forties, served to emphasise their different standings on the social ladder.

Unlike him, the head office DI was married. McGettigan had little time for the notion of matrimony. The concept of

monogamy remained anathema to him, whereas variety in relationships spelled utopia. On the question of sex, McGettigan
inclined towards the school of the three Rs – raw, rough and regular. He doubted that his views would be shared, or approved of,
by the man now heading up the investigation. Sounding out his
contacts in the Phoenix Park HQ, McGettigan discovered that the
DI had wed into wealth, taken a young woman of considerable
beauty for his bride. No one, apparently, knew much about the
life they shared together. A closed book was how one contact
described the relationship. The word coming down to
McGettigan cast Connolly as a man of firm conviction, a man of
unshakeable integrity, a man who viewed his role of detective
inspector as a vocation. Straight as a die, another called him.
Connolly had made few enemies on his rise through the ranks,
had a successful record in his investigations, and was popular
with his colleagues.

These were the sort of attributes bound to get McGettigan's
back up. Connolly's looks, and the confident way he walked, gave
the head-office detective a distinguished, suave appearance that
put McGettigan in mind of one of those successful chief-executive
types you often saw peering out from newspaper pictures as they
addressed shareholders at a corporate AGM. His voice, cultured
and articulate, always held in check, gave little clue as to what
was going on inside his head. According to yet another of
McGettigan's HQ connections, an assessment delivered with
awe-like reverence, Connolly had a mind that was both practical
and moralistic, and was regarded by the top brass as the acceptable face of law enforcement.

Fuck him, was McGettigan's reaction to what he'd discovered.

Working side by side with Connolly for three days now, the
antagonism remained but a thaw of sorts had begun. In spite of
the pent-up resentment, McGettigan found himself admitting to
a measure of grudging respect for the methodical way the detective inspector went about his work.

Connolly had asked to be introduced to any locals with a
connection, however tenuous, to either crash victim. It was a task
McGettigan would gladly forego. How would his acquaintances

react when he came knocking on their doors? What would they say when he introduced them to Detective Inspector Connolly? Hostile? Co-operative? He was about to find out.

With Connolly by his side, he walked up the concrete stairs to the fifth floor of Block G, Setanta Mansions. In all the times the sergeant had visited the flats he'd never once found the lifts in working order. Today was no different. Setanta Mansions consisted of four seven-storey blocks that had been constructed back in the late 1960s as part of the answer to Dublin's inner-city housing problem. Following a fanfare opening, the poorly designed complex quickly fell into disrepair and neglect, its disgruntled residents proving to be a thorn in the side of the local authorities and the law.

With a strong hint of urine fragrance in their nostrils, McGettigan and Connolly made their way along an open balcony liberally sprayed in graffiti, and stopped outside door No. 5-G, home to Derrik and Ruth Holland. Derrik Holland was employed as a foreman at the Dallard Road industrial development. Enquiries at the site earlier in the day confirmed that Holland had reported in sick.

McGettigan knew a little about the Hollands. He'd been called to No. 5-G the previous Christmas. A row had broken out between Ruth Holland and the other tenants in the complex. Neighbours objected to what they described as a vulgar display of Christmas illuminations on the Holland flat and balcony area. Given the state of neglect and slovenliness in evidence all about the place, the complaint struck McGettigan as being a bit rich but his sympathies were with the objectors. However, as long as he wore the uniform, he couldn't be seen to take sides. In the role of diplomat, not one of the sergeant's stronger attributes, he had reminded them that Christmas was the season of goodwill, understanding and tolerance. Somehow, an uneasy truce had been achieved, but he had no doubt that a similar row would break out next December.

Today, pounding rock music came from inside the flat.

McGettigan pressed the door bell, waited.

'Hell of a racket,' Connolly observed.

'Status Quo,' McGettigan replied.

'Oh, I see. Always like this, is it?'

'No, I mean the group; that's Status Quo... playing the music.'

Connolly raised his eyebrows and was about to comment when the door opened. Mrs Ruth Holland, a pretty 30-something, wearing nothing but a man's blue shirt, struck a provocative pose in the doorway. Both men reacted with surprise at the amount of leg on display and the ample bust so clearly outlined beneath the garment. 'I suppose you've had complaints about the music,' she said, looking at McGettigan's uniform.

'No, Mrs Holland, no complaints this time,' the sergeant said, his eyes greedily soaking up the sight in front of him. 'We wanted to have a word with your husband. Heard he's home sick.'

'Sick? Oh yeah. You'd better come in, he's in the front room.'

The place was stifling hot, in stark contrast to the biting outdoor chill. Derrik Holland wore a sweatshirt, boxer shorts and a Burger King 'Smile' hat. If Bruce Willis ever needed someone to play the part of an ugly younger brother in one of his movies, he'd find that person in Setanta Mansions. Holland held a can of beer in his hand while several other empty cans lay scattered on the multi-stained carpet by his bare feet. As soon as he saw the visitors, he turned off the music. 'What've we got here? Two little piggies,' he said, sounding the worse for wear from drink. 'What yo'want?'

'Heard you were unwell,' McGettigan said.

'Yeah, that's right, unwell. Pain in the bollix. To hell with work. Me and a few mates had a win on th'Lottery. Part of a syndicate. Have to celebrate, know wha' I mean. I'd offer yiz a drink only I don't want yiz contaminating the bleedin' stuff.'

McGettigan ignored the comments. 'Mind if I take off my overcoat? It's like an oven in here.'

'Strip to your jocks for all I care.'

McGettigan and Connolly took off their coats. The sergeant had begun to sweat profusely. 'This is Detective Inspector Connolly with me,' he said by way of introduction. 'He wants to ask you a few questions.

'A *Detective Inspector* no less,' Holland said. 'I *am* impressed.'

Connolly spoke for the first time. 'I'm investigating the murder of Fr O'Gorman and I was—'

'Oh, so the rumours are true,' Holland cut in. 'The PP was deliberately done in then, was he?'

'Yes, he was, and we believe some of the equipment from the site where you work was used to push his car off the road.'

'Hey, don't look at me, pal,' Holland snapped, appearing to sober up rather quickly.

'We know the site was locked up on the night of the accident.' Connolly said, wiping sweat from his forehead. 'Who's got keys to the gates?'

Holland puffed out his cheeks, grimaced. 'I've a set. The architect and developer have sets.'

McGettigan, content to allow Connolly continue with his line of questioning, was busy peering into the kitchen through a partially open door. Ruth Holland was sitting on a high, four-legged stool looking at a television, a drink in her hand, her legs crossed above the knees. McGettigan could not tell from his angle whether or not she was wearing underwear. He was intrigued. She was no Sharon Stone, for sure, and the setting couldn't be further removed from the famous scene in 'Basic Instinct', but the sergeant found himself getting hotter and hotter under the collar. A quick succession of lewd thoughts flicked through his mind. He would like to prise those thighs apart, give her the benefit of his sexual prowess and not charge her a penny for the experience. He was disappointed when Connolly concluded the interview.

Back inside the car, Connolly asked the sergeant what he made of Derrik Holland's answers. 'Hard to tell,' McGettigan replied, realising how much he had been distracted by Ruth Holland.

'I think you ought to do a little more sniffing around there,' Connolly suggested.

'Oh, I will,' McGettigan said, visions of Ruth lingering on in his mind.

'Find out if Derrik Holland really had a win on the Lottery.'

Tom Moran's wife, Brenda and daughter, Olive, sat mute in the hospital's coffee shop. For four days now, on and off, they had waited in the small cheerless cafeteria, sipping cups of indifferent coffee, eating snacks they didn't want; forever glancing at the clock on the wall, they waited to hear news from the intensive-care unit.

Fr Jack O'Gorman was already buried, his troubles in this life over, but Tom Moran lived on. On life-support he had, against all odds and predictions of imminent demise, continued to cling to life. From time to time his wife and daughter had been allowed to look at him, but such occasions only added to their distress. They might as well have been looking at a modern-day Egyptian mummy for all they could see of him. Crisp, white bandages everywhere. If it weren't for the sight of five toes sticking out from a plaster-clad foot, they might have doubted his very existence beneath the voluminous folds of swathing. Tubes leading from a collection of upturned plastic bottles, suspended from T-bars, dripped fluid into his veins. Blips of sound and colour from an array of monitoring equipment, which included a ventilator, nebulizer and infusion pump, kept track of his life signs.

The sight of Fr Patterson gangling through the door of the coffee shop succeeded in bringing a little animation to their faces. He eased his lanky frame into the booth beside them, ordered a cup of tea, and attempted to make conversation. Through Tom, he had got to know Brenda Moran on a nod-and-hello basis but he knew Olive a little better.

As choirmaster, Fr Patterson had been aware of Olive from day one of rehearsals. At twenty-seven, she was just a year younger than him. He'd found this out while chatting with her father. Tom Moran liked to talk about his daughter and never lost an opportunity to sing her praises. He talked about how she liked to attend flower-arrangement classes, how fond she was of reading and how she worked as a qualified Montessori teacher. Of more interest to the curate, however, was the information that Olive was not currently doing a line with any boyfriend. On the odd occasion when she visited her father in the church, he'd made an effort to talk to her but invariably found himself tongue-tied. She always responded with a friendly smile, a kind word, but never lingered long enough to allow a decent conversation to develop.

But these brief meetings had been enough to set his heart racing. She was never far from his thoughts, day or night. Especially at night. He would lie alone in his bed, close his eyes, conjure up her image, mentally undress her. He'd touch her luxuriant, chestnut hair. Run his fingers down its full length to the point below her shoulders. He'd kiss each feature on her soft oval face; those dark green eyes, the finely sculptured nose, the high cheeks, the chin that tapered to an elegant cleft and the mouth, her best feature, so sumptuous and full.

Talking now to the mother, he tried, unsuccessfully as it turned out, to keep his eyes off the gentle curvature of Olive's breasts. 'I called to visit Tom... they told me that you and Olive were here.'

'Very good of you to take the trouble, Fr Patterson,' Brenda Moran said. 'Tom will appreciate your concern. I'll tell him when... when...' Brenda choked back the words, unable to say any more. Olive reached over and clasped her mother's hand, offered the curate a tight smile. 'Thanks for coming, Father, very thoughtful of you.'

'No problem, Olive. Didn't know what else to do.'

'I know what you mean,' Brenda Moran said.

'I know this is an awkward time for you, Mrs Moran,' he said, 'but while Tom remains here in hospital, our church has no sacristan. And... well, the thing is, I was wondering if you might consider giving us a hand... on a temporary basis, you understand... until Tom is back on his feet again. What do you say?'

'Oh, I don't know, Father. It's very good of you to ask me, but it's a big responsibility... and without Tom, I'm not so sure...'

'I think it's a great idea,' Olive enthused. 'It will help take your mind off Dad's condition. You've done the work in the church before when Dad was away and you know as much about it as anyone. I'll be able to give you a hand with the chores.'

Discussions between mother and daughter went on for some minutes before, finally, agreement was reached. They would, on a temporary basis, take over Tom Moran's duties in the church. After a little further innocuous chit-chat, Fr Patterson took his leave of the two women and made his way towards the coffee shop exit. Passing through the doorway, a sudden impulse made him look back. Seeing them both stare back at him, he felt foolish. In an effort to hide his awkwardness, he gave them a little wave.

At that precise moment, he caught sight of a young man sitting behind their table. The man was staring, unabashed, at Olive. Long, unkempt, dark blond curls fell across the man's forehead and cast a shadow across the eyes. Olive Moran, aware that the priest's gaze had shifted, turned to see what had caught his attention. As soon as she looked at the man behind her, the stranger averted his gaze. Olive was used to having members of the opposite sex stare at her and saw nothing untoward in the young man's behaviour. She smiled back at Fr Patterson and gave him a little child-like wave. His face reddened. Feeling foolish, he grinned back at her, waved one more time and finally departed the coffee shop.

Chapter 5

One of Emma Boylan's firmly held tenets in journalism proclaimed: something will always turn up. This belief rarely let her down. Sometimes, though, you had to help make it happen, stir things a bit, prod people into action, make a nuisance of yourself. This morning she had an inkling that her ability to create that 'something' would be put to the test.

The fact that Lonsdale rarely featured on the national news headlines made its new-found infamy all the more startling. Revelations that one of its most prominent citizens, a man of the cloth, had been killed, and the heinous nature of the crime, ensured that the colourless Dublin suburb's days of anonymity were well and truly at an end.

Emma managed to squeeze into a parking space opposite a bus-stop shelter. On both sides of the street, brightly painted shop fronts glistening in the harsh, steely light. Pedestrians went about their business, shoulders hunched against the cold, breath steaming about their mouths. Customers entered and exited a Spar Supermarket; four young men loitered outside a bookie's shop, playfully punching each other, making suggestive gestures behind the backs of women who passed by on the footpath. Nowhere was there evidence of brooding, no sign that Lonsdale was burdened with grief over the recent loss of its parish priest.

Before getting out of her car, Emma took time to acquaint herself with the immediate geography of the area. Apart from the shops, the main thoroughfare contained uniform two-storey houses with reddish-brown bricks on the bottom half, pebble dash on the top. Wedged between these houses, a dreary, three-storey building stood, its windows dark and dirty, its slated roof bowed, its chimney slightly tilted and soot-coated. It didn't require any great powers of deduction on her behalf to work out that it housed Lonsdale's arm of the law.

All the city's suburbs once boasted similar structures, though in recent times most of them had fallen victim to the developer's breaking ball. Those that remained had been renovated and brought into line with the needs and requirements of the twenty-first century. Lonsdale, it appeared, had missed out on this urban-renewal effort. A pity. It would only be a matter of time, Emma suspected, before she needed to visit the building, an event she would put off for as long as possible.

Some distance down the street from where she'd parked, she could see an impressive gothic-style church behind secure iron railings and granite posts. Observing the building, she saw two elderly women emerge from its interior, both wearing heavy coats and scarves, one of them hugging herself to keep warm against the early March chill. In marked contrast, a young man wearing jeans and skimpy fleece approached the church entrance. He hesitated for a moment and glanced around furtively before entering the building. Emma smiled to herself. The young man, she suspected, hadn't wanted to be observed by his peers going into a church in the middle of the day. To be caught praying would do little for his street cred.

To one side of the church, on the same enclosed site, an old-fashioned two-storey house stood. This building, Emma recognised once more without putting too much strain on her powers of deduction, was the parochial house. The well-maintained building had a separate entrance to that of the church. Its austere granite exterior had been softened somewhat by the judicious use of palm trees and shrubbery. This location, she decided, would be as good a place as any to begin her enquiries.

Caroline Blackman did not conform to the preconceived notions Emma held in regard to how a priest's housekeeper ought to look. For one thing, Caroline Blackman was a lot younger than the stereotypical housekeeper. She was pretty, had a well-proportioned figure, dressed with care and spoke with an English accent. Emma guessed her age to be somewhere in her late twenties, which would make her eight or nine years younger than Emma herself.

Initially, the housekeeper did not want to engage in conversation, telling Emma that it was parish policy not to talk to the media. Never one to accept rejection easily, Emma switched to charm offensive, remaining rooted to the doorstep until eventually she was invited inside.

Sitting in a stately drawing room, filled with dark furniture, silver ornaments, rich drapes and elaborately framed paintings, Emma made small talk to begin with. 'You're not Irish?' she said. 'I'd say London, would I be right?'

'Half wrong, half right,' Caroline said, her voice showing signs of regret for having allowed the journalist inside. 'My mother was Irish, so that makes me Irish too, I suppose. But you're right about London... I've spent most of my life there... Islington.'

'So, what brought you back to the ould sod?'

'My mother lived in Ireland... she died five years ago. I came home to nurse her... and stayed.' This pronouncement was spoken in a tone that let Emma know the subject was not open to discussion. Emma duly changed tack. 'You must have been greatly shocked to discover that Fr O'Gorman's death was not an accident.'

'Yes, like everyone else, I'm stunned.'

'Any idea who might be responsible?'

'No.'

'To your knowledge, did Fr O'Gorman have any enemies?'

'Enemies? I don't believe he had any... *enemies*. There are people in Lonsdale who didn't exactly see eye-to-eye with him.'

'Anyone in particular?'

'Well, there's our curate, Fr Patterson, for one. Himself and the PP couldn't agree on what day of the week it was, argued all the time but they could never be termed enemies.'

'What did they row about?'

'Huh, what didn't they row about? In fairness, the fault lay mostly with the intransigence of the parish priest. But the clash of personalities, coupled with age difference and opposing attitudes to doctrinal matters – everything from *Humane Vitae* to the question of women priests – ensured conflict. But it was the ordinary day-to-day matters that caused most dissent.'

'How did this manifest itself?'

'Well, for example, when Fr Patterson took over as choirmaster, he introduced a few modern hymns to the repertoire. The changes were welcomed by the parishioners but frowned on by the parish priest. And then, the introduction of girls to serve on the altar at Mass time, a role traditionally confined to boys, met with equal disapproval.'

'Must have been difficult for you, caught between the two of them.'

'It was hell for all of us. In the end, Fr Patterson moved out, took up residence in a small rented house down the street from here. For the past year and a half this fragile arrangement had, in spite of ongoing hiccups, survived. Truth is, they respected each other but would never admit as much.'

'And this curate, Fr Patterson, he's moved back here now, has he?'

'Well yes, yes he has... only moved back in a few days ago.'

'Is he here now? I'd like to have a word with him.'

'No, he's out on his rounds.'

'Anyone else who mightn't have been all that fond of Fr O'Gorman?'

'Well, yes,' Caroline said. 'The anti-blood sports lobby; they strongly disapproved of his involvement with coursing.'

'Yes, I've read about that. Tell me, do you know anything about the objections Fr O'Gorman lodged against George Duggan's application for planning permission?'

'Just what was reported in the local papers.'

'It must have strained relationships between the two men.'

Caroline nodded. 'The two of them had a right old barney. I was in the kitchen at the time, couldn't help but overhear every word.'

'So, George Duggan would have had a good reason for holding a grudge against Fr O'Gorman?'

'You would have thought so, but no, that wasn't how it turned out. There was a coolness for a couple of weeks but they made up. Duggan called here about a month after the row, apologised and offered his hand in friendship. They sat here drinking whiskey for hours after that... got tight as ticks.'

'And they remained friends?'

'Right to the end. Fr Jack had been asked to be the celebrant at the wedding of Duggan's daughter, Yvonne. As things turned out,

Fr Patterson did the honours. And now, Ms Boylan, if you don't mind, I've got to get on with my work.' Emma wanted to probe further but when the housekeeper moved to the drawing room door and held it open, Emma was left in no doubt that the interview had come to an end.

Chapter 6

The Kozy Kitchen displayed its lunch menu on a sandwich board outside its front door. The choice on offer was sufficient to entice Emma inside. The ambience, a hybrid that fused French bistro and traditional Irish kitchen, met with her approval. Small in size, the dining area had lots of lace and gingham, plain timber chairs and tables, and black flagstones on the floor. The rich aroma of food emanating from the kitchen won favour with Emma's taste buds.

Halfway through her main course – warm sesame chicken salad – a familiar voice interrupted her musings. 'Well, I declare, if it isn't Emma Boylan.' The dulcet tones belonged to Detective Inspector Jim Connolly. Emma nodded her hello, desperately trying to swallow the strip of chicken she had just put into her mouth.

'Mind if we join you?' he asked. 'All the other places are taken.'

Still struggling to clear her mouth, Emma smiled and nodded her acquiescence. Connolly, enjoying her moment of discomfort, introduced his companion. 'This is Sergeant McGettigan, he's the one responsible for law and order in these parts.'

Emma, who had by now forced the food down her gullet, spoke at last. 'Gentlemen, I'd love you to join me… nice to meet you, Sergeant McGettigan.'

'Pleasure's mutual,' McGettigan said, squeezing his bulk into a seat on the opposite side of her table.

Connolly winking at the sergeant. 'Watch her,' he said, 'she's a press hound, an intrepid sleuth. Give her half a chance and she'll take over your investigation.'

'Not true at all, Sergeant,' Emma replied good-heartedly, accepting Connolly's backhanded compliment. 'I'd like to meet the person who gets the better of the Detective Inspector.'

McGettigan gave a mirthless chuckle. 'What's this, a mutual admiration society?'

Connolly held up his hands in a gesture of explanation. 'This young lady and I happened to exchange a little co-operation on a recent operation, that's all. Didn't always see eye-to-eye but our motives were always for the best.'

As Connolly spoke, the sergeant scrutinised Emma, his eyes soaking up every detail, his expression non-committal. 'So, tell us, Ms Boylan, are you and the Detective Inspector thinking of teaming up together again?'

'That would depend on whether there's anything to warrant us pooling our resources.' Emma turned to Connolly and looked him in the eye. 'Is there any reason?'

Connolly flicked back a few strands of silver hair that had fallen out of place and smiled. 'No, Emma, much as I regard your skills, I'm confident that myself and the sergeant are more than adequate for the task in hand.'

'What we don't need,' the sergeant said, buoyed up by Connolly's comments, 'is someone muddying the waters for us. Best leave it to the professionals, that's my advice to you, Miss.'

Emma was about to jump all over the sergeant when, mercifully, the conversation was interrupted. A young, red-haired waitress put plates of food in front of the two policemen. 'Have youse brought in the person that killed the parish priest yet?' she asked, looking at the sergeant.

'Our investigations are ongoing, Mary,' he replied, annoyed that the waitress, a person he obviously knew, should be so familiar in front of the others. 'We're following a definite line of enquiry and expect to have a result before too long.'

'Huh, Sergeant, sure the dogs in the street know who murdered the ould devil. I can't think why yis don't just go out to Duggan's farm and arrest the fecker. Everyone knows Duggan done it.'

'Now, now, Mary,' the sergeant said, trying to remain calm in front of company, 'you shouldn't be listening to the rumour-mongers, and you shouldn't go spreading malicious gossip.'

The waitress's attitude towards McGettigan was obstinate and sullen. She treated his dismissal of her concerns with a shrug of contempt. Small and wiry, with a freckled, boyish face, she might have been considered attractive had she taken just a little more care with her appearance. But clearly, how she came across to others did not bother her unduly. 'Right, Sarge,' she said acidly, 'whatever you say... but I'll tell you this for nothing: you and me both know who the guilty party is. Just 'cos he's rich and lords it over the rest of us doesn't mean he should get away with it.'

A silence followed the departure of the waitress. Emma and Connolly looked to the sergeant, wanting to hear how the man in uniform would react to what had just been said. McGettigan shifted uneasily in his seat, toyed with the food on the plate in front of him, before speaking. 'Ah, you wouldn't want to listen to Mary Dunne. She's like the rest of them around here, wants to be judge, jury and executioner; not willing to let a simple matter like evidence or proof get in the way.'

Emma took advantage of the sergeant's discomfort. 'Is George Duggan the prime suspect?' she asked.

Before McGettigan could answer, Connolly cut in. 'This is hardly the place to discuss such matters, Emma. The sergeant and I are not prepared to comment at this juncture on any aspect of the investigation. Now why don't we enjoy our meal, talk about more pleasant things.'

Much to Emma's annoyance, no further opportunity arose to bring the topic back to the subject uppermost in her mind. Even so, she did not consider the accidental meeting in the Kozy Kitchen a waste of time. Discovering that Detective Inspector Connolly was working on the case was good news. From experience, she knew she could trust him and, providing she played her cards right, get him to pass on some worthwhile titbits.

As for Sergeant McGettigan, she could tell he was hostile towards her. Well, fair enough, forewarned was forearmed; she would grant him the same respect she conferred on Rottweilers, and tiptoe around him with the greatest of care.

One other positive outcome had arisen from the shared lunch break: she now knew who her next contact should be.

Olive Moran's efforts at flower arrangement were quite impressive. She had once attended classes on the subject and was glad to have the opportunity to display her talent. She had just about completed the task when she heard footsteps approaching. 'Afternoon, Olive,' Fr Patterson said, making his way from the sacristy to the altar. 'You've a flair for the flower arranging, I see.'

'Chancing my arm, Father. The flowers *are* pretty though, just freshly cut; it'd be hard to make them look bad.'

'You're too modest, Olive, I can see you're a dab hand at this sort of thing. I knew you and your mother would be well able to look after St John the Baptist's needs while your Dad is in hospital. And speaking of the good man, how's he doing?'

'Mum's by his bedside right now, that's why she's not here. The doctors say there's been a slight improvement. We're keeping our fingers crossed.'

As Olive Moran spoke she experienced the oddest sensation; she thought she felt the curate's eyes scanning her body, mentally undressing her. She felt her flesh crawl, tried to dispel the notion. Her imagination playing tricks on her, surely? Giving him the benefit of the doubt, she moved to the pulpit. She had already dusted the pulpit but she hoped her activity would encourage him into action of his own. As this thought passed through her head, the curate startled her.

'Hey, what are you doing up there?' he shouted.

'What do you mean Father? I'm dusting the—'

'No, not you, Olive,' he said, pointing to the choir gallery in the back of the church. 'Up there, look, there's someone there.'

Olive turned her head, saw the movement. 'It's a man, I see him,' she said. 'What's he doing—?'

'Hey, you,' Fr Patterson shouted, 'no one's allowed up there…'

'He's leaving,' Olive said, 'he's going down the back stairs.'

Fr Patterson moved quickly from the altar and strode towards the rear of the church. He pushed open the heavy timber door that led to the porch. The small door leading to the choir gallery stood ajar but there was no sign of the intruder. 'Damn it,' he hissed, showing fluency with language unapproved of in ecclesiastical circles. He hurried to the main porch and stepped outside the building.

There was no sign of the man. Apart from an extremely rotund woman making her way into the church, there was no one in sight. 'Excuse me,' he said to the woman, 'Mrs O'Reilly, isn't it?'

'Yes, Father, I'm Maggie O'Reilly.'

'Tell me, did you see a man come out of the church just now?'

'Aye, I surely did, Father. Knocked me flat on me backside he did... no manners at all, took off like the devil was after him.'

'What direction did he go in?'

'River Street... a right pup.'

'Did you recognise him?'

'No, never saw him before. From the flats, I'd say – a ruffian, youngish, scruffy hair, no coat. What was he doing in the church?'

'I don't know, Mrs O'Reilly, I wish I did.'

Back inside the church, the curate told Olive how he had missed the man. 'Whoever it was, I doubt he wanted to join our choir.'

'There's something going on that I don't understand Father. First the parish priest is killed and now... now someone's spying on you.'

'Don't you worry about me, I can take care of myself. Whoever was up in the loft probably came in for a quiet snooze, could've been suffering from a hangover, wanted somewhere he wouldn't be disturbed.'

'Or he could be a junkie,' Olive said, agitated. 'What if he came in here to give himself a fix or whatever it is they do. There's a whole gang of junkies and drop-outs in Setanta Mansions. Could be one of them. He could be violent, Father, out of his head on crack or speed or whatever he's on.'

'I doubt that, Olive. At worst he might have been waiting for a chance to rob the collection boxes.'

'Should we tell Sergeant McGettigan?'

'No, I don't think we need bother him at this stage.'

'I don't know, Father. I'm worried.'

'Well, there's no need to be, we're in no danger. Trust me.' Without further comment, Father Patterson returned to the sacristy. Olive Moran stared after him, less than satisfied with his reassurances.

Almost half an hour since leaving the restaurant, Emma fed the parking meter and remained in the same spot she'd found on her arrival in Lonsdale. She'd learned precious little from the verbal exchanges between herself, Connolly and the local sergeant, but she had been intrigued by what the red-haired waitress had said. Most of the lunchtime diners had already left the restaurant but one or two stragglers had yet to make their exit. It was Emma's hope that the waitress would appear as soon as the last customers vacated the premises.

While waiting, Emma decided to try out the car's stereo system, something she had not had a chance to do since buying the Hyundai. Her old car had an audio-cassette player (seldom used) but this one boasted a CD deck and a four-speaker surround-sound system. Vinny, who loved the idea of music while driving, had already taken the car for a spin and had put the sound system through its paces. His verdict: not bad. Now it was her turn. She selected one of the CDs he had left in the car, inserted it into the deck and pushed the play button. Seconds later she was swamped by the sounds of Waylon Jennings (one of Vinny's favourites) – *Get your tongue out of my mouth, I'm kissing you goodbye.* Listening to the lyrics confirmed her worst suspicions in regard to her husband: his taste in music was definitely suspect. She was about to skip to another track when her eyes caught sight of movement outside the church. She let down her window to see more clearly.

A young man emerged from the front porch of St John the Baptist church, running on to the street, bumping into a stout woman in the process, almost knocking her off her feet. The woman waved her fist at the man who made no attempt to stop or apologise. He continued on his erratic way, veering into a side street before disappearing from Emma's vision.

Within seconds, another man emerged from the church and stood outside the main entrance. He was looking to see where the first man had disappeared to. Wearing a red quilted jacket, grey polo-neck sweater, navy sweatshirt and navy chinos, the ensemble appeared strangely at odds with the wearer. Emma concluded that he had to be a cleric; even in lay clothes you could always tell. Looking bewildered, he beckoned to the fat woman who appeared none the worse for her encounter with the first man. After an animated exchange of words, the cleric and the woman made their way into the church.

It was only after they had disappeared from view that Emma remembered seeing the young man earlier in the day. When she first parked in the square, she had noticed him entering the church. At the time, her attention had been drawn to him because of his lack of appropriate clothes for the cold climate. His second appearance struck her as curious. Why would he spend the best part of two hours in a church in the middle of the day?

As Emma pondered this question, the waitress, Mary Dunne and another young woman appeared at the front door of the Kozy Kitchen. Emma watched them light up cigarettes and stand chatting. A few minutes elapsed before the two women parted and went their separate ways. This was Emma's cue to get out of her car. She crossed the street and followed the waitress. There was no fear of losing sight of Mary Dunne; her red hair stood out from the other pedestrians using the footpath. Walking quickly, Emma soon caught up. 'Excuse me,' she said, tapping the girl gently on the shoulder, 'I was hoping I might have a word with you.'

'Jesus, you put the heart crossways in me,' the waitress said, pressing one hand to her chest. 'D'you make a habit of creeping up on people and scaring the livin' daylights out of them?'

'I'm really sorry,' Emma said, pulling a contrite face, 'but you served me lunch in the Kozy Kitchen... I heard Sergeant McGettigan call you Mary Dunne... I was interested in something you said.'

'Oh yeah, I remember you. You're one of them detectives helping the sarge sort out the murder, right? Nothing to sort out if you ask me; everyone knows George Duggan had the parish priest killed. End of story, final answer.'

Emma, not bothering to correct Mary Dunne's mistaken assumption that she was a detective, walked alongside the waitress, watched her light up another cigarette, finding it difficult to hold a conversation. 'What makes you so sure it was George Duggan?'

Mary blew out a whorl of smoke and glanced sideways at Emma. 'Duggan's the killer,' she said knowingly, 'because the reverend PP was banging the arse off his wife.'

'Nobody can prove that, surely,' Emma said.

Mary snorted. 'Don't have to prove it 'cos it's a bleedin' fact. Last year, the PP and Duggan's wife stayed overnight in the same hotel during the annual coursing meeting in Clonmel. Need I say more? Their relationship goes back for years. Our most reverend PP is the father of her daughter Yvonne.'

'What?'

'What I said. Fr O'Gorman is Yvonne Duggan's real father. With all the fuss around Yvonne's marriage, George Duggan could take no more. He flipped. End of story. I'm just surprised he didn't kill his slag of a wife while he was at it.'

'How do you know all this?' Emma asked, trying not to let her excitement show.

'I just know, that's all. Everyone in Lonsdale knows it but they're all too shaggin' hypocritical to open their gobs. And now if you don't mind, I'd like you to frig off and leave me alone, OK?'

Emma attempted to continue the conversation but it was obvious that Mary Dunne was saying no more. Pressed by Emma, she descended into a harangue of foul language. Emma had no choice but to make it back to her car. What she had heard put a whole new complexion on the murder of Fr Jack O'Gorman. But what credibility could she attach to the story the waitress had told her? All of a sudden, the murder of a parish priest looked as though it could be far more sensational than it had first appeared. On days like this, Emma was glad she chose to work as an investigative journalist.

Chapter 7

Lying in bed, two pillows supporting her head against the head-board, Caroline Blackman thumbed through one of her mother's dog-eared diaries. The ritual had become something of an obsession over the past number of years. In many ways it brought back childhood memories and hazy recollections of characters from favourite fairy tales. Back then, myths and legends had the power to transport her to magical castles and far-flung lands inhabited by wondrous creatures, witches, wizards, goblins, golden-haired princesses and handsome heroes.

And now, decades later, reading from the old battered copy-books had a similar effect – the power to cast hypnotic spells.

Before going to sleep she willed herself to crawl inside her mother's head, to explore the vast collection of memories contained there. What she unearthed in that labyrinthine maze proved far more potent than any fables conceived by Aesop or the brothers Grimm. These accounts were the stuff of reality. Goblins and witches were still in evidence but they had been transmogrified to real-life, flesh and blood, monsters. Sadly, the golden-haired princesses and handsome heroes had all but disappeared.

There were times when she laughed out loud, hearing her mother's laughter echo through some other-worldly portal as, together, they shared some hilarious episode from the past. The chronicler had poured her heart out in pen and ink, writing accounts of friendships, passion, unrequited love, wanton lust, loyalties, trust, happiness, sadness; but mostly the words described how a brave spirit had been destroyed by exposure to a series of life's great betrayals.

A noise from downstairs reminded Caroline that she was not alone in the house. Fr Patterson had a propensity for bumping into things, knocking objects over, creating noise and generally displaying an awkwardness that was at times endearing, but more often than not, his amiable incompetence got on her nerves. Since his return to the parochial house and his occupation of the bedroom suite directly below her own, she had become familiar with the racket. It had all been so different with Fr O'Gorman. He never made a sound and, for that matter, never tolerated others making sounds either.

Caroline's own suite was originally fitted out as a guest room. The intention had been to keep the suite in readiness for special dignitaries who chose to visit the parish. Bright and comfortable with plush carpet flooring, it had its own en suite bathroom with shower, central heating, a dressing table and most importantly, as far as Caroline was concerned, a comfortable double bed. That she, a mere housekeeper, should occupy this suite was not something that had been envisaged by the Bishop of the Diocese when he sanctioned expenditure for the extensive refurbishment a decade earlier. Back then housekeepers did not, as a rule, reside in the parochial house.

In spite of her favourable conditions, something bothered her, something intangible, something she couldn't quite put her finger on. This apprehension, she suspected, might be connected to Emma Boylan, the woman she had admitted to the house earlier in the day. Would this reporter be the one to force certain people in Lonsdale to face up to some ugly deeds that had been air-brushed from their collective consciousness? Would this investigative journalist be clever enough to uncover the rotten core beneath the respectable veneer of some of Lonsdale's most prominent citizens?

The prospect of such exposure both excited and frightened her. If the journalist was as smart as she looked, then the next few weeks could very well be revealing. But now, adjusting her pillows once more, it was time to dismiss all extraneous thoughts from her mind and decide on which section of her mother's diary to read.

Extract from the diary of Nelly Joyce – aged 10
Date 3rd July 1962.

Dear Diary
    Haven't written for two days. Here's why.

Our Lady's Industrial School for Girls burned to the ground last night.

It was an awful thing to happen.

Earlier that night, I was asleep in Dorm A on the top floor.

Mother Josephine woke me up.

The other girls were still asleep. Anne Marie Burke was snoring like a pig.

Mother Josephine put her finger to her lips like she always does when she wants to take one of us from the dorm. She is favourite nun with all the girls.

I'm lucky she picks me more times than my friends.

She brought me to her own room and let me into her bed.

It's big and soft, not like the hard beds in the dorm.

She says I can pretend she's my real mother.

She puts her arms around me and hugs me and kisses me.

I love Mother Josephine every bit as much as I would love a real mother if I had one. I hate when she picks one of the other girls.

Went to sleep in Mother Josephine's arms.

Woke up when I heard screaming. My eyes were stinging.

Someone shouted the word Fire.

Mother Josephine was really scared. She pulled me out of bed and told me to run back up to my dorm.

Outside her bedroom was full of smoke. Mother Josephine started to choke.

I could hardly catch my breath.

Sister Agnes and Sister Aquinas were banging on the doors and screaming at everyone to wake up and get out of the building.

Sister Theresa wanted to know what I was doing on the wrong floor.

Mother Josephine told her she found me sleepwalking and was bringing me back to the dorm. Sister Theresa said I couldn't go back upstairs because it was too

dangerous. She told Mother Josephine to get me out of
the building quick.

I was rushed through the smoke and taken down to the
ground floor.

A crowd waited outside in the dark but I couldn't see
any of my friends.

Flames were leaping out the windows. A fire brigade
came.

Mother Josephine caught hold of Sister Mary Martha
and asked what was holding the other girls back.

Sister Mary Martin said they couldn't leave the
building in their nighties and were getting into their
day clothes.

The fire-brigade men started to hose water on to the
building but the flames leaped through the roof and
there was a sound like thunder when the whole roof
fell into the building.

Everyone screamed. I started to cry. None of my
friends came out.

A fire-brigade man wrapped a blanket around me.

Another man took me to a car and drove me away.

I was brought to a house where a man and woman in
nightclothes made me cocoa and gave me a fig roll
biscuit.

I kept asking what happened to my friends but they
didn't know.

They put me in a nice bedroom but I couldn't sleep for
ages and ages.

When I woke up this morning I was given a lovely
breakfast. Had cornflakes for the first time in my life.
They were delicious. Mr and Mrs Williams were really
nice to me. Mr Williams told me he had very bad
news. Thirty five-girls had burned to death in the fire
and two nuns with them.

I bawled my eyes out.

This was the worst thing I'd ever known.

While I was crying I heard Mrs Williams and Mr
Williams whispering.

Mr Williams said it was all the nuns' fault. He was
giving out yards.
I saw a newspaper with a big huge picture of Our
Lady's School in flames on the front page. When Mr
Williams saw me looking at it he took it off me. He
said I should not upset myself.
He told me some people from Our Lady's would come
to sort things out.
I asked him could I stay with him and his wife. I said
I loved the nice food she gave me and I promised to
be a good girl and help her to keep the house nice
and tidy. Mr Williams looked very sad and said he
didn't know.
I'll finish for now and pray for my friends and ask God
to let me stay with the Williams's.
Goodnight Diary.
P.S. I just remembered that the diaries I wrote before
the fire are burnt in the flames but I'll write whenever I
get the chance.
Goodnight again Diary.

Caroline closed the copybook. Her eyes were misted. Even
though she had read this entry many times, it always had the same
effect on her. She became that ten-year-old; she lived through the
events described on the yellowing pages, but her reaction to what
happened differed greatly to that of her mother all those years
ago. Her mother had been an innocent child, believing in the
goodness of those whose job it was to protect her. As an aban-
doned child, she had been placed in the Industrial School along
with other wards of court and young female offenders that
nobody wanted or cared about. Cursed with the benefit of matu-
rity, Caroline understood the enormity of what had been perpetrated against those young girls. They perished in a raging inferno
because modesty had been foolishly elevated to a priority above
that of safety.
    Caroline switched off her bedside light and wiped a tear from
her cheek. As always, other episodes described by her mother,
events from later on in her life, took hold of her sleepy brain.

These images would hold sway in her consciousness until she eventually found release in sleep.

Not yet dressed for bed, Fr Patterson sat at the desk in his room putting the finishing touches to Sunday's sermon. Not one of his better efforts, he feared, but it would have to suffice. His mind was not on matters religious. A myriad of unconnected thoughts tossed about in his head like interchanging objects in a juggler's hands.

He wondered about the intruder he had chased from the church earlier in the day. What was that all about? He had inspected the choir gallery himself later that afternoon, half expecting to find syringes and traces of drugs, but found nothing.

A more intractable problem concerned his feelings for Olive Moran. With Olive's father, Tom, critically ill in hospital, her visits to St John the Baptist Church were now a daily feature. Tom's wife Brenda, to whom he had offered the job, spent most of her time by her husband's bedside. This meant, in effect, that Olive had become the *de facto* sacristan.

Accepting that he had contrived to bring about this situation, he was forced to face up to other profound considerations: his vocation to the priesthood and his vow of celibacy. He sighed. For far too long he had thought about women. Mental impressions of their bodies and how they were put together, how they moved, were ever present in his head. He had asked God to help cleanse his mind of such absorption, to give him strength to fight his most feral cravings, but his preoccupation with such thoughts stubbornly ignored all entreaties. His fantasies demanded gratification. He remained celibate, at least in the technical sense, provided he ignored masturbation and the multiple infringements enacted on a daily basis inside his head. Familiar with the oft-quoted statistic about 99 per cent of men succumbing to masturbation and the other one per cent being liars, he tried, unsuccessfully, to ignore the sense of ever-present guilt and frustration he felt. At 28 years of age, permanently lost in a wilderness of moral confusion, he remained a virgin. The realisation that the male organ had other functions apart from urination plagued him; it was a thought never too far removed from his mind... or his hands.

Just thinking of Caroline in the room above him, naked between the sheets of her bed, induced stirrings in his loins that cried out for relief. But with Caroline, his feelings were pure lust and nothing more. They were akin to the feelings he felt for Yvonne Duggan: lust, rampant lust. He had been flattered when Yvonne Duggan had asked him, and not the parish priest, to be the one to instruct her husband-to-be into the Catholic faith. During these discussions he had found his mind wandering on several occasions, imagining Yvonne Duggan and Alec Cobain having sexual intercourse. His mind conjured up visions of sweaty bodies entwined, Yvonne's luscious lips indulging in oral sex and Alec fondling her breasts and taking her nipples in his mouth. It was all he could do to stop himself from getting aroused.

But with Olive Moran, the feelings went deeper, a lot deeper. There was of course a degree of lust involved, he accepted that, but there was also something far more profound. He wanted to be with her, to feel her soft curvaceous body next to his own, to kiss her soft lips, whisper endearments into her ears, make love to her. Was she a virgin like himself? No, probably not. He had heard enough in the confessional to know that most of the young girls were having sex on a regular basis nowadays, some of them at it from the age of twelve. Olive had never presented herself in his confession box and for that he was grateful.

It was time to undress and go to bed. First thing in the morning he was due to meet the diocesan auditor. That should take no more than two hours at most. When he finished with the accounts, he would take Olive Moran to one side. He would come right out and tell her of his feelings. She would probably be shocked at first but he felt sure that once she understood the seriousness of his intent, she would warm to the idea. He would make it plain that he was not looking for a sneaky affair, that he wasn't interested in a bit on the side, no clandestine meetings, no hiding around corners.

For her he was willing to give up the priesthood, renege on his sacred vows, endure the shame that would be heaped on him. It was a sacrifice well worth making. Doing the right thing was an important factor. He felt reasonably confident that Olive Moran liked him. True, he was no film star, but he wasn't altogether unattractive. He had seen her steal the odd glance in his direction and she must have seen the loving way he looked at her. Yes, he thought, closing his eyes, tomorrow he would change his life, and hers, for the better.

Chapter 8

Emma Boylan's verbal duel with her boss, Bob Crosby, had not gone too well. Subject matter: initial probe into the murder of Fr Jack O'Gorman. Speaking to each other over the phone did not help. Negotiating Dublin city's chaotic traffic while talking into her mobile served to acerbate the situation. Emma should have known better. Face-to-face exchanges with Crosby were always preferable. After listening to her summary of findings, his assessment had been terse. 'You've got nothing,' he said, with a dismissive snort.

'But...'

'No buts, Emma. What you've got is just gossip, belly-button fluff, innuendo, horse manure, nothing worth wasting printer's ink on.'

'But Bob, I have—'

'Emma, I'm sorry,' Crosby cut in, sounding anything but contrite, 'I'm up to my rollicks here, OK? Come back to me with facts, real facts that will excite the readers. But remember this: if we're to name names in newsprint we need a case tighter than a camel's arse in a sandstorm, OK?'

Before Emma could reply, Crosby cut the connection.

'Ugggh! Men,' she hissed, pounding her fist on the steering wheel. In a quick reversal of mind, she smiled. She'd heard his hoary old quip about the camel a thousand times but it still made her smile. Crosby's gruffness was mostly surface but beneath the crusty exterior, she liked to think a fair-minded person took refuge.

Crossing over the River Liffey on O'Connell's Bridge, Dublin City's most central nub, Emma decided that a change of plan was called for.

Five minutes later, she found a parking space north of the river in St Michan's Street. Free from the car, her lungs greedily inhaled the mid-morning, crisp-edged air. The March climate felt invigorating, steely sunlight filling her with a sense of well-being. Organic smells wafted from the fish market and the vegetable market to either side of the road as she crossed on foot into Chancery Street. She used this short cut whenever visiting the Four Courts via the rear of the building. The Four Courts, an eighteenth-century architectural masterpiece, never failed to provide her with invaluable research assistance. Housing the Irish Law Courts and Law Library, its great domed central mass represented one of the city's most recognisable landmarks. She secured a visitor's pass to the Probate Office and conducted a search there. Twenty minutes later, feeling pleased with herself, she left the building with the required information.

The next hour was spent crisscrossing the city. She visited the Land Registry office in Nassau Street, a large earth-brown building overlooking the Trinity College grounds. After that, she drove back across the river via Butt Bridge to the Custom House. Her search there in the Planning and Land section had taken longer than expected but after half an hour she unearthed what she had come for. One last fact-finding exercise remained: a visit to the Registry of Deeds office in Henrietta Street. Her trawl there had been difficult but after several false leads, she succeeded in her quest.

Time for a bite of lunch. Emma decided to grab some pub-grub in Swan's Drink Emporium, a lively theme bar situated near the Parnell Square intersection with Bolton Street. The place was crammed but she managed to squeeze into a spot at the counter. Over a bowl of soup, lasagna and a mug of coffee, she brought a degree of order to the list of discoveries she'd made that morning. Barely registering what passed down her gullet, her concentration focused on this new information.

Bob Crosby's harsh words had spurred her into painstaking footwork. What she'd got was still as dull as the telephone directory, but the fresh data would provide her with the basis for a new direction. She now knew exactly who she should talk to in Lonsdale.

It was midday by the time Fr Clive Patterson finished with the church audit. The three hours with the accountant had been more genteel than anticipated. Even when discrepancies surfaced in the books, the probing remained calm. Before leaving the meeting, he'd asked the auditor what would happen when the accounts were presented to the Bishop. The auditor, a small wizened man with bald head and bottle-end glasses had smiled. 'Why, nothing, of course,' he answered, as though replying to the dumbest child in a school classroom.

Earlier that morning, before breakfast, he had paid special attention to his appearance. He'd taken a bath, washed his hair, shaved, paid extra attention to dental hygiene, sprinkled deodorant liberally on those areas of the body he considered vital, dressed in his best casual wear and subjected himself to a ruthless scrutiny in the bedroom mirror. Of late, he had taken note of what young men in the city were wearing, determined to keep abreast of the latest styles. His recent purchases had, he believed, met with current fashion dictates. His assessment of the image: not bad, not bad at all. Even Caroline Blackman had raised an eyebrow in reaction to his appearance. She thought he'd made the special effort to impress the Bishop's accountant and he had seen no reason to dissuade her from that mistaken assumption.

But now, with the accounts out of the way, walking into the sacristy, he felt less confident. The words he would deliver to Olive Moran had all seemed so cool the night before. He'd spent ages formulating lines, searching for the right words, anticipating Olive's reactions. Now he was having difficulty getting the various parts of his lanky body to conform to each other, let alone deliver eloquent words with any degree of flair.

In an effort to instil confidence in himself, he strode onto the altar area, whistling a current pop song, something he had never done before. He could not see Olive but he could hear a vacuum cleaner at work in the small side-altar area. 'Hello, Olive,' he called out, trying to sound nonchalant, crossing towards the side altar. Partially hidden, he could see the contours of a female rear-end and the back of a skirt peeking from behind the baptismal font.

His salutation had been drowned out by the whining of a vacuum cleaner. A shaft of light, pouring through a stained glass window, reflected its strong colours on that area of dress visible to him. For one insane moment he thought about sneaking up and grabbing the tantalising vision in both hands. He dismissed the irrational thought. Instead, he walked over to where the lead from the machine had been inserted into its socket and unplugged it.

Silence descended.

He waited, wide smile on face, for Olive to appear from behind the baptismal font. The smile turned to shock when Mrs Brenda Moran, not her daughter, turned to face him. She looked him in the eye with a puzzled stare, then lowered her sights to the plug in his hand. 'Oh, Father Patterson, it's you. Why have you unplugged the Hoover?'

He felt foolish standing there with the lead in his hand. 'I'm sorry, Mrs Moran, I... ah, I thought you... ah, what I was going to say above the noise was: how's Tom?'

'Nice of you to ask. He's showing signs of improvement. I'd be with him right now except Olive insisted on seeing him today.'

'I thought she went at nights?'

'Yes, she did, Father. It helped to give me a break... suited me, to tell you the truth, but y'know what young people are like. Anyway, she decided to switch things around for reasons best known to herself. I hope you don't mind her filling in for me when I can't make it here?'

'No, no, quite the contrary... what I mean is... it doesn't matter which of you... all labourers are equal in God's eyes when they toil in His orchard.' He wanted to stop blathering, knowing he was spouting absolute rubbish, but had difficulty in doing so. 'What I mean is: as long as the work gets done, that's what matters, isn't it?'

'Yes, Father, I'm sure you're right,' Mrs Moran said, looking at him in a strange, questioning sort of way. 'And now if you'll put the plug back, I'll be getting on with the work.'

'Oh, yes, sure,' he said, bending down to reconnect the Hoover. 'See you later then.' Feeling a complete idiot, he made a quick exit to the sacristy. He could feel, rather than see, Mrs Moran staring at him. 'Shit, shit, shit!' he hissed through clenched teeth, using the kind of language he abhorred when uttered by others. But he didn't know what else to say so he repeated the word over and over like some crazy mantra as he made his way back to the parochial house. He was furious with Olive Moran. *How could she do that to me? Now I'll have to go through the whole exercise again. 'Shit, shit, shit!'*

The Duggan farmhouse was not visible from the road. Emma drove around the perimeter wall searching for an entrance. Why was it that there was never anybody about to ask for directions when you needed them? The wall, eight feet in height and constructed with layers of fitted stone, looked as though it had been there for centuries. She was about to use her mobile phone to check the location with her father when finally she hit upon the entrance.

A series of steel bars formed a cattle grid that stretched between stone pillars on either side. The car's tyres rattled the grid bars as she crossed onto a gravel driveway. Heading along a single-track lane she passed through a tunnel of winter trees, their bare branches bereft of leaves, their skeletal twigs rimmed with a residue of white frost from the previous night. Emerging from the wooded area, she swung the car round a sharp bend and found herself in open country. Three-plank timber fencing on her right and a single-strand electrified wire fence on the left guided her through a flat expanse of drab pasture. The absence of livestock added an overall barren, desolate dimension to the scene. Several cement-cast drinking troughs, spread higgledy-piggledy across the land, put Emma in mind of flattened headstones.

One further turn along the narrow lane brought the Duggan residence into view. Tall pines framed the building and provided a screen that partially blocked out a row of farmyard buildings in the background. Beneath a chill, buttermilk sky, the afternoon light did little to breathe warmth on the period-built farmhouse. Emma drove into a gravel courtyard, the Hyundai's tyres making a crisp crunching sound on the granules. Frosty air nipped at her cheeks as soon as she got out of her car. Reacting with a body shiver, she buttoned her fleece jacket and tucked her scarf more tightly around her neck. She had only gone a few steps when the sound of barking dogs filled the air, the racket coming from one side of the house. Always wary of dogs, she was relieved when

Thelma Duggan, with two greyhounds secured to leashes, approached her. 'Hello, can I help you?' the woman asked.

'Yes, I hope so,' Emma replied, 'I'm Emma Boylan. My father, Arthur Boylan, acts as your solicitor. I work for the *Post* newspaper and I was hoping to have a chat with you.'

'Yes, yes, of course,' she said, sounding less than sure. 'Weren't you on the television recently? Yes, yes, of course, you're the journalist who won that award for something or other. Didn't realise you were Arthur's daughter. Fancy that.'

'That's me all right,' Emma said, feeling bad for having used her father by way of introduction. 'I was hoping you could spare a few minutes to talk with me.'

'Yes, yes of course... but, well, the thing is, you've caught me at a bad time. These two beauties must have their afternoon constitutional so—'

'I wouldn't mind walking with you, that way we could—'

'No, Emma, it might upset the dogs. I'll tell you what: why don't you wait inside the house, I'll be back in half an hour. George is out for the day but my daughter Yvonne will put the kettle on for you. She's just back from her honeymoon. Herself and Alec stayed here last night... had a good lie-in this morning... breakfast in bed no less... but they're up now.'

Before Emma could accept or decline the offer, Mrs Duggan approached the front door and rang the bell. Moments later a tall, good-looking woman opened the door. Wearing subtle makeup and dressed in a stylish petrol-blue trouser suit, she appeared to Emma as though she was about to leave the house. Except for age and weight, she bore a striking resemblance to Mrs Duggan. 'Hi, Mum,' she said, 'who's your friend?'

Introductions and explanations were made and Emma was invited into what Yvonne Cobain (née Duggan) called the breakfast room. 'Coffee or tea?' she asked.

'Coffee, thanks,' Emma said, taking a seat at a table in the brightly lit room. Yvonne busied herself making the coffee, all the while content to indulge in inconsequential chatter. A few minutes later, complete with two mugs of steaming hot coffee, she joined Emma at the table. 'I suppose you're here because of the death of our PP?' she asked.

'Yes, the parish priest; it's a big news story at the moment...
I'm trying to get a feeling of how his death affects those who knew
him. I believe your mother trains his greyhounds.'

A flash of irritation crossed Yvonne's face. 'I'm so sick of those
bloody greyhounds.' She was about to elaborate on the subject of
her mother's dogs when her husband appeared. A well-built man
with good looks and an engaging smile, he was wearing a blue
pinstripe suit, white shirt and burgundy tie. Yvonne did the introductions while he set about getting himself a coffee. By way of
explaining his formal attire, Yvonne told Emma he worked in the
Financial Centre. 'I'm going with him,' she said, 'but we'll wait a
few minutes 'till mother comes back with her blasted dogs, then
you can have her all to yourself.'

Alec Cobain winked at his wife and gave Emma the benefit of
his smile. 'If anyone can give you the lowdown on the dastardly
deeds taking place in these here parts,' he said, 'then it has to be
my favourite mother-in-law.'

As though on cue, Mrs Duggan, minus her canine friends,
entered the breakfast room.

Chapter 9

Thelma Duggan poured a measure of Remy Martin VSOP into a Waterford Crystal goblet and glanced inquiringly at Emma. 'You sure you won't have a shot?'

'No thanks, Mrs Duggan, I'm on my second mug of coffee...'

'Ah, come on, there's a chill outside that'd cut you to the bone.'

'Honestly, Mrs Duggan, I'm fine.'

Emma settled down on a low sofa and thought about her strategy for this interview. With the house to themselves, circumstances would never be better. Meeting the newlyweds had been interesting but it did nothing to add to the knowledge she already possessed in regard to the murder.

As soon as Yvonne and her new husband had left the house, Thelma Duggan ushered her from the breakfast room into a warm, spacious living room. Guarded by a firescreen, ash logs and coal burned brightly in an open fireplace. The room itself, which was probably once called the parlour, had a lived-in appearance that normally wouldn't appeal to Emma but did in this instance. It was the sort of room her husband Vinny, with his appreciation for all things antique, would feel right at home in. Brass objects and furniture showed signs of the green incrustation and the long-polished shine that Vinny had taught her to associate with genuine antiquity.

Thelma removed the firescreen from the front of the fireplace and placed it beside an ornate brass coal scuttle. 'There now, that's better,' she said. 'Now we can have a cosy chat in comfort. I suppose you'd better tell me exactly what you want to talk about.'

'Thanks, Mrs Duggan, I was going to—'

'Please call me Thelma.'

'Sure, thanks, all right, Thelma. I was going to ask you about the land your husband tried to develop for housing.'

'Oh,' Thelma said, taken aback by the question. 'What about it?'

'I believe you and Fr O'Gorman jointly owned that land.'

'Where on earth did you hear that?'

'It's recorded in the Land Registry office.'

Thelma subjected Emma to a hard stare. This was not the sort of cosy tête-à-tête she'd envisaged. 'You've been digging into our affairs, I see.'

'Looked up a couple of files, nothing more,' Emma said, trying to sound casual. 'Didn't do anything that any member of the public couldn't have done with equal ease.'

'Well, look, Emma, seeing as how George employs your father as his solicitor, you probably have access to all our files so I suppose I can talk openly to you... after all, you're on our side, right?'

Emma tried not to let her annoyance show. 'That's not how it works, Thelma.'

'What? You're *not* on our side?'

'It's not that. My father would never allow me to see his files... and as to whose side I'm on; I'm not on anyone's side... except the side of truth.'

A derisive smirk appeared on Thelma's face. 'Very noble of you, Emma... high moral ground and all that... and from a journalist.'

Emma ignored the sarcasm. 'It's not like that, Thelma, I simply try to establish the facts, let them speak for themselves.'

'Well, in that case I've nothing to fear. I'll tell you the sorry saga behind the twenty acres. No mystery really; as you say, it's there on the records for all to see. Some years ago, myself and Fr O'Gorman purchased the land. He came from a wealthy family, did you know that?'

'No, I didn't know that.'

'Yes, his people were quite wealthy... extensive farmers from the Midlands. Good breeding. Saw to it that their only son, Jack, never wanted for anything; always willing to supplement the meagre income he got from the church. And then, when his father passed away just over six years ago, he inherited £190,000. That's what in today's Euro money?'

Emma made a quick calculation in her head. 'About two hundred and forty thousand Euros; quite a lot of cash.'

'Certainly is and no mistake. He asked my advice on how best to invest it. I had from time to time drawn his attention to invest-ment schemes that gave good returns, schemes that avoided shelling out too much to the taxman. I saw the twenty acres as a great investment opportunity.'

'You advised him to buy it?'

'Yes I did. He liked the idea, asked me to come in on the deal.'

'Why would he do that?'

'Because of his position as parish priest.'

'What difference would that make?'

'He didn't want to be publicly linked to the purchase.'

'What did he intend to do with the land?'

'D'you know, I don't think Fr Jack was ever sure,' Thelma replied, putting more coal on the fire. 'He could see the long-term potential for housing development.'

'He was right about that,' Emma said. 'The demand for expansion in this part of the city is unstoppable.'

'Quite right, Emma, but it wasn't something he wanted to get involved in straight away. Initially, he just wanted to use the land for the greyhounds, set up our own trials for the dogs, run our own private coursing events.'

'Is that what happened?'

'Well, yes. At first, we used to walk the dogs there, raise the odd hare, let them loose, give them a taste for the kill.'

'A taste for the kill?' Emma asked. 'How'd you do that?'

'Simple,' Thelma said, glad to steer the conversation her way. 'We use an impaired hare... let the dogs after it, ensure a kill.'

'Impaired hare? What does that mean?'

'We'd break one of the hare's legs after it had been snared.'

'Break it on purpose?'

'Yes, it slows the hare down... allows the hounds to catch it, gives them a taste for blood.'

'But it's so cruel,' Emma said, genuinely shocked. 'How could anyone do such a thing?'

Thelma shrugged her shoulders indifferently. 'It's no more

cruel than what happens every day in the wild. That's nature...
survival of the fittest.'

Emma was sickened by what she had heard. She wanted to
banish the ugly images of blood-letting from her mind, return to
the subject of the twenty acres. She held the mug of coffee to her
lips, sipped slowly, using the time to refocus her thoughts. 'How
did it happen that your husband's name appeared as the person
seeking planning permission?'

'That's a bit complicated to explain. Like I said before, Fr Jack
didn't want his parishioners to know he had an interest in the
land. He was concerned by the scandals levelled at the Church
nowadays, all this clergy-bashing that has become so prevalent in
the media. He was anxious to avoid drawing attention to himself,
you know... this talk about the Church's vast wealth... while the
poor remain with us... and the pittance paid out to victims who
were abused by rogue priests. He once said to me – how can I
preach about it being harder for a rich man to get into heaven
than it is for a camel to pass through the eye of a needle, while I
am seen as a fat cat myself? So, he made an arrangement to hide
his involvement by agreeing to let George's name appear as the
front man.'

'He signed the land over to your husband?'

'Purely a book transaction, a convenience that is used in similar cases when a real owner wants to remain anonymous.'

'So, let's suppose there was a dispute, how would Fr
O'Gorman prove his entitlements?'

'All parties to the agreement signed legally binding covenants.'

'What would happen if one of the parties were to meet with,
let's say, an unfortunate accident... or die?'

'If anything happened to me, Fr Jack would automatically get
my share and if anything happened to him... vice versa.'

Emma took a deep breath. 'I see,' she said, intrigued by this
nugget of information. 'But, on the basis that you and the parish
priest were the owners of the twenty acres, why did Fr O'Gorman
object to the proposed development? Why did he allow your
husband to go ahead with plans to develop the site and then,
when most of the preliminary work was completed, pull the
plug?'

Thelma Duggan's mouth pursed, her eyeball-to-eyeball appraisal of Emma was cool and critical. 'I'm not sure I ought to answer that.'

'Why is that?' Emma asked, her journalistic instincts now on full alert.

Thelma held the goblet in front of her face, gazed into the fire's refracted light on the facets of the cut glass, before taking a swig of the brandy. Several moments elapsed before she spoke. 'Without going into detail, I can tell you this much: Fr O'Gorman has a nephew, Christopher White, only son of his late sister, Gemma.'

'I thought you said Fr O'Gorman was an only son?'

'Yes, that's what I said; he was an only son but he had a sister. And, as it turns out, she had an only son. Gemma was an odd one by all accounts. She defied her family by announcing her engagement to someone they considered unsuitable. His name was White and he worked in the music business... managed a band that nobody had ever heard of. Well, needless to say, her parents were furious. They refused to attend the wedding and would have nothing to do with her, not even when she gave birth to Christopher.'

'What did Fr O'Gorman think of the situation? Did he support her?'

'He rarely spoke of his sister but I suspect he had little time for her after she married White. He never wanted anything to do with his nephew, Christopher. Once, just once, I remember Fr Jack mentioning Christopher... we were both a bit boozed at the time... he said the lad was a ne'er-do-well fellow. Wanted nothing to do with him.

'All that changed about six months ago. Somehow or other, Christopher discovered that his uncle had inherited wealth over the years. He seemed to think that through his late mother, he was entitled to some of that wealth. Christopher also discovered that Fr Jack was part owner of the twenty acres we're talking about; probably found out the same way you did. He made contact, put the squeeze on his uncle for cash. This was about the same time as the final stages of planning procedures were nearing completion.

'But, as with all developments nowadays, a group of malcontents opposed to the project materialised. Christopher White was aware of this unease and saw his chance to threaten his uncle. He warned Fr Jack that he would inform the parishioners that their beloved parish priest was involved in the development unless he coughed up a lot more cash.'

'Blackmail?'

'Yes, in essence, that's what it was. Fr Jack panicked, gave him money through a "go-between" to keep him quiet. The poor man was terrified in case his role in the development became exposed. He came to George and told him to scrap the project, said he was afraid of repercussions further down the line. Well, this was like a bolt out of the blue as far as myself and George were concerned. As part owners, we had invested time and money in the project. The financial rewards would have been quite substantial for us, so we argued with him, tried to make him see sense. George and Fr Jack had an unholy row, the first time they had ever had words. George steadfastly refused to scrap the plans. Two days later, Fr Jack lodged objections to the scheme and the rest, as they say, is history.'

Watching Thelma drain the last drop of brandy and place the glass on the mantelpiece, it was obvious to Emma that her hostess wished to conclude the discussion. Nevertheless, she risked one more question. 'Before I go, Thelma,' she said, rising from the sofa, 'can you tell me if Fr O'Gorman ever met with his nephew, this Christopher White?'

'No, I don't believe the two men ever met face to face. As far as I know, White hasn't shown his face around these parts... but then again, he could be in our midst and none of us would know.'

Emma shook hands and said goodbye, thanking Thelma for her hospitality. Thelma smiled but it was apparent to Emma that something was bothering the farmer's wife.

Motoring back to the city centre, Emma tried to put a construction on what she'd been told. Her initial thoughts that George Duggan might have been behind the murder because of jealousy no longer appealed to her. Both Thelma and George Duggan had a far better motive than jealousy. They appeared to have gained a chunk of very valuable real estate as a result of the priest's demise. But would the Duggans, who were financially sound in their own right, go to the lengths of killing someone to add to their wealth? She would have to keep an open mind on that for the moment.

And what of Yvonne Cobain? Emma thought about the graceful daughter of the Duggans, wondering if she had ever been exposed to the rumour that Fr Jack O'Gorman was her real father. Trying to assess the effects such a rumour would have on a young bride intrigued Emma. Would Yvonne let her new husband know? What would Alec make of it?

But it was the revelation concerning Christopher White that most intrigued her. Here was a young man who appeared to think his mother had been diddled out of her inheritance. He was already blackmailing the parish priest, receiving sums of money, so how would it benefit him to murder his uncle? A bit like killing the goose that laid the golden eggs. The truth was, Emma admitted reluctantly, she hadn't got a handle on this investigation.

Not yet.

Her report to Bob Crosby was going to be a slim one.

Chapter 10

Music bellowed from McCann's Arch Bar. As the only public house in Lonsdale to feature regular *seisiúins*, it tended to attract the younger set. Even so, a few of the older residents, long-standing fans of traditional Irish music, propped up the bar, soaking up what was on offer. They ignored the designer drinks and shorts being consumed by the younger revellers all around them, fortified instead by Guinness, humming along with the familiar tunes and ballads.

George Duggan, who could never be considered a music fan, sat in an alcove to one side of the stage, sipping a gin and tonic. After a day that had not gone well for him, he felt in need of some alcohol sustenance. He chose McCann's, a pub he rarely frequented, because he was unlikely to bump into his friends or business associates there. The people he mixed with gave their patronage to the Mill House, one of Lonsdale's most sedate watering holes.

He attempted to blot out the music coming from the stage. His thoughts returned to a lunchtime meeting he'd had with solicitor Arthur Boylan in the Berkeley Court, one of Dublin 4's most fashionable hotels.

Before sitting down to dine in the hotel's plush Palm Court Café, he had felt the need to use the hotel's toilet facilities. Washing his hands he glanced in the mirror and noticed two small particles of tissue paper stuck to his face. 'Damn it,' he said, remembering nicking himself while shaving that morning, something he'd done on a regular basis lately. To stop the blood flow he had torn away two tiny portions of toilet roll and applied them to his face, fully intending to remove them before leaving the house. He had forgotten to do so. Annoyed with himself, he removed the offending blood-caked particles, hoping not too many people had noticed them.

The meeting turned out to be a disagreeable experience. They'd barely finished their soup when Boylan imparted the first instalment of his bad tidings. 'I've had correspondence from Fr Jack O'Gorman's nephew, a Mr Christopher White,' the solicitor informed him, dabbing the corners of his mouth with his napkin. 'He's going to contest his uncle's will.'

'How does that concern me? Fr O'Gorman left nothing to me, or my wife for that matter,' George replied.

'Oh, it concerns you all right,' Boylan said. 'Fr O'Gorman may not have named you in his will but White claims that you and your wife unlawfully stripped his uncle's assets and cheated him out of his investments.'

'What?'

'According to White, the priest's last will and testament fails to show the sort of wealth that should be evident. His contention is that you and your wife are responsible for the deficiency.'

'Absolute rubbish. All my business dealings with the parish priest were above board.'

'Clearly, Christopher White doesn't think so. He cites a number of investments and life policies that name your wife as beneficiary in the event of Fr O'Gorman's death. His biggest gripe, however, concerns the twenty-acre site you recently sought planning permission for. He claims the land lawfully belongs to his uncle.'

'That's a load of codswallop.'

'Maybe, but he claims he has documents that say otherwise.'

'I don't care what he's got. Fr O'Gorman and my wife signed a legal covenant in respect of the land in question.'

'Yes, I know that,' Boylan said, before stopping to allow the main course to be served. Tasting the food, both men assured the head waiter that everything was satisfactory before they returned to the subject. 'White's solicitor sent me photocopies of the covenant.'

'So, where's the problem?'

'I'm not so sure it'll stand up to scrutiny.'

'It was drawn up by O'Gorman's solicitor.'

'Yes, George, it was, but it's open to interpretation.' Arthur Boylan put his knife and fork down and spoke in a tone that failed to hide his irritation. 'Why in God's name didn't you come to me with this business over the covenant in the first place? I would have advised you, pointed out the shortcomings in the document. Not much point having me as your solicitor if you don't consult me on a matter as important as this.'

And now, some eight hours later, sitting in the alcove of McCann's, with the sound of accordion, tin whistle, and bodhrán assailing his ears, he admitted he'd made a mistake. But all was not lost. In a week or so, Boylan would establish whether Christopher White was prepared to pursue legal action or not. In the meanwhile, he and his wife would have to wait and hope that White backed off.

He decided to have one more drink before making his way back to the farm. One of the floor staff, a pretty girl in her teens, took his order and, minutes later, placed a gin and tonic in front of him. She thanked him with a winning smile when he rewarded her with a generous tip. The clean-cut alcoholic beverage, with its slice of lemon and ice, had the ability of easing the turmoil in his head. The sounds from the stage appeared to mellow somewhat. Except, that is, for the sound of the accordion. It still grated. Of all musical instruments, it irritated him most. Hearing the offending noise issuing from the instrument's metal reeds reminded him of the saying: A gentleman is someone who knows how to play the accordion... *but doesn't*. His sentiments exactly.

Halfway through his drink, the pub's proprietor, Donnie McCann appeared in front of him, a scowl on his face. 'I'd like you to leave the premises,' he demanded, taking hold of the unfinished drink.

George stared at him in disbelief. 'What? What's this? What the hell are you saying?'

'You're not wanted in this pub. If I'd clocked you coming in I would've refused you in the first place. As it is, several customers have complained about your presence and have threatened to walk out.'

Bewildered, George Duggan stared at McCann, not understanding what was happening. He had known the publican all his life and while they weren't exactly bosom buddies, they had always been civil to each other. 'What's got into you, Donnie? If this is some sort of a wind-up, well I—'

'Mr Duggan,' the publican cut in, 'here's your money back. Now please get out, leave before your presence here causes a riot. The people of this town don't take kindly to having someone like you in their midst.'

Now, Duggan understood. They were blaming him for the death of the parish priest, accusing him of murder. With this realisation came a hush in the pub. The musicians and the singers were mute. All conversation in the premises came to a standstill. Apart from the pounding of his heart and the swishing sound of an overhead fan, the world appeared to be on hold. The young waitress who had served his drink moved towards him and placed the tip he had given her on the table in front of him. Before turning her back on him she gave him a look of absolute loathing and pointedly wiped her hands with her service cloth. He opened his mouth to speak but couldn't formulate the words to express the outrage he felt. In the continuing unearthly silence, Donnie McCann stretched his arm, ramrod straight, and pointed his forefinger in the direction of the exit.

Like some dream sequence played out in slow motion, he arose from his seat and moved towards the door. A sea of faces reproached him. In the midst of this walk of shame, all those hate-filled faces appeared to merge into soft focus, presenting themselves as one unified, silent vision of condemnation.

Outside McCann's, he had difficulty coming to terms with what had happened. The sounds of musicians starting up again inside the pub left him in no doubt about the reality of the situation. Except for two dogs sniffing each other's rear-ends beneath the spill of light from a lamppost, he was alone. A cold breeze gusted on the dark street.

Had anyone been there to see him make his way unsteadily to the car park, they would have said he was drunk. In some respects he was drunk, but the stupor had not been induced by over-consumption of alcohol. The realisation that he had gone from being regarded as one of Lonsdale's most respected inhabitants to that of social outcast was enough to make him feel dizzy.

Caroline Blackman got into bed, switched on the reading light and opened one of her mother's battered copybooks. Earlier, in McCann's Arch Bar, she had kept her alcohol consumption to a minimum. Even so, she had taken a drink of water and two aspirins before undressing, lest one of her habitual headaches decided to disrupt her sleep. She had enjoyed the music and song in the pub but could have done without the cigarette smoke that permeated the premises and, even now, continued to sting her eyes. Like everyone else in the pub she had witnessed George Duggan's ignominious exit. She had met George Duggan in the parochial house on a few occasions in the company of Fr O'Gorman. She neither liked nor disliked him but she didn't agree with the humiliation meted out to him in front of so many people.

Flicking through the pages of the diary, she strove to put the incident from her mind. Finding the page she wanted, she looked at the photograph of her mother she had placed there on her last reading. The black-and-white print showed Nelly Joyce as a young woman, aged about 20, maybe 21. It had been given to her along with an assortment of other souvenirs days before death had brought a lasting peace to her mother.

There was no denying the striking resemblance that existed between the old photographic image of her mother and her own looks. The dark-lashed eyes in particular, large and wide-set, were unmistakably products of the same gene pool. The nose too, with its subtle upturned tip, and beneath it, a top lip that arched upwards to reveal even front teeth, bore clone-like similarities. Her mother had been beautiful in an understated sort of way. This realisation caused her to re-evaluate the opinion she had held of her own looks for the greater part of her life – an opinion that cast her in the role of plain Jane. Accepting that her mother was beautiful, and accepting that she shared those looks, it followed that she couldn't honestly think of herself as plain. She kissed the photograph, told her mother she loved her, put the print to one side and began to read.

Extracts from the diary of Nelly Joyce – aged 18
Date 14th August 1970. Carysfort Training College.

Dear Diary

The weekend, T.G. No classes. Weather great.

Decided to wear my new miniskirt.

The nuns go bananas when we wear anything above the knees in class.

Felt 'with it'. Seamus picked me up at the College at 4 o'clock.

He's got a car – only good thing about him!

Not much of a looker. Bad skin. Pock-marked face.

Saw 'Butch Cassidy and the Sundance Kid'. Fell madly in love with Robert Redford. Towards the end of the film Seamus tried to kiss me. I wouldn't let him. Not in front of the Sundance Kid.

After the pictures he took me to a Chinese restaurant in Wicklow Street.

Heard all about his job as a barman in a pub in Booterstown. Boring!

Went back to his flat. He has a really decent record player.

Seamus opened a bottle of wine – one he nicked from work.

We sat on the bed and kissed. I kept my eyes shut and my lips clenched.

Called a halt when he groped between my legs.

He was annoyed but said he respected me because of my high moral standards.

Hypocrite! We finished the wine and played more records. When I played 'Band of Gold' by Freda Payne, he asked to look at the Claddagh ring on my finger. I let him take it off, told him the story behind the ring's two hands and the heart between them.

Worn on the right hand with the heart pointing towards the nail, it means the girl is free to marry. Worn on the left hand pointing away from the nail, it means she is engaged.

He noticed I wore mine on my right hand and got all misty eyed.

One day, says he, I want to marry a teacher.

I told him if he didn't get me back to the College by the 9 o'clock deadline I'd be expelled and never get to be a teacher.

Drove me back and left me at the gate but held on to the ring.

He said he would give it back if I agreed to go out with him again.

I told him to get lost. We argued. He left without giving the ring back.

Met up with my pal Esther Clarke and some of the Seniors.

I told them I never wanted to see Seamus again. They wanted to know why.

I told them that Seamus had got my ring.

They fell around the place laughing. I didn't see what was so funny.

When Esther realised I didn't get the joke, she told me that the expression 'ring' was used as a slang word meaning virginity.

I went scarlet. Told them they were all filthy-minded sluts.

They laughed all the way to the dorm. I felt completely stupid.

Goodnight Diary.

Caroline Blackman closed her mother's diary. The passage she had just read was one of the few entries that brought a smile to her face. Other entries from the period when Nelly Joyce was studying to be a schoolteacher depicted a vulnerable teenage girl full of romantic notions, with little sophistication and no proper mechanism to guard against the problems that lay ahead for her. Away from the protection of her foster parents, she'd been alone in the world with no siblings or close relations to confide in or share her anxieties.

Caroline switched off the light and snuggled down on her pillow. Unconsciously, she felt the Claddagh ring on her right hand, and allowed the fingertips of her other hand to caress its crowned heart-shape ornamentation before shutting her eyes.

Chapter 11

Unwilling to divest himself of his overcoat, Detective Inspector Jim Connolly sat in his temporary office, brooding, unhappy with the world, disillusioned with his own domestic situation. Alone in the cold, dreary, damp barracks building, ensconced in McGettigan's lair, he hunched his shoulders, shivered and cursed silently. A small two-bar electric heater, the kind found nowadays at car-boot sales, sat forlornly in the corner of the room throwing out its pathetic measure of warmth. The contrast between this office and the centrally heated home he had left less than an hour earlier could not be more pronounced. And yet, the physical discomforts inherent in Lonsdale's police station were as nothing when compared with the soul-piercing chill that existed within the walls of the house he called home.

He had made it across the city ahead of the early morning traffic build-up, before Lonsdale had come to life, before most of the inhabitants had stirred from their nocturnal slumber. On the drive, his over-burdened brain formulated a freshly minted theory. The half-baked hypothesis demanded that he should get away from his house, away from the problems bedevilling his marriage, if he hoped to bring a semblance of peace to his troubled mind. The trick was to immerse himself in work, get stuck into this latest murder case, lose himself in the madness that was part and parcel of all such cases.

As a theory, it wasn't bad – not up there with Einstein, admittedly – but not bad all the same. However, Connolly knew life didn't easily conform to theories, no matter how sensible they might sound. Already, his best intentions were forfeit, his mind refusing to heed his wishes. Without success, he tried to blot out domestic issues and focus exclusively on the Fr O'Gorman murder. Instead, dark images from the previous night's row with his wife hogged the lion's share of his contemplation.

His marriage to Iseult Smyth-O'Brien, a match once described by his parents as being made in heaven had, in more recent times, seemed more likely to have been concocted in hell. That his parents should so readily have approved of him marrying the lovely Iseult should, in itself, have been warning enough. After all, throughout his life they had opposed every worthwhile thing he'd otherwise ever wanted, while at the same time pushing him towards things he didn't want.

They had strenuously opposed him when he decided to pursue law enforcement as a career. They'd been aghast. What on earth would their friends think? It had led to major upheaval in the family. Is the boy mad, they'd asked? Hadn't he got top grades in college? Hadn't he secured enough points to have his choice of university faculties?

But, against all advice, he had followed the dictates of his heart and mind and joined the police force, became a member of the *Garda Síochána*. It was a dream he had cherished since earliest boyhood. His parents did not, and would not, understand. They were slightly ashamed of him. When asked by their friends what career their son Jim had chosen, his parents would simply answer by uttering the word *law* and leave it at that. Even after he'd progressed through the ranks, even after he'd made it to detective inspector grade, they still felt their son had somehow failed them.

But when he'd shown up on their doorstep with Iseult on his arm, and they'd discovered that she was one of the wealthy and well-connected Smyth-O'Brien family, they approved wholeheartedly. Like himself, they were dazzled by her youth, her elegance and beauty, but for them it was the fact of *who* she was that impressed most. Such paternal endorsement should have set the alarm bells ringing. It failed to do so. The truth was, his infatuation with Iseult blinded him to the more salient realities of life.

And now, ten years later, it had all gone terribly wrong. The marriage had run its course. If he were to be totally honest with himself, he would have to admit that problems were evident from day one. He just hadn't wanted to acknowledge them at the time. On return from their honeymoon, Iseult's first act had been to bring him to see the house *Daddy* had bought for them.

Daddy's wedding present. Surprise, surprise!

The gesture had annoyed and embarrassed him. He had wanted to provide for his wife without being beholden to anyone. When he intimated this to his new bride, she pooh-poohed the idea. 'Don't be silly, darling, of course we'll let Daddy help. We couldn't possibly live on your pittance of a salary.' That had sparked off their first row but it hadn't changed her reliance on Daddy for extra comforts. Her father continued to spoil her shamelessly, buying her cars, horses and expensive items for the house.

Iseult found excuses not to accompany him to functions associated with his job, preferring to devote all her time to social activities connected with her own anointed circle. He had studiously avoided allowing word of his marital stress to surface outside the four walls of the home. This led to incorrect perceptions being formed by those he mixed with in the outside world. His colleagues mistakenly believed he purposely avoided bringing her to police-related occasions. He had heard the whispers: *Connolly doesn't want us to set eyes on his young wife; he's over-protective; afraid that some of us younger bucks will run away with her.* Yes, he'd heard the whispers. All of them contrary to the facts. He did nothing to set the record straight. Better they believed that than to know the humiliating truth.

His hapless marriage had stumbled along from year to year, barely tolerable, both parties attempting to avoid unpleasantness, until six months ago. At the time, he had been working on a heavy caseload that took up all his waking hours. This gave Iseult something else to complain about: You never spend any time in the home any more, she would say, making irritating childlike pouting gestures – You're wed to your job... it's all you really care about... what about me?... what about me, me, me?

And so it went. On and on. Relentless.

There was, however, one area of the marriage that remained constant and good. Perversely, it seemed to him, their sex life did not suffer. They made love with the same passion that had drawn them together in the first place. Physically, they were compatible, capable of indulging in bouts of wild, erotic passion, comfortable with each other's sexual needs.

And then, six months ago, this singular aspect of compatibility had shattered and broken down too. He assumed she had found another lover. It was not something she confessed to, not something he could prove… not then. She informed him that she desired to sleep in a separate bedroom. That was it, no reason given, no excuses offered. Perplexed, he sought explanations. He got none. Her only reaction was to freeze him out with a sullen stare. All his efforts at meaningful dialogue had been to no avail. The irony wasn't lost on him: he had the ability to extract confessions from the most hardened criminals during interrogation sessions, but remained hopelessly ineffectual when facing his wife.

In more recent months, she had gone away for weekends without telling him where she was going. She had begun to spend more and more time away from the house in the company of her friends, sometimes not coming home for two or three nights on the trot. He was tempted to find out where she was staying, discover exactly who she was staying with, but he resisted. It was a course he could have easily put into action, something he was trained to do, but he held back, resisted the urge. Better not to know, he told himself. Ignorance was bliss; wasn't that what they say? If he did know what she was up to, he would have to do something about it. And he didn't have the appetite to embark on that kind of action.

Last night changed all that.

His mind was about to rewind on this, the most recent and saddest episode of his very own domestic soap opera, when Sergeant McGettigan pushed through the door. 'You're in early,' the sergeant said, taking a seat in front of what used to be his desk.

'Well, you know what they say about the early worm.'

McGettigan smiled, his eyes introspective. 'Well now, if the early worm wanted to keep abreast of the latest developments in this part of Dublin's fair city, that worm would really need to have been here last night.'

'Why? What did I miss?'

'Aaaah-ha! You haven't heard then?'

'No, but I can see you're dying to tell me.'

'Aye, I will, but I'm going to plug in the kettle first, make myself a coffee, get the ould stomach ready for the day. You want a cuppa?'

'Yes, I could certainly do with a brew, thanks.'

Connolly watched McGettigan leave the office and allowed himself a sardonic little chuckle. The man was a mess. He looked as though he'd slept in his uniform. His hair had not been combed, stubble of beard glistened on his cheeks and chin, a half-smoked cigarette remained wedged behind one ear, his shirt collar gaped open, unbuttoned, incapable of spanning his expansive neck, and his eyes looked bleary and sunken behind dark circles.

And yet, if Connolly could believe the snippets of gossip doing the rounds in the station, McGettigan was quite the lady's man. The sergeant had earned a reputation as a 'hammer man', a term Connolly understood to mean someone who sought sexual favours from any woman foolish enough to fall for his line in flattery and deception. Apparently, McGettigan was such an animal. It mattered not a whit to the sergeant whether his conquests were married or single, whether they were young, old, white, coloured, pretty, plain, Catholic, Protestant, Jew or agnostic; nothing mattered so long as they satisfied his hunger for gratification.

Connolly was pondering this state of affairs when McGettigan sidled back into the small office, a mug of coffee in each hand. 'Now I'm ready to face the world,' he said, placing one of the steaming mugs in front of Connolly. He sat down, downed most of his coffee at a gulp and nodded with satisfaction. 'Not bad, not bad at all, even if I say so myself.'

Connolly took a tentative sip from his mug and was pleasantly surprised. It was good. 'So tell me, Sergeant, what did I miss last night?'

'Fun and games down at the Arch Bar. Donnie McCann – he owns the premises – decided to throw George Duggan out of the pub.'

'Why?'

'Because Donnie McCann and some of his regulars have decided that Duggan killed Fr O'Gorman.'

'That's a dangerous assumption to make.'

'You can say that again. McCann and a hardcore mob of hotheads are meeting in his pub this morning.'

'What? A lynching party?'

'Something like that, yes.'

'In that case, we'd better do something.'

'I intend to,' McGettigan said, polishing off his coffee, placing the empty mug on the desk. 'I'm going to talk to McCann before he opens this morning, read the riot act, bawl him out, knock some sense into his thick skull.'

'Subtle approach, eh?'

'Only language he understands. Might be helpful if you came along. He just might take notice of someone like yourself, top brass and all that.'

'Good idea, I'll go along with you.'

'Great. See you later, say 10 o'clock,' McGettigan said, retrieving the cigarette butt from behind his ear as he ambled out of the office.

Connolly continued to sip his coffee, lapsing into a reflective silence, putting what McGettigan had just told him on temporary hold, allowing his thoughts to return to events closer to home... to Iseult.

In his mind's eye, he pictured her as she looked on their first date. She'd been so beautiful. Stunning. Her face flawless, every feature looking as though it had been modelled in exquisite porcelain, the head perched delicately above a long graceful neck, crowned with gold strands of hair, neatly swept back and held in place with a dark-green velvet bow. In time, he would discover that the perfection he fondly likened to sculptured porcelain could be every bit as cold and unyielding as that very china-clay substance.

He had arrived home last night shortly before midnight. The house was in darkness. Iseult was absent. He showered and went to bed, read a few pages of Elizabeth George's novel, *Deception On His Mind*, before turning out the light and bedding his head down on the pillow. Less than five minutes had elapsed when he heard a car pull into the driveway. He heard doors slam and the sound of two people talking and laughing.

One of the voices belonged to Iseult.

He got out of his bed, went to the window and peered down into the courtyard in front of the house. Sensor lights, activated by the car's arrival, cast an eerily colourless sheen on the scene. A man placed his arm around Iseult's waist and playfully swung her around, lifting her feet off the ground. Holding on to the window frame for support, Connolly watched them move unsteadily towards the front door, leaving him in no doubt that they were both well and truly inebriated. Talking loudly and shrieking with laughter, they disappeared beneath the front porch. Silence followed.

What were they doing?

A new sound emerged. A slow rhythm sound, almost inaudible at first, grew in volume. Thump, thump, thump. He could hardly believe his ears; *Daddy's* girl was being unceremoniously screwed against the front door of *Daddy's* house. Lest there be any doubt, he identified the familiar grunting and groaning sounds coming from Iseult, sounds that, until that moment, he had foolishly believed were exclusively his to hear.

It was at this point that his brain snapped.

And now, next morning, sitting in McGettigan's dingy office, he forced his mind to blot out what had happened. He wanted to forget the confrontation he'd had with his wife and her lover.

It wasn't easy.

Subliminal flashes shot through his head. There was no escaping the ugly scene. He saw himself throw a punch at the man who, being the worse for alcohol intake, sprawled backwards, his manhood exposed, a stupid grin fixed on his face. His wife screamed abuse at him, thumped him with her fists before going to the aid of the fallen paramour.

After that he had gone inside the house, locked the door, and returned to the bedroom. From his window he watched Iseult help the man back to the car. Some time later, with his wife behind the wheel, the engine roared into life. He watched her negotiate a three-point turn, allowing the bumpers to hit the kerb stones on each turn, before making her exit.

He had not heard from her since and had no idea where she had gone. Considering the amount of drink taken, it was a miracle she had made it to her destination without crashing or being pulled over by the law. Just the sort of publicity he didn't need. He had no idea what the next move would be but sooner, rather than later, he had no doubt some developments would occur, another ugly twist would emerge on the downward spiral his marriage was now consigned to.

In the meanwhile, he would attempt to return to his new-found theory, try to refocus his energies into resolving the Fr O'Gorman murder.

Chapter 12

It was a grey, dismal morning, the kind that might easily coax one to remain in bed. Emma Boylan, however, would never let something as trivial as the weather upset her plans. For the third time in as many days she found herself parked in Lonsdale, peering through the windscreen, underwhelmed by the vista on offer. Slate-grey clouds stretched blanket-like above the buildings while the cross on top of the church steeple dissolved into the underbelly of the layered masses.

She switched off the ignition.

Her mood, akin to the oppressive atmosphere engulfing Lonsdale, was decidedly dark. She had good reason to feel out of sorts. Before leaving her apartment earlier that morning she'd lost out in a confrontational phone call with her editor in the *Post*. Bob Crosby had left her in no doubt about how he felt in regard to her progress to date. 'If you can't get me something worthwhile, something I can go to print with in the next day or so, I'll have no choice but to assign you to another project.'

Never one to accept a rebuke with grace, Emma had strenuously argued with him but she was long enough in the newspaper game to appreciate his point of view. He needed fresh headlines, he had a newspaper to fill, readers to consider and the all-important circulation numbers to protect and enhance. Knowing this did little to alleviate her growing frustration. Today, she decided to set herself some priorities: she would:

—talk to the right people
—ask the hard questions
—demand answers.

First stop: the parochial house. She'd missed Fr Patterson on her last visit; that put him on top of her list for this morning's itinerary. She was about to get out of her car when, as though on cue, she saw the curate making his way from the parochial house to the side porch of the church. Emma, a believer in the serendipity theory, smiled. *It's an omen, Divine intervention.*

She locked the car doors and strode purposely to the front entrance of Saint John the Baptist Church. Rain had begun to fall as the church's heavy timber door creaked and yielded to her push. In the semi-darkness of the porch area, she brushed against an elderly lady by the holy-water font. The woman, in the act of blessing herself, used her wet fingertips to spray Emma.

Endowed with this gratuitous benediction, Emma entered the nave, sat in the rearmost pew, lowered the kneeling board and knelt. She had fallen by the wayside as far as religious beliefs were concerned but she found herself making the sign of the cross and silently expressing the blessing she had learned as a child. *In the name of the Father, and of the Son, and of the Holy Ghost.* The simple exercise still managed to bring with it the same feeling of comfort she remembered from those almost forgotten days. But now, the chill in the air dissipated her evocation of past wholesomeness. The church's interior, gloomy and damp, was empty except for her own presence and that of a young woman who appeared to be replacing small white curtains on the central altar's tabernacle.

Within minutes of Emma's vigil, Fr Clive Patterson made his appearance on the altar. Wearing a red quilted jacket, navy check shirt, indigo denim jeans and desert shoes, the 'cool' ensemble had the effect of accentuating the cleric's elongated, angular physique.

The church's acoustics amplified and slightly distorted the dialogue between Fr Patterson and the woman. Emma could not be sure whether they were aware of her presence. They certainly acted as though they were alone. Reading their body language, Emma detected a nervousness in the priest, his movements jerky and unco-ordinated. Deciphering the female's movements proved more difficult. When Fr Patterson reached out to hold the woman's hand, his gesture was rejected. By now the voices were slightly louder, the church's vaulted ceiling and stone-cut pillars creating an eerie echo that endowed their words with an other-worldly dimension.

Just as Emma's ear had adjusted to the sounds, rain began to beat against the stained glass windows. It became increasingly difficult to pick up on what was being said. Even so, it was obvious that the two people on the altar were engaged in some sort of disagreement. Within minutes, the rain eased. The voices remained low, so that Emma had to concentrate her hearing to make out what was being said.

'Look, Fr Patterson,' the woman said. 'I'm sorry if I gave you the impression that I fancied you. I was glad when you offered the job to my mother... I was grateful to you. That's all there was to it.'

'I'm... I'm sorry Olive, I know... I know this is all a bit... a bit sudden,' the priest said, his words faltering. 'What with your father lying in hospital and all that, I've picked... I've picked a bad time to tell you how I feel. I'm not great with words... you've heard my sermons... I know I'm saying all the wrong things. But I've never felt this way about a living soul before so I'm... I'm—'

'Please stop this, Fr Patterson.'

'Call me Clive, please!'

'No, I won't. You're a priest and what you're saying is all wrong. If you didn't look so serious I'd think this was a wind-up, an elaborate, practical joke.'

'Don't mock me, Olive.'

'But you can't... you can't be serious?'

'I've never been more serious in my life.'

'Jesus...'

'My feelings for you are profound.'

'Stop... stop it, please!'

'I love you, Olive.'

'No, no you don't.'

'In time, you'll come to feel something similar for me.'

'I'm not listening to this... please—'

'We can get away from here, create a new life, get married, have children, be happy.'

'I don't want to hear this.'

'But you must—'

'You're a priest, for God's sake. Listen to yourself. Do you hear what you're saying?'

'Yes, I do, and I've thought about all that. I've decided to quit the priesthood.'

'This is madness… madness, do you hear—'

'There's nothing I wouldn't do for you, Olive.'

'I don't want you to do anything for me. I just—'

'Will you at least think about what I've said?'

'No,' the woman said angrily, striding away from him.

'Please, Olive, come back, listen to me, you've got it all wrong; just listen. Wait!' Fr Patterson shouted after her, following her off the altar and into the sacristy. 'Let me explain how it will work…'

Emma, who hadn't realised she had been holding her breath, exhaled loudly. She had barely a chance to take another breath before Fr Patterson reappeared. With a dazed look on his face, he gazed towards the back of the church where she sat but appeared not to see her. Zombie-like, he shuffled around by the side of the altar, approached the central aisle and slumped down on the front pew. With his elbows pressed against his knees he cradled his head in his hands. Emma could see his body shudder.

He was talking to himself. Mumbled tones. Indistinct. Emma wondered what she should do. Simple choice. She could do the decent thing: make a quiet exit, approach him at a more opportune time. Or, she could do what her journalistic instincts urged her to do: tackle him there and then while he was still vulnerable, get him to talk to her. Wondering which options to pursue, she heard the curate's voice take on a strident tone. 'I could kill her, I could kill her,' he said despairingly, each word forced through clenched teeth. 'Jesus, I've offered her my immortal soul… had it thrown back in my face.'

Emma's mind made up, she decided to let him calm down a little first, then talk to him. Within minutes, his sighs had subsided and his words, though they continued, had become whispers. She was on the point of moving when the appearance of a woman on the altar caused her to wait.

At first she thought Olive Moran had returned but as the woman came closer to the priest, she recognised Caroline Blackman. 'Come, Fr Patterson,' the housekeeper said, 'I want you to come into the house with me now. Olive's told me what happened. She says you're not feeling well, asked me to get you.

So, come along, pull yourself together; we can't have the parish-ioners seeing you like this.' Caroline glanced around the seats to see if anyone was present. She froze when she picked out the lone figure of Emma. 'What are you doing here?' she asked, a chal-lenge in her voice.

Emma got out of the pew and made her way towards the front of the aisle. 'I saw Fr Patterson enter the church and came in here to talk to him. When I saw he was busy I waited until he was free.'

'You were here all the time? Listening... you heard...?'

'Couldn't help overhearing,' Emma admitted.

Fr Patterson looked at Emma, then at Caroline. 'Who's this?' he asked Caroline, his eyes barely focusing.

'Someone you don't need to bother with, Father,' Caroline answered, fixing Emma with a scornful look. 'It would be best if you left us now, Ms Boylan. In future, I suggest you telephone the parochial house, have the decency to make an appointment. Good manners cost nothing.'

Before Emma could utter a word in her defence, Caroline Blackman clasped the priest above the elbow and levered him towards the sacristy door. Emma shook her head, as if to clear her brain. She had just seen one very unhappy curate profess his love to Olive Moran, daughter to the man who had driven the car that killed Fr O'Gorman. What did it mean? It could be conceived as a connection of sorts to the murder, she supposed, but it didn't help to clarify anything. On the contrary, seeing Olive Moran reject the curate's offer of love only served to muddle, rather than eluci-date, the thoughts in her head.

Chapter 13

Emma walked to her car, sat behind the wheel, gave her head the tiniest shake and blinked her eyes twice. Reality check. She switched on her Sony micro-cassette recorder and outlined in as much detail as she could recall the encounter she'd just witnessed. After completing her verbal report, one niggling detail stubbornly refused to go away. A vague instinct told her that another person – other than herself, other than the priest and his housekeeper – had been present in the church, observing. Her thoughts lingered on this notion for a few minutes before she consigned it to that segment of the brain that stored irrational fears and half-baked ideas.

She called Connolly on her mobile, asked if they could meet. He agreed, on condition that they didn't meet in the barracks. Emma had no problem with that; it suited her admirably and meant she could avoid confronting McGettigan. Last time she talked to the sergeant, he'd made it abundantly clear that he regarded her as a nuisance. Connolly suggested a coffee in the Kozy Kitchen. Emma agreed.

Ten minutes later they sat opposite each other, armed with mugs of steaming hot coffee and sticky buns. Connolly was first to mention the parish priest's murder case. 'Been reading your reports in the *Post*,' he informed her, a twinkle in his eyes.

Emma smiled. 'Hope you found them helpful.'

'Helpful? No, not really.'

'Oh?'

'Little in the way of new developments for your readers. So, when I got your call, I said to myself – Emma Boylan has got to be desperate. Right?'

'I'm never desperate, Jim.' Emma answered, unfazed by his directness. 'But, yeah, I suppose it's fair to say you're partly right... partly wrong. I suspect you've run into a few dead ends yourself or you wouldn't have agreed so readily to meet me?'

'Touché,' Connolly said, his smile still in place. 'They're a tightknit lot here in Lonsdale.'

'Yeah, thick as thieves. I've noticed,' Emma agreed.

'They don't exactly trip over each other to offer information.'

'Nope, not to cops, they don't.'

'Tell me about it. It's like pulling teeth.'

'More painful, I'd have said,' Emma offered.

'How did you make out with them?'

'Better than you, it would appear.'

'Really?'

'Heard some juicy gossip, one or two facts.'

'Such as?'

'Well, I've heard things I shouldn't have heard and I've dug up buckets of information in relation to property ownership and the like.'

Connolly raised his eyebrows. 'But nothing substantial, right?'

'I wouldn't say that; I've heard plenty… just haven't been able to string it together… as yet.'

'Ah ha, thought so! That's why I'm glad you contacted me. We've co-operated in the past with good results. Might be an idea to pool resources on this one. What say you?'

Emma pretended to think about it before answering. 'Yes, I'm in favour of some sort of arrangement.'

'Same rules as before?'

Emma nodded. 'Makes sense. I can go into areas that you can't; I can ask questions you can't; I can bend a few rules… and I can let you have the fruits of this labour. In return, you can—'

'—bring you up to speed on all the official developments ahead of your rivals. There's just one condition, Emma.'

'Huuum, I thought there might be. What?'

'You don't go to print with what I give you until I say so, OK?'

'Could be tricky.'

'Tricky or not, that's the deal. You want in?'

'Sure, why not.'

'So, Emma, who goes first, you or me?'

'You first,' Emma said. 'I want to see if you and McGettigan have got anything worth bothering about.'

Connolly outlined the progress he'd made since taking charge of the Fr O'Gorman murder case. Most of what he had to say was already known to her but there was one item that was new: paint samples taken from the wreck of the parish priest's car matched the paint from machinery working on a development site adjacent to the scene of the crash. 'We now know exactly how the car was pushed off the viaduct,' Connolly said. 'We can say for certain that two drivers were instrumental in bringing about the crash. Derrik Holland, the site foreman, says the place is locked up at night. Says no one had access at the time of the crash.'

'This Derrik Holland,' Emma asked, 'reliable, is he?'

'Questionable. Nasty piece of work, I'd say.'

'What makes you say that?'

'Well, for one thing, he's given up his job; claims to have won the Lottery. McGettigan's running a check to see if he's on the level.'

Connolly's account of the disturbance in McCann's Arch Bar on the previous night intrigued Emma. She listened with growing interest as the detective told her about George Duggan's enforced exit from the premises.

When Emma's turn came to keep her side of the bargain, she gave a brief, and selective, outline of her own findings. After recounting the events that had taken place in the church, Connolly pursed his lips. 'You might have hit on something there,' he said. 'I have the curate down on my list for further investigation. I've talked to him already, found him a bit flaky. Word has it he didn't see eye-to-eye with the PP. D'you know what I'm thinking, Emma?'

'No, tell me.'

'I'm thinking that we're both missing some important element, something that holds the key to this whole damn thing.'

A pause in conversation followed while they both sipped coffee and allowed their thoughts free rein. Sitting opposite Connolly, discussing a case, reminded Emma of the last time they had co-operated. The outcome in that instance had been successful as far as the law was concerned. She'd made all the banner headlines she could wish for. Her recent *Investigative Journalist of the Year* award had been awarded for work on that case. But success had come at a high price, way too high a price. A nightmare.

She had been expecting at the time. Her first baby. Vinny had been so excited, so protective. He'd taken to the notion of fatherhood very seriously. It should have been a wondrous experience for both of them but that wasn't how it turned out. Tension crept into their relationship. Vinny, with the backing of her own parents, had begged her to give up her job during the pregnancy. She had refused. Became very defensive. Women got pregnant all the time, she declared, it didn't mean the world had to stop spinning. She was a modern woman, she would cope, damn it, she wouldn't let a little thing like a baby on the way interfere with her career. As it turned out, she was wrong.

The story she'd been working on had been ugly, menacing, fraught with danger. With visions of front-page headlines foremost in her mind, she had exposed herself to unnecessary risk.

The unthinkable had happened.

On a visit to meet with Connolly in a city centre shopping centre, she'd been pushed down the escalator. Hospitalisation followed. She received immediate attention in intensive care, but the internal damage had been too great; she lost the baby. The whole world, it seemed, had screamed its warning but she'd remained deaf to it all. She had persisted in believing that she was above the weaknesses of others... that she was wiser, more intelligent, and less susceptible to such adversities. It was a grand conceit, a conceit that had cost her the life of her baby.

In the immediate aftermath, Vinny had been wonderful. He tried to hide his own hurt while offering her every support and encouragement. Never once did he so much as hint at attributing blame or responsibility for what had happened. He was willing to pick up the pieces, attempt to put things right, hope for another chance at parenthood. But Emma had never managed to dislodge the awful pall of guilt that enveloped her. In the days that followed the tragedy, she had drifted into a state of depression, returning to her parents' home, shutting out the world, feeling sorry for herself, allowing guilt to eat into her soul. Connolly had been the person who finally got her to shake off her despondency. He had come to visit her; used his persuasive powers to shock her into facing realities. For that, she would always be thankful to the detective inspector. A bond of trust had been established between them, a bond that she would never abuse. Well, not if she could help it.

Her thoughts returned to this latest case and her working relationship with Connolly. She watched him use his knife to cut off a thin sliver of sticky bun and then, using the tips of his fingers, gingerly place it in his mouth. He caught her watching him, raised questioning eyebrows, inviting her to make comment. She duly obliged. 'I'm going to talk to Olive Moran,' she said. 'I want to ask her about her father. After all, Tom Moran was in the car when it crashed. Sheer luck prevented Moran from going the same way as his passenger. If that had happened we'd now be looking at a double murder. Seeing Fr Patterson talking to his daughter, proposing marriage to her, got me thinking; could there be some sort of connection there?'

'You could be right, Emma. For my part I'm determined to track down this fellow Christopher White. I'd like to hear his side of the story before I move on the Duggans.'

Emma showed her surprise. 'The Duggans – plural? You think both of them could be involved?'

'In the absence of any other evidence, they're the prime suspects. They are the only ones so far with a plausible motive.'

'On the question of motive, I agree,' Emma said, 'but I don't think either of them murdered his Reverence. However, I am inclined to go along with your earlier assessment.'

'Which assessment was that? Connolly asked.

'That we're overlooking some big element, something that's slap-bang in front of us... but, for some reason, we're not seeing it.'

Chapter 14

Caroline Blackman had done her best to calm the curate. His confrontation with Olive Moran would have seemed comical were it not for the devastating affect it wrought on the man. Her own reaction had been one of surprise; she'd been aware that the curate had an eye for young women but she had no idea he carried a torch for Olive Moran in particular.

She had been flummoxed when Olive came knocking on the door, telling of her trauma in the church. And then, seeing Fr Patterson slumped in the pew spewing out words and disconnected phrases, she needed all her skills in the art of persuasion to get a rational response from him.

It had taken ingenuity to get him to go to his room. He looked a wreck, his eyes unfocused, glassy, vacant. The fragments of his ramblings that were coherent let her know that he wanted to burn his dog collar and clerical garb, leave the church, claim his freedom, join the human race as a full-blooded male, lose his virginity post-haste and get even with the 'bitch' who had rejected him.

After she'd got him to lie down, she left his room, closed his door and hoped he would sleep for a while. What they would say to each other when he emerged from his room, she didn't even want to contemplate. She could not help but have some sympathy for his lamentable inadequacies in the human relationships department. Love, he was discovering, was the strongest emotion of all, just a step away from psychosis, capable of twisting the soul inside out, of wrecking the careers of men and women foolish enough to get caught up in its unforgiving stranglehold.

But in Fr Patterson's case, the situation, though sad, was comical at the same time: here was a man who organised pre-marriage courses for couples about to enter into matrimony, who patently hadn't a clue himself in regard to initiating the most basic steps of male/female relationships.

Sipping coffee, thinking about the episode, wondering what Emma Boylan made of the event, Caroline heard Fr Patterson coming down the stairs. He had been in his bedroom for less than an hour; not long enough, she feared, for him to revert to his normal self. She was pleasantly surprised. He appeared to have regained some measure of composure. His ill-chosen casual attire had been discarded in favour of a three-piece tweed suit and an open-neck shirt. His features, though a little drawn, had almost returned to normality.

He looked at her, searchingly. 'I want to apologise for what happened.'

'That's OK, Father, glad to be of assistance.'

'It must have been embarrassing for you.'

'Not to worry, Father.'

'Don't know what came over me. But I do know this: it's brought me to my senses, helped me to make up my mind about what I should do.'

Caroline noticed the vein throbbing in his temple and the quiet, seething anger, barely held in check. 'Father,' she said, 'I wouldn't go rushing into making decisions too quickly, you need time—'

'No, Caroline, I've had all the time I need. I'm off to see the Bishop, tell him I'm leaving the priesthood.'

'What? Leave the priesthood?'

'That's what I said. I've made up my mind.'

'That's a bit extreme, don't you think? Have you thought this through? What will you do? How will you make a living?'

'I don't have the answers yet but whatever I do has to be a darn sight better than the life I'm leading now. I want to serve God… all I ever wanted – still have the vocation – but my bodily needs refuse to surrender to that calling.'

'But, Father—'

'—and you don't have to worry about your own job; your contract is with the Bishop. I imagine they'll appoint a new parish priest straight away, now that I've decided to go.'

Caroline nodded, accepting that there was little point trying to talk sense into him in his present frame of mind. 'Come back after you've talked to the Bishop, tell me what happened.'

A speculative expression appeared in his eyes. 'Yes, Caroline, I'll make contact as soon as I can. I'm taking my clothes and some personal belongings with me now. I need to get clean away from *here* – get my head together. I'll always remember your kindness. All I ask is that you don't think too badly of me – all those crazy things I said a while back.'

'We all say things we don't mean. I've forgotten already.'

'God bless you, Caroline. Pray for me now and again, OK.?'

'I will, of course; you do the same for me!'

Olive Moran sat on the chair beside her father's bedside. In a room to himself, wired to all sorts of contraptions, most of the heavy bandages had at last been removed. His face, and the ruddy complexion she had associated with him all her life, now looked like an alabaster cast. Even though he remained unconscious, she talked to him about everything that came into her head. Could he hear her? She didn't know for sure, but she felt better talking to him. It gave her hope. Seeing him lying there, unresponsive, unmoving, being kept alive on a respirator, was breaking her heart, breaking her mother's heart, putting great strain on the family, and the family finances.

In that regard, her own job as a Montessori teacher, partly suspended since her father's hospitalisation, would have to be reinstated on a full-time basis. She needed the money. Simple as that. The supplementary income her mother earned from work in the church helped, even if there was a downside to the arrange-ment. It meant her mother could not put in as much time working at her beloved pottery as she would have liked. Two craft shops in the nearby Blanchardstown shopping centre bought items of pottery from time to time and paid the going rate. However, the cost of the electricity required to keep the kiln operational, coupled with the outlay for glazes, earthenware clays and equip-ment maintenance, all but obliterated the meagre profits her mother made from the enterprise.

To bring in more income, Olive would have to take up her full-time teaching job again. There was only one drawback: as a Montessori teacher, a job she enjoyed and got total fulfilment from, she would not be able to help her mother out at the church and she would not be able to visit her father as often as she would like. All these things she considered, and mentioned to her father, as he lay still in his hospital bed. The absence of a response made her realise how much she had depended on him throughout her life.

He had encouraged her to take up teaching in the first place. Guided by his insights into the educational system, she had learned the importance of the teacher's role. She felt at ease with children, comfortable in the knowledge that she was good with them. In their presence she displayed a sense of humour and projected a positive outlook on life. So, why was it that when it came to adult relationships, she found it so difficult to make long-term friends, both male and female? She had dated a few men in her time but all such encounters had ended in disillusionment for her. Problem was, she measured all men against the qualities she saw in her father and in doing so, invariably, they came up short.

Her thoughts were drawn back to the unpleasant event in the church. She wondered what her father would think of her latest would-be boyfriend, Fr Clive Patterson. Shock? Horror? Disgust? Probably all three. Even now, several hours later, sitting by her father's bedside, she had difficulty thinking about it. It had all been so unexpected. Finding herself on the altar with a man – a priest – and being proposed to by that same priest had to rank as the most bizarre incident in her life. She had been aware of the looks he gave her when she sang with the choir. It was hard to put into words the unease she felt when his gaze appeared to encompass her. She decided it would be in everyone's best interests if she did not turn up for tomorrow's choir practice.

After saying goodbye to her father, Olive waited half an hour outside the hospital for the bus that would take her across the city to Lonsdale. She had purchased a magazine from the newsagency kiosk in the hospital lobby but failed to summon up enough enthusiasm or energy to read a single article.

What little energy she possessed she would need for later. She would have to talk to Emma Boylan when she got to her house, something she did not look forward to. Agreeing to talk to the journalist had been a mistake but it was too late to cancel now. She thought about the telephone call she had received from Emma

Boylan and how the journalist had cajoled her into a meeting.

Olive closed her eyes and dozed into a superficial sleep. A jumble of unrelated scenes drifted through her mind as the bus stopped, started, slowed down and crawled through the city's evening traffic, making its tedious way towards Lonsdale. A hand tipped her shoulder, forcing her to open her eyes. A gawky lad, a neighbour of hers named Sean Finn, stared into her face. She could smell potato crisps on his breath, salt-and-vinegar flavour. 'Hey, Olive,' he said, a toothy smile on his face, 'your bus stop is next. You were asleep. Didn't want you to miss it.'

Olive thanked him and made her way to the front of the bus.

The walk to her house, past the Setanta Mansions and through the Weston housing estate, would only take twenty minutes. She inhaled deeply, filled her lungs with cold air and walked with renewed vigour. A fresh breeze ruffled her hair, stinging her face with what felt like ice-tipped needles. It was the kind of weather she had often heard her father refer to as *bracing*.

A car passed by and stopped about twenty-five metres ahead of her. Someone offering a lift, she thought. But even as this thought entered her head, she became apprehensive. She didn't recognise the car. It didn't belong to any of her neighbours or friends. And why, in the fading light, had it not got its lights on? She was being foolish, she told herself, allowing herself get spooked by the appearance of the car, but recent accounts in the media of young women disappearing without trace after accepting lifts from strangers in cars flashed through her mind. Feeling ever more fearful, Olive had come abreast of the stalled car when she saw Mrs Duggan, accompanied by two greyhounds on leashes, emerging from the dusk, walking towards her on the other side of the road. Olive breathed a sigh of relief. Passing the car without so much as a sideways glance at its occupant, she waved to Mrs Duggan and said 'good evening'. Mrs Duggan, appearing to be dragged along by the dogs, seemed preoccupied. She might have nodded in her direction but Olive couldn't be sure.

Olive had only walked a short distance when she heard the sound of the car approaching her from behind. The driver had waited until Mrs Duggan and her dogs were out of the way before following her. For a second time, the car passed her by and pulled to a halt some twenty metres ahead of her. The apprehension she felt earlier now turned to fear. She knew with certainty that it wasn't her overwrought imagination playing tricks on her. Someone really was stalking her. In the encroaching twilight, houses on both sides of the street had become great, dark hulking shapes, unfriendly, crowding in on her. Mature trees in front gardens cast gloomy shadows, their branches looming ghostly above her, moved by the strengthening breeze in what seemed like a conspiracy to frighten her. She forced herself to walk past the car, holding her breath, anticipating the worst. Nothing happened. No one jumped out at her, no one attacked her.

Ten metres past the car, nearing the front gate of her home, she heard footsteps behind her. Assailed by a vision of impending dread, trapped in the inexplicable logic of nightmares, she couldn't move. Snap out of it, move, some inner voice bellowed, its insistence stabbing at her brain. It worked.

She propelled herself into action.

Running now, her legs were barely able to sustain the exertion. She couldn't breathe, gulped for air, heard her heart pound. From behind, she heard the heavy footfalls gaining on her with every stride.

Her gate was only half a dozen strides away. Seeing it gave her the impetus to push forward. A silver-coloured car stood parked outside the gate.

She pushed past the car.

Her arms reached out for safety.

In that very moment, when safety seemed assured, someone grabbed her from behind. Too terrified to scream, she felt her legs buckle.

Her attacker pounced on her like a rugby player crashing over the line. She was squashed to the ground. From somewhere she found the strength to struggle. Her effort proved futile. The back of her head appeared to explode. Pain, accompanied by a thousand shafts of blinding light, fragmented and dissolved. An expanse of empty darkness followed, blocking out all consciousness.

Chapter 15

Coal nuggets and timber logs blazed brightly in the fireplace, generating more than enough heat to warm the compact living room of the Moran household. Brenda Moran and Emma Boylan sat in easy chairs, sipping tea and chatting amiably. To one side of the fireplace, a television showed Sky News, the volume switched low. Brenda Moran's eyes stole ever increasing glances towards the digital clock displayed on the corner of the screen. Eight o'clock, it read. 'I can't understand why she's not here,' she said. 'It's not at all like our Olive to be late.'

'Oh, I don't mind waiting, Brenda,' Emma lied smoothly.

'Olive always lets me know if she's going to be late.'

'I'm sure there's a good reason. The bus could have broken down. She might have had to wait for ages for another one to come along.'

'You could be right,' Brenda said, unconvincingly, 'it's just that it's been dark now for some time.' She continued to glance at the time counter, her mild concern gradually turning to a look of apprehension. 'She could have stayed on longer than usual with her dad. Or maybe she called into the church after getting off the bus. There's a choir practice in the morning; she might have decided to leave the hymn sheets ready for Fr Patterson. Then again, she might have met someone on the bus and decided to go for a coffee.'

'There, you see,' Emma said, sounding positive, 'there could be any number of reasons for her being delayed.'

'I know, I'm being silly; after all, she's a big girl, 28 next birthday, mature enough to look after herself. Still, it's not like her to make an appointment and forget about it. I don't know what you must think of her.'

Emma remained polite but after waiting another hour it became more difficult to convince herself and Brenda that everything was all right. She liked Olive's mother, a good-looking woman in her mid-fifties, slender build, hair that showed evidence of over-reliance on colouring agent, and large-framed glasses that dominated a fine-boned face. Rather than write the evening off as a total waste, Emma decided to stick it out for a while longer. She suggested to Brenda that it might be a good idea to contact the hospital, establish what time Olive left her father's bedside.

Brenda readily agreed and made the enquiries. She was informed that Olive had left the hospital at approximately 5.45pm. 'I'll phone the parochial house,' Brenda said to Emma, 'see if Olive's been to the church.' After waiting a few seconds, phone pressed to her ear, she shook her head. 'No answer... just keeps ringing.'

Emma, who was by now finding it difficult to hide her impatience, decided on some action of her own. 'Look, I'll tell you what, Brenda; why don't you let me take you to the parochial house, see if Olive's there. If she's not, we can have a look in the coffee shops, ask around if anyone has seen her, what do you say?'

'Well, if you're sure you don't mind.'

Five minutes later, Emma pulled in through the gateway that led to the parochial house. The stone-cut building, dimly lit by two lamps perched high on the perimeter wall, looked forlorn and not a little forbidding. Emma parked the car and got out. A stiff breeze made herself and Brenda hunch their shoulders in unison. 'Brrrrr... awful bloody night,' Brenda remarked, bracing herself against the dropping temperature.

On the way to the parochial house Emma had glimpsed a quarter moon as it played hide-and-seek behind fragmented, fast-moving clouds, but now the pale crescent had disappeared entirely into the dense veil of darkness. Barely visible in the background, St John the Baptist's steeple, picked out in the spill of the two lamps, soared into the night sky, the granite monument to Christendom casting ghostly, elongated shadows on to the church grounds.

Making their way up the path to the front door of the parochial house, their footfalls crunched loudly on the gravel path, the sound echoing eerily on the surrounding walls. Senses sharp, Emma stopped suddenly, took an audible intake of breath, and nudged Brenda. 'I just saw a light in the church,' she said, pointing to a stained glass window above a side-porch entrance.

'You couldn't have,' Brenda said. 'The church has been locked for the past two hours. If Olive was in there she'd have switched on the main lights. Anyway, I don't see any light.'

'You're probably right,' Emma said, feeling foolish, 'there's certainly nothing there now. It must have been a reflection on the glass... headlights of a car, most likely.'

An old-fashioned outdoor light, the kind seen on farmyard outbuildings, illuminated the parochial house's front door. Emma stood slightly back as Brenda Moran rang the bell. Seconds later, Caroline Blackman opened the door. Seeing who her callers were, she looked surprised, then wary. She greeted them by name, a quick fleeting smile for Brenda, a scowl for Emma, and asked them to step into the hallway. Brenda Moran explained that Olive hadn't come home from her visit to the hospital. 'I thought she might be here... in the church, that is, but I see the place is in darkness. Have you seen her at all this evening?'

'No, Mrs Moran, I haven't seen her. And as you said, the church is locked up for the night.'

Emma, seeing the jaundiced looks coming her way from the housekeeper, explained why she was accompanying Mrs Moran. 'Olive had arranged to meet me over two hours ago and, like her mother, I'm concerned that she hasn't shown up. We were hoping she might be here.'

Caroline looked sceptical. '*Here?* Why would she be here?'

'Well no, I mean in the church,' Emma said by way of clarification. 'Just now, before you opened the door, I thought I saw a light.'

'You couldn't have,' Caroline said, testily. 'I locked the doors myself. I always make sure there's no one inside before closing the doors.'

Emma, seeing no point in delaying any longer, was on the point of leaving when Brenda Moran stopped in her tracks. 'Wait a minute,' she said, a note of urgency in her voice. 'Olive mentioned something to me the other day about an intruder in the choir gallery. She said Fr Patterson chased a man out of the church, gave her an awful fright at the time. Maybe he's in there now, maybe he's got Olive in there.'

This was the first Emma had heard about an intruder. 'Did you know about this?' she asked the housekeeper.

'Yes, yes I did,' Caroline replied, 'but I don't think there was anything sinister about it; just some fellow having a snooze in the gallery, suffering from a hangover, most likely.'

'I'm not so sure,' Brenda Moran said, pushing her oversize glasses higher on the bridge of her nose. 'I think we should take a peek inside the church just to make sure everything's in order.'

'Are you serious?' Caroline asked, looking at Emma and Brenda in turn. 'You don't really suppose there's someone hiding in the church?'

'Only one way to find out,' Brenda said. 'Let's have a look.'

'Count me out,' Caroline said. 'Let's wait for the morning.'

'Suit yourself,' Brenda said, 'but I'm not waiting a minute longer. If someone's in there I want to know.' She extracted a key from her pocket and looked to Emma for support. 'You coming with me?'

'Yes, why not,' Emma replied, surprised by Brenda's spirited decision.

Two minutes later, Brenda turned the key and lifted the latch of the door that allowed them entrance to the sacristy. Familiar with the room's geography, Brenda found a switch. 'That's better,' she said, relief in her voice, 'this place can be a bit spooky in the dark.' She reached to a switchboard full of meters, fuses and switches, and pulled down a lever, her action bringing about an abundance of extra light. 'Main switch,' she informed Emma, knowingly, 'lights up the whole building.'

Emma followed Brenda to the side of the central altar and down the aisle through the main body of the church. Two rows of antiquated electric lights with yellowing globes provided dim illumination. The place looked even gloomier to her now than it had on her previous visit, and felt just as cold. The air was tinctured with the whiff of mildew and seeping dampness. They could hear the wind buffet the windows and high pitched roof, its velocity increasing, sounding for all the world like a furnace in full flame. There were other sounds too. Age-old timber roof trusses and arch-braced collar beams creaked and crackled under the pressure of the wind, sounding to Emma's ear like an old ship being tossed about on a rolling swell.

Without warning, Brenda yelled at the top of her lungs: 'Anybody here? Hello! hello, anybody here? Are you here, Olive?' Her words echoed around the church's cavernous interior.

No answer.

'She's not in the church,' she said to Emma.

'Hadn't we better take a look in the gallery?'

'Yeah, I suppose we'd better, OK. Have to be careful though, the light on the stairs is on the blink.'

Their footsteps reverberated around the nave of the empty church as they made their way to the main entrance porch where the door to the choir's gallery was situated. Even though the light fixture didn't work in the narrow stairwell, a spill of illumination from the main lights allowed them to pick their way up the steps. Once there, a quick glance told them it was empty.

Emma advanced towards the front of the gallery and let her eyes scan the church's interior. The building's architectural features, with its traditional cruciform layout, looked cold and uninviting. Not the sort of location she would willingly allow herself to be incarcerated for a night. Looking out over the side aisles, the central altar and the two smaller side altars, it did not appear as though a living soul, apart from herself and Brenda Moran, was present. Multifaceted shadows, cast by timber-ribbed, vaulted ceilings, pointed arches and clustered pillars conspired to create a feeling of other-worldly decay. 'There's nobody here,' Emma said to Brenda. 'Let's get the hell out of here.'

Her words had barely been articulated when the place plunged into darkness. Emma's scream, amplified by Brenda's more raucous yell, challenged the all-encompassing blackness. 'What's going on?' Emma asked, feeling a prickling sensation on the back of her neck.

'Don't know,' Brenda replied, her words choked in fright, 'but there *is* someone else in the church.'

'Christ, I can't see a friggin' thing.'

Brenda shrieked, this time grabbing hold of Emma's arms. 'Listen. Listen, Emma, I swear I heard someone moving. You hear it?'

Involuntarily, Emma sucked in a lungful of chilled air and shuddered. Above the sound of her own heart thumping, she could hear the wind howl outside; hear the timber creak in the roof and the barely audible murmur of traffic in the distance. What she couldn't hear was evidence of anything that sounded human. She was about to say as much when the unmistakable sound of running feet echoed from below.

Brenda gasped.

Emma stifled a scream. When she spoke, her words were little more than a hoarse whisper. 'I heard that; you're right, we're not alone.'

Another jarring noise rang out.

'Someone's crashed into something,' Brenda said in a loud, frightened whisper. The word *bollocks*, bellowed by a male voice, reverberated around the church's interior. Running feet again. More silence. Standing next to Brenda Moran, Emma felt the muscles tightening in her stomach as tension took hold. She became aware of the tight grip that Brenda had on her arms.

'We've got to get out of here,' Emma urged, freeing herself from Brenda's grip. Her eyes had adjusted to the darkness, but it was still virtually impossible to discern one object from another. A faint glow of light from the exterior lamps and night traffic did little more than indicate the shapes of the stained glass windows. A tiny red flame flickered in the church's sanctuary lamp, its meagre glow less bright than that of a single candle. Emma remembered from her days as a good practising Catholic that the sanctuary lamp remained lit twenty-four hours a day, every day of the year, with the singular exception of Good Friday. This knowledge provided little comfort to her now.

'I'll lead the way,' Brenda offered, her voice recovering somewhat from the fright. 'I know my way around this place; hold on to my shoulder and I'll try to get us down the stairs.'

Emma allowed herself to be guided through the darkness, taking short, floundering steps, attempting to sense her way towards the spiral stairwell. The steep descent meant that Emma had to hold on to the hair on Brenda's head if she wanted to remain in contact. With snail-like progress and much laborious breathing, they inched their way downward, step by step, in circular motion until, at the halfway stage, their progress abruptly ended.

Brenda lost her footing.

Emma, in turn, lost her balance and found herself stepping into thin air. She tumbled forward. Yelling aloud, her body crashed against the conical walls, bouncing off one side, then the other. Vaguely aware of Brenda's painful wails beneath her, Emma's head caught a corner angle of solid stone step. Her torturous scream died as she landed heavily on top of the already prone figure of Brenda. But Emma had no sense of this, her consciousness having decided to take an enforced leave of absence.

Chapter 16

McGettigan blamed the beer. He'd never had trouble getting it up before. Margaret Harris, the woman fondling his flaccid manhood, might not have been the most attractive woman on the planet, but the alcohol in his system had succeeded in softening her features to something approaching beautiful. The sergeant, familiar with the old song – *I've never gone to bed with an ugly woman, but I sure woke up with a few* – readily identified with the chauvinistic lyrics, but felt that perhaps in Margaret Harris's case, the song's sentiment slightly overstated the case. He was more concerned with how the alcohol had softened his most proud possession to marshmallow limpness.

Definitely the beer.

For a forty-three-year-old woman, Margaret Harris was in fair shape. She had an agile body, pendulous breasts with dark nipples, full rounded hips, and long shapely legs, assets she employed to full advantage in the pursuit of his pleasure. Serious makeup masked her face and long, luxuriant hair – the product of a weekly high-maintenance session in the beauty saloon – swished about her head like a pony's mane, tantalising, but failing to elicit the desired response from his erogenous zones. McGettigan found it hard to credit that this woman, supposedly happily married to bank manager Ted Harris, could be so knowing in the ways of seduction. With the exception of the prostitutes he took his pleasure with in the city's massage parlours from time to time, he'd seldom experienced a woman who could attend to his carnal needs with such enthusiasm and wanton abandonment.

She was all over him, kissing, sucking, caressing, changing positions, all the time moaning deep-throated encouragement, begging to be shagged senseless. Her breasts moved rhythmically as she straddled him, rode him like a jockey, her brush bouncing up and down on him, coaxing, cajoling, teasing, torturing him. Her tongue flicked expertly over those parts that normally responded wildly to such torrid encouragement. But for some inexplicable reason his body, or at least that part of his body that should have stood proud for such salacious anointing, decided to shirk its duty, half-heartedly rising, twitching, mocking him, then limply flopping like an asphyxiating fish. The drink; it had to be the drink.

It had all looked so promising earlier.

He'd been sitting at the bar in the Mill House, enjoying a pint of lager, talking bar-room politics with Joe Berry, the barman, when Margaret Harris sat down on the stool next to him. He had clocked her earlier in the pub in the company of three other women, all of them appearing to be in particularly good spirits. Without any encouragement, she joined in his banter with the barman, accepted a drink from the sergeant when offered, and insisted on buying a round back. Over the years, McGettigan had got to know Margaret Harris and her husband Ted, but he had certainly never thought of them as friends. They were part of the horsy set, the sort who placed policemen in the same category as domestic servants, stable hands and road workers. He'd had a few run-ins with Ted Harris on account of the state of his depleted overdraft. Nothing too serious, but enough to stifle friendship developing.

He knew Margaret on a nod-and-hand-wave basis and wondered from time to time if her husband, the staid Ted, ever talked to her about his customer's bank accounts. McGettigan didn't think so, but the thought of Harris discussing his dismal finances was enough to dissuade him from cultivating a relationship with the banker's wife.

So, it was a surprise when she came on all friendly towards him at the bar counter. She sat half on, half off the high stool, the hemline of her skirt riding above her knees, playing further up her thighs with every move. She laughed at his jokes, her knees touching against his, her eyes holding out a promise that was too good to ignore. McGettigan, sensing that his luck might be in, excluded the barman from further conversation, and upgraded his charm offensive to ramming speed.

As the counter area of the bar became more crowded with late-night drinkers, she suggested that they move to one of the alcoves. He readily agreed, feeling light-headed, intoxicated by the notion that the bank manager's wife was openly trying to seduce him. She had come up to him, bold as brass, and picked him up. It was a good feeling, a reassurance that he could still impress the ladies.

He was on his fifth pint of beer and she had just ordered another brandy when his soaring self-esteem came crashing down to earth. The intent behind her cordiality became evident. It was his services as a law officer that interested her. In conspiratorial tones she told him about being caught speeding on the N3 approach to Blanchardstown in her husband's Mercedes. She had not told Ted about the incident and didn't want him to find out. 'Can you fix it for me?' she asked. The request came as a bitter blow to McGettigan's ego.

Margaret had caught the look of disappointment on his face, pressed her fingers against his leg, just above the knee, and winked at him. 'I'm more than willing to make it worth your while,' she said, with a look in her eyes that could only mean one thing. McGettigan, an expert in deciphering the language of lust, read the signal loud and clear. 'I think I can sort out the speeding ticket,' he said, leering at her with lecherous intent.

'And I think I can make the sexiest man I know in uniform a happy puppy,' the bank manager's wife replied. After that, they had one more round of drinks before arranging to meet at McGettigan's house in River Street.

They made their way separately to the River Street residence. As had been arranged, McGettigan got there half an hour before Margaret's arrival. The house's interior was like a tip-head. It had been a few weeks since he'd had female company and he'd been a bit negligent in the cleaning department since then. Normally, it didn't bother him too much how the place looked, not being overly concerned with what his visitors thought, but having the bank manager's wife come to his house... well, that was a bit different, a bit special. Wouldn't do to have her feel she was slumming. He wished he'd had a little more notice. The kitchen was impregnated with the stale smell of boiled cabbage and bacon, sour milk, dirty dishes, and the lingering odour of cigarette smoke. Definitely not a place for the faint-hearted, but he felt sure an inspection of his kitchen would be the last thing on her mind. Still, you never knew with women.

Hurriedly, he attempted to tidy the more obvious displays of sloppiness, paying special attention to the upstairs bedroom. There was a chill in the air, not conducive to what he had in mind. He bounded down the stairs to the kitchen, took hold of the mobile Dimplex heater and brought it back to the bedroom. Maximum output, he hoped, would generate enough heat to warm the room. He gathered several pairs of smelly socks from the floor, along with various items of clothing, old newspapers and beer cans, and deposited the lot in the spare room. The bed itself, not made for several days, got a hastily pulled together makeover.

As heat kicked in from the Dimplex, he became aware of a smell and stuffiness in the room. He thought about opening a window but quickly rejected the idea. With a strong, icy breeze blowing outside, all heat would dissipate if he dared open a window. Damn it, he thought, she would just have to put up with the smell; better that than the cold.

It occurred to him, as he tried to whip the place into some kind of shape, that being a bachelor had one serious drawback. It meant not having a woman to wash, clean and keep the place tidy. But the downside to having a full-time woman – *ie*, a wife – was far too high a price to pay. It would curtail his freedom to play the field, something he could never contemplate. Once, just once, back in his early twenties, he had almost marched up the aisle, but luckily, he had come to his senses in the nick of time, seen the light and 'done a runner'. There had been some recriminations at the time, forcing him to lie low for a while, but he did not let it affect the rest of his life. That salutary experience had taught him a lot about women. Enough to stop him from ever making the same mistake again.

Margaret Harris, when she arrived, asked to be shown to the bedroom straight away. So far so good, he thought. Once there, her nimble fingers helped undress him in double-quick time. Between kisses, she told him that her husband Ted had, in recent years, lost all interest in her. 'He's more keen to straddle that damn horse of his than throw a leg across me. Gets his kicks from sitting high and mighty in the saddle, having people refer to him as Judge Harris at the greyhound events. Thinks he's Lord-fucking-muck, part of the old Lonsdale set, a cut above the rest of us. He's so full of shit.' Expounding on the subject of her marriage difficulties, she told the sergeant about her discovery of a cardboard box that Ted had hidden in their garage, a box that contained teenage pop magazines and photographs of boy bands. 'I tell you, the man has lost his marbles, reverted back to his childhood.' All this said while she gently cupped his testicles with one hand. 'Imagine, at his age, interested in kid's music.'

It might have been this information that sowed the seeds of McGettigan's inability to perform to his full potential. Instead of responding to the all-knowing touch of her fingers, his thoughts returned instead to the petty confrontations he'd had in the past with the woman's husband. He'd been forced to grovel in front of the bank manager to secure an ongoing overdraft facility. It had been humiliating.

What he'd just learned made him think of Ted Harris in a whole new light. Margaret's benign impression that hoarding pictures of pretty boys signalled a yearning in her husband to return to his youth didn't sit right with him. In McGettigan's devious mind, a cesspool conditioned to dealing with the more obnoxious foibles of others, a far more sinister scenario took shape. What if Ted Harris was a closet paedophile? What if the pompous prick was gay? A tantalising thought. If it were true – something he desperately wanted to believe – it would dramatically change the status of the relationship that existed between him and the bank manager. Payback time with knobs on. He would lean on the smug bastard, intimate to him that he was wise to his sordid, deviant ways. The threat alone would ensure Ted Harris never pushed him around again.

None of these thoughts, however appealing, helped improve his efforts at lovemaking. Feeling desperate, listening to the whinnying sounds coming from Margaret Harris's throat, knowing that he'd failed to sustain an erection for more than ten seconds at a time, he closed his eyes and tried to imagine it was Olive Moran who moved on top of him.

The delusion began to take hold of his senses.

It was working.

Yes, yes, yes, he could feel an anticipatory thrill, an urgent stirring in his groin. Yes, God, yes, now he was standing proud, rampant, rock-solid, ready for action. Marshmallow softness transmogrified to Brighton rock. Margaret gasped, impressed with what she saw. But it wasn't Margaret he was hearing. In his imagination Olive Moran was the one speaking to him, the one providing prick-engorging endearments. 'What a big truncheon you've got,' she gushed.

'All the better for you to gobble, my dear,' he answered.

'Yummy, yum yum, just look at the big upstanding boy we've got here. I want to take it and—'

A ringing telephone interrupted their lovemaking.

'Fuck it,' McGettigan said through gritted teeth, 'it's the direct line from the station... have to answer it.'

Margaret, in the process of pulling a condom over the sergeant's rampant member, cursed beneath her breath as she felt his manhood shrink and shrivel once more beneath her fingers. McGettigan, no longer entranced by the beauty of the imagined Olive Moran, watched as Margaret turned away from him and slipped out of the bed. He snarled into the phone, with a series of yeah's and no's before banging the instrument down.

'What's wrong?' Margaret asked, retrieving her scattered clothes from where they lay on the floor.

'Caroline Blackman,' McGettigan said, 'she says there's a problem down in the church.'

'At this hour of the evening?'

'Yeah, God damn it! Someone broke into the place.'

'What're you going to do?'

McGettigan frowned. 'Have to go and check it out.'

'Pity... and just when things were looking up...'

'Yeah, well, maybe we can do it again, what do you say?'

'We'll see.'

'Yeah, right, I think we could be good for each—'

'You *will* sort out my speeding fine, yes?'

'I'll see what I can do.'

'I hope you'll do a little better than that.'

'I said I would, didn't I?'

'Good.'

'There's just one condition.'

'And what might that be?'

'Later on... I'd like to finish off what we started tonight—'

'We'll see.'

McGettigan smiled. 'You'll have to do better than that.'

'Fine, sort out my ticket first... then we'll see.'

Chapter 17

Her name was being called. A distorted, fractured signal coming from a distant galaxy, spiralling through a dark vortex before penetrating her brain. She struggled to establish where she was. Dreaming? Dead?

Impossible to say. Someone was shaking her, slapping her face. 'Wake up, Emma, you're OK,' an insistent voice coaxed. Words began to register with increased clarity. Pinpricks of colourful light exploded in effervescent cascades behind her eyes.

She blinked, opened her eyes. An unfocused world slowly materialised.

'What… what happened?' she asked.

'You're back with us,' a woman's voice said.

Emma recognised the woman. Memory flooded back. She had been descending the stairs. She remembered the darkness… and the fall. 'Brenda, it's you. Where are your glasses? What happened?'

'We tumbled down the stairwell… broke my glasses.'

'I fell on top of you?'

''Fraid so. Flattened me. Hit your head on the way down.'

Emma felt the swelling on the back of her head, 'Ouch, that hurts.'

'You've been out for about five minutes.'

'I don't appear to have done too much damage,' Emma said, clasping Brenda's hand. 'Thanks for breaking my fall.'

'Huh, like I had a choice.'

'Sorry. Hope I didn't hurt you too much.'

'Just a sprained ankle… bruised shin.'

'I'm really sorry, Brenda, I—'

'At first, lying there in the darkness, you on top of me, I thought every bone in my body had been crushed.'

Mention of darkness prompted Emma's next question. 'Who put the lights on?'

Caroline Blackman provided the answer. She entered the porch area through a swing door in the partition that separated them from the main body of the church. 'I turned them on,' she said, looking at Emma. 'I wondered why the two of you were taking so long; looked out to see if you were coming back to the house. Saw the church in darkness, knew something was wrong. I plucked up enough courage to get the flashlight and take a look. I switched on the main lights and shouted your names. Got no answer. I was beginning to think you'd both left the church when I heard a moan coming from the porch. I dashed down the central aisle, came in here and saw the two of you in a heap. You were out cold, Emma. Mrs Moran filled me in on what happened.'

Brenda Moran took up the commentary. 'Caroline ran back to the house, called Sergeant McGettigan, told him what had happened. He should be here any moment.'

Caroline Blackman nodded in agreement. 'While we're waiting,' she said, 'why don't both of you come back inside the house? I'll make us a cup of tea, or maybe something a bit stronger; what do you say?'

Brenda was about to accept the offer but held her tongue when she heard the sound of heavy footsteps approaching. Sergeant McGettigan pushed through the swing door and stood before them. One of the buttons on his uniform remained undone and a small portion of shirt appeared to have prevented his fly zip from reaching the top. The unmistakable smell of sour beer, cigarettes and bodily sweat accompanied him into the church, a vaporous glow almost visible in the chilled night air. He looking displeased with the world as he gazed at the three women, treating each one of them with contemptuous appraisal. 'What's this all about then?' he snarled. 'A grand reunion of the Children of Mary?'

His attitude brought a sharp rebuke from Brenda Moran. 'It might help if you were to keep a civil tongue in your mouth and your brain zipped up, Sergeant McGettigan. Just who the hell do you think you are? Strutting about the place, throwing your weight around and talking down to your betters?'

There was a momentary pause before McGettigan responded to this unexpected rebuke. 'I'm here because I got a call to come here so don't give me grief, OK?' He ran his fingers across the stubble on his cheeks and chin while his eyes, creased into narrow slits, bore into them with a look of unbridled aggression. 'I've more important business to attend to, so if you'll be good enough to tell me what this is all about?'

Emma, incensed by his unwarranted rudeness, opened her mouth to unleash her annoyance but a wave from Brenda's hand dissuaded her. 'Your behaviour, like your manners, is lamentable,' she told him, speaking quietly, each word articulated so as to show her displeasure. 'You're here, Sergeant, because there's been a break-in at the church. A man ran out after we'd entered and unlocked the side door.'

'You'd a look at this man?' McGettigan asked.

'No, we didn't,' Brenda replied.

'Invisible, was he?'

'No, the lights went out. We heard running, heard a man swearing.'

'And this voice – the one swearing – it was a man's?'

'Yes, Sergeant, a male voice, no doubts about it,' Brenda replied.

'OK,' McGettigan said, 'tell me exactly what happened.'

'I thought we just did,' Brenda said, casting her eyes upwards.

'I need to hear the sequence of events.'

Emma related everything that had transpired from the moment Brenda and herself had entered the church until the moment they had fallen down the stairwell. McGettigan lit a cigarette, then surprised them by asking if they could all move into the main body of the church and take a seat.

'I've a problem with your story,' he said, as soon as they had moved. 'You say you heard running while you were in the dark?'

'Yes, that's right,' Emma confirmed.

'Could you pinpoint the location?'

'The sounds came from the nave,' Emma said.

'You're sure?'

'I think so. We were a bit disorientated at the time.'

'The footsteps ran towards the altar,' Brenda said. 'I'm sure he escaped through the sacristy door.'

'It was open?'

'Yes, I didn't lock it after we entered.'

'That's the bit I don't understand,' McGettigan said, flicking ash on the floor. 'If you heard the intruder in the main body of the church during the blackout and you heard him bolt for the sacristy, then who switched the main lights off? I'm right in thinking that the master switch for the lights is in the sacristy?'

'You're right, Sergeant,' Brenda said, nodding her head, considering the implications. 'You think there was more than one person here?'

'Could be. Tell me: what were you doing in the church at this hour?'

Brenda told him about Olive's visit to the hospital and her failure to return home. She explained why Emma Boylan had been in her house and how they had decided to look for Olive. 'I don't know where she is,' Brenda said.

'Telephone your house,' McGettigan said. 'Find out if she's returned since you left.'

Using Emma's mobile, Brenda made the call. There was no answer. At McGettigan's suggestion, they were about to leave the church when, walking in front of the central altar, he stopped suddenly. 'Something's just occurred to me,' he said, in a move that put Emma in mind of the television detective, Columbo. 'When the two of you – Ms Boylan and Mrs Moran, that is – came in first and went towards the gallery, the main lights were on, yes?'

'Yes, we've already established that,' Emma said.

'Well, if that's the case,' he said, ignoring her interjection, 'why didn't you see anyone? If, as it now appears, there were two people in the church at the time, how could you miss seeing them?'

In spite of her misgivings about the sergeant, Emma had to admit he had a valid point. 'It means that whoever was here managed to find somewhere to hide,' she ventured.

'OK, let's suppose I buy that,' McGettigan said, 'how did one of them slip back into the sacristy to switch off the lights without you seeing him?

'It could have happened while we were in the porch area,

while we were climbing the stairs to the gallery,' Brenda suggested. 'We couldn't see too much of anything at that point.'

'Yes, you could be right,' McGettigan admitted, 'or there might have been someone on the outside, an accomplice, who simply came in through the sacristy door, turned off the lights and allowed his friend to escape. The trouble with both theories is that there still had to be someone inside the church all along. So, why didn't you see him... or them?'

'Because whoever was here hid themselves,' Brenda said.

'Where?' the sergeant asked.

Brenda glanced around the church's interior. 'Could have concealed himself by lying low in the pews.'

'No, I don't think so,' Emma cut in. 'I'd a good look at all the seats while walking through the church at the time. I'd have spotted someone if they were there.'

Caroline Blackman pointed to the pulpit. 'Could have hid there.'

McGettigan nodded, dropped the butt of his cigarette on the floor, trod on it with his foot and made his way towards the pulpit. Adjacent to one of the four pillars that marked out the transept, the pulpit represented the church's most impressive fixture. Hand-carved timber panels encased the pulpit's octagonal shape, each rectangle displaying biblical scenes surrounded by exquisite decorative borders. McGettigan mounted four steps and stood on the platform. 'Doesn't look like anyone has messed around here,' he said, 'but I'd better have a look at the confession boxes before I call it a night. I'll take a look at the one on the right-hand aisle,' he said. 'Maybe one of you could check out the other one.'

Brenda, followed by Emma, made her way towards a confession box with the name 'Fr O'Gorman' displayed above the central door. Seeing Emma look at the name, Brenda explained that nobody wanted to remove the name on the box until a new parish priest was appointed. Sergeant McGettigan, with Caroline Blackman in his wake, examined the triple compartments of Fr Patterson's confessional and found nothing to arouse suspicions.

Emma pulled one of the side doors of Fr O'Gorman's confessional open. She hadn't been inside a confession box since her schooldays but everything appeared normal to her. A timber partition, complete with a small, square, grill-covered window and kneeling board towards the base, separated the confessor's compartment from the priest's central section. The misgivings she had as a child in regard to entering this confined, darkened world of professed guilt, contrition and penance came back to her with all the nauseating force she once associated with the rite.

Brenda Moran opened the opposite penitent's door and, finding nothing out of the ordinary there, moved to examine the central division. Before pulling the door open, she pushed aside the heavy velvet curtain that cloaked the uppermost opening. The scream that followed made everyone jump. Letting go of the material as though it burned her hand, she stumbled back from the door. 'There's someone inside,' she croaked, trying to catch her breath, 'Couldn't see properly... darkness... but, oh! Jesus, sweet Jesus, there's someone there... on the priest's seat.'

McGettigan came running. 'What's up?' he shouted,

Emma answered. 'Brenda says there's someone in there.'

'OK, all right, stand back all of you,' McGettigan ordered, 'he could be dangerous.' Approaching the door, he asked in a loud voice if there was anybody there. Hearing no reply, he gingerly pulled the curtain to one side. His gasp confirmed Brenda's story. 'Keep back everybody,' he ordered, 'I'm going to open the door.'

Cautiously, the sergeant slipped his fingers into the brass fitting that served as a handle and pulled the door towards him. It had only opened a few inches when a great thumping sound startled them. The door shot open, crashing into McGettigan's legs. A naked body tumbled to the floor. A woman's body. All of them, except for the sergeant, screamed.

The still form lay on its back, the face partially hidden by strands of chestnut hair. McGettigan knelt and felt for a pulse in the woman's wrist and sighed. 'Dead,' he said. He cleared strands of hair from the face. 'Oh, Christ, no,' he cried, instantly recognising the victim.

By now, Emma, Caroline and Brenda had ventured closer and looked at the face. At once, they recognised Olive Moran. Brenda shrieked loudest. She flung herself down beside the body. 'Noooooooooooooo,' she wailed. The once beautiful face of her daughter was now a mask of terror, the eyes not fully closed, a tiny fraction of irises showing beneath the lids. In death, Olive Moran appeared to be cowering as though warding off some awful evil, the murderous reflection of her killer still embedded on the retina. Bluish-purple discolouration was evident on her neck, chest and arms.

Hearing Brenda's cry, Emma froze, the cold coming from within, a chill that went beyond the merely physical. Every fibre of her being wanted to reject the image confronting her. She squeezed her eyes shut, as if doing so could somehow banish the awful vision. It didn't. Growing nausea and suffocating fear clawed at her insides. She forced her eyes open again, attempted to collect her thoughts, struggling to accept the reality of the situation. What she was experiencing, she told herself, was as nothing when compared with the anguish Brenda Moran must be feeling.

McGettigan and Caroline looked on, momentarily paralysed. A shocked silence. Emma hunkered down to place her arm around Brenda's shoulder. There were no adequate words for a situation like this so Emma gently caressed Brenda. McGettigan, regaining his composure, spoke to Emma. 'Can you take Mrs Moran away, please? The proper authorities will have to come and secure the scene.'

Emma glared at the sergeant, a look that let him know he was out of order, rude and insensitive. For a moment, nobody said anything. Only the sound of Brenda's muffled sobs, as she kissed her daughter's face and ran her fingers through the matted hair, could be heard. Several minutes elapsed before Brenda allowed Emma to shepherd her away from the spot where Olive lay. Trance-like, Brenda's eyes stared into the middle distance, her legs moving in unco-ordinated motion, as she held on to Emma.

Behind them, Sergeant McGettigan had already begun to make the calls that would set Lonsdale's second murder investigation in motion.

Chapter 18

Saturday morning had all the hallmarks of the morning-after-the-night-before. And what a night it had been. After all, it wasn't often that Emma could claim to have had the experience of skulking around a darkened church, falling down a stairwell, knocking herself out and then, as if that were not enough trauma, seeing the dead body of Olive Moran tumble from a confession box. She had written her exclusive and got it to the *Post* in time for the morning edition. The editorial people, who retained photographs of Lonsdale and its church from the time of Fr O'Gorman's death, recycled the prints to accompany her front-page story. Rival newspapers, who had missed out on the story on their first editions, were forced to bring out later editions, unashamedly plagiarising Emma's account and passing it off as the work of a 'Special Correspondent'.

It had been past one o'clock in the morning when Emma finally made it back to the apartment. Vinny had been brought up to speed on her breaking story and had insisted on waiting up for her. Slumped in front of the television, watching an old black-and-white film on the movie channel, he sprung to life when she arrived home, kissed her tenderly, poured a drink, and temporarily disappeared into the kitchen while he rustled up a light snack for both of them. She kicked off her shoes, rested her aching feet on a footstool, closed her eyes and thanked God for granting her the comfort of a good home and an attentive husband. She felt tired, drained and desperately in need of sleep.

Fifteen minutes later, they devoured one of Vinny's specials – hot pasta with Parmesan and ricotta cheese, heated to melt into a creamy sauce and garnished with basil. Went down a treat. Dirty dishes were put on hold. The bedroom beckoned. Once there, they indulged in their favourite activity with an eagerness that took both of them by surprise. Where the reserve of energy had come from, Emma had no idea. That was one of the things about making love she found amusing: didn't matter how exhausted you felt; when the chemistry was right and the juices flowed, the body invariably found a way to respond.

With only five hours of sleep, not counting time out for romance, she was now back in Lonsdale. Specifically, she was sitting in front of Detective Inspector Jim Connolly's desk discussing events from the previous night. Connolly had telephoned her earlier. The call could not have been more timely; she'd already planned to make contact with him first thing, but since he had precipitated the move, she saw no advantage in letting him know that.

Connolly poured a cup of coffee from a percolator and pushed it in front of her. 'I've already examined the crime scene,' he informed her, 'and I've seen the preliminary report from the pathologist.' He picked up a folder from his desk top and extracted a single sheet of paper. 'According to this, Olive Moran died from strangulation. A firm object was used to crush her thyroid cartilage and fragment the cricoid cartilage. Considerable force would've had to be exerted to cause such damage.'

'Jesus Christ!' Emma said. 'The poor woman.'

'And the poor mother. I've spoken with Mrs Moran.'

'Couldn't have been easy,' Emma said, sympathetically.

'It wasn't. She's had to be sedated. She's in a dreadful state.'

'Can't blame her. First her husband, now her only daughter.

Connolly nodded, his expression grave. 'Makes you wonder. How much punishment can one person take?'

'Yeah, it's terrible,' Emma agreed, taking a sip of coffee. 'As you know, I was with Brenda Moran when we found Olive.'

Connolly nodded again. 'I've been briefed by Sergeant McGettigan but I'd like to hear your version of events.'

Emma gave her account of the occurrences leading up to the discovery of the body. Connolly was anxious that she repeat the earlier conversation she'd overheard between Olive Moran and Fr Clive Patterson. Emma recounted, as accurately as she could, the scene she'd witnessed in the church, trying to dredge up every last word that had been uttered. When she'd finished, Connolly remained silent for several seconds before commenting. 'You actually heard the curate say, "I'll kill her" – his *actual* words?'

'Yes, but I wouldn't read too much into it.'

'Why is that?'

'You had to be there… hear his intonation.'

'His *intonation*?'

'Yes, you see, when he spoke the words, it sounded more like an expression of frustration than any real desire to actually *kill* somebody.'

'So why has he disappeared?'

'He's disappeared? I didn't know that.'

'Yes, Emma, he has. According to Caroline Blackman, Fr Patterson decided to visit the Bishop yesterday. He hasn't come back.'

'You've contacted the Bishop?'

'Of course. Talked to him earlier. He confirms that Fr Patterson called. The curate arrived at four o'clock, unannounced and with no prior appointment. The Bishop was unable, or unwilling, to see him. Apparently Fr Patterson didn't take kindly to being refused an audience… became abusive, had to be ejected from the episcopal palace. No one has seen hide nor hair of him since. I need to find him, hear what he has to say for himself.'

'Fr Patterson is a very disturbed man,' Emma said, 'but I can't believe he'd kill Olive Moran – he's not the type.'

A dark smile flickered across Connolly's face like a fleeting shadow. 'Not the type?' he said. 'There *is* no specific type when it comes to murder. People who murder don't go around advertising the fact. You, of all people, ought to know that, Emma.'

'I know Jim, you're right, of course, but according to you, Olive Moran was choked to death. Could the curate, who professes love for her, do that? I don't think so, do you?'

'I don't know, Emma. Don't they say that love and hate are two sides of the same coin?

He paused for a moment, as though his mind had temporarily been distracted by thoughts of some inward, personal struggle, before returning his attention to Emma. 'Besides, there's something else I find odd about Olive Moran's body. I've talked to the assistant State Pathologist and she has given me the benefit of her preliminary observations. According to Dr Tara O'Reilly, Olive Moran was sexually assaulted.'

'What? You're serious?'

'That's what the pathologist thinks. She's not sure whether it happened before or after Olive Moran was killed. But it was the nature of the sexual assault that bothers me.'

'The nature of the attack? How's that?'

'I can't tell you that, Emma, it's one of the factors we're holding back from the public. Could help us later in our investigations.'

'Look, Jim, you can tell me; I'll keep it off the record. You've trusted me before and I haven't let you down. It's a two-way street – I tell you what I know, you tell me what you know, we both benefit – so give!'

'OK but if what I tell you leaks out, I'll never take you into my confidence again. You clear about that?'

'Gave you my word, didn't I?'

'Very well, then,' Connolly said, still hesitating before deciding to confide in her. When he spoke, Emma noted the pained expression in his eyes and how his voice, low and precise, had become grave. 'Traces of semen were found inside Olive Moran's mouth. The odd thing is, her genitalia had not been interfered with. Strange, is it not? Olive Moran was smothered, then stripped – presumably to protect the killer. That way, the killer assumed there'd be less likelihood of us finding fibres or hairs on her clothes to identify him.'

Hearing these revelations, Emma felt sick. 'Olive was forced to endure oral sex before being killed?'

'Looks that way. Except we don't know at this stage whether she was alive or dead when the act took place.'

Emma thought about this, trying to retain a measure of objectivity. 'If, as you say, the killer stripped Olive to remove clues he might have left on her clothing, it makes no sense to subject her to oral sex, an act that allows you to analyse the semen for DNA.'

Connolly nodded his head in agreement. 'None of this makes sense. We find a match for the DNA sample, we nail the killer.'

As Connolly outlined his plans to apprehend the killer, Emma's thoughts were concerned with the notion of Olive Moran being subjected to oral sex. It was a revolting thought, one that gave her a sinking feeling in her stomach. There was no comfort in believing that Olive might have been dead when this violation took place. Either way the offence was barbaric. She forced the thoughts from her mind and refocused on Connolly's words.

'...First,' he said, using his index finger for emphasises, 'the parish priest is killed, right?'

'Right,' Emma agreed.

'And now,' he continued, using his middle finger this time, 'Olive Moran is found dead in his confessional.'

'Has to be a connection,' Emma said.

'Yes, but I'm damned if I can see it. Who is the killer?'

'A lot of people seem to think George Duggan killed the PP.'

'I checked out that angle. A big zero. Yesterday evening, George and Thelma entertained their daughter Yvonne and her new husband to dinner in their house. I've talked to the newly-weds; they confirm the story. Perfect alibi.

'As for Fr Patterson, the situation is somewhat similar. We don't know where he was yesterday evening when Olive Moran was killed, but he has an airtight alibi for the day that the parish priest met his end. So, if both murders were the work of the same person, it lets George Duggan and the curate off the hook.'

Emma thought about this for a moment. 'There's got to be a reason why someone would place Olive Moran's body in Fr O'Gorman's confession box.'

'You're right,' Connolly said, 'I just can't figure out what it is.'

'It's clear to me that the late parish priest is the common denominator. He is a confessor – has the power to forgive sins. What if he refused absolution to some sinner and that penitent is now set on revenge? Suppose that sinner confessed his sins in the *same* confession box where Olive Moran's body turned up dead?' Emma stopped. She noticed a dimple appear along the laughter line of the detective's right cheek.

'As theories go,' Connolly said, 'that's about as far-fetched as I've ever heard. And even if something like that was behind what's happening, why would this sinner take Olive Moran's life?'

'I don't know, Jim, I'm clutching at straws. It was a dumb idea.'

'You're right, Emma, dumb idea.'

'Don't hear you coming up with anything better. What's the story with Christopher White?'

'Ah yes, the parish priest's lesser-spotted nephew. Easy to see him as a suspect in the Fr O'Gorman case; had the best motive of all – money. Problem with that is this: White, to my knowledge, doesn't even know Olive Moran. So, why on earth would he want to kill *her*? It'd be different if Thelma or George Duggan were attacked; they represent the enemy as far as White's concerned. Still, I'd like to have a word with him just the same.'

'You haven't found him, then?'

'No, Emma. Turns out he's a smart bugger. Deals through his solicitor on all matters. I contacted his solicitor, a pleasant enough fellow, but he has been instructed not to divulge White's whereabouts. I've contacted all his known addresses but he appears to be continually on the move. It's a pain, but I'll track him down eventually. Right now I'm trying to see if Olive Moran had any boyfriends that we don't know about; find out who talked to her on the bus yesterday evening. I'm going to meet her teaching colleagues in the Montessori school, see if they can tell me anything of relevance.'

'So,' Emma said, with an air of finality, 'the truth is, we haven't a clue who killed Fr O'Gorman or Olive Moran. What are you going to say to the media when you face them later today?'

Connolly shrugged his shoulders and tried to put a brave face on the situation. 'Tell them we're following a definite line of enquiry… that we're hoping our investigations will yield positive results over the next few days.'

'You're relying on the theory that the first forty-eight hours after a murder represents the optimum chance to collar the suspect?

'Yes, Emma, but it didn't happen after the parish priest's death and now, a little more than twelve hours after Olive

Moran's death, I have to admit – at least to you– that I'm not holding my breath.'

Time: 12 o'clock noon.

Location: the assembly hall in Lonsdale's sports complex.

The event: a press conference to report on the circumstances of Olive Moran's death.

Sitting at the top table, Sergeant McGettigan and Detective Inspector Jim Connolly took turns to address the assembled media personnel. Emma Boylan sat towards the back of the room, content to let others ask the questions. McGettigan, she could see, was revelling in his moment in the spotlight. Spruced up for the television cameras, clean-shaven, hair groomed, tunic, shirt and tie all spic'n'span, his transformation nothing short of miraculous. He puffed out his chest, looked directly into the camera lens and gave expansive answers to questions, while adding little of interest to what was already known. When fielding awkward questions from the press corps, he hid behind a bluster of words, stringing together long, meandering sentences that served to confuse rather than elucidate.

Emma could not help but notice that Connolly appeared to inhabit a private world of his own while McGettigan spoke. She had never seen him look so out of sorts. He appeared to be unfocused, troubled, as though some sort of personal turmoil was affecting him. Feminine intuition told Emma that the inner conflict she saw in Connolly's demeanour had nothing to do with events in Lonsdale.

As soon as Connolly's turn came to speak, his eyes snapped into sharp focus, banishing whatever dark place he'd been to, the transformation even more remarkable than McGettigan's shiny makeover. The detective inspector was back on top of his subject, sounding assured and confident. Listening to him, Emma could not help but observe the marked contrast of styles that differentiated the two policemen. With what seemed like the greatest of ease, Connolly imparted sensitive information to reporters hungry for worthwhile facts. With hair thinning on top, silver flecks flicked down by the temples, a handsome, well-cared-for face and assertive hazel eyes, Connolly looked and sounded composed, all vestiges of his earlier despondency totally vanished.

After twenty minutes, the conference came to an end. Emma, as she had suspected before the event took place, learned nothing she didn't already know. The ironic thing was: she knew far more about the case than had been revealed to her fellow journalists. While her colleagues asked questions, scribbled notes, held up recorders and took photographs, she remained unaware of the person sitting directly behind her. Like the others, he had a pen and pad in front of him but, instead of taking notes, he drew a series of small crisscross lines and inserted X's and O's in the boxes created.

Chapter 19

Arthur Boylan liked to keep Saturdays free from work. His only break from the never-ending chore of dealing with people's problems, his only opportunity to read the newspapers. This morning, as was the custom most weekends, his wife Hazel cooked and placed a fried breakfast in front of him. The sort of fare described in hotels as "Full Irish". A dietician's nightmare. Hazel enjoyed watching him devour his fill of rashers, sausages, eggs, black pudding and tomatoes with such evident relish. Using a slice of fried bread to soak up what small particles remained, he dabbed his lips with the serviette, caressed his tummy with his hands and declared himself well satisfied.

He offered to help Hazel stack the dishwasher and, as expected, received the usual dispensation. This little nicety enacted, he moved from the kitchen into the living room and sat down to read the *Post*. He already knew about the discovery of a body in the church in Lonsdale – it had been the top feature on the television news and all radio news bulletins – but he wanted to read his daughter's account of what happened. With his own personal interest in the goings-on in Lonsdale, courtesy of his client, George Duggan, it always helped to get the full background details.

He was moved by Emma's powerful depiction of Brenda Moran – the mother whose anguish and grief at the loss of her only daughter – represented a despair of unimaginable proportions. The fact that Brenda Moran's husband remained in hospital on life-support during this, the blackest period of her life, served to inflict more pain on an already impossible situation. He was still reading Emma's article when Hazel announced that he was wanted on the telephone. Over the years he had established an unwritten rule: calls were not taken on the weekend unless they concerned matters of grave urgency. Hazel enforced this convention to the best of her ability, becoming a shrewd arbitrator of what constituted 'urgency' and what did not. On this occasion her instincts let her down. The caller, George Duggan, had somehow convinced her that it was imperative he speak with her husband.

Arthur Boylan took the call, barely concealing his annoyance. Without preamble, Duggan got to the purpose of his call. 'I want you to start proceedings against Donnie McCann.'

Arthur extended a world-weary sigh down the line. 'Who is Donnie McCann?' he asked.

'Proprietor of the Arch Bar in Lonsdale.'

'I see. What's he done to upset you?'

'Defamation of my character.'

'Oh! How'd he do that?'

'Forced me to leave the premises in front of all the other customers. Took my drink and marched me out to the street. Never been so humiliated.'

'What'd you do to cause this?'

'Absolutely nothing!'

'Must've done something?'

'Nothing! Pure victimisation, character assassination. Claims some customers objected to him serving me – said I was a killer. Well, now, with the murder of Olive Moran, it must be obvious to everyone – including Donnie McCann – that I'm not the one going around bumpin' people off. Jesus, the very idea, it's preposterous! Well, it's comeuppance time for McCann. I want you to sue the bastard, oppose the granting of his liquor licence and make him regret the day he decided to mess with me.'

Arthur Boylan was getting impatient. 'Look George,' he said bluntly, 'all this can wait till Monday. Talk to me then, I'll see what can be done, OK?'

'No, damn it, Arthur, it's not OK. You're my solicitor. I want action. I don't take kindly to being fobbed off 'cause you can't be bothered. If you don't want my business, just say so. There are plenty of other solicitors out there who'll jump at the chance to act on my behalf.'

'Yes, George, there are, and you're free to do as you wish. However, if you *do* wish to retain my services, I will be more than willing to talk to you Monday morning. Your decision.'

George Duggan hung up.

A wry smile crossed Arthur Boylan's face. He visualised the spectacle of Duggan being drummed out of the Arch Bar and experienced a degree of empathy with the publican. As for Duggan's threat to take his business elsewhere, he doubted such a thing would happen, and even if it did, it wouldn't bother him in the least. In truth, he fully expected Duggan to be waiting for him at his office first thing Monday morning, their little tiff brushed aside. And when that happened, Duggan would be made aware of the latest correspondence from Christopher White's solicitor. Its contents, Arthur felt confident, would have the effect of softening George Duggan's cough.

Caroline Blackman slid between the sheets, opened her mother's diary and flicked through the pages until she found the passage she was looking for.

Extracts from the diary of Nelly Joyce – aged 21
Date 18th May 1973. Johnstown National School.

Dear Diary
   Spent the morning drilling my 15 eight-year-old boys, preparing them to meet the Inspector.
   Inspector arrived at 2.30pm. Big, middle-aged man. Bald. Squint.
   He picked on Dara Herron, a remedial pupil, to read.
   Dara stopped after the fifth line, grabbed me and spewed vomit down the side of my dress, on to my legs and shoes. I wanted to die.
   The Inspector offered to mind the class while I went to clean myself.
   Rushed to the washhand area in the staff room and whipped off my dress.
   Used a wet towel to clean off the soggy mess.
   Before putting it back on I bent down to wipe my legs and shoes.
   Someone approached from behind, gave me an awful fright.

I swung around and saw the teacher from 3rd grade staring at me.

I was stripped to bra and panties, felt mortified.

I roared at him to get out. He just smiled.

I'll only leave, says he, if you'll agree to come to the pictures with me tonight.

I roared at him again, told him to get the hell out of the room.

He smiled and left, but not before giving me another quick glance all over.

Put my clothes on. Ran back to the classroom.

When the Inspector saw me, he asked the boys to give me a round of applause.

He said my pupils were a credit to me.

After the Inspector left, I bumped into the 3rd-form teacher waiting outside my classroom door. I apologised for having shouted at him. He said he was sorry too and wouldn't have barged in on me if he'd known I was undressed.

I blushed.

He just smiled and asked me again if I would go out with him.

I said I'd think about it. He said that was good enough for him.

Don't know what I'll say to him if he asks me out again.

He is gorgeous, the finest thing I've seen on two legs in these parts. One or two of the other female teachers claimed he has a bit of a reputation as a ladies' man.

His nickname is Cherry Picker.

I sort of like that.

Goodnight Diary.

Caroline Blackman closed the copybook. She had read that passage so many times, pictured the scene in the classroom, it was almost as though she had been there. From other earlier diary entries, she had got to know quite a lot about her mother's place of work in Johnstown, a large boy's school with seven teachers and a headmaster. Caroline could tell from her mother's entries that she enjoyed her job there. At twenty-one, away from her foster parents, earning wages and independent, Nelly Joyce had everything going for her. She had been lucky to share a flat with two girls her own age, and the girls appeared to look after her like she was a sister.

What really intrigued Caroline about this particular entry in her mother's diary was the mention of the man's nickname – Cherry Picker. Later on in the diary entries, the same nickname was used over and over again; never once was the man's real name alluded to. It was puzzling, but it was common enough for people to avoid using real names when writing their diaries. Another thing she found fascinating was her mother's apparent lack of understanding in regard to the nickname itself. Even allowing for the fact that this diary entry was written back in 1973, surely her mother couldn't have been so innocent or naïve as to miss the connotations associated with the words 'Cherry Picker', especially when the words applied to someone with a reputation for being a ladies' man.

Caroline rubbed her eyes and was about to turn off the bedside lamp when she changed her mind. It had been a long day, she was tired but a compulsion, more insistent than her tiredness, enticed her to turn to another entry from her mother's diary.

Extracts from the diary of Nelly Joyce – aged 21
Date 25th May 1973. Johnstown National School.

Dear Diary
    10.45 am. Morning.
    Cherry Picker approached me outside my classroom. Asked me out again.
    (Only one week since he first asked me for a date. I've got so used to the nickname, won't call him anything else – except to his face, of course.)
    Nearly wet myself when he spoke my name.
    I'd decided to say no but my 'no' came out as 'yes'.

I blushed scarlet. His face lit up. Asked me what I'd like to do. I was so flustered I didn't know what to say. He decided for both of us.

Dancing! We would go to the National Ballroom in Parnell Square.

4.30pm. The flat.

Tried on every stitch in the wardrobe. Nothing worked. Nothing!!!

Tears, tantrums, despair.

6.15pm. Maura and Eva in from work.

Maura offered me her slinkiest underwear.

Eva had a go at my face, plucked and shaped my eyebrows, applied eyeliner and mascara, added rouge to my cheeks, used her own special strawberry blush on my lips and attempted to knock my hair into shape.

8.15pm. Date arrived.

He looked smashing. Expensive suit, smart shirt and tie. Neat shoes.

The dance was terrific.

During one smooch, Cherry Picker's hands slid down to my bum – pressed me hard against him. He was aroused – the dirty devil!!!

I felt dizzy with the erotic thoughts.

We gazed into each other's eyes – didn't need to speak.

2.45am. Morning. Home again.

Still tingling with excitement.

He dropped me off at the door but not before some prolonged snogging.

He is a hell of a kisser.

I'm in LOVE! I AM MADLY, PASSIONATELY, INSANELY IN LOVE!.

I'm the happiest girl alive tonight (or should that be this morning).

Have to finish writing now, turn off the lights and get under the blankets.

I will hug my pillow and pretend it's him – can still taste his breath, feel his tongue, his lips, feel that special part of his body press firmly against mine.

Dear God, please let me be this happy for the rest of my life.

Goodnight Diary X X X.

Chapter 20

The mid-morning burial service was drawing to a conclusion, the atmosphere as dark as the leaden sky overhanging Lonsdale's cemetery. Olive Moran's plot was situated between the parish's older burial ground – a jumble of old crosses, mottled with lichens and mosses, tilting at various angles – and the newer, more symmetrical series of well-kept plots that formed the latest extension to the graveyard. Mourners clustered into the narrow spaces that divided the surrounding graves, reciting a decade of the rosary. Some encroached on to the pebble-covered surfaces of neighbouring plots, their presence in danger of disturbing flower-pots, withered floral bouquets and plastic domes of weather-bleached artificial blooms. From time to time, audible sobs could be heard above the murmur of prayer. Brenda Moran, nestled by two teary-eyed sisters and a brother, looked lost, marooned in some forlorn world of her own, mouthing responses to the prayers but not participating on any serious level with what was happening.

It was a large, well-attended funeral. A group of school children stood together by the edge of the old grounds, their bare legs pressed against brambles and tufts of weeds. Dwarfed by a Celtic cross that was smeared with a recent splattering of bird droppings, they appeared lost and bewildered, as though not fully understanding the significance of what was happening, nor cognisant of the fact that they would never see their Montessori teacher again.

Emma Boylan, scanning the faces on the opposite side of the burial plot, caught sight of Mary Dunne. The redhead waitress from the Kozy Kitchen shielded a lighted cigarette in a cupped hand as she brought it to her mouth. This was the person who had told Emma that Yvonne Duggan was not George Duggan's daughter, suggesting instead that the parish priest had been the biological father. And now, Mary Dunne stared at George Duggan, his wife Thelma, their daughter Yvonne and their new son-in-law, Alec Cobain.

Standing in front of Emma, to one side of Brenda Moran, the Duggan family talked quietly to each other, sharing the palpable grief all around them, oblivious to the scrutiny coming their way from Mary Dunne. As the wooden casket was lowered into the open grave, Yvonne Cobain flicked a tiny blood-soaked particle of tissue from her father's clean-shaven jaw line. It didn't appear to bother Yvonne that the result of her father's mishap in the bathroom should flutter through the air and land on Emma's arm.

Emma recognised Caroline Blackman in the crowd, suitably attired in sombre clothes for the occasion and, to her side, Sergeant McGettigan. The sergeant had discarded his uniform in favour of a grey, double-breasted suit. Emma suspected that Detective Inspector Connolly was somewhere in the crowd but she didn't see him.

Prayers and blessings complete, mourners moved to shake Brenda Moran's hand, sympathise with her, offer what little solace they could. Emma, who had paid her respects earlier, made her way towards the cemetery exit. She felt unaccountably sad, unable to get the mental picture of Olive Moran out of her head. She had only met the young woman briefly and could not claim to know her, but there was something heart-rending in the manner of her departing this world. It seemed inconceivable to her that Olive could have done or said anything in life to deserve such a premature and terrifying end.

Caught up in these sad thoughts, Emma hadn't noticed Thelma Duggan moving alongside her as they both passed through the cemetery's outer gateway. 'I was probably the last person to see Olive alive,' she said to Emma. 'I saw her walking home, coming from the bus. I still can't believe what's happened.'

'Have you told anybody about this sighting?' Emma asked.

'Yes, I did. Soon as I heard the news I phoned Sergeant McGettigan. He came out to the house with Detective Inspector Connolly. Told them what I knew.'

'And were you able to help?'

'I don't know about that, but Detective Connolly seemed very interested in the fact that I had seen a car acting suspiciously around the same time.'

'A car? What do you mean?'

'Well, at the time, of course, I didn't link the car to anything untoward, never gave it a second thought. But since then... after all that's happened, I've been trying to remember exactly what I saw.'

'What makes you think the car was acting suspiciously?'

'A number of little things. I was walking towards the church with two greyhounds. That's the point where I turn about and head for home. I should have exercised them earlier but got delayed by something or other. Anyway, I saw Olive Moran making her way home from the bus stop. And then, I saw a car pull to a stop ahead of her. I remembered that the car had no lights on. That in itself was odd because it was getting quite dark at the time. I thought that perhaps the driver had stopped to offer Olive a lift but no, she walked past the car. I would not have given it a second thought except for an even odder occurrence. On my return walk with the dogs, I saw the car again. Frightened the life out of me, it did. Could have killed myself and the dogs.'

'How was that?'

'This time the car approached from the opposite direction, headed back towards the church. But here's the queer bit; it was fully dark by this stage and yet the car still had its lights off. The street lights had come on by then but they're pretty useless. How the hell could the driver see properly? Could have killed anybody walking on the road.'

'Sounds to me like he did kill somebody; Olive Moran.'

'Yes, it's scary to think Olive might have been in the car... maybe dead already... being driven to the church.'

'Did you get a look at the car's number plate?'

''Fraid not. Detective Connolly asked me the same thing. Told them same as I'm telling you.... I didn't think to look.'

Thelma stopped at the spot where she had parked her car, waiting for the rest of her family to catch up before getting in. Emma took the opportunity to put one last question to her. 'Could the driver have been Fr Patterson?'

Thelma stared wide-eyed at Emma. 'That's the very same question the detective asked. What *is* this about Fr Patterson that has people asking these silly questions about him?'

'It's just that Olive Moran and Fr Patterson had a little "difference" the day before her death.'

'Are you trying to tell me that because of a silly rumour, you think Fr Patterson might have something to do with Olive Moran's death? Is that it?'

'No, not exactly, but the curate has managed to disappear at a most inopportune time. Only natural to wonder whether or not he might've tried to contact Olive.'

Thelma grunted disdainfully. 'Nonsense! Father Patterson is a lovely young man. There isn't a bad bone in his body or an evil thought in his head.'

Emma saw no point in pursuing this line of enquiry any further.

Yvonne Cobain, who by now had caught up with her mother, offered to give Emma a lift back to the church. Emma accepted. Yvonne and her mother sat in the front seats, Emma and Alec Cobain in the back. 'Dad has his own car,' Yvonne explained to Emma. 'He's going for a drink with some friends before coming home.'

The conversation in the car was stilted and centred on expressions of regret for the passing of Olive Moran. Alec remained quiet, never once bothering to utter a word. Yvonne, who had removed her jacket before sitting in the driver's seat, tossed the garment behind her, apparently forgetting that Emma was sitting there. Emma couldn't decide whether Yvonne was being deliberately rude, scatterbrained or merely trying to show off the expensive Italian designer label, MARELLA, displayed on the garment. She decided to give Yvonne the benefit of the doubt and hung the jacket on the back of the driver's seat, amused to note the scattering of hairs Yvonne had neglected to brush free from the material. She smiled, now convinced that Yvonne was inclined to be careless in her attitude to both people and to the clothes she wore.

Back in her own car, Emma tried to think what her next move should be. Seeing Mary Dunne at the funeral, and remembering what the waitress had once said to her, had given her an idea. It was a wild idea, perhaps an insane idea, but the more she thought about it the more she wanted to put the idea to the test.

Chapter 21

Brenda Moran's two married sisters, along with their husbands, sat in her living room. Talk was quiet. The women sipped Baileys, the men drank Millers from cans. Brenda had left them to their own devices half an hour earlier, telling them she needed to be alone for a while. Every so often, the sisters threw expectant glances at the door, worried by her non-return. Their husbands, avid Manchester United fans, discussed the Premiership League and the European football fixtures without enthusiasm or conviction. Every so often they stole furtive glances at their watches, keen to get their enforced visit to Brenda's house over with, but anxious at the same time to offer moral support to their spouses by their presence.

Brenda would have preferred it if they had gone away, left her alone, stopped looking at her with pitying eyes. They meant well, she knew, but it didn't help. Nothing helped. She sat alone in her studio, a timber-framed annex, built specifically to cater for her love affair with pottery. Her special space; the one area where she found solitude. Tranquillity. She felt whole here, in touch with her spiritual self. Pottery represented more than a hobby; it allowed her to express her innermost thoughts and aspirations in three dimension. Allowing the wet clay to yield to her fingers as it spun into shape on the potter's wheel imbued her with an almost mystical power; not altogether unlike that of giving birth. Once created, there was the pleasure of decorating the object with glazes and then, finally, preparing it to meet the world by subjecting it to a baptism of fire in the kiln.

She removed her glasses, wiped tears from her eyes, and looked at the rows of pottery she had so lovingly given life to. Resting on shelves that Tom had erected, each creation remained mute and inanimate, dead as the beautiful daughter she had just buried beneath the damp clay of Lonsdale's graveyard. Visions of

Olive overwhelmed her, incidents from earliest times. She saw Olive as a child, plain as day. There she was, blowing out candles on her birthday cake, crying after she'd fallen and cut her knee; squealing with delight on discovering that her father had let go of her when she learned to ride a bike. She saw Olive in her confirmation dress, looking like a child bride; smiling, happy, acknowledging the proud beams of delight on her parents' faces. In a series of fast, ever-changing pictures, Olive developed from child to teenager and then to young woman.

Always beautiful. Always independent. Always full of life. Wonderful years. Never failing to show respect and love for her parents, especially her father, placing him on a pedestal. Nothing had happened in the intervening years to diminish her respect for him.

Brenda was glad that Tom was spared the pain of knowing about their daughter's death. He would lose his mind if he knew what had happened. This thought brought a bitter smile to her face. With Tom connected to a life-support machine, he had, it seemed to her, already lost his mind. Another thought; maybe, just maybe, she too would lose her mind. The two people she cared most about were taken from her: Olive dead, her husband unconscious. But he wasn't dead, and she would hold on to the slender hope that soon he would get well again.

She had loved Tom Moran from the day she first met him. He was, she remembered, so handsome. He had swept her off her feet with a winning smile. A year later she walked down the aisle with him, a virgin bride, wed to the most wonderful man in the world. Their union had been blessed a year later with the birth of a daughter. They christened her Olive. They would have liked another child – a brother or sister for Olive – but that hadn't been part of the Almighty's grand design. Even so, they were content with the treasure they had been given and loved her unconditionally, a love she had returned a thousand-fold.

But now, Olive was dead. Tom, only a whisper away from a similar fate. It wasn't fair, it just wasn't bloody-well fair.

A well of anger exploded inside her.

She moved to the rows of pottery. She took down a vase from the top shelf, stared vacantly at it for a moment, traced her finger over its glazed spiral Celtic swirls, then smashed it to the floor. Next, she grabbed a large, sunflower-design pitcher, a favourite of hers, and broke it into smithereens against the side of her kiln. The kiln, a second-hand monstrosity she had unwisely purchased, was too big for her needs and cost a fortune to run. It now became the focus of her fury. Olive had often joked about it, claiming it drained the national electricity grid every time it was switched on. Now, in an uncontrollable rage, she pulled the heavy front door section open and dislodged the racks that held her most recent, unfired creations. Item after item went hurtling through the air. Cups, mugs, jugs, teapots, coffee pots, plates, candlestick holders and flowerpots all destroyed in a blur of activity.

She was screaming at the top of her voice when her sisters came rushing into the studio. Horrified by what they saw, dodging flying objects, they took hold of her. Still struggling, screaming profanities, her eyes wild and unfocused, it took their best efforts to quieten her down. The ravages of the past few days had etched themselves on her face and body, making her look far older than her years. She continued to shake all over, sobbing great body-wrenching sobs, muttering about how unfair it all was, blaming God for what had happened.

Arthur Boylan tidied his desk in readiness to go home. A glance at his Omega watch confirmed an end to his working day.

His secretary rang through. 'George Duggan is in reception. Wants a word with you.'

'Damn,' Arthur fumed. 'Tell him I'll see him in a minute or two.' He slammed the phone down and cursed again. A bad taste remained in his mouth from his last verbal exchange with Duggan.

The unmistakable whiff of drink accompanied Duggan as he entered the room and sat in front of Arthur's desk. Something in the solicitor's expression let Duggan know that his alcohol-tainted breath had been observed. 'I went to Olive Moran's funeral earlier today,' Duggan said by way of excuse. 'Had to have a few drinks with some of her relations; all part of the mourning process.'

'You didn't drive here, I hope?' Arthur asked.

'What if I did?'

'Cops round here don't take kindly to anybody caught over the limit.'

'If they pulled me over, I'd let them know I had connections, tell them they'd be transferred to Bally-go-backwards if they as much as looked crooked at me. Always works.'

'Didn't work too well when you were caught feeding banned substances to your cattle.'

'I got off, didn't I?'

'Only after I went to the ends of the earth to dig up a decent defence.'

'It's what I pay you for.'

Arthur Boylan sighed, his exasperation showing. 'What was it you wanted to talk to me about, George?'

'I told you the other day but you were in no mood to listen.'

'So, tell me again.'

'I want you to stop Donnie McCann getting a liquor licence for his pub, and I want to hear about the latest correspondence you got from Christopher White's solicitor.'

'Right, well, let's just forget about McCann's liquor licence, shall we. You'd be asking for trouble, turn everyone in Lonsdale against you.'

'They're already against me.'

'True enough, so why antagonise them further? Forget McCann, OK?

'Huuumph, yeah, OK.'

'Now, this other business. I've heard from White's solicitor. He has discovered an insurance policy taken out by his uncle Fr Jack O'Gorman that names your wife, Thelma, as the beneficiary in the event of his death.'

'So what? My wife advised the PP on several investment schemes. It's only natural he would want to reward her should anything happen to him. What's the problem?'

'Christopher White believes this policy document, coupled with the land registration papers, gives you and your wife a motive to murder his uncle.'

'Motive, my arse,' Duggan said belligerently. 'Neither I nor my wife killed anybody. That's the first thing, OK? Second thing:

everything Thelma did for the late parish priest, in regard to his finances, was above board, one hundred per cent lee–git. So, I don't have anything to worry about, right?'

'Wrong!'

'What do you mean *wrong*?'

'I've examined the covenant your wife and Fr O'Gorman signed.'

'And...?'

'I have to tell you it's flawed.'

'Flawed? What the hell are you saying?'

'Just this: should White contest its legitimacy, he'd stand a good chance of getting a result.'

'What the hell—?'

'Listen, I'm saying he could be awarded a settlement...'

'You mean money?'

'Yes, he could expect to get half the value of the twenty acres.'

'Well, he can whistle. I won't give the shagger a penny.'

'You might have to. Don't forget, with outline planning permission, we're talking millions.' Arthur let Duggan digest that for a moment before continuing. 'The insurance policy is for twenty grand. It's airtight, no problems there as far as I can tell.'

'So, what's he on about?'

'Leverage.'

'Leverage? I've lost you.'

'He wants to force a deal. He'll drop all legal action, make an out-of-court settlement with you on the land question.'

'Oh, he will, will he?

'Yes.'

'How much?'

'Two million, straight cash deal.'

Duggan leaped from his chair. 'Is the man stone mad or what? Does he think he's dealing with a complete gobshite? Why on earth should I give a blackmailer two million, tell me that?

'Sit down, George. Calm down and let's sort this out.'

Duggan flopped back into his chair. 'Why should I give this jumped-up-Johnny anything at all?'

'To stop him taking you to court. To stop him stirring it up with the murder investigators. Apparently, he's prepared to send a photocopy of Fr O'Gorman's insurance policy, naming your wife as beneficiary, to the press if you refuse to play ball.'

'Play ball? Jesus Christ, I'll play ball all right. I'll cut them off him and ram them up his arse. I can't believe I'm hearing this.'

'I'm only telling you what his solicitor told me.'

'He can't do that, can he? He can't put something like that, something private, into the newspapers.'

'Yes, he can. He knows the sort of headlines it would generate. I can try and get an injunction against its publication but I doubt if I can keep it from the press indefinitely.'

'You're joking,' Duggan said, hoping to see his solicitor smile.

Arthur Boylan did not smile. 'I'm pointing out what could lie ahead.'

'Fine, just fine,' Duggan said, menacingly, 'so what do I do?'

'Do not accept Mr White's deal. It's blackmail. If you did, he would, in all probability, be back looking for more money within a year. Your best chance is to face Christopher White in the courts.'

'But you've already said he could get a result. I can't have that. There must be some other way around this problem. I lose millions no matter which way I jump.'

'There's always a slim chance you could win a court battle. If you retained the services of a top barrister, it might be possible to come out on top. You could probably settle on the steps of the courthouse. I doubt if he has the money to mount a long-term legal battle at the level this would be conducted. If that turned out to be the case, it's possible you could win by default.'

'Quite a gamble.'

'Well, that's the choice, George.'

'Can you get White's solicitor to arrange a meeting between myself and White?'

'Meeting head-to-head without your respective solicitors is not very clever. I could try to arrange it, yes, but I would strongly advise against such a course of action. What purpose would it serve?'

'Well, I could wring Christopher White's neck for a start,' Duggan said with a sardonic snigger.

'I'm glad to see you can still make jokes,' Arthur said, exasperatedly.

'Just wishful thinking, Arthur. Seriously, I want to meet the bastard face to face, see if he's the kind I can do a deal with. If I can, I will. If I can't, then we'll face each other across the courtroom.'

'I still advise against a head-to-head,' Arthur admonished.

'Your advice is noted. Now please see if you can line up a meeting between the two of us.'

Chapter 22

The man sitting in front of the computer cocked his head away from the monitor, his attention distracted by a song coming from the radio. His fingers ceased their rapid movement and paused above the keyboard as he listened. The radio disc jockey was featuring 1950s rock 'n' roll hits on his programme. Golden oldies, he called them; vintage recordings by Little Richard, Fats Domino, Chuck Berry and other artists from that era. But it was the sound of Jerry Lee Lewis that grabbed the computer operator's undivided attention.

As a boy he remembered his father playing old vinyl 45s by Jerry Lee Lewis. He hated the American singer, really hated him. The songs represented a musical time-warp that his father had never emerged from.

And now, listening to the piano-thumping rock 'n' roller, the contempt he harboured for his dead father re-ignited. He thought about the singer's nickname – The Killer – and smiled. It was, he decided, the supreme irony that he could now justifiably use that appellation for himself if he wished to. What would the old man say? He smiled again, thinking, it'd probably kill the old fart, if he wasn't already dead. But even without the baggage from the past, he had earned the name *Killer* in his own right.

He had, after all, killed a person. Actually done the deed himself.

He had eliminated Olive Moran. He'd planned her death like a hi-tech computer game, familiarising himself with all the right doors, avoiding the hazards, remaining alert to every move. In the end he had easily outwitted her, left her with no way out, watched her forfeit her life. Game over!

Earlier, watching the evening news on television, he'd been pleased with his own contribution to the top item. Olive Moran's murder had gripped the nation. The media had got everything it needed – sex, beauty, religion and death. He felt proud. If he had one regret it was that the pictures of Olive Moran splashed across every newspaper and television screen didn't do her justice. He had seen her in a far more personal way, he had looked into her eyes, seen her soul. She was indeed a beautiful person but she had to die, there was no getting away from that fact. And it was manifestly just and proper that he should be the instrument of that justice.

Reliving the action gave him a surge of satisfaction, almost as good as the action itself. Putting her body into the confessional had been a cool move. Arranging it so that she fell out from the darkened cubicle could not have been more perfectly stage-managed. That the body should be naked added extra spice to the game. Nice touch. He commended himself. Even now, he found it hard to hide his elation. She had made it so easy, too shit-scared to offer any serious resistance. He could still see her eyes as they stared at him before he snuffed her life out; eyes, full of unimaginable terror, her body paralysed, her mind uncomprehending. He had held her as she went limp in his arms, intoxicated by the smell of fear coming from her.

Exhilarating. His wildest fantasies realised. Dark gothic surroundings, a flickering sanctuary lamp and a flashlight to illuminate the scene, a surreal atmosphere admirably suited to his purpose. He'd peeled off her clothes, striptease fashion, slowly, item by item, until all her hidden secrets were revealed. Indescribable pleasure. Contact with the smooth flesh had sent sexual charges through his body. She had become cold and stiff, a fact that forced a bark of laughter from him. In America, a dead body was called a 'stiff'. Perfect description. He too had been stiff, his erection standing ramrod straight, defiant, demanding gratification.

He'd counted on Olive Moran's mother calling Sergeant McGettigan when her daughter failed to return from the hospital. Mrs Moran had, however, arrived in the church a little sooner than anticipated. But the real surprise had been the sight of the reporter. That was something he had not planned for.

Since then, he had read what the reporter had written in the *Post* about the murder. There was no doubting her ability as a journalist. Grudgingly he bestowed credit on her, pleased with how she had made his handiwork read in print. Her descriptions were accurate. He had seen her several times in Lonsdale in the days leading up to his final destination with Olive Moran but, until her picture appeared next to the by-line beside her reports, he hadn't known who she was. That had all changed now. She was clever, he could tell from the conjecture outlined in her articles in regard to what motives might lie behind the two recent deaths. But, like the detectives investigating the cases, she placed too much emphasis on the link between the priest's death and that of Olive Moran. There was a link, of course, but from everything he'd read and heard, nobody, including Emma Boylan, had made the proper connection.

Thinking about the incisive nature of Emma Boylan's investigation, he felt a twinge of unease. Could she be a threat to what he'd planned? McGettigan and Connolly represented bit-players, mere drones; pissing against the wind as far as he was concerned, clueless, buzzing around in a hundred different directions at once, all of them wrong.

But Emma Boylan was different. Queen bee.

Her antenna, he could tell, was more acute than the plodders from the law, raising the prospect that maybe, just maybe, she could get lucky and stumble on to the real game plan.

He would have to do something about her. It wouldn't do if his plans came unstuck prematurely because of a snoopy press reporter. It was imperative that he complete his mission. Nothing must deflect him from the path of retribution. A great injustice had been perpetrated by certain people in Lonsdale and he had taken on the responsibility for delivering appropriate justice.

He switched off the radio, poured himself a vodka and Red Bull and returned to the computer game he'd been working on. Computers had made him a rich young man. As a games designer he had struck it rich with two of his earlier creations. He'd been lucky. Back in the mid-'90s there wasn't such tremendous competition out there. Up against 'Doom', 'X-Wing' and 'Dune II' he had scored with an even bloodier game. He called his creations 'Maggots' and 'Maggots II', a concept in games that broke new ground, both technically and stylistically.

Back then he was the new kid on the block. Success beyond his wildest dreams. His repulsive, bloodsucking bugs had imprinted themselves so forcefully on the young players that his games remained top sellers to this day. He had sold the rights for a cool million dollars plus a 1 per cent royalty on all sales. A master stroke. Right now he was working on the creation of a new game. Going up against such blood-letting games as 'Silent Hill' and 'Resident Evil', he needed to be at his best but his concentration was far from focused.

This inability to apply his mind he put down to the reporter. He could not stop thinking about Emma Boylan. Computer games allowed him to wallow in blood, guts, gore, and all manner of bodily membrane but, no matter how clever he was in simulating horror, death and mayhem, it still remained mere animation. The 'high' no longer high. Now, with the smell of real death and fear in his nostrils, the visions he conjured up on his monitor didn't seem such big cheese.

Emma Boylan could pose a threat. That made her a worthy opponent. It qualified her to participate in his game. A challenge was always good; it kept him on his toes, alert, careful, but most of all, lethal. In the end he would win; there could be no other result, but first he had to decide on a strategy. Easy peasy. First step would be to control what she reported in the *Post*. No problem there. He would hack into her computer network, find out what she was writing before it went to press. Easy for someone like him. He had the right tools; the sniffers, the scanners, the password crackers. He had all the cutting-edge program designed to seek out vulnerabilities in software networks.

Watching Emma Boylan's movements over the past few days, he noted that she seldom had anybody with her. Good. He knew her car, a silver Hyundai Coupé. He had seen her park it in the same space on successive days. It would be easy to get to her, take her in, then out of the game. What he had done to Olive Moran remained vivid in his mind. Maybe he would do a similar number on the reporter. Why not? She was a good-looking woman, nice figure – no Lara Croft, admittedly, but pleasant enough on the eye just the same. Fuck her; yes, he sure would like to fuck her.

The smile was back on his face. His erection screaming for attention.

Later, later!

With Emma Boylan under his control he would have the ability to see to it that she uncovered no new developments. Dead reporters tell no tales. He needed two weeks, three at the most, to achieve his goal, but there was no rule that said he couldn't indulge his wildest fantasies during that period. Besides, he was the one making the rules.

It called for careful planning. Not a bother for him. He was a games designer; knew all the moves. Planning, combined with guile, wit and speed of intellect were, he acknowledged without a hint of modesty, his strongest points. He was laughing again.

While Emma Boylan was on the trail of a murderer, he would be on her trail. The supreme irony of it appealed to him. A good contest was in store. He would stalk her, take her, and play her like a cat playing a mouse. He would zap her from the scene. He thought about how she would look once her clothes were removed. Naked. He would do it all with her. Everything. But, should he do it while she was still alive or wait until she was dead?

Jerking off always helped clarify his thoughts.

Perhaps he would just knock her out at first, promise to spare her life if she performed certain acts. His mind brimmed over with a series of lewd images. Fleeting doubts vanished. He would stop Emma Boylan's investigation while, at the same time, satisfying the sexual hunger now consuming him.

Emma Boylan's disappearance would work to his advantage. It would add to the confusion and throw the whole murder investigation into chaos. While the detectives were chasing around in circles, he would complete the mission he had set himself. Emma Boylan would represent a pleasant diversion, relief from the serious business of eliminating his remaining marks.

Chapter 23

Emma Boylan's learning curve was steeper than expected. She would be first to admit that her knowledge on the subject of DNA left a bit to be desired. Like most people, she knew in general terms how DNA worked and how its application had revolutionised crime investigation. She'd downloaded reams of information on the subject from the internet but there were still some aspects on specific procedural techniques that were unclear to her.

She contacted the ever-reliable Detective Inspector Jim Connolly. A self-proclaimed expert on the subject, he was one of the people pushing the Government to establish a nation-wide DNA database. 'I've no time for left-wing pinkos and civil-liberties groups who argued against holding DNA files,' he confided to Emma.

'They have a point, surely?' Emma ventured.

'Wrong, Emma. Current restrictions mean that certain bodily samples such as blood or semen can only be obtained if the person in question consents. Advantage, criminal.'

'So if someone decides not to co-operate, that's it?'

'More or less, but when a person refuses to give samples, a court of law is entitled to draw an inference and use it as corroborative evidence.'

Expounding further on the subject, Connolly mentioned the name Lifeline Diagnostics, an organisation specialising in biological relationships. This was the information Emma had been seeking. If she had come right out and asked for it specifically, the detective would have demanded to know why. Better, she decided, that he did not know how she planned to use his information – at least not until she satisfied herself that she was not on a wild-goose chase.

She found Lifeline Diagnostics's laboratory in a back street, tucked discreetly behind the walls of Dublin Castle. Sitting in a small but expensively furnished office, she faced forensic scientist Simon Tubridy, a mild-mannered man in his late forties. Immaculately dressed in a three-piece suit, all courtesy and charm, he eyed her approvingly. He had agreed to see her on the strength of a lie she'd spun, a deception that had him believe she was assisting DI Connolly on a current investigation.

'What exactly can I do for you, Ms Boylan?' he asked.

'I need to establish that a certain man is the biological father of his daughter.'

'I'm sorry, Ms Boylan, but Lifeline Diagnostics do not accept standard civil paternity or civil biological relationship cases from the public.'

Emma explained, in conspiratorial tones, that what she sought was pertinent to a criminal investigation, an undercover operation. For a moment it looked as though the forensic scientist had seen through her deceit. A heavy silence hung between them. But when Tubridy finally spoke, she could tell he had given her the benefit of the doubt. 'What you need to do,' he said, 'is obtain swab samples from both subjects.'

'In the case I'm dealing with I'm afraid it's not possible to get swab samples,' Emma said, beginning to feel out of her depth. 'Are there any other ways to do the test?'

'Look, Ms Boylan, I think there are a few things you should know about DNA before we proceed any further,' Tubridy said, his initial charm waning as he launched into a crash-course on the subject. 'Everyone is born with a unique genetic blueprint known as deoxyribonucleic acid – what we call DNA.'

'A bit like a supermarket bar code,' Emma said, hoping her simplistic analogy would give him an opening to impress her with his superior knowledge on the subject. Sure enough, her strategy worked.

Tubridy blinked his eyes twice in fast succession. 'No, Ms Boylan, DNA is a science; it is nothing remotely like a supermarket bar code.' This remark was followed by an exasperated sigh. 'Let me explain: a child gets one half of its genetic makeup from the mother, the other half from the biological father. In DNA testing, we first establish the genetic markers that the child shares with the mother. The markers that do not match the mother will match the biological father. You with me so far?'

'Yes, I think so,' Emma said, feigning a dumb-female smile.

Tubridy glanced at his watch, exhaled loudly. 'You... *think* so?'

'Yes, but what happens when there are no samples available from the mother?'

'It works like this: if the alleged father contributes half the child's genetic makeup, then he's the real father. However, the system has limitations. The absence of shared characteristics is not absolute proof that people are unrelated. In difficult cases, we like to test other family members to give us more genetic information in order to form a firm conclusion.'

What Emma had heard from the forensic scientist did not fill her with confidence as far as her next move was concerned. Seeking the help of Lifeline Diagnostics had sprung from something Mary Dunne had said; the bit about Fr O'Gorman being Yvonne Duggan's real father. And then, at Olive Moran's burial, when Yvonne flicked a blood-soaked fragment of tissue from George Duggan's shaven face on to her sleeve, the possibility of paternity testing took root. Later, getting a lift back from the graveyard to her own car, she collected a few stray strands of Yvonne's hair from her jacket.

'I've brought two samples,' she said, producing two envelopes from her handbag. Quickly, she explained what was in the envelopes and asked if they would suffice for the DNA testing she required. Tubridy examined the contents and shook his head. He explained in elaborate, mind-numbing, technical detail that his laboratories were not equipped to carry out the tests on account of the nature of the samples.

Emma was about to retrieve her samples when he told her that there was a way to achieve what she required. There was a laboratory in Britain, he informed her, that could help, providing it went through the proper channels. For reasons Emma couldn't divulge, she rejected this offer. Dejected, she shook hands with Tubridy, said goodbye, thanked him for his help, and opened the door to leave. 'Wait,' Tubridy called out, 'I have another idea.'

Emma moved back into his office and watched as he scribbled

on a page of his desktop notebook. 'I suggest you get in touch with the name I've written here,' he said, giving her the note. 'He's an old friend of mine, a professor in the science faculty at the City of Dublin University. Just tell him I sent you.'

It was the telephone call from the hospital that transported Brenda Moran back to the real world. Good news. Her husband Tom had come off the mechanical ventilator and had regained a degree of consciousness. She attempted to dress herself, taking renewed care with her appearance. She felt a dazed dread, afraid to believe the good news in case it turned out to be a false hope.

Sleep had eluded Brenda Moran in the days and nights since Olive's death. Mentally, emotionally and physically, she had taken about as much punishment as it was possible to sustain without going over the edge.

On her way into the hospital reception area, she encountered Sergeant McGettigan making his exit from the lifts. The sergeant, wearing his uniform, stopped when he saw her. 'You've heard the good news?' he asked.

'Yes, that's why I'm here. I've been told he's off life-support.'

'Aye, indeed he is, nothing short of a miracle. I've just been in to see him, let him know the world hasn't forgotten him. He's still heavily sedated so I'm not sure he recognised me or heard a word I said. I'll call back when he's feeling a bit better. I'm sure he'll make a full recovery in no time at all.'

'Please God you're right, Sergeant. What worries me now is how he's going to react to Olive's death. How do I tell him? I'm so relieved he's on the mend, of course I am. Like you say, it's a miracle, but I'm dreading the moment when I have to tell him about…'

'I think you should hold it from him until he gets out of hospital.'

'You think so?'

'Sure, best idea, Mrs Moran. Put it off for as long as you can, that's my advice. It's all going to be such a terrible shock to him. Remember, he probably has no idea that Fr O'Gorman is dead.'

'Right. Good day to you, Sergeant.'

McGettigan's words annoyed her. His motives for visiting Tom were all too transparent. The sergeant wanted to question

Tom about the fatal crash and couldn't wait to interrogate him. She grimaced, dismissing McGettigan's advice to take it easy and not rush things, advice he apparently believed did not apply to himself.

Tom Moran looked ill. Very ill. That was her first thought. He lay still in his bed. Gone were the tubes, the electrodes and the sensors that had become so much a part of his existence in recent weeks. Gone too, the sound of nerve-tingling blips from machinery charting his every heartbeat. Gone also, the life-force series of undulating peaks and valleys on the monitor screen that had so frightened her at first.

She had prayed for this day. But now that it had come about, he appeared more vulnerable than ever, left to his own devices, the crutch of modern technology withdrawn. She tiptoed to the chair by his bedside, sat down and gazed at his face. His eyes were closed. His face, so pale against the starchy white bed linen, looked death-like, the effect making her wonder for the briefest moment if... but before the thought had fully formed, she saw the almost imperceptible rise and fall of his body.

'Hello, Tom,' she said, taking hold of his hand.

No response.

'Tom, can you hear me? It's me, Brenda, I'm here.'

She felt a reaction in his fingers, saw a slight movement from his closed eyelids. She felt a lump in her throat. Tears fell. She didn't want him to see her cry but couldn't help herself. She was having difficulty holding herself together. Suddenly, his eyelids flipped open. Colourless eyes looked at her. She could tell that he recognised her. She bent over to kiss his cheek, trying not to let her tears fall on to his face. 'Tom, oh my God, you're back with us, back with me, I'm so happy. How... how do you feel?'

His mouth contorted in a series of grimaces, his lips barely opening and closing. All she could hear was a low guttural sound that seemed to emanate from deep down in his throat. His Adam's apple bobbed up and down, an expression of pain in his eyes. Brenda spoke in comforting tones. 'It's all right, Tom love, don't try to talk, we'll have all the time in the world for that later.' She talked to him for several minutes, trying to conjure up bright happy images, careful to avoid all mention of Olive.

Getting no response made it difficult to continue and she was glad when Mr O'Mara, one of the hospital's chief neurological consultants; entered the room. She had spoken to him on previous visits and liked his manner. His smile now, as always, allayed her fears. 'He's going to be fine, Mrs Moran,' the consultant said, sitting on the side of the bed, able to look at her and the patient without effort. 'He's a little drowsy right now because of medication.'

'But he knows it's me, doesn't he?'

'I'm sure he does, but you have to understand what he's gone through. He's been unconscious for a long time so we have to allow the brain some time to adjust. As I've explained to you previously, our probes have found that the temporal region of the brain has been churned about quite a bit. It's this area that houses his perceptions of smell, sound and taste, so it's natural for him to have difficulty with these senses at first. You're going to have to give him time. Time is the great healer.'

'What about his voice? He's having trouble speaking.'

'It's been some time since the voice box performed its function, so we have to be prepared to expect some hesitancy in that department. The femoral artery suffered damage in the accident. This could affect his memory. It's possible that his brain is not capable of remembering or identifying sounds just yet, thus impeding the signals required to form sound patterns. Given time, other parts of the brain should take over the defective segments so, Mrs Moran, until these matters sort themselves out, we can only watch, wait and pray.'

'Will he be able to speak or not?'

'Yes, I believe he will, Mrs Moran, but I won't lie to you; it could take some time and even then, there's the possibility of impediment. We just don't know enough about the brain, and in the end, it's the brain that informs all the body's other organs. Like I told Sergeant McGettigan, the next few days and weeks will be crucial.'

'You discussed his condition with the sergeant?' Brenda asked, irked by this revelation.

'Had no choice, I'm afraid. I protested, of course, but the sergeant pointed out that your husband is a witness in a murder investigation.'

'Well, Mr O'Mara, I know you mean well but I don't want anybody bothering my husband until I give permission, and that includes McGettigan or any other detectives that come sneaking in here behind my back. Hasn't he suffered enough? Tom deserves a little peace after what he's been through.'

'I couldn't agree with you more, Mrs Moran. I shall see to it that your wishes are observed.'

In the silence that followed this exchange, they both noted that the patient had closed his eyes again.

Chapter 24

Extracts from the diary of Nelly Joyce – aged 21
Date 14th July 1973. Johnstown National School.

Dear Diary

Lost my virginity last night. Honest to God! Should I laugh or cry?

What happened was this—

Went to the pictures, saw 'The Sting'. Fell in love with Robert Redford all over again. He's fabulous. Those eyes!

Went back to Cherry Picker's flat. Stayed the night.

Before going to bed, he insisted on having a bath. I was already between the sheets when he came into the bedroom.

Kissed and cuddled like mad.

After a while, he says he'd like to put it in me.

I wanted that too but I told him I was terrified of becoming pregnant.

It won't happen, says he, Once the goolies are exposed in a hot bath before intercourse, it acts as protection, he swore.

I wasn't convinced. Said no.

Got highly excited after a while. Changed my mind. Begged him to do it!

Didn't enjoy it, not a bit. A huge disappointment!

Pain was terrible. As bad as getting a tooth out – every bit as bloody.

When he finally got it inside me I cried with pain.

He pushed it in and out until he was finished, moaning and groaning – said it was wonderful.

He thought my cries were uncontrollable passion.

I was glad when he rolled off me.

Maybe I'm abnormal. Everyone says sex is great. Well, it's not.

I've read about women who are frigid, women who get no pleasure from sex. That's me. I'm frigid. I must be!

Still love him madly but I'm dreading the next time he asks me to make love.

Goodnight Diary.

Extracts from the diary of Nelly Joyce – aged 21
Date 22nd July 1973. Johnstown National School.

Dear Diary

Went back to Cherry Picker's flat this evening.

Snogged hot and heavy as soon as we got inside the door.

He suggested we go to bed. I said yes. He said he would have to have a bath first, expose his nuts to the hot water, prevent little babies coming along.

I laughed and told him to stew them good and proper.

After five minutes, I joined him in the bath.

We splashed about like bold children.

We helped dry each other and got into bed.

We kissed each other all over until we were both dying for it.

This time it was wonderful.

I lost all control and screamed with pleasure as I reached orgasm.

I think I frightened him.

He clamped his hand on my mouth to shut me up.

Do you want me thrown out of the place? he says. There's other people in the house, you know. I'm out of here in a flash if the landlord hears a complaint.

One hour later he dropped me back at my flat. We kissed on the doorstep.

He said I was the loveliest woman in the world. Said he would always love me.

I told him he wasn't half bad himself and that I loved him too.

I'm so happy I don't know if I can sleep or not!

I just know Cherry Picker is the man for me.

I feel sure that one day soon he will ask me to marry him. When he does I will have my 'yes' ready for him!

On that happy note I'll say goodbye for another day.

Goodnight Diary.

Extracts from the diary of Nelly Joyce – aged 21
Date 10th September 1973. Johnstown National School.

Dear Diary

Dr Carroll gave me the bad news.

I'm sorry, he says, your urine test came back positive – you're pregnant.

Wanted to die.

I'll have to tell Cherry Picker tomorrow. He's not going to like it, especially after all the trouble he had taken to prevent this happening.

He'll support me but it's going to be difficult for both of us.

I'm sick, sick in my heart with what's happened.

I've been Stupid! Stupid! Stupid!

Goodnight Diary.

Extracts from the diary of Nelly Joyce – aged 21
Date 11th September 1973. Johnstown National School.

Dear Diary

Met Cherry Picker after school in his flat. He knew something was wrong.

I told him about my visit to Dr Carroll. He put his head in his hands, said nothing for ages. I cried.

We'll have to get rid of it, he says. I didn't know what to say.

If I could just become un-pregnant everything would be great.

He said he knew a way to bring about a miscarriage. You have to have a bath in scalding hot water, says he, and drink a bottle of gin.

I told him it sounded a bit like the hot baths he used on his testicles.

He was more sure about this.

Said he saw it in a Michael Caine film called 'Alfie'.

He said he knew a medical student who might be able to help.

We hugged before going back to the flat.

He said that he would always stick by me.

For a magical moment I almost forgot the awful trouble I was in.

He made no attempt to make love.

I've told no one else about what's happened.

I'll get into bed now and try to work out what to do.

Goodnight Diary.

Caroline Blackman closed the diary and turned off her bedside lamp. Reading about her own conception was eerie and disturbing. Thinking about the dreadful sorrow and misery her conception had meant for her mother left a hollow pain.

She had read all of the diary entries several times over the course of the past five years but their potency never dimmed. These forays into her mother's past vividly set out the terrible consequences that followed on from the fact of being pregnant out of wedlock back in the 1970s.

Her mother had worked in the Johnstown National School until the sixth month of her pregnancy. When she could no longer hide the changes taking place in her body, she had a visit from the school manager. He dismissed her, said her very presence represented a bad example to the pupils, parents and teachers. He asked who the father was but she refused to divulge any information in that respect. The man referred to as Cherry Picker would lose his job as a teacher if his identity became known. That would have been in neither of their interests.

According to the diaries, Cherry Picker helped her financially during this dreadful period. Her flatmates had been furious with her at first but stood by her, helping her in every way they could. They had to make sure their landlord never saw that she was pregnant, knowing that if he did, he would force her to leave the flat straight away.

Her foster parents, Mr and Mrs Williams, received a letter from the school manager informing them of Nelly's disgrace. Two days later they sent her a suitcase stuffed with the few possessions she owned and a note telling her never to darken their door again. On top of all her other problems this rejection had been heartbreaking. They had taken her in when the Industrial School burned to the ground and they had given her a good and loving home. They had paid for her education and had supported her in every way they could. It seemed inexplicable and unpardonable, given their previous laudable actions, that they should turn their backs on her at this, the most critical point in her life.

It was through her two flatmates, Maura and Eva, that contact was made with a home for unmarried mothers in London. Two weeks before the baby was due, Maura and Eva and the man she called Cherry Picker went to the ferry port in Dun Laoghaire and saw her safely on to the boat for Holyhead. Between them they had provided the money for her fare and had even managed to scrape together forty pounds in cash for her.

Caroline Blackman pictured the scene in Dun Laoghaire: her mother, an unfortunate twenty-one-year-old, naïve when it came to the ways of the world, going to a country where she knew no one, with forty pounds in her pocket, terrified of what lay ahead. Caroline herself had been present at the ferry port that day, inside her mother's belly, as yet unborn, unaware of the terrible upheaval her presence there was causing.

In her bed now, alone in the parochial house, Caroline allowed the images so vividly recorded in her mother's diary to project themselves like some old movie on her mind's eye. She experienced a sense of guilt for the unwitting part she herself had played in her mother's plight. Her nightly excursions to her mother's past reinforced her resolve to do something positive by way of absolving that guilt. But there were other people, apart from herself, who had been far more instrumental in making her mother's life a pure hell. In the five years since the poor woman's merciful release from earthly suffering, she had been successful in discovering the names of those prime tormentors.

Caroline wanted to sleep but her mind refused to shut down. She thought about her job as the parochial housekeeper and wondered how long more she would have to endure that role. A new priest would take up residence in the parochial house in the morning. The Bishop was determined to get things back to normality in the parish. That was fine as far as she was concerned, her own mission in Ireland would be accomplished soon enough. When that happened, she would leave the place, go back to London, take up her life again and put the ghosts from the past to rest once and for all.

Chapter 25

Emma Boylan sat opposite Connolly in the Kozy Kitchen. He had phoned her earlier, made the mid-morning appointment, said he wanted a word. Sounded ominous. The expression on his face now confirmed her suspicion that the word would not be complimentary. In all the time she'd known the detective she had never totally succeeded in reading the expressions that, from time to time, marred his strong, agreeable features. She wondered if it was this ability to remain inscrutably enigmatic that made him so good at his job.

She remained tight-lipped while a waitress placed mugs of coffee in front of them. The waitress, Emma noticed, was new, at least new to the café; she hadn't seen her there before. No sign of Mary Dunne. Connolly, looking suave and dapper as ever, sipped his coffee, unintentionally creating a frothy moustache on his upper lip as he did so. Emma resisted the urge to smile as he used his napkin to clean his mouth, giving him the benefit of her best quizzical expression. It never failed to get a response.

'I'm annoyed,' he said at last.

'Not with me, I hope?'

'Yes, damn it, with you.'

'Really?' she replied sheepishly. 'What have I done this time?'

'You know damn well what you've done.'

'Enlighten me.'

'You talked to Simon Tubridy in Lifeline Diagnostics.'

'Oh, him. Yes, I—'

'—told him you were working with me.'

'Well, we are sort of working together on—'

'No, Emma, we are not, I repeat *not*, working together. I will not allow you to go around saying—'

'OK, all right,' Emma interrupted cautiously, 'I might have stretched the truth a little. No big deal. We *are* co-operating on an investigation, aren't we? Anything I dig up, I tell you, right?'

'Wrong! Damn it, Emma, you know better than that. Have you any idea the sort of trouble you'd land me in if this got back to headquarters?'

'Sorry, Jim, hadn't thought of that. How'd you find out?'

'As it happens, I visited Lifeline Diagnostics twenty minutes after you'd been there, talked to Simon Tubridy. He mentioned you, seemed impressed with your looks if not your brains, said you told him you were working with me.'

'And how did you react?'

'Wanted to strangle you for a start. Had to play along but I was furious, really furious. If I denied it, Tubridy would have contacted my superiors to ask what was going on. What in God's name were you playing at?'

'I said I was sorry.'

Connolly allowed a silence hang between them for longer than necessary. When he spoke, it was apparent that the matter had not been dispensed with. 'Tubridy said he passed you on to his professor friend in the University. Further embarrassment! I couldn't very well ask him what that was about – seeing as how it was supposed to be my investigation – so you'd better tell me what you've been up to... in my name.'

Emma attempted to make amends. She told him about the samples she had secured from George Duggan and his daughter, Yvonne. 'I want to establish whether they are father and daughter – biologically, that is. I talked to Professor Joseph Larrigy in the University; he'll get back to me within a week or ten days with the test results.'

'I suppose you told him you were working for me?'

'No, I didn't.'

'Well, I suppose I should be thankful for that much at least.'

'Not really, I'm afraid. You see, the professor automatically *assumed* I worked with you because of Tubridy's referral.'

A flash of irritation crossed Connolly's face. 'You'll have me crucified yet, Emma. What the hell is it with women this weather? As if I haven't enough troubles on my plate already, what with...' He paused, shook his head ruefully as though regretting the words he'd just spoken. After a heavy silence he continued without much enthusiasm. 'So tell me, if you prove that George

Duggan is not the biological father of Yvonne, where exactly does that get us?'

Emma liked his use of the word *us*. 'It could mean that Fr O'Gorman is the real father.'

'So what?'

'It creates a link between his murder and that of Olive Moran.'

'How do you make that out?'

'Olive was found dead in his confessional, remember?'

'So?'

'I'd say the killer is trying to send us a message.'

Connolly grunted disdainfully. 'And I'd say you've been watching too many detective shows on TV.'

'You're not trying to tell me there's *no* connection?'

'Oh, there's a connection all right, I just don't know what it is yet.'

A brief silence ensued while they both remembered their almost untouched coffee mugs. Emma availed herself of the opportunity to ask another question. 'Any news on the whereabouts of Christopher White?'

'Gone to ground. Better chance of sighting Elvis. However, we have managed to dig up some info on him. Seems he's a bit of a hippie. He last stayed in a new-age commune down on the Dingle peninsula in Co. Kerry but nobody there could tell us where he's moved on to. He's supposed to be a wizard with the new electronic technology – uses computers to manufacture music – which probably explains why most of the stuff we hear today is such god-awful crap. Anyway, we've tried to trace him through the techno-business and failed so far. Oh, they've all heard of him all right, proclaimed him as a genius but, with a little prompting, they admit he's a bit on the flaky side. Trouble is, he's always one step ahead of us. The sooner we talk to him, the happier I'll be.'

'What about our other elusive suspect?'

'The curate?'

'Yeah, any news on his whereabouts?'

'Hey! What am I?' Connolly asked with a sardonic chuckle. 'Your phone-a-friend or what? I ask the questions around here.'

'Thought you might know something.'

'Well, as it happens, I know diddly squat. Even the Bishop doesn't know where the curate's got to. His Lordship suggested that he may have gone on a retreat. Seemingly quite a few priests go on retreats every now and then to top up their faith. The trouble is, from our standpoint, these retreats are held inside the walls of contemplative monasteries or theology seminaries, cut off from the outside. They believe in total seclusion: no newspapers, no radios, no televisions.'

'You think that's where he's gone... a retreat?'

'I don't know, Emma. For all I know he could have taken up residence in a city brothel; you never know these days. People do the oddest things... I ought to damn-well know.' Connolly stopped, as though lost in his own world momentarily, before returning his gaze to Emma. 'I've decided to put out a public announcement – papers, radio, television – asking him to contact us.'

'Not much help if he's somewhere that doesn't get any of these things.'

'Yes, you could be right, but I'm sure there's someone in those places who keeps in touch with the real world.'

'Are you going to say he's a suspect in the Olive Moran murder?'

'We'll just say we need to eliminate him from our enquiries.'

Connolly finished his coffee and called for the bill. Before leaving he chastised Emma once more for using his name to mislead people. He insisted that it didn't happen again. Emma nodded her agreement, while under her breath adding the words – until the next time. Smiling, they took leave of each other; Emma going to her car, Connolly to the barracks.

Emma was about to pull on to the street when a movement to one side of St John the Baptist Church caught her eye. A man beside a blue VW Polo, with a mobile phone to his ear, turned to look in her direction before getting into the car. The incident would not have registered with her had it not been for the fact that she thought there was something familiar about the man.

She switched on the ignition and drove on to the street, still racking her brains in an effort to recall why the man's appearance should strike a chord with her. She had only gone quarter of a mile when, in a flash of inspiration, it came back to her. She'd seen the man with the mobile phone on two previous occasions, both times in the vicinity of the church. That she should see him for a third time struck her as too much of a coincidence.

Christopher White! The name flashed on in her brain like a neon sign. Could the person Connolly was searching for be here, right under his very nose? The more she thought about it, the more she convinced herself she was right. She jammed on the brakes, stopped the car, made an erratic U-turn and raced back towards the church. She intended to confront the man. Direct action, best idea, bound to get results. If he denied he was White, there was little she could do, but if he admitted it she would... shit, she didn't know what she would do in that event, but it didn't stop her forging ahead with her plan.

There was no sign of the blue VW Polo. She drove up and down the adjacent streets, carefully scanning left and right but not finding what she was looking for. Admitting defeat, she found a parking space outside the police station, got out of the car and headed for Connolly's office.

McGettigan greeted her in his usual abrupt manner. 'I suppose you want to see super Dick?'

'No,' she answered mischievously, 'I'd like a quick word with Detective Inspector Connolly.'

'Too bad, Ms Boylan, right now he's not available.'

'Look, I know he's here; I saw him come in less than ten minutes ago. Maybe you'd let him know I'm here, I won't keep him a minute.'

'No can do, Ms Boylan. Right now he's getting some grief from his better half and some bloke in a pinstripe suit.'

'His wife? Here?' Emma asked.

McGettigan glanced around to make sure no one except Emma could hear him. 'Yep, breezed through the place like we were dirt, and the bloke with her – looked like an accountant or solicitor – followed behind like a pet poodle. She's a bit of all-right, that's for sure, but she looks as though she's about to have his guts for garters.'

'I see,' Emma said, having difficulty imagining the scene described by the sergeant. She had never met Connolly's wife and was intrigued that she would come to Lonsdale to see him.

McGettigan was enjoying the situation. 'I know I'm only a lowly uniformed sergeant,' he said, his expression laced with sexual innuendo, 'but do you think I might be of service to you... Ms Boylan?'

Emma ignored his suggestive leer with contempt, but she had little choice but to talk to him. She described the young man she had seen on three occasions and told of her search for his blue VW Polo. 'I believe the person I've seen is Christopher White.'

'Do you indeed?' McGettigan said, now treating her with a little more seriousness. He fetched a chair for her, told her to sit down and asked her to give him details. He wanted times, locations and a more accurate description of the man. When she relayed as many details as she could recall, he thanked her and said he would talk to Connolly as soon as the detective was free.

Emma was glad to get back to her car. She'd had enough exposure to the beefy sergeant's lust-hungry and fawning persona, an experience even less pleasant than being subjected to his more customary abrasive personality. His less-than-subtle mood swings didn't bother her one way or another, she just wanted him to pass on her message to Connolly.

That Connolly's wife should come to his place of work fascinated Emma. Why would a wife travel across the city when she could see her husband at home on a daily basis? Odd, to say the least. Emma wondered if she should stick around for a while, maybe get a glance of the woman. She'd heard Bob Crosby once describe Iseult Connolly as a 'real beaut'. Connolly himself never made any reference to his wife, at least not in Emma's hearing, a factor that made her all the more curious. As a delaying tactic, Emma dictated some thoughts into her pocket recorder, updating an article she'd been working on for the next day's edition of the *Post*. Ten minutes later, the recording complete, and with no sighting of Connolly's elusive wife, she switched off the machine and headed, reluctantly, for a meeting with her editor.

Because wisdom will not enter a deceitful soul,
nor dwell in a body enslaved to sin,

For a holy and disciplined spirit will flee from deceit,
And will rise and depart from foolish thoughts,
and will be ashamed at the approach of unrighteousness.

It would take more than the Wisdom of Solomon to restore the full measure of mental equilibrium sought by Fr Patterson. The Holy Abbot, Brother Urban, had pronounced him dead – spiritually speaking. The hope was that he would be reborn after an intensive twenty-one-day stay with the friars. The retreat in the Old Order of Carmelites, a nineteenth-century monastery on a cliff edge overlooking Donegal's most northerly coastline would, he had been promised, reinvigorate the spirit and bring him back to life.

He had donned the friar's habit and subjected himself to a regime of spiritual awareness, prayer, fasting, penance, and exposure to the message contained in the Bible. For hours at a time he lay prostrate on polished floorboards, contemplating the words he had read earlier in the Holy Book, trying to apply the Lord's message to his own pitiful existence. Determined to reclaim his soul, he sought forgiveness for the sins he had committed.

But even in this hallowed place, the Devil continued to ply his evil trade. From time to time, even while mouthing prayers, his mind reverted to type, conjuring up bad thoughts. Aware that his prayer had been subjugated to lustful longings, he tried all the harder to redirect his thoughts to a higher plane. For the most part, this action had been successful. Other times he had fallen, succumbed to thoughts of bodily pleasures. Just once, he had been plagued by an insistent stirring in the groin area but, after praying fervently and forbidding his hands to venture near the source of temptation, the crisis passed. And now, after six days, the impulses for carnal desire had become less pronounced.

His thoughts once more dredged up words from the Book of Wisdom, words he felt sure applied to him especially. Repeating them over and over brought him comfort, allowed him to believe he would truly be born again, only this time without the weaknesses inherent in his old manifestation.

For *the fascination of wickedness obscures what is good,*
And roving desire perverts the innocent mind.

Chapter 26

'Explain!' Crosby demanded, pushing a copy of the *City Herald* across his desk. 'How come this tabloid runs an exclusive on the Lonsdale murders? What's happening here, Emma?' He got up from his desk, stalked the room, hands gesticulating like an orchestra conductor in the climactic throws of Tchaikovsky's 1812 Overture. 'You've practically taken up residence in Lonsdale so how come you missed this? Explain.'

Emma had seen the *City Herald* before receiving Crosby's call to come to his office. She'd been rattled too, furious to have missed it. The headline read – Fr O'GORMAN LIFE POLICY SHOCK. The text told how Mrs Thelma Duggan, claiming to be the priest's beneficiary, had tried to cash an insurance policy just three weeks after his mysterious death.

Crosby glared at her. 'How did you miss this? he asked.

'I didn't *miss* it. If you read further down the article, you'll see that Fr O'Gorman's nephew, Christopher White, submitted a photocopy of the policy to the *City Herald*. Nobody, not even your friend Detective Inspector Connolly, has been able to make contact with White.'

Her answer failed to mollify him. 'Well, seeing as how you read the full article, it won't have escaped your attention that the solicitor acting for Thelma and George Duggan is Arthur Boylan – your father, Emma.'

'So?' she asked, cryptically.

'Christ, Emma, your old man is on the inside track on this one. Surely you could have used that contact to get hold of the story. And don't tell me about client confidentiality and all that baloney... blood's thicker than water – you should have got this one, Emma.'

She was taken aback by Crosby's comments. He could be abrasive at times, unreasonable and demanding but, until now, she had always believed him to be fair-minded, possessing scruples and a degree of integrity. Suggesting she use her father as a source crossed that line of ethical behaviour. Crosby could not miss the reaction on her face. He stopped pacing, sat on the side of his desk and favoured her with a conciliatory glance. 'Sorry, Emma, I shouldn't have said that,' he offered, holding his hands up in mock surrender. 'It's unworthy of me.'

'Yes, it is. It's—'

'—It's just that I'm so bloody annoyed. So far, thanks to you, the *Post* has led on this story – we've made it our own – and it bugs me to see some Gonzo hack steal our thunder.'

'I know, Bob. Feel like that myself. But there's a way we can grab back the initiative if we jump fast.'

'I'm listening.'

Emma reminded Crosby about the searches she had carried out in connection with the ownership of the land Fr O'Gorman had purchased while using George Duggan's name to hide his identity.

Bob appeared disappointed. 'Emma, we agreed not to go to press with that. Duggan would sue us if we tried to suggest, without proof, that there was anything illegal in the transaction.'

'It's different now.'

'Different? How's it different?'

'Read the article in the *City Herald* again. Note that Christopher White says he has other, more serious, revelations to release at a later date. I believe he's talking about the land deal.'

'So why is he holding back on it?'

'I've a far-out idea on that Bob... want to hear it?'

'Shoot, can't be any more daft than anything else I've heard.'

'I think White has gone to the *City Herald* with the insurance story to let George Duggan know he'll do the same with the twenty-acre land deal. He's banking on Duggan paying out a sizeable chunk of cash to keep the story away from the media. It's his way to get money.'

Crosby's expression softened as he paused to let this sink in. 'You're saying that if Duggan refuses to play ball, White will talk to the *City Herald*.'

'I could be wrong but, yeah, I think so, Bob.'

'And you're saying I should spike their story beforehand?'

'Yes, Bob. I think we should run with it *now*.'

'George Duggan will sue our asses.'

'Not if we write it in a way that covers us. We can use photo-copies of the documentation I uncovered, give all the facts as we know them, let the readers make up their minds.'

Crosby raised his eyebrows, grimaced, said nothing. He returned to his own side of the desk and flopped heavily into his seat. She could tell he liked the idea but the possibility of litigation bothered him. In recent months the *Post* had had to pay out two huge settlements and run a number of front-page apologies. The paper's board of directors, never happy at the prospect of shelling out cash in this fashion, had hauled Crosby over the coals. At the same time, he was supposed to win circulation battles with his rivals. He had risen to the challenge, was brave and resourceful, ran with breaking stories that caught the public's imagination. Sometimes, however, beating the competition meant that accuracy suffered. And when that happened he got a roasting in the boardroom.

'Write the story, Emma,' he said after silent deliberation. 'Put what you have together and we'll see how it plays with "legal".'

'Will do, Bob. Mind if I work from home? Less distraction there.'

'I don't mind where you write it as long as it's good.'

'Right; talk to you later.'

'Yeah, fine, Emma. Oh, by the way, about earlier... you know... I was out of order – sorry.'

'Apology accepted. You can be a cantankerous old pain in the ass at times but I forgive you.'

Crosby laughed, something he rarely did lately. 'Hey, watch your mouth, young lady. Have some respect for your elders. Go on, get out of here, write me a good front page.'

Vinny Bailey drove down the ramp to the car-park beneath Hubband House, the building that housed his apartment. He had spent most of the morning attending an art auction in Aunt Sally's Attic, an antique shop off Molesworth Street. He'd gone there in the hope of buying a James Barry self-portrait that took his fancy when he viewed it some days earlier. As an antique and fine-art dealer, Vinny made a comfortable living specialising in the purchase and sale of paintings. Back in his student days at the College of Art and Design, he had learned to appreciate aesthetic values in works of art. Later, expelled from the college prior to sitting his final examination (his youthful exuberance having brought him into contact with the Irish Republican movement), he rounded off his education in his father's studio. Working under Ciarán Bailey's guidance, he had developed a love of paintings and *objet d'art*.

Today, though, things had not worked out. The painting he sought to purchase, a modest-sized oil on canvas, executed in the neoclassical style, fetched more than Vinny was prepared to pay. Disappointed, he had come away from the auction empty-handed.

Reversing his car into his parking spot he was surprised, and delighted, to see Emma's car parked in its allotted space. It meant she was home for a change. He couldn't remember the last time he had seen her in the apartment during the day. More recently, it seemed to him, she spent an inordinate amount of time across the city in Lonsdale. He knew how serious she took her work but he worried that she might be overdoing it.

A year had passed since she had lost their first baby and in that time she had buried herself in work, refusing ever to mention the subject. During the early part of her pregnancy he had been critical of her role as an investigative journalist, warning her that for the sake of her unborn baby, she should give up her job until after the birth. She had reacted like a bull to a red rag. And then, in the course of pursuing her career, she had lost the baby. He had been devastated, still was to this day, but he avoided levelling any criticism at her.

There seemed little point in recriminations; what had happened had happened and couldn't be rectified. He had tried to pick up the pieces, get on with his life as best he could. He wasn't so sure that Emma had done likewise. Granted, outwardly, she put on a brave face for the world, but sometimes, when she thought he wasn't looking, he saw that melancholy look in her eyes. He did not intrude, knowing she would have to confront whatever demons haunted her in her own way. She had suffered enough and didn't need him to lay any more guilt on her shoulders than already rested there.

Walking along the car park's ramp towards the apartment entrance, thoughts of Emma uppermost in his mind, he failed to notice a car making its exit from the basement area. A squeal of breaks brought his mind back into focus. He jumped to the side of the ramp. Shaking with fright, he waved his apology to the driver. The car, a blue VW Polo shot forward to the exit, smoking its tyres. The glance he got of the driver, though obscured by windscreen reflections, let him know that the person behind the wheel was a young male. In that millisecond, the scowl displayed on the driver's face was not lost on him. Vinny shook his head – I deserved that, he thought, annoyed with himself for being stupid enough to walk out in front of the car in the first place.

The incident was forgotten as soon as he saw Emma. Working on her laptop, she didn't notice him until he put his arms on her shoulders. She jumped with fright. 'Oh, Vinny, I didn't hear you come in.'

Vinny kissed her. 'What has you home this hour of the day?'

'I'm putting an awkward piece together for tomorrow.'

'And it's not working out?'

'Right. It's a hotchpotch piece at best. I'm trying to make it sound more substantial than it really is.'

'A silk purse out of a sow's ear?'

'Something like that.'

'Why write it then?'

'Crosby's on my back, looking for miracles.'

'Oh, dear!' Vinny said in mock sympathy.

'Yesterday it was Connolly's turn to harangue me.'

Vinny was enjoying this. 'You poor thing.'

'That's why I came home, had to get away, get some peace and quiet, try to string a few strands together.'

'And then I come home and spoil it all.'

'No, Vinny, I'm glad you're here. You're not... well, you're different... because—'

'—because I'm your husband. Is that what you were going to say?'

Emma punched him playfully. 'I was about to say – you're here when I need you… and I need you now. I'd like to run a few things by you, see what you think.'

'Sure, I'll be glad to help, but you know me – as a journalist, I make a good antique dealer.'

Emma smiled. 'True, Vinny, very true, but there's nothing wrong with your logic or common sense. I'll let you read it as soon as I've finished it.'

'Right, Emma, but there's a condition.'

'A condition? Ah, come on, Vin, you sound just like the others.'

'Never! I just want you to promise me that as soon as you download your story to the *Post*, you'll come with me for a meal… a decent meal in a decent restaurant. Agreed?'

'Agreed.'

Emma worked the PC keyboard until she was reasonably satisfied that the piece hung together in a coherent way. She used the scanner to make copies of the legal documents connected with the article, saved them as J-peg pictures before dragging them onto her final file. She printed hard copies of the lot and carefully read everything, checking it line by line, word by word.

Satisfied that it was as good as she could get it, she handed the pages to Vinny. He went into their lounge area and shut the door. Twenty minutes later he emerged. 'Looks fine to me,' he said, handing her the pages back, 'but George and Thelma Duggan are not going to be too pleased.'

'I'm too hard on them?'

'No, I wouldn't say that exactly, not if they've done what you say they've done. One thing's for sure, they don't come out of it with any great credit. To be honest, Emma, I don't blame this nephew fellow – White – for trying to stop them. Its perfectly obvious from reading your article that the Duggans stood to benefit from the parish priest's murder. With planning permission, that land has got to be worth millions. Whether you like it or not, your article points the finger of suspicion in their direction.'

'I could be up shit creek,' Emma acknowledged, 'but I don't think I've said anything libelous. Anyway, the legal boys in the

Post will have to check it out before they let it roll. The funny thing is, Vinny, if the Duggans decide to go after me, their solicitor is my own father. Wouldn't that be hilarious, a sort of Boylan versus Boylan.'

'Would that be allowed?'

'No, not really, but it's an interesting thought.'

'Well, let's hope it doesn't comes to anything like that.'

'It won't.'

'Good, then send it down the line and let's think about where we're going to eat this evening.'

Before logging off, Emma scrolled through her e-mails. One item in bold type let her know she had a new message. The words, *DUGGAN, MORAN & BOYLAN*, came up on the screen, accompanied by an attachment symbol. Emma opened the message. It was a one-liner.

GRAVESIDE PICTURES TAKEN AT OLIVE MORAN'S BURIAL.

See attachment.

Emma was puzzled. Who had sent this to her? She double-clicked to download the attachment and waited several seconds as a colour photograph slowly materialised. *What the hell...?* Her own image, along with those of the other mourners around Olive Moran's grave, stared back at her from the monitor. The photograph had been taken at the precise moment that Yvonne Cobain decided to flick the speck of blood-dried tissue from her father's face.

Why would someone take such a photo? Why would they download it on to her system? She decided to print a hard copy of the e-mail and its attachment. She would show it to Crosby in the morning. If he could shed no light on its meaning, she would take it to Connolly. One way or another, she would not rest easy until she knew what the mysterious message meant.

Parked down the street from The Pavilion Restaurant, a lone male sat behind the wheel of his car listened to a Raging Speedhorn CD. One hour earlier he had watched Emma Boylan and her man – her husband, he presumed – go into the restaurant. That she should have a husband complicated his plans. It meant he had to factor this extra element into his calculations. But he didn't mind, not really. If anything, this new dimension made the challenge all the more exciting. Like a good computer game, it was the unexpected hazards that brought heightened enjoyment. He had dreamed up a dozen scenarios for Ms Boylan's demise, all of them appealing, but none involving her partner.

Hacking into her computer network had been a master stroke. Hacking was a favourite pastime of his, a trade he had developed with the help of the 'games' people he worked for. Like all the major software organisations, they ran programs to identify security holes in order to stop malicious hackers intent on exploiting their product. He had put together all the tools necessary to gain access to the most sophisticated networks.

He had become a member of The Cult of the Dead Cow, one of America's most controversial hacker groups, and had obtained their LophtCrack password-cracking program. The cult's BO and BO2K programs gave him freedom to run riot in other people's systems. The initials BO had nothing to do with body odour and everything to do with the more unsavoury aspects of computer piracy. BO stood for 'Back Orifice', a program designed to allow hackers back-door access to other users' systems by planting a 'Trojan Horse' in their software.

And that's what he had done with Emma Boylan's system. He had simply sent her an e-mail with an attachment, knowing that as soon as she double-clicked it on to her system, he had control of her files and programs. The beauty of the Back Orifice system was that it worked like any other program, once installed. He could now monitor every item that went through her network without her even knowing about it.

As 'Knives and Faces' blasted out from his speakers, he tapped his fingers on the steering wheel and thought about his premature meeting with the man in Ms Boylan's life. The dopey bollix had nearly walked under the car. Could have been killed there on the spot. He was glad that hadn't happened. That would give him no pleasure at all. The fun of snuffing out a life lay in knowing that person, in planning each step of the game, in hunting down the quarry and experiencing the adrenaline rushes that accompany the final death throes.

All seven minutes plus of Death Row Dogs had blasted its way to conclusion when his vigil outside the restaurant came to an end. He watched as his two 'players' got into their car and moved into the traffic. The wait had been good for him. It gave him time to think, time to construct a perfect strategy. He now knew exactly how this little game would terminate. And once that was out of the way he would get back to the more serious business that awaited him in Lonsdale.

Chapter 27

Extracts from the diary of Nelly Joyce – aged 22
*Date 21st April 1974. The Little Flower Home for Unmarried
Mothers, Finsbury, London.*

Dear Diary

Ann-Marie is one week old today. Gets cuter by the
minute.

Mother Superior spoke to me about work. I have to
clean the dorms, make beds, look after the nurseries
and help in the kitchen and laundry.

She says that when I feel stronger I can work in the
print room and do some outdoor work in the garden.

As long as I can be near Ann-Marie, I'll do whatever
she asks.

Got a letter from Cherry Picker.

He enclosed £20. Said he got my letter telling him all
about the baby's birth.

He's worried in case I get too attached to her before I
give her up.

Mother Superior told me people would come to look at
the babies in two days' time – Saturday. I dread it.

Hope no one picks Ann-Marie. Problem is, I can't get
out of here until she's adopted. I'd like to know her
better before she's taken.

I'm not great at praying but I've asked God and the
Blessed Virgin to do me this great favour – let me keep
my baby. I notice pictures and statues of Saint Thérese
of Lisieux all over this place. Decided to ask her for
help as well.

I will write to Ann-Marie's Dad and invite him over to
see his beautiful baby.

I need to know what the plans are for our future together.

Ann-Marie is crying. Must go now!

Goodnight Diary.

Date 28th April 1974. The Little Flower Home.

Dear Diary.

I feel locked out from the real world.

Made friends with some of the girls here. One girl, Janet, from Leeds, says she can't wait to have her baby adopted. She wants to get back to college. Others, like me, dread the parting.

Work in the print room is OK. We print Memoriam cards.

There's a dark room and photographic equipment where we print hundreds of small pictures of the person who's dead.

It's odd dealing in deaths with so much new life all around me.

A photographer took a picture of each mother and baby today.

Janet says the pictures are intended for the adoptive parents.

According to her, they like to see what the child's mother looks like, to know what kind of stock the child came from.

Janet is bitter on the subject, says they want to make sure we're sound of wind, limb and piss, like some kind of f***ing animals.

Cried my eyes out thinking about this.

Don't have the heart to write any more today.

Going to pray again. Is anyone listening?

God, are you there???????

If you are, please look down with pity on me.

Goodnight Diary.

Caroline Blackman closed her mother's diary. It was impossible not to feel her pain. Some of the words, written in blue ink, were partially obliterated. It didn't take any great stretch of the imagination to realise that tears from her mother's eyes had fallen on the page.

Caroline sat up in bed, pulled a drawer open in her bedside locker and extracted a small passport-sized photograph. It showed Nelly Joyce holding Ann-Marie. Now, as always, she had difficulty in reconciling the fact that she had been that tiny baby; that Ann-Marie had grown into Caroline Blackman. Her adoptive parents had, apparently, disliked the name Ann-Marie and chose to christen her Caroline instead. She had been told from an early age about her adoptive status. But it was only after the death of her real mother, Nelly Joyce, that she had discovered the grim circumstances surrounding her own adoption.

In one particularly poignant entry from Nelly Joyce's diary, the mother of three weeks described the day that Ann-Marie was taken from her. It was the one entry Caroline did not feel strong enough to re-visit.

Mervin and Stella Blackman had come to The Little Flower Home on a Saturday, two weeks into Nelly's stay there. Like other visitors, they strolled from one cot to the next like viewers in an art exhibition, peering at each infant in turn.

On that particular day, Nelly dressed Ann-Marie in a pink and white dress she had knitted herself. Seeing how lovely her baby looked in her cot, Nelly decided she would talk to the Mother Superior the following day and tell her she had changed her mind about the adoption.

But the next day had been too late.

By then, Ann-Marie had already been taken from the Home. Nelly was never informed which of the visitors had chosen her baby but she had noted one couple in particular taking special interest in her baby. They had stood out from the other visitors on account of their stylish, expensive clothes.

For days afterwards Nelly had been inconsolable, refusing to eat, refusing to speak. The Mother Superior, through perseverance, had managed to help her out of her depression. Within a few weeks, a job had been found for her as a junior teacher in a school in London's Hammersmith district. The Mother Superior had gone out on a limb to secure the position for her, concealing the tragic circumstances behind the work application. Nelly, though grateful, wanted to return to Ireland but the school manager in Johnstown had ensured that wouldn't happen.

Three months after taking up her job in Hammersmith, the father of her 'lost' child came to visit her. The reunion, which lasted two weeks, had been a bittersweet experience. The spectre of the absent Ann-Marie hovered above them like a dark cloud. Even when they made love, their pleasure was dimmed by a shared feeling of guilt. Condoms, not freely available in Ireland at the time, had been used frequently during the short visitation. On other occasions they'd relied on withdrawal.

Nelly begged him to come and work alongside her in Hammersmith. He declined. He was due a promotion back home, he had told her, pointing out how useful the extra money would be for both their sakes. Reluctantly she accepted that what he said made sense.

Alone once more, living in a one-room bedsit above a barber's shop off Gledstanes Road, she tried to come to terms with her enforced separation. Despair, never far away, was held in check with hopes and dreams for the day when they could share a life together as husband and wife, a respectable couple, able to put their past difficulties behind them forever.

Caroline sighed.

Her mother's hopes and dreams had never materialised.

A noise from downstairs brought her reverie to a sudden halt. She could hear a key being turned in a lock. The sound came from the door in Fr O'Gorman's room. Her absorption with her mother's past had led her to temporarily suspend real time. But now, her thoughts focused on the parochial house's main bedroom, a room that hadn't been used since the parish priest's death. Today, when the new curate, Fr Kelly, arrived to take up duty in the parish, he indicated that he would use the master bedroom.

She had shown him Fr Patterson's room, thinking it the most appropriate, but he made it clear that he wished to occupy the

bigger room. Fr Kelly's looks put her in mind of a eunuch character she had seen in an old film about ancient Rome. She couldn't
remember the name of the movie, but images of an orgy came to
mind; images of scantily clad nymphs tending to lecherous males
while gluttonous eunuchs looked on, drinking wine and dangling
grapes above their cherubic lips.

It was Fr Kelly's shape and way of speaking that led her to
equate him with the stereotyped eunuch depicted on celluloid, but
it was a characterisation that she readily admitted failed to reflect
the man's haughty manner and imperious demeanour.
Overweight, with a full-moon face, his skin had a pinkish sheen
and was smooth as a baby's bottom. In his forties, she guessed, he
was bald except for two small patches of hair above each ear. His
voice, faintly effeminate, had a tendency to emit small whistling
sounds when enunciating certain words. He never once offered to
shake hands, a factor that pleased her because, instinctively, she
knew the palms of his hands would be moist and sweaty.

His attitude to her was 'correct' – neither friendly nor hostile.
He promised not to get in her way or make impossible demands
of her. He explained that his appointment to Lonsdale was of a
temporary nature. From the way he said this, she could tell that it
couldn't be temporary enough as far as he was concerned. He
made no reference to the death of Fr O'Gorman or the disappearance of Fr Patterson. It was as though these recent unpleasant
events had been responsible for forcing him into this 'temporary'
posting.

Caroline dismissed thoughts of Fr Kelly, closed her mother's
diary, and reached out and switched off her bedside lamp.

Chapter 28

Vinny slept like a baby, his head partially hidden beneath the duvet, his breathing regular as clockwork. Untroubled. Emma smiled. She envied her husband's ability to sleep soundly regardless of the circumstances. She herself was less fortunate. Awake since the alarm's 6.30 morning call, she had already showered and dressed.

First objective of the day: to mould her face into something more presentable than the image glaring back from the mirror. The ritual began with the application of foundation and moisturising cream, followed by the faintest touch of eye-shadow and eyeliner. Delicately applied mascara and lip gloss completed the daily miracle. She tried to ignore the shadows, still evident, beneath her eyes. Harder to ignore were the encroaching crow's-feet at the corners of her eyes that her mother liked to describe as smile lines. Emma didn't agree. To her, their appearance brought little joy and less to smile about. Besides, if her mother was so comfortable with her appearance, how come she paid such exorbitant prices for wrinkle concealer?

Moving downstairs, she poured herself a glass of pure orange juice, put two slices of bread in the toaster and coaxed the coffee percolator through its paces. As the morning's ritual proceeded, she found time to place her laptop on the kitchen table and clicked on to the *Post's* website. Her article on the Duggans' land deal jumped out at her. Top story. She read it carefully, checking the quality on the reproduction of the accompanying documentation and photographs. The story held together. Thelma and George Duggan would consider it a hatchet job. Emma tried not to give in to a feeling of guilt. Her hope was that its publication might flush out the person or persons responsible for the murders. She did not want to believe George or Thelma Duggan were responsible but all this land business and life-policy endowments put them in the frame.

Emma closed the laptop, finished breakfast and prepared to leave for the office. She looked in on Vinny, leaned down to kiss him on the side of his face. He opened his eyes, pulled her towards him and kissed her on the lips. 'Forget about work today,' he said, with a boyish grin. 'Let's spend the day in the sack, pretend we're hibernating bears, what do you say?'

'I say you're a daft bugger and remind you that hibernating bears are sexually inactive during their winter sleep.'

'Huh, not much fun in that, then.'

'No, and now if you don't mind I've got work to do. See you about seven this evening, OK?'

'Yeah, sure. No, no, wait a minute, listen. I'm in and around the city centre later this morning. How about a bite of lunch together?'

'You're a gas, Vinny; if it's not sex, it's your stomach you're thinking of.'

'Pray tell, what could be more enriching for the soul? Meet me in FXB's restaurant in Pembroke Street, around one o'clock, say?'

'Yes, good idea, fine. Will you book a table?'

'Sure. See you at lunchtime, then.'

Brenda Moran decided to make an early morning visit to the hospital. She needed to get away from the house in order to preserve what little vestige of sanity remained to her. Olive's death was driving her round the twist. Too many reminders. Everywhere she turned in the house, Olive was there; each image, each memory, choking her emotions, tearing her apart.

Enough. She'd had enough.

She made it through the city's congested streets before the morning traffic reached its peak, parked in the hospital car park and headed into the building. She hoped to see improvements in Tom. Although he'd regained consciousness, he had not as yet regained command of his speech. On her last visit, conversation had remained one-sided. She had relied on his eye movement and hand grip for responses. But had he understood a word she said? Hard to tell. She had not as yet broached the subject of Olive's death. That bothered her. Surely he missed his beloved daughter? Could it be that the brain damage the neurological consultant hinted at had obliterated his memory?

Still pondering these questions, she entered his room. What she saw stopped her, mid-stride, in her tracks. The shape of a woman filled the chair by Tom's bedside, her back to Brenda, the woman's hand gently caressing the patient's hand. For one insane second, Brenda panicked, thinking that perhaps she'd entered the wrong room. But no, the face in the bed definitely belonged to Tom. In that heart-stopping moment of bewilderment, she watched as the woman's head slowly turned and looked at her. It was Thelma Duggan. The expression on Thelma's face mirrored Brenda's own surprise. For a moment neither woman spoke. Thelma Duggan was first to find her tongue. 'Why, hello, Brenda,' she said, a tremor in her voice. 'I'm sure Tom never knew he had such devoted women in his life...'

'What are you doing here?' Brenda asked, staring at her with barely concealed hostility.

Thelma vacated the chair she'd been sitting in and offered it to Brenda. 'George had business in the city this morning,' Thelma said with a smile that failed to reach her eyes, 'so I jumped at the chance to come visit Tom. I'd heard he regained consciousness.'

Brenda sat in the chair and looked at her husband. 'Yes, he has, but he needs all the rest he can get... especially *this early* in the morning.'

'Oh, I didn't bother him at all. As you can see, he's still asleep.'

'Yes, indeed, but... but it's still a bit soon for him to have visitors.'

'I'm sure Tom would make an exception for me,' Thelma said, remaining close by the bed. 'Old friends and all that.'

Brenda contrived to make her lips into what approximated to a smile. She did not consider Thelma Duggan a friend. Quite the opposite. She remembered first moving to Lonsdale with Tom, in the immediate aftermath of their honeymoon, and being introduced to George and Thelma Duggan. The Duggans had invited them to their farmhouse for a meal, ostensibly as a welcome-to-Lonsdale gesture, but Brenda had never doubted that the invitation had been little more than a vetting process, a ritual applied to all newcomers. The evening had been pleasant enough but she felt that Thelma had been too familiar with Tom, cracking risqué jokes and making comments about the honeymoon with less-than-subtle innuendo.

Months later, as Brenda got used to the city and made friends in Lonsdale, gossip filtered through to her that suggested Thelma Duggan's virtues were open to question. It was said that she granted her favours to the more 'dashing' males in the area with impunity. Brenda had tried to ignore such gossip but it was harder to ignore the special attention Thelma lavished on Tom. She had made known her misgivings at the time to Tom but he had brushed the matter aside. 'You're listening to the wrong people,' he insisted. 'I just want to make friends in the city and Thelma Duggan is being helpful... she knows who's who.' Thelma had introduced him to the greyhound set and he had welcomed the sport and its followers with enthusiasm.

On one occasion, during the time she was pregnant with Olive, a friend had told her, jokingly, that she'd better keep an eye on her husband if she didn't want the Duggan woman running off with him. It bothered her at the time that anyone would say such a thing, even in jest. She trusted Tom one hundred per cent. The mere suggestion that Thelma would even think about luring her husband from her was enough to germinate a dislike for the woman.

Earlier this morning, before setting out for the hospital, Brenda had picked up a newspaper and caught sight of the front-page headline. Seeing that it concerned the death of Fr Jack O'Gorman, she quickly scanned through the piece. She did not think of herself as uncharitable or vindictive but, reading about the Duggans' skulduggery, she had to admit to a sense of self-righteous satisfaction.

Even without the benefit of the *Post's* front-page story, seeing Thelma by Tom's bedside had rekindled the barely concealed animosity. 'Look, Thelma, I appreciate your visit to Tom,' she said, trying to sound unruffled, 'but he's going to remain asleep for a while, so there's no need to wait around. I'll tell him you called, give him your best wishes.'

The abrupt dismissal made Thelma visibly flinch. Whorls of crimson appeared in her cheeks. 'Yes, Brenda, you're right of

course. I'll leave now, let you be the one he sees when he wakes.'
Thelma stopped talking, bent over and kissed Tom on the forehead before continuing: 'He's always had you to protect him from
the likes of me, hasn't he? Good to see nothing's changed.'
Thelma walked towards the door but turned to look back at
Brenda before leaving. 'Goodbye,' she said, a gleeful smile on her
face.

Brenda made no reply, taken aback by the sheer invective
Thelma had managed to invest into the single word, *goodbye*. For
the first time, she realised that her feelings for Thelma Duggan
were no different than the feelings Thelma had for her.

Vinny had not meant to sleep on for so long. He had intended to
get out of the bed as soon as Emma left, but the allure of an extra
five minutes proved irresistible. And now, half an hour later, he
hurried towards his beloved Citroën in the underground car park,
berating himself for being late for an appointment he'd arranged
the previous day. He was about to unlock the driver's door when
he noticed the car's uneven tilt. On closer examination, he saw
that the rear tyre was flat. 'I don't bloody-well believe it,' he
hissed, shaking his head dejectedly. He hated changing wheels.
'Damn it,' he said aloud, kicking the offending tyre to vent his
frustration, hoping there was nobody around to witness his
predicament.

With an exaggerated body-heaving sigh, he went to the back
of the car, extracted the spare wheel and lifting equipment and set
about the task with all the enthusiasm of a death-row prisoner
awaiting execution. He loosened the wheel nuts a little before
getting down on his knees to place the jack in position under the
chassis. Unsure about where the head of the jack should be
placed, he flustered about, knocking caked mud from the general
area, before finding what he hoped was the correct location.

He had just begun to project the jack upwards when he sensed
a sudden movement behind him. Before he had time to look
around him, a white blur of activity shot past his face. Something
clammy pressed against his mouth. He struggled to stand upright.
An arm grip around his neck held him down. He was aware of his
body becoming limp. An all-consuming vaporous smell, smoth-

ering in its intensity, distorted his senses. The car park spun around, creating a rainbow of brightly coloured streaks of illumination, revolving, pulsating, alive, consuming him whole. His last memory was that of a male figure shimmering above him, a hallucinatory figure that appeared to melt and flow like some Hans Bellmer surrealist drawing come to life.

And then, nothing.

Chapter 29

'Bailey? Let me see. Yes, Madame, we have a reservation in that name,' the waiter said to Emma, glancing down his nose at the booking list. 'Would Madam like me to show her to the table or would—'

'Table please,' Emma cut in.

No sign of Vinny. She had consciously arrived ten minutes late to make sure Vinny would be waiting for her. It was a habit she had developed over the years for restaurant appointments. Until today, it had been an unnecessary action as far as Vinny was concerned. He always got there ahead of her. They had a little running joke on the subject. 'Nice men don't *come* first,' Vinny would say, quickly adding, 'except where grub is concerned; in which case, I'm willing to make an exception.' It never failed to bring a smile to her face.

Not today.

It would take more than a one-liner to cheer her up now. The morning had been a mixture of highs and lows – with the lows winning out. Reaction to her story on the Duggans' land deal received massive coverage on television, radio and the media in general. Bob Crosby bestowed a 'well done' on her, his highest accolade. The compliment would be good until the first time she failed to measure up to his impossible demands.

Glancing alternatively from her watch to the restaurant's entrance door, she decided to give Vinny five minutes. If he failed to show by then she would kill him. Well, no, she wouldn't kill him – not actually – but she would make his life miserable – big time. She decided to call him on her mobile phone. Before punching in his code she noticed a text-message sign flashing. It was from Vinny; it read –

PROBLEM! CHECK YOUR E-MAIL. VINNY.

Emma looked at the message for several seconds, not knowing what to make of it. Vinny never bothered with text messages. He hated them. She dialled his code. With the bollocking she intended to give him already rehearsed, she waited impatiently for him to respond. He didn't answer. Instead, his answering service kicked in. Not like Vinny at all. He wouldn't do this to her, not unless something extraordinary had come up. She tried to think. What could the matter be?

She read the text message again. Puzzling. Why would he want her to go to her e-mail? Vinny knew she never took her laptop to restaurants. He also knew her mobile phone did not have the capability to access e-mails.

So, what was he up to?

She got up from her table, made her excuses to the head waiter and exited the restaurant. She was furious, hopping mad. Muttering obscenities under her breath, she headed back to the apartment, her frustration registering with every gear change. Her mood worsened as she neared home, her mind consumed with variants of the words she would use to devour Vinny. Whatever was contained on Vinny's e-mail, it had better be damn-well good.

With great reluctance, Abbot Urban summoned the curate to his study. He needed to probe a sensitive issue with the young man and decided to use his own personal quarters for that purpose. Fr Patterson appeared unaware of the singular honour bestowed on him, thinking only, how cold the place was. With twin embrasure windows overlooking Donegal's wild Atlantic coastline, the Abbot's book-lined study represented the heart of the monastery. It was from here that all decrees concerning the operational practices of the Order emanated. For twenty-two years now, the octogenarian Carmelite monk, like some elongated mystical figure set free from the canvas of an El Greco painting, enjoyed the solitude offered to him behind the heavy timber doors, only occasionally allowing others to invade the space.

He had read about the death of Olive Moran and was aware of the request by the investigators to speak to Fr Patterson. Even contemplative Orders, like his own, were forced to visit the realities of the outside world. It was, to his mind, a vital if unpleasant necessity. Discovering that a participant on the retreat was front-page news came as quite a shock. He couldn't remember anything remotely like this happening before.

The Abbot had observed Fr Patterson's progress over the short period the curate had already spent in prayer and meditation. What he saw was, to his mind, the personification of a soul in turmoil. That some deep-seated problem was disturbing the young man was painfully evident, but it was a problem Fr Patterson had come to the monastery to resolve, a matter between the curate and God.

Abbot Urban, feeling every day of his eighty years, ran his fingertips over his wispy white beard and spoke in soft whispers. 'I hope you don't mind me breaking into your meditation, Fr Patterson,' he said kindly, 'but I believe it might help if you were to talk to someone at this point, what do you say?'

'Of course, Holy Abbot, what would you like me to talk about?'

'I'd like you to share the oppressive burden I perceive to be weighing so heavily on your conscience.'

'I wouldn't know where to begin, Holy Abbot,' Fr Patterson answered, finding the sound of his own voice strange after his days of enforced silence. He sat on a hard, straight-backed wooden chair, facing the venerable old monk, glad of the opportunity to open his mouth again, relieved to be able to converse with another human being.

Gentle probing from the Abbot encouraged him to list all his real and imagined weaknesses. He told of the persistent doubts that plagued him on many aspects of faith. Like some unholy litany, he itemised the sins of impurity that had bedevilled him throughout his priesthood. Trance-like, he talked about his obsession with the appeal of the flesh and his longings for female company. He wanted to serve God, he earnestly assured the Abbot; he wanted to live up to his vow of chastity, but his body craved relentlessly for the satisfaction that only a woman could provide.

'I understand, my son,' Abbot Urban said, his eyes closed, his head nodding ever so slowly, inducing an almost hypnotic spell on the priest. 'Tell me, Fr Patterson, is there a particular person, a woman perhaps, who, more than any other, holds a special place in your heart?'

Not expecting this question, Fr Patterson paused for a moment before answering. 'Yes, Holy Abbot, there was.'

'Was? I see. Why do you say – *was*?'

'Because she is no more.'

'No more?'

'I have exorcised her from my life.'

'How did you achieve that?'

'I'd rather not say, Holy Abbot.'

'Why not?'

'Coming here represents my break with that part of my life.'

'I see. And to that end, have you been successful?'

'Yes, I think so.'

'You only think so?'

'I've taken measures to cut her out of my life, Holy Abbot. Her hold on me recedes daily. With God's help, I'm learning to live without her, to forget the ways of sin she provoked in me.'

'I see, I see. But it seems to me, Fr Patterson, you apportion blame to this woman, not yourself.'

'In what way?'

'You reproach her for your own weaknesses of the flesh.'

'I gave way too readily to temptation. I allowed myself to be led astray, to be diverted from the path of righteousness. I recognise that. I accept that the fault lies within me.'

'You do?'

'Yes, Holy Abbot, and having recognised it, I sought to eliminate the source of temptation... the very occasion of my sin.'

'And how did you go about that?'

'I banished the source.'

'You mean the *woman*?'

'Yes, I've banished her from my life.'

'You are talking about Olive Moran, yes?'

Fr Patterson flinched. Hearing Olive Moran's name on the Abbot's lips brought about a shocked intake of breath. A wave of panic contorted his face, his eyes transfixed on Abbot Urban's face. 'I don't understand how... how you know about my... my fall from grace... with Olive. But it's all in the past now... I've severed all connections.'

'You did?'

'Yes, Olive Moran no longer exists.'

Now it was Abbot Urban's turn to allow shock to register. His hands opened outwards like a book; elongated fingers, thinned by age, splayed fanlike in a gesture of inquiry. 'She no longer exists? Are you saying that this woman no longer lives, that you have put an end to her existence?'

'Effectively, yes. I had to make a choice – God or Olive Moran. I chose God. Olive was expendable, God wasn't.'

'So you know she is dead?'

'Dead? What... what's this? Who's dead?'

'Isn't that what you've been telling me?'

'Sorry? I've lost you. I don't understand.'

'Olive Moran was found murdered in St John the Baptist Church the same day you visited the Bishop. But you know all this, don't you?'

Fr Patterson stared at Abbot Urban for several seconds, as the kernel of a silent scream began to distort his face. No sound came from the open mouth. Instead, the curate appeared to crumble in on himself before falling in a dead faint from his chair to the floor.

Emma rushed through the operational sequences required to access her computer. 'Come on, come on, damn it,' she hissed impatiently as the different stages appeared and dissolved on her monitor. Back from the restaurant, she'd been confronted by the sight of Vinny's car in the underground car park. Seeing the flat tyre and the implements for changing the wheel scattered on the ground, her heart began to race. She rushed from the car park, trying not to give credence to the thoughts in her head, and made her way into the apartment.

Now, torturous minutes later, her e-mail flashed on the screen.

MESSAGE FROM VINNY.

Her index finger stabbed at the mouse, clicking twice to access the message. A new line of type appeared.

HI, EMMA, OPEN THE ATTACHMENT.

Emma shifted the cursor on to the attachment icon and clicked twice. A picture of Vinny's face slowly materialised on the screen.

He looked awful, his eyes filled with anger, his expression disagreeable. Emma watched, not understanding, her breath coming in short, shallow gasps. In a live-action sequence, the focus panned from Vinny's face down to his hands. No sound accompanied the action.

The camera operator lingered on the hands for several seconds, clearly showing the wrists bound together in handcuffs. 'Jesus!' Emma cried aloud, before clasping a hand over her mouth. 'What the hell…?' she shouted at the computer, her voice taking on a shrill sound. She continued to watch the slow-moving picture. A close-up of the hands remained on the screen but she could tell that Vinny was moving, walking slowly towards some out-of-focus object. Within seconds the object became clear. It was a miniature guillotine, the kind used in offices for cutting paper. A hand – not Vinny's – could be seen pushing a carrot into the contraption. The blade snapped down, dissecting the carrot in one swift movement.

Emma gasped for breath. She watched as Vinny's little finger was placed in the same spot where the carrot had been seconds earlier. The blade descended. Before the sharp edge reached the finger, the picture dissolved. The monitor went blank. Emma, half crying, half screaming, pounded the desk in front of the computer. 'Help me, somebody,' she croaked, shaking her head, unable to accept the images she had just seen. 'No,' she wailed, 'what the hell is going on?'

She had begun to shake when a male voice came from the computer speakers. 'Emma Boylan,' the disembodied voice said, 'have I got your attention? Mmmm, thought so. Good, that's good! Now listen and listen good. I've got a few demands for you and the paper you work for. Firstly, I want you to report no new developments in regard to the murders in Lonsdale. You may repeat what's already on the record – stuff you've already written – but you must not print a single word that is new. Do as I ask and nothing will happen to lover-boy here. Disobey this request and I'll sever one of his fingers and mail it to the *Post*. I'll sacrifice one finger for each new revelation you report. I need ten days to do what I must do. If you've disobeyed me and I run out of fingers before I've completed my work, I shall have to think seriously about what other bodily parts I can chop off – tongue, toes, ears, even his dick. You dig?' There was a pause and the sound of stifled laughter before the voice spoke again. 'One other thing, Ms Emma Boylan. Do not go to the cops with this. If you do, I'll speed up the process of cutting your husband down to size. Please believe me when I say – this is not an idle threat. One peep out of you to our friends in blue and I'll take delight in mutilating him – snip, snip, snip! You dig?'

Emma heard a chilling peal of laughter before he continued.

'Contact your editor. Don't use the phone. Talk to him face to face, no other way, OK? By using your password he can see this little presentation on his own terminal. It'll be interesting to see how much value he places on the limbs of your husband. But be warned; I mean what I say. I'll contact you tomorrow with new instructions. OK? Talk t'ya!'

Emma knocked her chair back from her desk and stared at the blank screen. Her hands gripping the edge of her desk, she tried to take in what she had just heard and seen. She could feel her heart pound, feel her throat constrict, making it difficult to breathe. How long she stood in this stupefied position she'd no idea, but some tiny part of her brain had switched to autopilot. She closed down the computer, left the apartment, and headed for her car in the basement. Her instincts told her to get to Bob Crosby without delay.

Chapter 30

The look on Caroline Blackman's face said it all. Fr Patterson's appearance on the doorstep was the last thing she expected. Wearing dog collar and clerical garb, the curate looked at her from under his brows. 'Hello, Caroline,' he said. 'Is there anybody here at the moment?'

'No, no, I'm on my own. Fr Kelly is staying here but he's out for the rest of the day. Come in, tell me what you've been up to.'

He allowed himself to be ushered into the drawing room, the look on his face a mixture of relief and anxiety. Making small talk while Caroline busied herself fixing coffee and biscuits, he barely kept the nervous tremor in his voice in check. 'Didn't know about Olive's death till yesterday. Still can't believe it.'

'Where've you been? Outer Mongolia? Biggest story in the country. Saturation coverage – you couldn't miss it.'

'I've been on a retreat – searching for my soul, cut off from the real world. I'd no idea – poor Olive, it's just awful. That's why I'm here. Wanted a word with you before talking to the authorities; hoped you'd fill me in on all that's happened.'

'It's not a pretty story,' Caroline warned.

'Even so, I'd like to hear all the details.

In chronological order, Caroline outlined the events that had followed on from his departure from the parochial house on the day of Olive's death. The curate listened without once interrupting, his expression one of childlike incredulity. When she had finished, he shook his head sorrowfully. 'They don't think I've killed her, do they?'

'You mean Inspector Connolly, Sergeant McGettigan; that lot?'

'Yes. What do they think?'

'Hard to tell. They know about your row with Olive.'

'What? You told them! You told them about —'

'No Father, I didn't have to.'

'But who—?'

'Emma Boylan.'

'Who?'

'The reporter that's been snooping around here lately.'

'But how would she know?'

'She was in the church when you argued with Olive.'

'She was?'

'You don't remember?'

'No, I don't... all a blur really, but one thing I *do* know: I didn't kill anyone... least of all Olive Moran.'

'I know that, and I'm sure the police know it too.'

'So why are they so keen to talk to me?'

'To eliminate you from their enquiries.'

'And the parishioners.' What do they think?'

'Well now, Father, I'd say the parishioners are far too busy blaming George and Thelma Duggan for all the ills that have befallen Lonsdale.'

'The Duggans? What have they done?'

'You obviously haven't read today's paper.'

'No, like I said, I haven't seen —'

'Yes, that'd explain it. Well, our friend Emma Boylan has a piece in today's *Post* suggesting that the Duggans cheated the PP out of property he owned – the twenty acres by the church grave-yard – and that Thelma tried to cash in an insurance policy she'd taken out on Fr Jack.'

'But... but I didn't know that Fr O'Gorman owned land or...'

'Looks like there's quite a lot you and the parishioners were kept in the dark about. Anyway, when the locals read about the Duggans' involvement in the shady dealings, they got a bit excited, started running about like headless chickens. A meeting was held in McCann's Arch Bar. Got very heated. Donnie McCann set himself up as head vigilante, wanted to run the Duggans out of town. Wild West stuff. A few hot-heads were willing to be led by him but, luckily, common sense prevailed. The mob decided to hold off action until they received further clarification. They believe George and Thelma Duggan are behind all the recent skulduggery.'

'Which means they haven't had time to bother about me.'

'I'm afraid so. Sorry, Father.'

A smile, more like a facial tic, was evident on the curate's face. 'Sorry! Don't be sorry – praise the Lord for small mercies.'

'Amen to that.'

'But listen, Caroline, I'd like you to do me a big favour.'

'Of course, Father, anything.'

'Contact Detective Inspector Connolly – not McGettigan – let him know I'm back. Tell him I'll talk with him here rather than going to the station.'

'Of course I will. Good thinking. I'll call him straight away.'

'Holy Chrisssssssssst,' Crosby said, making a sound like a rapidly deflating tyre. Seeing the guillotine blade dissolve as it approached Vinny's finger, he turned away from the computer screen to look at Emma. 'I don't know what to say, Emma. This is bloody serious.' His observation, aimed at himself as much as Emma. 'We've got to talk to Connolly.'

'You heard the warning,' Emma said. 'One word to the cops and Vinny loses a finger.'

'Yes, but this madman holding Vinny doesn't have to know.'

'Seems to me like he already knows just about everything I do or say. He's managed to hack into our computer network… what else has he done that we don't know about?'

'Good point, Emma, but we have to do something.'

'Like what?'

'I think you should go home. I'll talk to Connolly. I'll be discreet, see if we can come up with something.'

'What about the *Post*?'

'What about it?'

'Are you going to stop reporting developments?'

'I don't know, Emma.'

'Of course you know; you're the editor.'

'Look, Emma, naturally I don't want any harm to come to Vinny but the newspaper can't be held to ransom. This decision goes to the board.'

Emma had not expected this answer. 'Are you telling me that you'd print something that endangers Vinny? You'd stand by while this maniac chops him to pieces in order to grab headlines?'

'I didn't say that, Emma.'

'Sounded like that to me.'

'All I'm saying is that I have to go to the board. Nobody wants to see Vinny get hurt… and please God it won't come to that, but we can't just shut down shop… you *do* understand that?'

'Even if it means exposing Vinny to—'

'I'll make sure that doesn't happen, Emma, I'll—'

'You had better, Bob, because if anything happens to Vinny, I'll hold you personally responsible.'

'Now, hold on a sec, Emma, that's ridiculous… that's unfair.'

'Is it?'

'Yes, damn it. *I'm* not the one holding Vinny. I'm not doing the threatening. Right? I'm just trying to do my job. I've told you I'll act responsibly. I can't see what else I can do.'

'You can give me a guarantee that you won't print anything that endangers Vinny.'

'Jesus Christ, Emma, trust me, you know I won't print anything like that but… well, fact is, there are no guarantees in our business; you ought to know that. Please take my word for it when I say I'll do everything in my power to prevent anything happening to Vinny, OK?'

Emma pressed her face into the palms of her hands and sighed. Naked fear churned up from her stomach. It was an unfamiliar fear, divorced from any thoughts for her own safety, arising from an increased feeling of helplessness. 'Yeah, Bob, she said wearily, her voice for once taking on an air of defeat. 'I'm asking the impossible, I realise that. I know you'll do what's right. I'm sorry for saying what I said just now. It's just that… I don't know what else to do. I feel so inadequate.'

Emma applied a paper tissue to her eyes and hung her head. Crosby, who had never seen her cry before, put his hands on her shoulders and pressed her to his ample chest. There was no need to speak; he allowed his gesture to convey the empathy he felt for her, to reassure her that everything possible would be done.

Vinny can't be sure whether the darkness is real or a manifestation of his fogged brain. Steep wooden steps creak noisily as he is forced to make his way down to a basement. Suffering from the effects of drugged liquid he had swallowed earlier under duress, his legs seem incapable of carrying his weight. His hands, securely manacled behind his back, are unable to avail themselves of the handrail for support. His inner consciousness alerts him to a fear, a fear that at any moment he could miss his footing and take a tumble. It is with some measure of relief that he makes it to solid ground. He wants to ask questions but his mind is in no state to formulate the required words. Instead he sways like a drunk, lost in a nether world, his eyes trying to make out the shape of what appears to be a wooden door in front of him. In a fleeting moment of lucidity, he is aware of the manacles been removed from his wrists. His arms, now free, fall numbly to his sides, deadened from lack of blood circulation.

Some instinct tells him that this is no dream; a nightmare perhaps, but one rooted in the real world. He is reasonably sure there is a man by his side, a man who has dominance over him.

The man's shape, appearing to move in blurred motion, unlocks the door that stands partially hidden near the base of the steps. Vinny feels himself being shunted bodily into a dark space. He falls heavily, the side of his face glancing off a cold, hard surface. His arms lack the strength to propel himself into upright mobility. 'Where the hell am I?' he calls out, his words sounding slurred and unfamiliar to him.

There is no answer.

He feels as though someone has prised a hole in his cranium and dowsed his brain with treacle. Intermittently, his consciousness fights to reassert its independence.

He scrambles unsteadily to his feet and sees a sliver of dim light. His pickled brain recalls the door he's just been pushed through. The effects are whatever drugs have been administered to him is wearing off. His sense of smell returns. There is mustiness all around him, the kind created by mould growing on damp stone.

With only the sliver of light to guide him, he moves less assuredly than a blind man towards the door. Feeling the yawning void in front of him with outstretched hands, he is aware of a clammy dampness soaking through his undervest. The sweat of fear. His fingertips make contact. It's a solid, heavy construction.

His hands search for a handle. There is none. He moves back, then rushes towards it, channelling all his weight into his shoulder before crashing against the structure. The door remains steady as a rock. Temporarily defeated, he sits for a while trying to get his breath back, his brain attempting to sort out how he had ended up in this situation.

A series of half-formed images, like reflected impressions on a fragmented mirror, help him piece together recent events. The flat tyre. The unpleasant mess against his mouth. The sickening sensation repeats itself. Bright lights swirl and dance inside his head, spinning into infinity.

A shimmering image, like that of a scene viewed through a snow blizzard, materialises. Impressions of an old-fashioned, stone-faced building with steps leading up to a front door is discernible. Is it a fragment of a dream or had he really walked up those steps and entered the house? He can't be sure.

Kaleidoscopic images flash through his brain. Indistinct. Ethereal. He remembers a mug of coffee being pressed to his lips, his head being jerked back, liquid being forced down his throat. Sounds. Shouting. Indistinct words, meaningless. A movie camera. A man talking to camera. A small desk guillotine, the blade stopping short of his finger. And then, the steps to a cellar. Sometime later, how long he had no idea, that same voice telling him something about Emma, threatening to subject her to unspeakable acts of sexual depravity. He blots out this recollection from his memory; he is in no state of mind to take it on board.

And still, his mind struggles to recover. Questions, so many questions. Is what happened connected to Emma's work? Is she in danger. Yes? No? He knows about her investigative work in Lonsdale but, unfortunately, she has never discussed the finer details with him. That puts him at a disadvantage, at a loss to understand the strategy behind his kidnapping. One thing, however, is obvious: he must get out of the cellar before his captor returns. With this thought in mind, he searches for a plan that might help him accomplish the task.

Chapter 31

Detective Inspector Connolly and Fr Patterson sat facing each other, one each side of the fireplace. Caroline, who had ushered them into the drawing room, decided to leave them to their own devices. 'I'll put the kettle on,' she offered, 'make some coffee, OK?'

'I'd prefer if you stayed,' Fr Patterson said nervously.

'Of course, Father, if that's what you'd prefer.'

The curate nodded gratefully, then reluctantly returned his gaze to the detective. Caroline, feeling a bit like 'piggy in the middle', sat on the three-seater couch, an old-fashioned chunky piece of furniture that both men had studiously avoided. The expression on Connolly's face let her know that he would prefer to be alone with the priest. *Well, tough titty, Detective,* she thought, *this is not my idea of fun either, believe me.*

Conversation remained painfully stilted, each word struggling for life before finding expression. The fault lay with the curate. Before answering questions put to him by the detective, he stole furtive, sidelong glances in Caroline's direction, putting her in mind of a small boy afraid to let go of his mother's hand on a visit to the dentist.

As the interview creaked onward, Caroline allowed her thoughts to stray far and wide, happily ignoring the men's conversation. Connolly distracted her wanderings when he stood up and extracted a small plastic container from his inside pocket. Curious to know what was happening, she cleared the clutter from her mind and watched with rapt attention.

'—so if you've no objections,' Connolly was saying, as he produced two cotton buds, 'I'll take the saliva sample now.'

'I've no objections at all,' Fr Patterson said, 'I just don't understand *why?* Why test me?'

'Purely procedural. We're taking samples from all those who were in contact with Ms Moran on the day in question.'

'But I wasn't here when poor Olive met with her…'

'We can't know that for certain.'

'Yes, you can,' Fr Patterson said, taken aback. 'You can check with the Bishop's palace; they'll confirm that I called.'

'I already have. They confirm that you talked to the Bishop's secretary. However, you could have come back to Lonsdale afterwards.'

'But I didn't.'

'Can you account for your whereabouts after leaving the palace?'

'Let me see… I got in my car… drove around… went nowhere in particular. Wanted to clear my head.'

'Got any witnesses… someone who might have seen you while you were… driving around?'

'No, I don't think so. It was late in the evening when I decided to go to Donegal. I didn't check into the monastery until some time before midnight.'

'We'll need to check that out. In the meanwhile, I'd like to proceed with this test. Like I said already, you are not obliged to—'

'And I said I had no objections,' Fr Patterson said testily, awkwardly getting to his feet. 'What do I have to do?'

'Just open your mouth; it's perfectly painless.'

Fr Patterson did as requested, his eyes finding Caroline, seeking her reassurance. She duly obliged with a tight little smile. Connolly gently inserted the cotton buds into the cleric's mouth and extracted a swab of saliva from inside his cheeks. This done, he placed the buds back in the slim plastic container. 'Just a precaution,' he said to the curate, placing the container in his jacket inside pocket.

Both men sat down again, their body language personifying the unease that existed between them. Connolly, in the process of winding-up the interview, was interrupted by the sound of his mobile phone. 'Sorry about this,' he said, 'damn thing is worse than a ball and chain.'

While Connolly took his call, Fr Patterson appeared to retreat into some private world of his own, his eyes unfocused, his fingers continually intertwining and circling each other.

Caroline's attention settled on Connolly. With only one side of the telephone conversation to rely on, she could tell that his caller was Sergeant McGettigan. Snippets of Connolly's conversation let her know that Bob Crosby, editor of the *Post*, wanted to meet with the detective urgently. The subject matter had to do with Emma Boylan, but the words were too cryptic, too fragmented, to allow her get the gist of what was being discussed. The detective had used the words 'immediate danger' and 'threats' more than once in the exchange.

As soon as Connolly finished the call, he confirmed what she already suspected. 'My presence is required back at base. Have to go straight away.' Before leaving he looked directly at Fr Patterson. 'Catch you later, Father. Clear up one or two details. Thanks for your co-operation.' Turning to Caroline, he took her hand and shook it. 'Thank you, Ms Blackman... got to run, I'm afraid. Good day to you.'

After seeing the detective to the door, Caroline returned to the drawing room and sat in the chair he had vacated. The curate was still in pensive mood. 'Come on, Fr Patterson,' she said, attempting to sound upbeat, 'you haven't been hauled away by the Gestapo or anything dramatic like that, so cheer up. Nobody thinks you're guilty of anything.'

'I already know I'm not guilty of anything,' he said, oblivious of her attempt to lighten the topic. 'I'm a little less sure about my innocence when it comes to matters spiritual. I've certainly broken more than my share of the laws in that respect.'

Caroline suppressed the urge to sigh. 'You're being too hard on yourself. You're a good man and I'm sure the Man above – if he exists – thinks the same.'

Fr Patterson smiled for the first time. 'If *He* exists,' he said, echoing her words. 'I've just been locked away in a monastery perched on the edge of the world, convincing myself that *He* does exist.'

'Well, good for you.'

'It's my response to this belief that bothers me.'

In no mood to involve herself in a theological discussion, Caroline changed the subject. 'What do you intend to do with yourself?'

'What do you mean?'

'Are you going to stay here?'

'I don't honestly know. I've got to see Bishop Gannon later today. He'll tell me what to do. My future – if I have one – rests in his hands.'

'Would you like to come back here, to Lonsdale, I mean?'

'No, not really. Too many bad memories.'

'So, what'll you do?'

'Make a clean break, start all over again.'

'You're probably right, Father; might do likewise myself.'

'Really?'

'Yes, really! Time I moved on, got back to my base in London.'

'What'll you do there?'

'Take up my life from where I left off five years ago.'

'You never did tell me why you left London…'

'A long story, Father; one I'm not sure I can talk about yet. But I did have a particular reason for coming to Lonsdale.'

'And what would that be?'

'I'll give you the brief outline, if you really want to know.'

'I'd very much like to hear it, please.'

'OK then, just remember you asked for this – a brief history of the trials and tribulations in the life and times of one Caroline Blackman. Let's see now, where to begin? I was adopted as a child and raised by adoptive parents. I was educated in Islington, London, and had a reasonably satisfactory upbringing there. My adoptive parents were well-to-do folk, quintessentially English, with the usual set of middle-class values and attitudes. So, from a materialistic point of view I saw little in the way of hardship or deprivation. However, my parents left me under no illusion in regard to my lineage; they let me know at every opportunity how lucky I was to have been adopted by them. It was a factor they took particular pleasure in when introducing me to their friends. I resented this; felt at times I was being paraded in front of their friends like a pet poodle.

'I was nineteen when I got the bug to search for my biological mother. Mad notion, really. Came out of nowhere, a compulsion to track her down. Wasn't easy. Seemed to me the authorities had placed as many obstacles as possible in my way. Even so, I was determined to let nothing hinder my search.

'After several false leads and as many disappointments, I eventually tracked her down; discovered she was living in Ireland. Quite a shock. Never occurred to me that she might be Irish, or indeed that I could be Irish. My mother's name, it turned out, was Nelly Joyce. She had worked in Ireland as a schoolteacher in a place called Johnstown. At the age of twenty-one she became pregnant outside of marriage.

'This was back in the '70s, a time when little tolerance existed for those unfortunate enough to break the rules. She was sacked by the school manager and forced to go to England to have her baby – *me*.

'After the birth, she had little choice but to give me up for adoption, a factor that broke her heart. She wanted to come back to this country, start teaching again, but found her way blocked.'

'Blocked? Why was that?'

'Her "shame" meant her name had been blacklisted throughout the entire education system in this country.'

'That's terrible... so, what did she do?'

'With financial help from some friends, including the man who had made her pregnant – my real father – she stayed on in England and managed to eke out an existence.

'I only found all this out when I came to Ireland to meet her. She had finally come back to the country she loved – in spite of what this country had done to her. When I eventually got to meet her, she was already dying. I spent three months with her, watching her waste away, watching cancer devour her. It's an experience I'll never forget. In that short period I discovered what a truly wonderful person she was. Gasping for her every breath, she never once uttered a bitter word against the people who could have helped her during those earlier, dark days. To me, she epitomised the true meaning of Christianity. It's a virtue I could never even begin to understand. After her burial, I decided to return to London, pick up the pieces, get my life back on track again.'

'But you didn't go back to London?'

'No, you're right, I didn't.'

'Why was that?'

'Because she left a diary behind. When I read it, I discovered the sort of life she'd experienced. I read about the people who loved her and the ones who betrayed her. The more I read, the more I wanted to know, to understand the forces that had dealt my mother such a tragic hand. I set about doing some research. Not being a native, it was difficult but I've a stubborn streak in me, a curiosity that won't be satisfied until I know all the answers. Decided I'd like to meet some of the personalities so vividly described in her diaries. That's why I came to stay for a while in this city.'

'You mean, some of the people your mother wrote about live here in Lonsdale?'

'Exactly! I felt I owed it to her to track them down.'

'And have you met any of them?'

'Yes. Indeed I have.'

'Do they know who you are… I mean, have you told them about your mother… that you're…?'

'No, I haven't told them… not yet, but before I leave this place they'll know who I am. I intend to make certain people aware that I know how my mother was treated by them. It's something I've vowed to do for her.'

'I'm not sure I like the sound of that, Caroline.'

'Why's that?'

'Why? Well, because you said yourself that your mother harboured no bitterness towards anyone. If I may be bold enough to offer you some advice: take a leaf from her book – leave well enough alone.'

'No, Father, I'm not like her. I'm nobody's doormat and I'm no saint, I don't hold with the notion of forgiveness and redemption or meekly turning the other cheek.'

Fr Patterson decided to offer further gratuitous advice. 'With all that's happening here lately, the last thing we need is someone to come exposing skeletons.'

'Oh, I'm not so sure about that, Father. I've encountered enough hypocrisy, evil and cruelty during my stay in this country to turn my stomach. I think it might be quite a healthy thing to explode a few myths. I intend to drag a few skeletons into the light of day, let the more decent folk around here see the sort of neighbours they rub shoulders with.'

'Is that wise?'

'You of all people, Fr Patterson, should know the value of confronting the truth, accepting reality. That's all I propose doing.'

'But why? Who will benefit?'

'Why, my mother, of course. My mother was given a raw deal while she was alive; I've decided that she's due some justice in death.'

Chapter 32

Bob Crosby sat uneasily in his favourite alcove in the Fitzwilton Club, nursing a gin and tonic he didn't really want. A fully paid-up member for over twenty years, he hadn't participated in any of the club's sporting activities for more than a decade. While others sweated off their aggression on the playing courts, he enjoyed the comforts of the lounge and the companionship of a few special friends. Detective Inspector Jim Connolly, the man he had come here to meet, was numbered among that select band.

Checking the time, he noted the detective was already fifteen minutes late. His glance at the watch coincided with Connolly's arrival.

'Sorry I'm late, Bob,' Connolly said, easing himself into a seat. 'On top of everything else, I had a little domestic crisis to attend to.'

'Don't tell me you're having trouble with the beautiful Iseult? Never could figure how you managed to snare that gorgeous creature.'

'Gorgeous creature? Yes, Bob, she's that all right, but you know what they say about the rotten egg... looks perfection on the outside but once you crack it, you discover...' Connolly let the phrase dangle as if expecting Crosby to finish it for him. With no riposte forthcoming, the detective sighed, furrowing his eyebrows. 'Try living with her,' he said with a feeble smile.

'What? What's this?' Crosby asked, not sure where the conversation was going. 'Don't tell me there's trouble in—'

Connolly raised a hand and splayed fingers to interrupt, his expression one of pain. 'Sorry, Bob, I don't think we should go there right now.'

'Having a difficult day, then, are we?'

'Difficult? Huh, I'd call that an understatement. Thanks to you, Bob, the natives are restless.'

'Thanks to *me*? What have I done?'

'I think you know, Bob – your front-page story. The piece by Emma Boylan; the story accusing the Duggans of cheating the late parish priest.'

'We made no such accusation in our story.'

'Don't split hairs, Bob. You may not have spelled it out in so many words but the inference was hard to miss. It fired up Donnie McCann enough to call every hothead in Dublin to his pub. Within minutes, we had a lynch mob baying for blood; took all my powers of persuasion to break them up.'

'So, you sent them packing... where's the problem?'

'They dispersed, yes, but for how long – that's the problem. I tell you, Bob, Lonsdale is at boiling point. I could have done without Emma Boylan's irresponsible, provocative reporting.'

'She'd love to hear you saying that.'

'I'm sure she would. Look, Bob, you're the editor; couldn't you have pulled it?'

'I could have but I didn't. *Mea culpa*. Bad call on my part. If I had spiked it, there'd be no need to drag you away from your work now... tell you about the other consequences arising from my decision.'

'Oh?'

'A sinister development. Emma's husband, Vinny, has been abducted.'

'What? You're serious?'

'Afraid so, Jim. His abductor's made contact, threatened to inflict bodily harm on him unless we meet certain conditions.'

'Conditions? You'd better tell me everything you know.'

Momentarily delayed while a waiter served a Guinness to the detective, Bob Crosby outlined what had happened. The expression on Connolly's face darkened. He remained silent throughout the narration, noting each detail, trying to understand how they linked up with the current upheaval. 'Where's Emma?' he asked.

'I expect she's trying to get her father to contact Christopher White's solicitor,' Crosby said.

'White?'

'Yes, White – Fr Jack O'Gorman's nephew.'

'I know who he is,' Connolly said irritably. 'What makes Emma think White is the one behind Vinny's kidnapping?'

'Actually, she's not totally convinced it's White, but he's the only suspect on the horizon. She thinks he is unhappy with her articles, sees her as the enemy, something like that.'

'Where's the logic in that, Bob? I've read Emma's article. If it comes down on the side of anybody, it's White. Why would he go after the one person who appears to be on his side?'

'Search me, Jim. None of this makes sense. Meanwhile, if I print any new developments in the case, Emma gets one of Vinny's fingers in the post. What the hell am I supposed to do? I can't just stop reporting the news.'

'What other choice have you, Bob? You're going to have to sit tight until we bring in whoever is responsible for this madness.'

'And when might that be?'

'Well, you said yourself that Emma believes the person holding Vinny will be through with his plans within ten days or thereabouts. That means he's active as we speak, so we're bound to get a whiff of something.'

'But right now you've got nothing, Jim; is that what you're telling me?'

'That's not altogether true; we've got one or two irons in the fire.'

'Such as?'

'We know what he's driving.'

'We do?'

'Yes. Emma popped into the station the other day, said someone was stalking her, gave McGettigan a description of a car and the driver. She didn't get the reg. number, unfortunately.'

'So, we find the car, we find the man.'

'Hopefully. I've put a tail on Emma. If we spot the car in her wake, we'll pounce. Meanwhile, I'd like you to show me the message sent by the kidnapper. Can you download it to my computer?'

'I could but I won't.'

'Why d'you say that?'

The message contains a virus.'

'How's that?'

'The bugger planted a Trojan Horse in the *Post* network when he sent it; gummed the whole bloody works up.'

'So much for modern technology.'

Crosby nodded. 'You said it.'

'Can it be sorted?'

'Hope so, Jim. The IT guys are working on the problem. Until we have a clean system, I don't want to send anything to anyone.'

'So, what do you want me to do?'

'Can you come to the *Post* building, see the message there?'

'Sure, that's fine by me, Bob. Is there any way I can get in without being seen? I don't want one of Vinny's fingers cut off on my account.'

Ciarán Bailey sat in the passenger seat, engrossed in deep contemplation, stealing occasional sidelong glances at Emma. He noted the deep concern etched on the face of his daughter-in-law. In the half-hour since she had driven from the city to collect him, he had fought a losing battle with the dark thoughts hovering at the edge of his brain. That something untoward could happen to Vinny was a concept he had difficulty coming to grips with. In recent years he had, on the odd melancholy occasion – usually after consuming too much of his favourite beverage – thought about his own mortality and the effect his demise might have on his son. Never once had he thought of the situation in reverse. A shiver ran through his frail frame.

Emma sensed his need for quiet as she drove away from Little Bray and headed back towards the city. Earlier, on her arrival at his studio, she found him working on the restoration of a large-scale oil painting on canvas. He was totally absorbed in his work, wearing his ubiquitous multi-daubed smock, immersed in an odour-filled world of brushes, palettes, linseed oil, turpentine, varnishes and tubes of paint. For a man in his seventies, suffering from the onset of angina, his stamina and enthusiasm for life never failed to impress her.

As soon as he'd seen her, he'd sensed something was wrong.

She had told him, as gently as possible, about Vinny's abduction. He'd listened with apparent calm, asking questions that concerned the circumstances leading up to Vinny's disappearance. He may not have displayed any histrionics but the concern in his eyes for his only son amply mirrored the pain he felt, a pain she herself could barely cope with.

And now, motoring through Dublin's slow-moving traffic, heading towards County Meath, she felt it necessary to bring her father-in-law up to date with all aspects of her latest investigation. Ciarán nodded, saying little, fully appreciative of the seriousness of the situation. Drained of colour, the face that normally bespoke a merciless pragmatism and intelligence now looked gaunt, filled with sadness, his cheekbones protruding, his mouth drooped at the corners, a visage that emphasised his frailty.

Emma was fond of Ciarán and knew her feelings were reciprocated. In the past, when the odd difference of opinion between Vinny and herself surfaced, Ciarán had more often than not taken her side in the discord. This did not mean the bond between father and son was strained; quite the contrary. Father and son worked together in total accord, each respecting the other's area of expertise. Emma tried to mask the anxiety she felt in regard to Vinny's position while, at the same time, respecting Ciarán's right to know the worst.

It was almost five o'clock by the time Emma and Ciarán made it to Arthur Boylan's office in the town of Navan. Emma wasn't altogether sure why she had decided to visit her father but it was better than doing nothing.

Arthur Boylan greeted his daughter and Ciarán Bailey with the usual *bonhomie* but there was no denying the question mark in his eyes. 'It must be something very special that brings the two of you here,' he said, ushering them to chairs. 'Not bad news, I hope?'

'It could be, I'm afraid,' Emma said, noting Ciarán's reluctance to speak. 'I'm hoping you might be able to sort something out.'

'Sort something out? Like what... exactly?'

As she had done a few hours earlier with Ciarán, she set about telling her father the circumstances, as she knew them, behind Vinny's abduction. Arthur reacted in much the same way as Ciarán had – disbelief on his face, finding it hard to express the fears he felt, at a loss to understand how this could be happening. 'How can I help?' he asked.

'I want you to get on to Christopher White's solicitors straight away. Arrange to meet them. Tell them it's a matter of life and death; get them to suspend client confidentiality on a temporary basis; tell them that everything is off the record. Can you do that?'

'It's not something they'll readily agree to, but I do know John-Joe Tallon; he's a senior partner. I could arrange to meet him, talk to him in confidence, see if there's anything that can be done behind the scenes.'

Ciarán Bailey, who, up until now, had remained silent during the exchange, held up his hand in a cautioning gesture. 'What if we're wrong about this fellow? What if White is not the one behind all this?'

'It has to be him,' Emma insisted.

'OK, Emma,' Arthur Boylan said, picking up his phone and punching the numbers, 'I'll contact Tallon, see what he has to say.'

Emma and Ciarán remained silent while Arthur was put on hold, their expressions expectant; their eyes fixed on the phone as though their lives depended on it. Arthur finally made contact, greeting Tallon with familiarity before broaching the subject of White. Almost immediately, he stopped in mid-sentence. 'I see,' he said twice into the mouthpiece, looking across at Emma, a dejected look on his face. A long silence ensued, only interrupted by Arthur with expressions like 'uuum,' 'yeah' and 'I see'. At length, Arthur replaced the phone and looked gloomily at his visitors. 'No joy, I'm afraid,' he told them. 'According to John-Joe Tallon, Christopher White dispensed with his firm's services three days ago.'

'What?' Emma asked. 'I don't believe this.'

'I'm afraid that's the story. White told them he wasn't satisfied with progress; decided to do the job himself.'

'He's totally flipped,' Emma said, 'gone completely mad.'

Arthur Boylan nodded. 'According to Tallon, they've been having difficulty dealing with White's volatile nature. In recent days they found his behaviour more and more bizarre – screaming obscenities at them, threatening to sort out all those who stand in his way.'

'Where does that leave us?' Ciarán asked.

No one offered an answer.

Shoulders hunched against the cold, Vinny blinks his eyes, peering into the nothingness that envelops him. The concoction used to drug him appears to kick in intermittently, overwhelming his senses, forcing his eyelids shut, inducing a state of slumber.

The dampness, the cold and darkness all around him does little to ease his discomfort. An all pervasive musty smell, coupled with the absence of sound and the deprivation of light, ensures his continued state of disorientation. His head aches. He needs to empty his bladder. Just one thought obsesses him: to escape and get word to Emma. To that end, he moves about, thumping the walls, trying to discover if there are any parts of the room that might have a hollow section or hidden door.

He finds none.

From time to time he pounds on the one and only door that holds him captive. Its heavy timber planks and enormous hinges remain solid and firm, unyielding to his best efforts. A barely perceptible sliver of light creeps beneath the door's base, the only indication that another world exists outside. His eyes have become accustomed to the dark, making it possible, with the help of finger touch, to make out certain features.

He is being held captive in a large, one-room basement bereft of any furniture or fittings. A row of paint cans, all with battered lids and various quantities of paint in them, stand by the base of one wall. A collection of jars stand beside the tins. An assortment of paintbrushes have been placed in the jars, steeped in what his nose tells him is turpentine. That is it. Not another thing.

He decides to use one of the partially empty paint cans to empty his bladder. While engaged in this act, he spots something on the floor that he hadn't noticed before. Dimly silhouetted inside the door, an object of indefinite shape has appeared. Quickly finishing nature's call, he hurries over to the shape, gets on his knees and reaches down for closer examination. It is a round tray. He uses his fingers to identify the objects on the tray. Sandwiches. He can feel the texture of bread, establishes that the slices have been buttered and contain some sort of filling. He lifts one of the sandwiches to his nose. Ham. A flood of relief shoots through him. This is a good development. It means that whoever is holding him captive is not entirely indifferent to his welfare.

There is another object on the tray. After a brief finger-frisking examination he identifies it as a flask. Excitedly, he unscrews the cup top and removes the stopper. A whiff of coffee assails his nostrils. His audible sigh of relief echoes around the empty basement walls. Until now, he hasn't thought about hunger or thirst, food and drink being the least of his worries. The sandwich tastes good. He pours hot coffee into the flask cup and sips it. It is strong, acidulous, but he doesn't mind. Greedily, he devours the sandwiches and washes them down with the coffee.

His thoughts stray to the world beyond the heavy planked door, to Emma in particular. He pictures her waiting for him in the restaurant; a scene that brings a smile to his face. He imagines her sitting at the table, glancing at her watch, getting more and more annoyed. She would have given him ten minutes, he suspects, fifteen at the most, before storming out of the place, cursing him to hell and back. It would not take long after that for her to realise something was wrong. She would have contacted Connolly.

Thinking about Emma, the atmosphere all around him changes. He no longer feels cold. The musty smell has evaporated. A warm glow of coloured light illuminates the entire basement. He can see everything clearly, every detail picked out in glowing technicolor, breathtaking in its intensity. Music, low at first, increases in volume until it swamps the room with a haunting symphony of tubular bells and xylophone bars. He looks around in wonderment, conscious of the fact that he is laughing out loud.

The door before him slowly opens. A blinding light forces him to shield his eyes with his arm. He can hear a voice. 'Vinny, Vinny, there you are.' The speaker is Emma. He lowers his arms. He can see her now, emerging from the blinding light. 'Emma, how did you get here; how did you find me?'

She smiles at him, a wicked, seductive smile. She is dressed in light summer clothes, the same clothes she wore on their honeymoon in Spain. 'This is not happening,' he says. 'This is some sort of hallucination, right?'

'I'm here,' Emma answers, 'that's all that matters.'

Vinny stands up, reaches out, puts his arms around her and kisses her fully on the lips. They press into each other, their hands claw, touch, probe, tease. Vinny gently lays her on to the floor. There is no need to speak. He can see all the love in the world in her eyes, feel his body respond to her touch with an urgency that screams for release. Magically, it seems to him, their clothes, along with their inhibitions, vanishes. He has never felt more liberated or unself-conscious. With wild untamed energy, they explore each other's bodies. Heat pours from her melting loins. Her tongue traces a line around his lips before sensuously sliding into his mouth, circling his own tongue in a fiery tango, her breath and his mingling as one. His hardness welds them together, merging their hearts beats, forging their souls to dissolve into one pulsating entity. Lost inside her, every nerve ending on fire, his heart thumps to the rhythm of their writhing bodies, emotions overflowing in a choreographed-like ballet of bold licentiousness.

'Emma, Emma,' he screams, as his body jerks and shudders in a final explosion of joyous delirium. His breathing comes in great gulps, his heart still racing, he holds on to her, his body now moist and limp, exhausted from their lovemaking. 'I love you, Emma, do you know that?' he whispers. He opens his eyes to see her face, to watch her expression.

There is no response. There is no Emma.

He is alone.

The shock of discovering Emma is not beside him, had never been beside him, is too much to take. He is the victim of illusion masquerading as reality. He feels cheated, ashamed that his mind and body have so easily been duped by the deception.

There is still light but it has become oppressive, threatening. Aggressive colours hurt his eyes, blood-reds, deep purples. Spearheads of garish colouration bombard his head. He screams. The walls around him are alive, breathing like living tissue. Large-cut stones appear to wrestle, to bulge and recede, as though trying to break free from their grouting. The mortar itself has become alive, wriggling and writhing with snake-like movement, hissing and spitting all the while. Terrified, Vinny's hands shoot to his eyes. He wants to shut out the sights. But there is no escape. The noise and vision penetrate his hands, ignore his closed eyelids. His head feels as though it is about to burst asunder. He curses the flask and its contents and lets out a long, wailing scream.

Chapter 33

Something vague and distant disturbed Thelma Duggan's sleep. She turned in the bed, struggled to emerge from that cotton-wool buffer zone that divides sleep from wakefulness. In this drowsy, half-conscious state, she couldn't place where the sound was coming from. Was it real? Imagined? Hard to tell. She had gone a little heavier than usual with the pre-bedtime tipple of brandy. Could it be responsible for playing tricks on her mind?

She prised her eyelids open. Familiar surroundings. The clock on her bedside table showed 1.30 am. She'd been asleep for barely more than an hour. But the noise; what could it be?

She stopped all movement, took a deep breath, held it, listened, her body rigid as stone, anticipating... what?

The dogs were barking. Well, that at least was real. Reassuring almost. But not reassuring enough to set her mind at rest. She exhaled slowly. Dogs barked for the slightest reason; like when a fox or badger strayed into the yard to scavenge food. Greyhounds, sensitive creatures at the best of times, frighten easily. They get spooked during thunder and lightning storms and howl in fear. Sometimes they bark for no apparent reason at all.

The noise she heard was difficult to pin down. Could it be George using the bathroom? He made such an ungodly racket, opening and closing closet doors, knocking objects to the tiled floor, letting the toilet lid bang down, always clatter, bang, clatter, bang.

For more than ten years now, herself and George had slept in separate rooms. Ostensibly, the arrangement had been arrived at because of his snoring, but the truth had more to do with the growing coldness between them in regard to sexual feelings. Encounters of that nature had become infrequent and awkward to the point of embarrassment.

There! She heard the sound again.

This time she was positive. It came from outside. It was real, not a figment of her imagination. Fully awake now, she strained her ears to listen. Above the yelping of the greyhounds she could hear another sound.

What was it? A door or gate banging against its frame?

She got out of the bed, put on her nightgown and slippers and left the room. She peeped into George's room. Loud snoring confirmed deep slumber. She moved to the landing and was about to venture downstairs when the guestroom door opened. Alec Cobain emerged, naked except for a pair of boxer shorts. If he was surprised to see her, it didn't show. 'The dogs are kicking up a hell-of-a-racket,' he whispered. 'I heard something moving outside.'

'Yes, so did I. Something's disturbed them. I'm going to take a look, see what's the matter.'

'Hold on a sec, I'll put something on, join you.'

'OK, but hurry.' Thelma moved to the bottom of the stairs and waited. She was glad Alec had decided to join her. Didn't do to take chances. She was pleased that Alec and Yvonne had stayed overnight. They had arrived earlier in the evening, concerned about the damning article in the *Post*, anxious to offer moral support in what was a difficult time for the whole family. The newlyweds had been upset by the implications of dishonesty and double-dealing levelled against Thelma and George.

Thelma listened.

The clamour from the greyhounds increased. She thought she smelled burning. Impatient to get outside, she wondered what was keeping Alec. As though on cue, he dashed down the stairs, still adjusting his trousers, almost tripping in his haste. 'Right, I'm ready,' he said. 'There's definitely something wrong outside. You'd better switch on all the outdoor lights.'

'Can you smell burning?' Thelma asked.

'Yes, I can, you're right; something's burning. Come on, let's hurry.'

Outside, an orange glow formed a halo above the farmyard. The crackling noise of fire filled the air. 'The sheds are ablaze!' Thelma shouted, running towards the yard gate. With Alec at her heels, they could now see flames leaping into the night sky. 'Someone's left the gate open,' she yelled, 'there's someone—'

Her words were obliterated by sudden movement. A group of dark-clad figures rushed from the farmyard, knocking her bodily to the ground in their haste. Alec, too, caught by surprise, was pushed out of the way. He yelled at the fleeing figures to stop but the stampede sped past him unchecked. Alec hurried to Thelma's assistance. 'Are you all right?' he asked, helping her to her feet.

'I'm fine; those brutes knocked me down. Oh Jesus! They've set fire to the sheds. Run back inside, Alec; call the fire brigade; call the police; wake George, get him out here fast. Hurry! We've got to release the dogs... oh my God, they're trapped.'

Thelma rushed towards the kennels. Timber crackled and sparked. A gentle breeze fanned the flames. Above the roar of the fire, the barking of dogs had reached a deafening crescendo. Braving the heat and smoke, she began pulling the bolts that opened the doors to each compartment. Two terrified grey-hounds sprang free from the first kennel, quickly melting into the darkness, barking wildly.

She opened the second and third doors. More dogs leaped to freedom, showing no inclination to stop and acknowledge their benefactor.

Almost overcome by the heat and smoke she forced herself on to the next kennel. Flames licked the door jambs. She managed to release the bolt and free two more terrified animals.

She had reached the fifth door when, overcome by the heat, she collapsed to the ground. She tried to get up, move forward, but she could hardly breathe. The heat was unbearable. She tried to call out the dogs' names, tell them she would free them, but she couldn't speak. Through the roar of the fire she could still hear the dogs; she imagined them calling to her, begging her to set them free. They were her friends; she couldn't let them down.

From somewhere she found the energy to push her body, crab-like, along the ground. With a supreme effort she reached up to the bolt on the fifth door and jerked it free. She was aware of two fleeting shapes leaping past her, moving like bullets, reflected light from the flames glistening in their eyes.

She wanted to move to the last door but her body refused. She was choking, desperately gasping for air, aware that two dogs remained locked in. One last thought shot through her mind before her world blanked out: why had the dogs in the sixth kennel stopped barking?

Barely conscious, she felt herself being dragged away from the heat. 'Her hair's on fire,' she heard someone shout. The voice sounded familiar. George; it was George. *Thank God he's got to me on time.* He wrapped material around her head. Everything went blank. *I can't breathe.* She could smell singed hair, feel her skin burn and blister. In an instant, the material was removed from her head. She could see again. George had taken a pyjama top away from her head. 'You're going to be OK,' he whispered reassuringly. 'We've sent for the doctor and the ambulance.'

She tried to ask a question, tried to find out if all the dogs escaped, but her mouth was not up to the task. Her thoughts remained fixed on the dogs. Like a scene played out in slow motion, two hounds chase a hare, turn it one way, then another way, before going in for the kill. After that, the scene evaporated, leaving her lost in a vast black wilderness of nothingness.

Unaware of the commotion taking place in the Duggan farmyard, Caroline Blackman was finding it impossible to sleep. It had been late when she got to bed; sometime after one am. For the first time in months, she found herself alone in the house, conscious of the quietness.

Earlier in the day, Fr Patterson had departed. He had an appointment with Bishop Gannon and had promised to let her know how things turned out. She could almost hear him spinning his contrite offering to the Bishop. It wasn't difficult to imagine the Bishop's response. Conditioned to forgive sinners, he would absolve the curate of his trespasses and offer him his old job back. Hell, he'd probably promote Fr Patterson to the post of parish priest.

She herself did not hold with the notion of confession, penance, redemption or forgiveness. She embraced the more negative forces. Betrayal, revenge and retribution were the constant bedfellows that held sway in her life.

Tonight, the big house was quiet, quiet as death itself. A shiver ran through her body. Somebody walking over her grave... or her mother's. She could not sleep; she could not banish the dark thoughts haunting her. Earlier, undressing for bed, she had decided not to look at her mother's diaries. She had come to her mother's most distressful period, a harrowing episode she was reluctant to visit again. And yet, some impulse, some force outside her control, let her know she would get no sleep until she revisited the scenes her mother had endured.

Extracts from the diary of Nelly Joyce – aged 22
16th September 1974. Johnstown, Co. Wicklow, Ireland.

Dear Diary
    First day back in Ireland. Staying with my old friend Maura in her flat.
    Her friend Eva got married, moved to Galway.
    Maura looks great. Invited me to stay as long as I liked.
    Told her I would only stay for a few days, until I got things sorted out.
    Cherry Picker arrived at 6pm. Maura, bless her, left us alone.
    He acted fidgety. Kissed me. Not the kiss I knew – different!
    I cooked the food that Maura left out for us.
    We talked. He was ill at ease, uncomfortable.
    At one stage he shouted at me – Why are you here?
    I had to tell him — I'm pregnant since your last visit to Hammersmith.
    He flew into a rage. Said I was trying to trap him and that I couldn't be pregnant by him. Accused me of sleeping around.
    I swore to God I'd been with no one, swore I loved him.
    Begged him to come back with me, said we could get married, hold on to this baby – be a proper family.
    He sneered. Pushed me away. Said he couldn't marry the likes of me, wanted proof he was the father. Called me a slut. Accused me of having no respect for myself.
    I was stunned, asked him — Why are you doing this?

He said he was engaged to a respectable woman, a woman of virtue.

I punched him. He pushed me away like I was dirt.

He left without another word.

Maura returned, found me sitting on the floor staring at the wall.

She held me, hugged me, talked to me.

She was so sympathetic. She managed to get me to bed.

Told me I could stay with her as long as I wanted.

She offered to travel back to London with me for a few days.

I will take her up on the offer.

I fear what I might do to myself if I am left on my own right now.

Goodnight Diary.

Caroline closed the tattered copybook. Reading this particular entry never failed to bring about a mixture of sadness and barely contained fury. That her mother should have been treated so badly made her want to strike out at the man who so callously cast her aside. That man – her biological father – had destroyed Nelly Joyce. He had taken away what little self-respect she'd possessed. And what of her mother's culpability in the affair? A question Caroline had, on occasion, posed herself. Nelly Joyce had been foolish, naïve in the extreme, not to have questioned her lover's bona fides. How could she not have seen through him? How did she let it happen?

But Caroline did not wish to be judgmental when it came to her mother's actions. It was all too easy, given the benefit of hindsight, to be critical of her mother's role in the affair. There were times when Caroline, reading various passages from the diaries, wanted to scream at her, shake her free from the romantic haze she'd allowed herself to inhabit, get her to see how things really were. But it gained her little to ponder on what might have been. What had happened had happened, and couldn't be changed.

Caroline pictured the scene of her mother's final humiliation. She could see the two of them, see him arriving at the flat, see him kiss her mother, even though he had already committed himself to marrying another woman. His kiss represented the ultimate act of cruel betrayal. A Judas Kiss.

It might have been a kindness had he killed her but, as it was, he condemned her to a limbo existence, unwed and pregnant for a second time, living on the edge of society, without the possibility of hope.

From reading subsequent entries, Caroline knew that her mother had returned to England two days later. What must have gone through the woman's head at that point? Unimaginable. Only one friend had stood by her. Maura, good as her word, accompanied Nelly back to Hammersmith and stayed with her for a week. After that, Nelly was on her own.

She continued to hold on to her teaching job until the eight month of pregnancy. As in the case of the first birth, she went to The Little Flower Home for Unmarried Mothers in Finsbury. Mother Superior Bracken, who knew her from the previous pregnancy, had taken a liking to the unfortunate Nelly Joyce and made her second stay at the home as comfortable as possible. But the pain of being separated from her second-born – after two weeks together – proved even more painful than the first time. On this occasion Nelly could not fool herself into believing there was a man, a father, back in Ireland who loved her and would make the pain go away. This time she knew she was on her own with absolutely nothing to look forward to.

And now, all these years later, Caroline had traced the whereabouts of the man who had been the author of her mother's downfall. She had traced him to the Dublin suburb of Lonsdale. The angry fire she had for so long stoked, blazed more fiercely than ever, consuming her like an out-of-control inferno. The time to confront her quarry was breathtakingly close.

Chapter 34

Confusion reigned supreme in Thelma Duggan's brain. This was not her house, not her room, not her own bed. The effort to open her eyes hurt. The sort of stinging she experienced after an all-night session in a smoky pub or restaurant, except this was worse. Much worse.

And the smells, the noise, the colours, all unfamiliar, all wrong. Foreign. Jesus, her world had become well and truly out of kilter. Her head throbbed. Searing pain. She was in the throws of as bad a hangover as she could ever remember. Trouble was, she hadn't been drinking, at least not to the extent her head would have her believe.

She was about to call out, summon help, when a young woman's smiling face loomed into vision, seeming to materialise out of nowhere. 'Ah, good, Mrs Duggan, you're awake then,' a lilting voice said, 'and how are we feeling this miserable wet morning, eh?'

'How are *we*?' I don't know... you tell me...?'

'Ah, you don't remember, is that it? Well, that's to be expected. You've had a rough experience but you're in safe hands now.'

'What? Where am I? Who are...?' Her throat hurt as the words came out in little more than a fractured croak.

'You're in the James Connolly Memorial Hospital in Blanchardstown. I'm Nurse Gallagher. You were admitted during the night suffering from smoke inhalation and some super-ficial burns to your face, scalp and hands – nothing too serious, I'm glad to say.'

Now, Thelma remembered. She remembered the flames, the figures darting past her, knocking her to the ground, and her efforts to free the greyhounds. 'The dogs? Are they all right?' she asked, her voice hurting as she struggled to enunciate the words.

Nurse Gallagher, a perky young woman in her twenties, raised her eyebrows. 'I'm sorry? Dogs did you say? 'Fraid I know nothing about any dogs but your daughter is here, waiting to see you. I'll get her for you; she'll be able to fill you in on whatever you want to know, OK?'

Thelma nodded, her mind striving for clarification, trying to remember what had happened prior to her passing out.

'Hello, Mum,' she heard a voice say. She hadn't noticed her daughter enter the room until she felt her hand being squeezed. 'How are you?'

'Yvonne, you're here. How did you get—'

'Don't try to speak Mum; save your throat. I came with you in the ambulance, been here ever since. You had us going there for a while but it's not as bad as we first feared. The doctor put some dressings on your face and fingers; he said you were lucky to have been pulled away from the fire before any real damage was done.'

Thelma could see her daughter staring into her face. 'I must look a frightful sight,' she said to Yvonne. 'Have you got a mirror?'

'It looks worse than it is,' Yvonne said, taking a small vanity mirror from her handbag. 'The doctors says all the burn blisters will disappear within a few days, so you see, there's nothing to worry about. Your voice will be back to normal when you've had some liquids.'

'Nothing to worry about?' Thelma said, reacting to the image of her face in the mirror. 'Oh, Sweet Jesus, will you look at my hair, it's fuzzy... some of it's gone. My face... I look like... like a lobster and you tell me not to worry.'

'Honestly, Mum, you're exaggerating. It'll all clear up in the next day or so. Your hair will grow back soon enough, just be thankful it's not worse.'

Thelma handed back the mirror and grimaced. 'Worse? Any worse, I'd be dead! I'll have to hide away from all my friends... don't want anyone seeing me like this. I look like the wreck of the Hesperus.' She shook her head despairingly, dismissing further debate on her appearance. 'So, tell me,' she said, her voice recovering some of its authority, 'have they discovered who's responsible... who set fire to the place?'

'I talked to Sergeant McGettigan. He arrived just before you were taken away. He has a witness who saw a group of men entering the Arch Bar about half an hour after you and Alec discovered the fire. It's fairly obvious that Donnie McCann is behind what's happened.'

Thelma nodded, her damaged fingertips feeling the gauze covering on her face. 'Always hated that bugger. I hope they put him in jail and throw away the...' She stopped talking, her eyes taking on a startled expression. 'Tell me, Yvonne, did all the grey-hounds escape?'

Yvonne hesitated a fraction before answering. 'Yes, yes, the dogs are fine, nothing to worry about at all.'

'You're lying, Yvonne. I can always tell when you're lying. The last kennel... did...?'

'I'm sorry, Mum. I suppose you're going to find out sooner or later. We agreed not to tell you but... well, two of the dogs didn't get out in time. They suffocated.'

'Oh no! Oh my God, the end kennel; I couldn't get to it. Poor Ballalley Runner and Carnival Princess... dead, I can't believe it... I don't believe it.'

'I know it's... it's terrible,' Yvonne said, looking at the tears in her mother's eyes, 'but you saved eight dogs. You risked life and limb for those animals.'

'Yes, but poor Ballalley Runner and Fr O'Gorman's dog, Carnival Princess. Gone, dead, I can't believe it.'

'Mum?'

'Yes, Yvonne; what?'

'You said that Carnival Princess was Fr O'Gorman's dog.'

'Yes, that's right. I'm just glad the poor man is not around to see what happened; it'd kill him.'

'Could it be,' Yvonne asked, failing to see the unintended black humour in her mother's reply, 'that whoever set fire to the kennels *wanted* to kill Fr O'Gorman's dog? Could that be what this is all about?'

Thelma was silent for several seconds, mulling over what her daughter had just said. 'No,' she said at length, 'I think it's purely coincidental. Nobody would deliberately destroy all the dogs just to get at... no, no, it's just a coincidence; a tragedy that Carnival

Princess happened to be one of the unlucky animals. Besides, if what Sergeant McGettigan says is true – if Donnie McCann is the culprit – what reason would he have for killing Fr Jack's dog? I know he hates George... despises me, but he looked up to Fr Jack, put him on a pedestal.'

'I don't know, Mum, but you'll have to admit it's mighty odd; first Fr Jack and now his dog.'

'Odd, perhaps, but I don't think it's got anything to do with what's happened,' Thelma's voice signalled an end to such speculation.

Emma joined Ciarán for breakfast. Neither felt hungry. Toast and coffee sufficed for sustenance. An insistent downpour pelted the kitchen window, creating a background noise that underscored their gloomy moods perfectly. By Emma's calculation, it had rained for the past eight hours without let-up. The dull, unrelenting deluge drained her energy, destroying the little hope she had that the nightmare she was living through would soon be over.

She had spent the night above the antique and fine-art studio, in what Ciarán still referred to as 'the lad's' room. Staying there, with nothing but the sound of the outside elements to distract her, allowed her to absorb what had once been her husband's private world. The room décor, unchanged since Vinny's bachelor days, reflected his interest in paintings, music, *objet d'art* and all manner of junk. Posters and paintings, leaning more to classical rather than modern influence, hung on the walls. Among the works of art, two small canvases, painted by Ciarán, depicted studies of Vinny as a boy and as a teenager. The boyish twinkle in his eyes, so vividly captured by the artist, had changed little over the years.

It wasn't the only thing about Vinny that hadn't changed. Staying in his room was like taking a trip down memory lane into his past. Looking at his old, discarded record collection, boxes of vinyl albums and singles, she could see that his taste in music remained time-warped in middle-of-the-road pop ditties, circa late '70s and '80s. For someone with an eye for all things aesthetic, his ear for music was, in stark contrast, remarkable for its lack of discretion or sophistication. Van Morrison, Kim

Carnes and Bob Dylan, Emma was familiar with, but the rest –
artists like J.Geils, The Allman Brothers and The Sweet – meant
nothing at all; she couldn't recall a single record by any of them.
But she didn't mind; she loved Vinny and was happy enough to
tolerate this atypical lapse of good taste. After all, she *had* taken
him for better or worse.

Thinking about 'worse', she hoped his present situation
would not turn out to epitomise that word. The downcast expression on Ciarán's face did little to encourage optimism.
Conversation with him across the breakfast table dwelt on the
lack of progress in regard to Vinny's predicament. Since driving
back from Arthur Boylan's office in Navan the previous evening,
his mood, like the oppressive weather, remained decidedly
gloomy. 'I just wish there was something I could do,' he said. 'I
feel so useless sitting here.'

'So do I,' Emma said, getting up from the table, smashing her
fist into the palm of her other hand. 'It's so bloody frustrating…
the not knowing, the waiting.'

'Perhaps you should ring Connolly,' Ciarán suggested. 'He
might have heard something by now.'

'No, I don't think so. He said he'd call me if anything
happened. I suppose I could—'

The telephone rang, stalling her in mid-sentence.

'You answer it,' Ciarán said, 'that'll be him… the detective.'

Emma grabbed the telephone and pressed it to her ear. 'Hello,'
she said, her eyes fixed on Ciarán. 'Who's this?'

'Ah, Ms Boylan, it's you. So glad to have caught up with you.'
The male voice on the phone sounded cheerful, almost as though
the speaker was renewing acquaintance with a long-lost friend. 'I
want you to do something for me. I want you to—'

'Is Vinny OK?' Emma cut in. 'What have you done with my
husband? Where are you keeping—?'

'Shut it, Ms Boylan. I'll do the talking,' the voice, no longer
friendly. 'Don't say another word unless I tell you to, OK?'

'Just tell me—'

'I said shut it. Now, listen. I want you to meet me in one hour's
time. I want you to drive to The Dead Man's Inn on the old Lucan
Road. D'you know where that is?'

'Yes but—'

'No buts, Ms Boylan. Be there in exactly one hour. Drive into the car park at the rear of the pub… and wait. If you're followed I'll know and I won't meet with you. Do something stupid like contact the law and your husband will suffer. You dig? Play it straight and I'll take you to him, set him free. 'Fraid I'll have to hold on to you for a few days… complete some business.'

'How can I trust you? How do I know—'

'Take it or leave it. Be there in one hour – alone, or all bets are off.'

'No, listen to me,' Emma said, but she could tell that the line had gone dead. She replaced the phone and faced Ciarán. 'I'm going to meet the person holding Vinny. I must hurry; he's agreed to release Vinny if I get there in the next hour.'

'I'm coming with you.'

'No, Ciarán, you can't. I have to go alone and I can't tell anyone. They're the conditions if I want to see Vinny alive.'

Ciarán's mouth opened to speak but for once he was stuck for words. Emma grabbed her keys from the table and rushed towards the door. 'Just sit tight,' she told her father-in-law. 'Don't talk to anyone, OK? I'll contact you as soon as I know what's what. Wish me luck.'

'Good luck, Emma.' He wanted to say more but she had already disappeared out the door.

Detective Sergeant Gogan's stint at being Emma Boylan's shadow had begun earlier that morning at 6am. Until 9.30am it had been a mind-numbingly boring stakeout. Sitting in his Mondeo, outside Bailey's Fine Art and Antiques shop in Little Bray, he had nothing to report for the first three-and-a-half hours. Watching rain run down the windscreen, he cursed the weather, he cursed his job and he cursed his lack of promotion to the rank of DI.

Alone in his car, he had gone through a full twenty-pack of cigarettes, pondering why his wife and two children were no longer content to live with him, and generally feeling pissed off with the world and all the shit it had seen fit to dump on him, down through the years. Over six-feet tall, Gogan, a gaunt angular man in his mid-forties, felt agitated, impatient, but most of all in need of a drink. To add to his discomfort, the left cheek of his bony posterior had gone through three stages of pins and needles and his long, spindly legs had rebelled against their cramped condition.

Conscious of an article he had read recently on the subject of budget-price aircraft seat space, the possibility of coming down with deep-vein thrombosis had taken root in his mind. That and a dose of piles was all he needed. Although in constant radio contact with Connolly's operation control centre, he could not stave off his feeling of despondency.

And then, just when the tedium had reached breaking point, his subject – Emma Boylan – emerged from the house and climbed into her car.

Action at last.

Following the Hyundai, being careful not to be observed by her, had taken his mind off the discomfort and the domestic strife that persisted in blighting his life. Dark skies, under which the city found itself cloistered, cast an almost macabre pall on the slow-moving ribbons of cars that surrounded him on every side. Interminable rain had reduced the traffic flow to a crawl, with commuters sluggishly inching their way through glazed streets on their way to work.

He could see their faces, expressions grimly set against the choking exhaust fumes enveloping them, listening to radios tuned to morning dross in their attempt to blot out the unrelenting drone of a thousand combustion engines; high-powered motors competing with each other to destroy the ozone layer and the very world they lived in. Observing all this morning misery, long faces and bad-tempered drivers, Gogan felt unaccountably happier.

Once away from the city centre, traffic eased marginally. Along water-polished roads, he followed the Hyundai as it headed west, passing through Kilmainham and on to Con Colbert Road before skirting Chapelizod, a once-venerable village that had long since been swallowed up and ingested into the city's urban sprawl. Using the car's cigar lighter, he lit up another cigarette and inhaled deeply. His lungs responded to the tar and nicotine intake as he watched Emma approach the old Lucan Road.

Where the hell is she going? A gentle tendril of smoke drifted from his mouth, its comforting haze all-embracing, when suddenly he had his answer. The Hyundai's left indicator blinked on and off as it slowed and entered the car park to The Dead Man's Inn.

Gogan ignored the turn-in to the pub and headed for the adjacent bypass instead. It meant temporarily losing sight of the Hyundai, but he had little choice. If Emma was being watched – as he suspected – then entering the car park immediately behind her would be a dead giveaway. By doing a loop, he could get on to the elevated bypass that ran parallel to the old road serving the pub. That way he could pull to a halt on the lay-by to the rear of the car park and observe activity from there.

He had circled around, reached the higher ground and was about to put this manoeuvre into action when he saw something that forced an instant re-think. A car remained stationary on the very spot he had intended using as his observatory position. He didn't need to be Sherlock Holmes to figure out what it meant. Someone had the car park under observation, waiting for Emma Boylan to arrive, watching to see if she had been followed. Luckily for Gogan, he spotted the parked vehicle in time, just before he engaged his indicator. A close shave!

Gogan sped past the stationary car, a blue VW Polo, stealing a furtive glance at its occupant as he did so. A man with blond hair sat behind the wheel, his face inclined towards the car park. Having escaped detection by the skin of his teeth, Gogan was anxious not to lose sight of his prey. Not easy under the circumstances. He could not risk circling back towards the pub but he had to find a way to keep the operation intact. He could request back-up – secure the services of another unmarked car – but the chances of it arriving in time could not be guaranteed.

Grappling with the problem, he pulled into an Esso filling station and cut the engine. He needed to do some quick thinking. Lowering his window, he cleared his throat and spat a whorl of smoker's phlegm on to the filling station's tarmacadam before deciding to make a call on his radio phone. Within seconds, he was patched through to Connolly.

Gogan could tell that the detective inspector was excited by what he had to tell him. Connolly said little and asked few questions until he had heard the full account. Gogan was about to ask what his next move should be when he caught sight of the blue VW polo. 'I've just seen him,' Gogan shouted excitedly into the radio phone. 'He's just whizzed past me, past the filling station.'

'Which direction is he headed?'

'He's on his way to The Dead Man's Inn.'

'Good! Follow him,' Connolly said. 'Keep out of sight but don't let him get away. I'll get another car there as soon as possible.'

'Right, but it's going to be a hell of a job staying out of sight.'

'I know, but do your best, I'll have someone there ASAP.'

Chapter 35

The comings and goings at Lonsdale's police station had increased tenfold since the murders began. What had for years been one of Dublin's most easygoing centres of law enforcement, dealing for the most part with trivial infringements and routine policing matters, had taken on an urgency that seemed at odds with the old, colourless building.

This morning, the grey monochromatic setting, shrouded in clouds and rain, was enlivened by the new-found activity but, more particularly, by the introduction of a singular splash of colour. Walking up the pathway that led to the front door, Ruth Holland, one of Lonsdale's more flamboyant dressers, had an altogether incongruous effect on the building; a bit like seeing an old black-and-white movie with one character picked out in full glowing colour.

In the company of Sergeant McGettigan, who used an old-fashioned black umbrella to ward off the elements, she was about to enter the building when Detective Inspector Connolly came rushing out the door, almost knocking the umbrella from the sergeant's hand in the process. Until that moment, McGettigan would not have believed the debonair detective capable of moving faster than walking speed. 'What's up?' he shouted, watching Connolly dart past him and sprint between the rain drops to his car.

'We've got him,' Connolly shouted back, before getting behind the wheel of his unmarked car.

'Got who?' McGettigan yelled.

There was no reply. Connolly was already speeding away from the barracks, his tyres smoking on the wet tarmac. McGettigan shrugged his shoulders and turned to the woman. 'Hot-shot detective from HQ,' he said, 'watched too much *Starsky and Hutch* in his youth.'

A rueful wrinkle appeared on Ruth Holland's brow. 'Yeah, he was the smug git you brought to our flat... thinks his S-H-Y-T-E doesn't smell.'

McGettigan suppressed the smile hovering on his lips. He didn't know which was the funniest: her notion that Connolly remained odourless after performing bodily functions, her incorrect spelling of the word shite, or the fact that she thought it more refined and ladylike to spell rather than enunciate the offending word. He made no comment, closed his umbrella and held the door open for her. She was about to enter when, for a second time, her way was blocked. Donnie McCann came barrelling through the door, in no mood to give way to anyone. The burly publican pointedly ignored Ruth Holland, while fixing McGettigan with a wrathful eye. 'You lot will be hearing from my solicitor,' he said, the words little more than a guttural growl. 'Harassing decent, law-abiding citizens instead of locking up murderers like George Duggan and his old slag of a wife.'

'I'll tell you what, Donnie,' McGettigan said, attempting his best Clint Eastwood grimace, 'when you're talking to that solicitor of yours, get him to advise you on how to hold on to your pub licence... Judge Dillon takes a dim view of those who set fire to other people's property and destroy animals. Besides, I fully intend to see that he takes it away from you.'

'Don't you go threatening me, Sergeant.'

'It's not a threat... it's a promise.' McGettigan loved using that line.

'You know what you can do?'

'Go ahead, Donnie, make my day, tell me.'

'Go fuck yourself.'

McGettigan guffawed. Before he could come up with a suitable Clint Eastwood-like rejoinder, the publican had already moved out of earshot. 'Sorry about that,' he said, turning to Ruth Holland. 'Dealing with gobshites like McCann is something of an occupational hazard in my line of duty.'

She made no reply, allowing herself to be finally ushered into the building, past the front desk and into a dimly lit conference room. The room, not much bigger than a broom cupboard, consisted of minimalist furnishings, a coffee table and two well-

worn, tubular steel-framed chairs. Institutional, pea-green paint
peeled from the walls in shapes not unlike dog's tongues, exposing damp patches that had soaked through the crumbling plaster-
work. There were no windows in the dark, airless space, the only
illumination coming from a double-tube fluorescent fitting, fixed
to a yellowing ceiling.

McGettigan pitched his umbrella tent-like on the floor, allowing its moisture to drip-dry on to the linoleum. This done, he
switched on a small mobile fan that sat on top of the coffee table
and gestured to one of the chairs, inviting her to sit down. Ruth
Holland hesitated, eyeing the surroundings with a look of disbelief, and shook her head wearily. Using a paper tissue, she dried
drops of rain that had splashed from the sergeant's umbrella on to
the chair before settling her curvaceous bottom on its seat. She
folded her arms defiantly beneath her chest, crossed her legs and
regarded the sergeant with a degree of hostility.

At thirty-four, Ruth Holland could be said to be a looker, if a
tad on the coarse side. She carried a little excess weight, a factor
emphasised by her tight-fitting red leather trouser suit. Her
lipstick overshot her lips and her head was crowned with an
abundance of blonde hair that owed little to Mother Nature, a
creation that might have looked more at home in Nashville,
Tennessee than Dublin's fair city. Hazel eyes, dramatically
outlined in heavily made-up spider-like lashes, drilled into
McGettigan, challenging the glances he threw in her direction.
She gave no encouragement to his amateurish attempts at banter.

McGettigan, conscious of his visit to the Holland flat at the
start of this investigation, could not easily forget her brash take
on Sharon Stone. If she'd been giving him the 'come-on' at the
time, a scenario he wanted to believe, what had happened in the
interim to alter her attitude? Time to find out. He reached into his
shirt pocket, withdrew a pack of Silk Cut. 'You want a drag?' he
offered.

'Yeah, sure, why-friggin-not.'

McGettigan shook two cigarettes free, struck a match, lit
them both, watched the reflected flame in her eyes and handed
one to her. His little play with the smokes and flame was, he
believed, dead cool. He'd seen some actor do it in an old movie

and fully expected to get the same sort of response he'd seen on the screen. It didn't happen. There was nothing in Ruth Holland's eyes; no come-on, no reaction at all. *Fuck it*, he thought, *the bitch isn't on for it today*. He took a drag from his own cigarette, inhaled deeply, cursing profoundly beneath his breath.

'So, Mrs Holland,' he said, putting thoughts of sexual conquest aside and adopting his sternest interviewing voice, 'what exactly is it you want to say to me that couldn't be said just as well over the telephone?'

'Remember the day you and that smug git called to Setanta Mansions?'

'Yes, we talked to your husband Derrik. What about it?'

'You remember what Derrik told you, or were you too busy looking up my skirt at the time?'

'You weren't wearing one, as I recall.'

'Hah, so I was right, you *were* lookin...'

'Look, look, Mrs Holland, what's this about?'

She pointed her cigarette at him. 'It's about lies, Sergeant.'

'Lies, is it?'

'Yes, Sergeant, lies. My husband Derrik is nothing but a dirty friggin' liar. He talked a load of crap when you called to the flat.'

'And how do you know what he told us was crap, Mrs Holland?'

'Because he's been feeding me a diet of bullshit and lies for months about some business deals he's got goin' for him.'

'How do you know this?'

'I decided to do a little investigation of my own.'

'I see.'

'No, you don't see,' she said, blowing a lungful of smoke into the already stuffy atmosphere. Her disgorged plume merged with McGettigan's contribution before being dispersed by the fan from one corner of the room to the other. 'I discovered that my husband was spending a lot of time in a certain well-known hotel in the city centre. I followed him one day. I watched him collect a key from the desk and take a lift to the fourth floor.'

'He was with another woman, right?'

'Are' ya goin' to let me tell you what happened or not?'

'OK, sorry, go ahead.'

'You see, I knew he went to the fourth floor 'cause I watched the numbers light up above the lift. So, I sat in the lobby watching the lift for ages, waitin' for him. Three hours later he gets out of the lift with a young scumbag, couldn't be more than nineteen or twenty. That's a laugh; three minutes with me and he's shagged out – limp as a wet dishcloth for two days afterwards... but he's able to get it up for this tart for three fucking hours. Brazen hussy. You know the type, overdressed, flash, all tits, thighs and come-to-bed eyes.

'I stayed out of his way and watched the two of them go to the desk. He started groping her arse as he waited for the bill. That was it. I went fuckin' ballistic, charged like a bull, kicked him, punched her, screaming me bleedin' lungs out. He nearly shit himself at first, than recovered and started punching me back. Security came and pulled us apart then threw the lot of us out. We continued fightin' in the car park. His slut disappeared. Anyway, the upshot of all this is that myself and Derrik are no longer livin' together.'

McGettigan crushed his cigarette butt in an upturned coffee-jar lid and looked at her through a haze of smoke. 'Why tell me this?'

'Because our marriage was fine until he got the money.'

'Oh yes, I remember. Derrik won money on the Lottery.'

'More bloody lies, Sergeant. Derrik didn't win sixpence on the Lott'ry.'

'He didn't?'

'No, not a brass farthing,' she said, blowing a smoke ring into the air between them and watching it form a perfect zero before dissolving.

'So, where did he get the money?'

Ruth Holland squared her shoulders and jutted her chin and jaw-line upwardly. 'The money he got was blood money,' she said, murder in her eyes. 'He got it for pushing Fr O'Gorman's car off the road.'

Emma checked her watch again. She had already waited five minutes in the car park behind The Dead Man's Inn. Five long, nerve-wracking minutes. Rain drummed on the roof of the car incessantly, forcing her to keep the air-conditioning at full blast to clear the fogging windows. She switched on the radio, heard the weatherman forecast continuing showers. Great, just great! She turned the radio off.

Minutes ticked by slowly.

Her brain raced in several directions at once. She'd begun to wonder if she wasn't on a wild goose chase. It came as a relief when a car entered the car park and flashed its lights in her direction.

She recognised the driver as the person she had observed outside Lonsdale's church, the person she'd chased and lost. Her heart seemed to miss a beat as she watched his car swing round in a semicircle, not bothering to stop, his hand gesture indicating that she should follow him.

This was a dangerous game, following a madman to God knows where, but Emma felt she had little choice. It was imperative to find Vinny, free him from the danger he had been sucked into. That this madman should take Vinny hostage, Vinny who had nothing whatsoever to do with any of this business, served to underscore the insane situation she'd found herself immersed in.

She recognised the village of Lucan as she crossed the old bridge that spanned the River Liffey, driving past the weir view, along the Barnhill Cross roads, still not knowing where he was headed. He was clever enough to use back roads, roads that presented less chance of encountering patrol cars.

Driving in a north-easterly direction, she noted a sign indicating the Royal Canal. A humpbacked bridge took her over the canal and on to more open landscape, but apart from several stud-farm nameplates, there was little to indicate what part of the country she was passing through.

Ten minutes into her journey she passed football grounds with a display board that read – St Peter's, Dunboyne. Now, at least, she knew where she was; Dunboyne, County Meath, a village on the periphery of Dublin city. She passed housing estates with all the predictable names: Chestnut Grove, Congress Hill, Beechdale, Woodview and Rivercourt, all interchangeable with each other, two-storey semi-detached piles, all neatly packaged, eight to an acre, and all mortgaged to the hilt.

Exiting dormitory land, she was led on to a winding lane that ran parallel to the Tolka River. By now the rain had eased to a soft drizzle. She'd followed him for more than a mile along the river banks when she saw the Polo take a sudden left turn and entered a densely wooded area. At the junction where he veered left, Emma saw a notice board with the word PRIVATE inscribed on it. She continued to follow the Polo. Driving along a narrow potholed roadway, through a canopy of oaks and ash, the world became a darker place. Shifting down to third gear, then to second, Emma remained doggedly behind the blue car, her Hyundai rocking and rolling over potholes that had grown to resemble small craters.

Quarter of a mile into the woods, Emma's fear increasing by the minute, a formidable granite wall appeared on either side of the single-lane road. A series of fortress-like pillars, standing defiantly at regular intervals, looked as though they were built to stop an advancing army.

Emma slowed down behind the Polo as it approached a pair of tall, intricately designed wrought-iron gates. Scripted in stone on a granite arch above the gates, she read the words TOLKA DEMESNE. As though by magic, the two great gates swung open. She assumed that the man in the Polo had a radio-controlled device that triggered the lock mechanism. After passing beneath the arch, she watched in her rear-view mirror as the gates gently swung inwards and locked themselves again.

A gravelled path, with weeds and grass forming a central ridge, led through extensive gardens. Emma watched the Polo swing to a stop in front of a stone-faced, three-storey manor house. Rain and drizzle had finally petered out but the walls and the roof of the building remained wet and dark; a dismal exterior with lifeless, black windows that seemed to suck the very life from its immediate surrounds.

The blond-haired man got out of his car. Emma did likewise, never taking her eyes off him. He approached the house and climbed a flight of stone steps. Without as much as a glance back at her, he stood before the main door and extracted a bunch of keys from his pocket. He was about to insert a key when he swung around and faced Emma. 'Well, come along then,' he shouted to her. 'If you want to see your dearly beloved husband, you'd better follow me.'

Emma stood immobile for a moment, like some animal caught in the beams of an oncoming car, before snapping back to reality. 'Yes, I'm coming,' she heard herself reply, her body unconsciously obeying some command from her brain to move up the steps.

Chapter 36

Had he blown his cover? Connolly didn't think so. Since taking over from Gogan in Lucan, he'd been careful to keep his distance from the blue VW Polo and silver Hyundai. Gogan remained discreetly behind him in case the need arose for a sudden change in tactics. Two squad cars rode shotgun at the rear. The rain helped limit Connolly's exposure. Other motorists used parking lights or dims in the dull-pewter light; his black Mondeo remained without illumination.

He used every twist and turn to his advantage, holding back when possible, losing sight of the Polo and Hyundai from time to time. The housing estates on the outskirts of Dunboyne presented the greatest difficulty but he felt sure he hadn't been spotted. In contact at all times with Gogan and the back-up uniforms, the operation was going smoothly, the objective within reach. Emma and Vinny would be rescued, the murderer hauled into custody.

He veered away from the banks of the Tolka River and entered the dense woods where he had seen two pairs of red tail-lights disappear some seconds earlier. Overhanging foliage cast mid-morning into darkness as he negotiated the potholed road through the trees. His lights remained resolutely off. A road sign indicated TOLKA DEMESNE. The name was familiar to him. Tolka Demesne had received much media attention in recent months. He radioed HQ and asked for all the information they had on the subject.

Connolly came to a halt in front of two gates. While considering what to do about this obstacle, the information he sought came through on his radio – Tolka Demesne, a pleasant female voice informed him, consisted of one thousand and forty-two statute acres and had belonged to the Plunkett-Dillon family for the past two hundred and eighty years. Since the death of Edward Plunkett-Dillon in 1998, the house and lands remained vacant. Held in trust by relatives, the property was put on the market.

In the year 2001, the Irish Government showed an interest in acquiring it. The intention was to refurbish the place and restore it to its former grandeur and then to utilise the facilities as a venue for entertaining foreign dignitaries. However, a last-minute hitch stalled the deal. The Trust decided that certain artifacts – including the contents of the library – should remain in their ownership. The Government shied away from the deal. To date, the problem remained unresolved.

In the past year the Trust leased the house and lands as separate lots for short-term periods. The house is currently leased to a Mr Albert Atkinson, probably an alias. No information is available on this person, except to note that his lease agreement expires in nine days' time.

Connolly stored the data away for further reference, got out of his car and approached the gates. They were locked. The opening and closing mechanism, he could see, was radio-controlled. He was glad Detective Gogan was present. Gogan had his faults, more than most in Connolly's opinion, but he had his uses too. One of those uses – his ability to crack security systems – would do nicely right now.

There was no mistaking the look of madness in the man's eyes as Emma tried to hide the growing fear inside her. 'Where's Vinny?' she asked.

'All things come to those who wait,' came the reply.

'I know who you are, so all of this is a bit stupid.'

His reply: a bark of laughter, a challenging stare, a dismissive snort but no answer.

'You're Christopher White,' Emma said. 'You're Fr O'Gorman's nephew, right? You're aggrieved that the Duggans cheated you out of your inheritance, right?'

Another derisive snort from him. Still no verbal response.

'Look, Christopher, this is not the way to go about putting matters right. You have a case against the Duggans... I can help you with it... I'm on your side, for God's sake. I know everything about—'

'Listen, lady, you know sweet Fanny Adams. I've read your scribbling; was impressed initially, gave you credit you didn't deserve. You're just as dumb as the cops. But that's hardly the point at issue right now.'

'No, the issue is—'

He cut across her. 'Just shut up. I need to check some things here.'

'Vinny? What about Vinny? I want to see him... now.'

'Vinny, Vinny, I want to see Vinny,' he said, doing a cruel imitation of her voice. 'You're bloody pathetic! You'll see Vinny when I'm good and ready to—'

'No, I want to see him now, you hear me? NOW! I demand—'

'I said shut up. Zip it or I'll close you down... permanently.'

Emma opened her mouth to reply but thought better of it. At close quarters, the mad aura surrounding him was almost palpable, but she could also see that he was handsome, in an oddball sort of way. Sandy-blond curls tossed back from his forehead framed a lean, pale face with sharply angled cheekbones, intense deep-set eyes that were chilling, a perfectly sculpted nose and a strong masculine mouth. He walked with an assured gait, his trim body moving at ease beneath designer jeans, stylish open-neck shirt and leather moccasins that might have been custom-made.

He paused to inspect each room off the hallway. Emma followed uneasily, finding it difficult to remain silent. The hall itself, a spacious area of dilapidated grandeur, covered by a garish carpet of autumnal gold and rust-coloured leaf patterns, featured a winding stairway that wound gracefully to the floor above. Emma's finely tuned nostrils detected a mouldy smell. A room, which Emma assumed to be the main reception, was impressive for its grand scale. Muted light leaked through partially closed shutters, throwing a dull sheen on the room. In addition to a high ornate ceiling, the walls were clad with rich wood panelling and the floor was covered in herring-bone-patterned parquet. It was the sort of place you could imagine once being the scene of elegant parties, sit-down dinners for the privileged classes, reeking with the smell of expensive cigars and exotic perfume. Little of that faded grandeur remained. It now stood cold, neglected and not a little forbidding. Almost bereft of furnishings, the room had rows of framed paintings stacked against the base of each wall. Dust-laden plastic sheets made it impossible to see the images depicted on the canvases.

Passing through a pair of sliding doors, Emma, still silent, followed him into a room with a grand piano standing in its centre. Sheets of white cloth covered the instrument's instantly recognisable shape. She identified other covered shapes: a concert harp, a harpsichord, music stands, bundles of sheet music and, lying on its side – a double bass.

Entering another room, on the opposite side of the hallway, Emma broke her silence. 'I demand to know—'

'And I demand that you keep your trap shut. You want no harm to come to lover boy, keep it buttoned. Dig?'

'Yes, but—'

'No buts, just button it.'

Emma cursed silently. She'd like to throttle the man. She wanted to talk, to ask questions, to scream at the top of her voice, but she forced herself to say nothing. Wasn't easy. The inspection continued. She wanted to ask what he was doing but desisted.

They were now in a library. Unlike the other rooms, it was partially furnished and had a more humane look to it. Emma got a faint whiff of stale cigar smoke. The walls were lined with book-packed shelves; a magnificent gold, white and blue rug covered all but the borders of a dust-laden timber floor. A crystal chandelier hung from an arched Rococo ceiling. Dust everywhere. Easy chairs, couches and small tables were scattered haphazardly around the floor.

An impressive white marble fireplace remained partially hidden behind an ornately carved walnut writing desk and a heavy kitchen worktable. The surface area of both tables was taken up with computer stacks, monitors, scanners, CD burners and other state-of-the-art multimedia hardware. Most of this equipment was unfamiliar to Emma. Cardboard boxes, all bearing well-known computer brands, were pushed untidily beneath the tables.

What Emma took to be the main computer monitor showed a screensaver with slow-changing, erotic images of the naked female form. A closed circuit television monitor, to one side of the main terminal, showed the entrance gates to Tolka Demesne, the same gates she had entered through five minutes earlier. She wasn't the only one with an eye on this screen. 'We've got visitors,' her host said, his voice hostile, the laughter gone. 'You've ignored my warnings, brought the cops. Dumb move, Ms Boylan; very, very dumb.'

Emma moved closer to the monitor. She recognised Connolly, saw him get out of his car, inspect the gates. 'I'd no idea we were being followed,' she said, trying to mask the surge of relief she felt. 'I swear I'd nothing to do with this.'

He didn't believe her. 'This dramatically reduces the odds of keeping lover-boy alive. We have a new game now – another level, not the one I planned. Pity – for you and his nibs, that is. For me, the challenge becomes more exciting, more dangerous. Top level. Let the blood spill where it may.'

'Look, Christopher, let's stop this nonsense now. That's Detective Inspector Connolly at the gates. He's got back-up. Stop this now. Tell me where Vinny is located and I promise I'll speak up for you... I'll—'

'You'll do nothing. Stay out of my way and I might just let him live. You dig?'

He kicked the chair away from the table and took command of the keyboard. Emma watched his long fingers, like those of a fine surgeon or concert pianist, flitting above the characters, tapping instructions into the computer at breakneck speed. 'If these guys want to play games,' he said, addressing no one in particular, 'they've come to the right place. Let's hear what the dumb fucks have to say for themselves.'

On the CCTV monitor, Emma could see a man talking to Connolly, their conversation relayed to the room via speakers.

'Detective Gogan, can you open them?' she heard Connolly ask.

'No sweat,' the man named Gogan replied, pointing to a small object situated high on one of the pillars. 'See the box up there? It's got a radio signal. I can manually manipulate the frequency, trick it into opening the gate.'

'Good,' Connolly snapped. 'Quick. We don't know how much danger Ms Boylan is in. We don't even know if her husband is in there or not.'

Emma looked away from the monitor. 'What are you going to do, Christopher?' she asked.

'Hey, what's with this *Christopher* crap? Don't come this buddy-buddy, palsy-walsy act with me. You *don't* know me, lady, you don't know anything about me, OK?'

'Fine, er... Mister... whatever you say. I just want to know what you intend to do now?'

'I want you to talk to these dickheads at the gate.'

'What do you want me to say?'

'I'll talk to them first. You listen, then do as you're told.'

'Whatever you say, Mr...'

She watched him run his fingers over the keyboard, heard him speak. 'You people at the gate, listen up.'

Emma's attention swung back to the black-and-white monitor. She saw Connolly and the man with him stop in their tracks and look to the camera and microphone in overgrown foliage above the gate's arch. There was silence for a second, then Connolly's voice sounded in the room. 'Who are you?'

'I'm the person holding the reporter and her husband. I told her not to tell you lot... the consequences for doing so are—'

'Hold on,' Connolly shot back. 'She didn't know.'

'Yeah, yeah, whatever! You want to see them alive, you'll do exactly as I say, OK?'

'I'll do nothing until I know Ms Boylan is unharmed.'

'She's unharmed.'

'Let me speak to her.'

'I'll put her on now,' he replied before turning to Emma. 'Say hello to your friends.'

'Detective Inspector Connolly,' Emma said, 'I'm fine so far.'

'And Vinny?'

'I haven't seen him yet—'

'And she won't see him,' the man beside Emma cut in, 'none of you will see him alive if you don't all do exactly as I say.'

'What do you want?' Connolly asked.

'I'll open the gates and allow you and those with you to approach the house. You stay in the cars until myself and Emma leave.'

'We can't allow you to do that. We have —'

'If you don't do *exactly* as I tell you, I'll kill Mr Bailey. I have radio-controlled explosives strapped to his body. I press the button and it's curtains for him... half this house goes up with him.'

'How do we know you won't still press the button once we allow you to get past the gate?'

'You're just going to have to trust me.'

'Can't go for that. I have to get—'

'You have no choice. Do we have a deal?'

Emma interrupted. 'I'm not going anywhere with anybody until I see Vinny... until I'm sure he's all right.'

The face of Emma's captor contorted into a grotesque sneer. He laughed as though he had heard the funniest joke in the world. 'You don't get it,' he said. 'None of you get it. I'm calling the shots here. I'm the one making the rules. You do what I tell you or you lose a life... and in this game you only get one life – fuck-up and you lose. Game over. Dig?'

'Can I see Vinny?' Emma asked.

'Not now. You come with me out through the gates. I'll give you the radio-control zapper that triggers the explosive. Once I'm through the gates, I'll let you out of the car. You'll walk back to the house, press the deactivating button. It has a short range so you'll have to be in the house for it to work. Press the correct button and this little crisis is over, you dig?'

'How do I know—'

'You don't know shit, OK? Tell your friends that everything is go.'

Emma thought for a minute, looked at the monitor. She could see the two detectives waiting at the gate. 'We'd better do as he says,' she told them.

A burst of manic laughter came from Emma's captor. He spoke to the tiny figures on the monitor screen. 'You heard the little lady; time to rock 'n' roll. I'm going to open the gates. You lot drive to the front of the house. You'll see two cars parked there already. Leave enough room for me to make a turn. Emma will be holding the explosives control mechanism. I'll have a gun to her head. If anything happens to either of us... you know what happens.'

On the monitor, Emma saw Connolly get into his car and pass through the gates. He was followed by the second detective in an unmarked car and, behind him, two squad cars. While this was happening, her captor was busy keying commands into his computer. Emma could tell that files were being deleted. The picture on the black-and-white monitor switched from the gate scene to a wide shot of the front exterior of the house. Connolly and the others were negotiating their cars into position.

'What now?' Emma asked.

'You take this,' he said, handing her a remote-control gadget. 'I'll tell you which button to press when the time is right.'

'This is an ordinary TV remote control,' Emma said.

'Correction: it *was* an ordinary remote control. I have reset it. Now move! Keep your mouth shut.'

Emma watched him open the drawer of the walnut writing cabinet and produce a small handgun. 'I won't hesitate to use this if I have to,' he said, taking the weapon in his hand. 'You play the game, you live… any messing, you get zapped – lights out; you dig?'

Emma knew very little about guns but the silver chrome-finished weapon, pressed against her temple, had the desired effect. The fear she felt caused her to shake. On command, she walked out of the house, down the steps, and across to the blue VW Polo. She was forced into the driver's seat. At first she thought she was being asked to drive but soon discovered that he wanted her to slide across to the passenger's side. It was his way of keeping the gun to her temple. As the car made its exit from the house, she saw Connolly sitting in his car, a grave look of concern on his face.

Once through the gates, the Polo slowed down. 'Out,' she heard him shout. 'Quickly, hurry before I close the gates again.'

'Which button… which button do I press?' Emma asked, waving the remote control in front of his face.

He started to laugh. 'Number one will get you RTE, two gets you Network 2 and three will get you BBC. It's just a remote control, you dumb fuck. Now get out of the car.'

Emma scrambled out of the car. 'What about Vinny?' she asked; holding the door ajar, trying to keep up with the car as it moved away.

'He's gone on the big trip to the sky.'

'You mad...' Emma stopped, seeing the gun pointed at her face. In a heart-stopping moment of clarity she saw his finger squeeze the trigger.

Chapter 37

Before hitting the ground, Emma saw flames emerge from the pistol. She heard a roar of manic laughter from her captor, heard the wheels of his car tear up gravel as it sped away.

I'm alive? Her eyelids blinked. *I am alive!*

She picked herself up, unsure what had happened. The gates were closing. Blind instinct forced her to scramble through the opening just in time. The Polo had already disappeared.

Shaking, she stood beside the tall gates, attempting to kick-start her brain. She felt as though she'd just been sucked up into a tornado and spat back down to earth again. A car approached. It took a second to realise the sound came from her side of the gate. It was Connolly. He jumped out of the car, hurried to her side. 'What the hell happened?' he asked. 'You look... Jeez, you look really shaken.'

'I just got shot,' Emma said.

'Shot? But you're...'

She started to laugh, uncontrollable laughter, mirthless guffaws that quickly turned to sobs. Connolly put his arms around her, gently pressing her close to him. Her body heaved great sighs. 'It's all right, Emma,' he soothed, 'everything's all right.'

She tried to speak, her lips trembling, her eyes unfocused. 'I tell you, I got shot, got shot by a toy gun... a bloody cigarette lighter in the shape of a gun... saw him pull the trigger... never been so scared in my life, Jesus!'

'We've got to get Vinny,' Connolly said.

Emma pulled away from him. 'There's no explosives... he gave me a television remote control... a trick, like the gun. It's all a goddamn game to him. There's no explosives.'

'What? You're sure?'

'Sure I'm sure. Check the remote control if you like. I dropped it the other side of the gate.'

'OK We'd better hurry back to the house; find Vinny.'

Emma started to shake. 'I think he's killed… killed Vinny.'

'I'm sure you're wrong, Emma. Come on, quickly, get in the car; let's get back to the house, find him.'

'He said Vinny had taken the big trip to the sky. He's killed him, Jim, I know he has.'

'We can't know that, Emma,' he said reassuringly, helping her into his car. Taking the wheel, he effected a hurried reversing manoeuvre and headed back to the house. 'I'll have the men search the house from top to bottom.'

Still in a daze, her eyes blinking frequently, Emma joined Connolly and his men in the search. The two uniformed officers were on the top floors, working their way downwards. Gogan took the first floor. She concentrated on the area she was already familiar with. Connolly remained close by her side. He listened as she explained how her captor had operated the computer, how she had watched them arrive on the CCTV monitor. 'We'll come back to all this later,' Connolly said, 'have our IT people take it apart, OK? First we'd better search the rest of this floor.'

Their search yielded nothing.

'Let's try the basement,' Connolly suggested, already making his way down a narrow stairway. Emma followed. The musty smell of dampness, a feature of the whole house, became more pronounced as they descended the steps. Pools of oily water mottled the floor. Naked bulbs hung from the ceilings. Connolly hit the light switch. Low-watt illumination glowed in the stair-well. A series of stone-cut archways led to a long, dark passage-way. 'You check out the rooms to the left,' Connolly said to Emma, 'I'll check the right.'

None of the doors were locked and all of the rooms had dim bulbs screwed into rusty wire-cage fixtures. The whole area was empty except for a few cardboard boxes and assorted household implements.

'Vinny, are you here?' Emma yelled out, startling Connolly. 'Can you hear me, Vinny?' Her voice reverberated off the bare walls. 'Jesus, it's freezing down here,' she said. 'Quiet as the grave.'

Connolly paused. 'Hey, what was that? I heard something.'

They listened. It really was quiet as the grave. The other officers were going through the house, opening and closing doors on the floors above them, but not a sound penetrated to the basement. Emma grabbed Connolly's arm. 'You're right, I hear something too.'

'It's coming from that end,' Connolly said, pointing to a stairwell at the opposite end of the passageway to where they had entered.

'Vinny, we're here,' Emma shouted, 'we're here.'

A muffled thumping sound came from behind a heavy, church-like timber door. 'He's in there,' she shouted, hoarse now with expectation, 'quickly, quickly, open it.'

Connolly pulled back a bolt and eased the door open. Seeing Vinny emerge from the dark brought gasps from both of them. He held his hands across his eyes, shielding them from unaccustomed light. 'Tell me I'm not hallucinating,' he said. 'Tell me this is not another dream.'

Emma threw her arms around him, unable to speak.

'You're a sight for sore eyes,' Connolly said. 'Let's all get the hell out of here.'

In the two hours since Vinny's rescue from Tolka Demesne, he had regained his strength, eaten solid food, drunk three mugs of coffee, allowed Connolly to debrief him, and reaffirmed his undying love for Emma. He had refused to go to the casualty unit, refused to see a doctor and refused to be bundled off to bed. The pupils of his eyes remained dilated, he had moments of aftershock, but he stubbornly insisted he was all right.

Emma did not want to leave him on his own in the apartment, worried that he could suffer a relapse, but she desperately wanted to know what progress Connolly and his team were making in capturing White. She wanted him apprehended, wanted it badly. She wanted to see him punished. *OK, so I'm vindictive, that's just too bad. He could have killed myself and Vinny.*

It no longer mattered whether the telephones or mobile were tapped so she remained in constant touch with Connolly. She had also phoned Vinny's father and her own parents to tell them the good news. They were overjoyed, wanted to come and visit Vinny straight away. With as much diplomacy as she could muster, she gently dissuaded them, saying that Vinny required a few days' peace and quiet. It wasn't a lie, but she knew Vinny had no intention of taking it easy for the next few hours, never mind the next few days. It simply wasn't his nature.

Far from wanting to rest, Vinny informed her that he wanted to bonk her brains out, do her every which way and then start all over again. It was this single thought, he informed her, more than anything else that helped him survive the darkest, most stressful, moments of his recent torment. The look in his eyes let her know he was serious. Odd, she thought. It was unlike Vinny to express his needs in such earthy terms. Perhaps his period in captivity had affected him more profoundly that either of them imagined. Time would tell, she thought, smiling to herself. But Vinny's amorous needs, not to mention her own, would have to be put on hold for a little while longer. Her immediate priority was bound up in the chase to find Christopher White.

She was about to call Connolly when the door bell of the apartment rang. A courier had a special delivery for her. She signed his docket and tore open the envelope. It was from Professor Joseph Larrigy at the City of Dublin University. He had sent her the results obtained from the DNA samples she'd given him. With so much activity in the past few days she had almost forgotten about the samples. She glanced over the covering letter before homing in on the information she required. According to the Professor, the DNA samples showed that George Duggan was not Yvonne Cobain's biological father. 'I knew it, I just knew it,' Emma said excitedly. 'I was right.'

Vinny, who had been in the kitchen brewing yet another coffee, heard her exclamation and came into the lounge. 'What did you know?' he asked. 'And what were you right about this time?'

'George Duggan is not his daughter's father.'

'Excuse me?'

'I've just received proof that George Duggan is not the biological father of Yvonne Cobain. You know what that means?'

'No, haven't the foggiest... well, except that I suppose it means someone has been doing the naughty thing with Mrs Duggan... other than Mr Duggan, that is.'

'Spot on, Vinny, ten out of ten. It means that Fr O'Gorman is Yvonne Cobain's real father.'

'It does? I see. How does it help with what's going on?'

'I'm not sure exactly,' Emma admitted, the excitement in her voice waning, 'but I'm sure it's the key to all that's happened. First, Fr O'Gorman is killed. Then, Olive Moran. Her body is placed in Fr O'Gorman's confession box. Christopher White admits to the crime. He killed his uncle to inherit his wealth but discovered the Duggans had beaten him to it. But why kill Olive Moran? Why *her*? If Yvonne Cobain is Fr O'Gorman's daughter – that makes her and White first cousins. It gives her a claim on Fr O'Gorman's wealth. So, why didn't White go after her instead of Olive Moran? What am I missing here, Vinny?'

'Beats me.'

'Yeah, right. It beats the hell out of me, too.'

Sergeant McGettigan cautioned Fr Patterson, read him his rights and placed him under arrest. 'I'm taking you in for the murder of Olive Moran,' he told the curate. Fr Patterson, who had invited the sergeant into the drawing room of the parochial house, groped for words. 'This isn't right,' he managed to say. 'I haven't kk... kill... killed anybody.'

McGettigan looked at him in open appraisal, shaking his head from side to side. 'I never would have pegged you for a killer and that's the God's honest truth, Father.'

'That's because I'm not a killer. This is all a mistake.'

'You know what, Father, I wish that were so, but there's no mistake. We have all the evidence we need to convict you.'

'Evidence? How can there be evidence for something I didn't do?'

'Look, Father, we know what you did to her; the DNA tests prove it.'

'What are you talking about?'

'You subjected Olive Moran to oral sex before you killed her.'

'What? Are you mad? Oral... Jesus! I could never do such a thing.'

'You're wasting your breath, Father. You see, we found traces of your semen in her mouth. How do you suppose that got there?'

Fr Patterson's face drained of all colour. He looked as though he was about to faint. 'I never touched Olive Moran in any shape or form. What you're suggesting is impossible.'

'So, the question remains: how did your semen get into her mouth?'

'It couldn't have.'

'But I'm telling you it did.'

'And *I'm* telling you, it's impossible.'

'Aye, so you say. It'll be interesting to see what a jury thinks. In the meantime you'd better come with me. I'll save you the indignity of handcuffs, Father. Is there anything you want to do here before you leave?'

'There's no one here except myself. The Bishop has put me in charge of the parish on a temporary basis.'

'Well, hadn't you better talk to the housekeeper, Ms Blackman, tell her about this little problem that has come up?'

'She's not here anymore.'

'Since when?'

'Since twenty minutes ago. I returned from visiting an old parishioner and discovered she's fled... taken her belongings, the lot. Left a note.'

'What did it say.'

'Nothing really. Congratulated me on being appointed temporary parish priest. Said she was sorry if she caused me any trouble and wished me well. That was it, really.'

'Can I see the note?'

'It's on the fridge door.'

McGettigan retrieved the note, read it and put it in his pocket. 'Right, we'd better go. You can lock up the place. I'll let you use the phone in the station to call whoever you have to.'

Connolly's interview with Derrik Holland came to a temporary halt as Fr Patterson was 'processed' and placed in custody. Connolly was content to let Sergeant McGettigan go through the loops, observe protocol. Later, he would interview the curate himself but his priority right now rested with Holland. Derrik Holland, he hoped, would help resolve the mystery surrounding the two recent murders. As so often happens it was a lucky break, rather than any clever police work, that brought about this development.

Ruth Holland's decision to tell Sergeant McGettigan about her husband's infidelities provided the key they had been looking for. With her help, facts that otherwise might not have emerged until much later, came to light. Derrik Holland, they discovered, no longer lived with his wife. Social security records showed he was currently unemployed and drawing the dole. With Ruth's cooperation, they searched all his known haunts, finally tracking him down to one of Dublin 4's new five-star hotels. He had booked into a luxury suite in the company of a woman half his age. For someone drawing social security payments he appeared to be doing well for himself.

Prior to Fr Patterson's arrival, Connolly had spent two hours interviewing Holland. At first, Holland tried to play hard-ball, giving smart-ass answers to questions, but Connolly's finely-tuned interrogation technique eventually achieved results. Once Holland discovered his wife had talked about his indiscretions, his bravado deserted him. What he had to impart clarified many of the niggling questions in relation to the investigation.

Initially, Derrik Holland had been contacted on the telephone by a man offering him a large sum of money. All he had to do was help push a car off the Dallard viaduct. The money involved proved irresistible. Holland claimed to be unaware of the identity of the car's occupants. He undertook surveillance work for the man, earning five times his normal wage. It was during this period that his wife had caught him *in flagrante* with another woman.

Connolly took up the interview where he had left off before the brief interruption caused by Fr Patterson's arrival in the station. 'You told me you were employed to do surveillance work. Can you elaborate?'

'I had to keep an eye on certain people for him.'

'You mean spy on people?'

'I wouldn't call it that. I told him where they were from time to time.

'Who have you watched?'

'I'd prefer not to say.'

'Look, Mr Holland, we are investigating two murders here. And you are implicated up to your eyeballs. It might lessen the jail term facing you if you co-operate. So, I'll ask you again; who were you keeping tabs on?'

'OK, I'll talk. Just remember I volunteered this information.'

'I will.'

'I was asked to keep an eye on Yvonne Cobain. I staked out her house in Grove Park, in Rathmines. My brief was to establish her routine... know where she worked; what time she left the house, what time she got back. I also had to keep a record of her husband's comings and goings.'

'When did you last report on her whereabouts?'

'Yesterday evening. I got a text message after that, telling me to call off the surveillance.'

'Can I see your mobile phone, see the message.'

'I delete all messages as soon as I've read them.'

'Tell me, did you do a similar number on Olive Moran?

'Yes.'

'Did you spy on Emma Boylan or her husband?'

'No.'

'And you've never met this man who hired you, face to face?'

'Correct. We relied on the telephone and the text messages.'

'So, how did he give you the money?'

'I met a "go-between".

'His name?'

'It wasn't a man. It was a woman.'

'I see. Her name, please?'

'Caroline Blackman.'

Chapter 38

'Emma, listen, I've got some information… thought I'd better call you,' Arthur Boylan said, speaking on the telephone from his office in Navan.

'What is it Dad? You sound… apprehensive.'

'I've had a call from George Duggan. The damn fool's ignored my advice and arranged to meet with Christopher White.'

'When?'

'Five o'clock this evening.'

'That's less than an hour and a half away. Where?'

'Duggan's house.'

'Thanks for letting me know, Dad.'

'You're not going to do something rash?'

'Don't worry. I've seen what he's capable of. I'm going to pass the information on to Detective Inspector Connolly.'

'Good. I was about to do so myself but I'll leave it to you.'

'Thanks again, Dad. Talk to you later.'

Emma contacted Connolly and arranged to see him within the hour. He had tried to put her off, said he was tied up on a new line of enquiry on the murders. She convinced him that what she had couldn't wait.

They met as arranged in the Kozy Kitchen. Connolly seemed out of sorts. 'This had better be good, Emma,' he said, fixing her with his most severe stare. 'I've a worrying development on my hands that I've put on hold in order to see you.'

Emma got straight to the point. 'Christopher White is meeting with George Duggan.'

'When? Where?'

'Within the next twenty minutes… in Duggan's house.'

'You're absolutely sure?'

'Of course I'm sure.'

'Right. In that case I'll go to the house, bring McGettigan along. It's time I had a serious chat with Mr White.'

'I'm coming with you.'

'No, Emma, you're not. I'm thankful for the information but I can't—'

'I have information on Duggan's wife that's vital to what's happening.'

'Look, Emma, if you're withholding information in a murder case, I can have you—'

'We're wasting time, Jim. Let's get the sergeant and move.'

Twenty minutes later, Emma pulled in behind Connolly and McGettigan as they parked in front of Duggan's farmhouse. Another car, a silver Nissan Primera, was already there. From previous visits, Emma knew that the Duggans parked their cars around the back, so the Nissan had to belong to a visitor. Emma, who had expected to see a blue VW Polo, suspected that White had changed cars to avoid detection.

Thelma Duggan answered the door. She seemed surprised to see them. 'We'd like to talk to Mr White,' Connolly said, without preamble. 'We have reason to believe you and your husband might be in danger from your visitor. May we come in?'

A look of concern crossed Thelma's face. 'Oh, Christ no, is he the...? Oh no! Come in. He's with George... discussing some business. I'll take you through to the study straight away.'

Thelma Duggan, followed by Connolly, McGettigan and Emma went through the kitchen and down a short hallway. Raised voices could be heard coming from behind a closed mahogany door at the end of the hall. Without forewarning, Connolly pushed open the door. George Duggan jumped to his feet and stared wild-eyed at the intruders. 'What the hell...?' he asked, fury in his voice.

A young man with his back to the door remained seated but turned his head slowly to look at the newcomers.

For a fraction in time the scene froze, like a still from a movie.

'It's not him,' Emma blurted out.

'I'm not *who*?' the man asked, standing to face Emma and the two men with her. He was small in stature, had nondescript features, dun-coloured hair with ponytail, and wore oversize grunge apparel that looked at least a decade out of style. George Duggan moved to his side and confronted Connolly, a look of intransigence in his eyes. 'What's the hell do you think you're playing at, Detective Inspector? How dare you and your gutter-press friend barge in here without... without...'

'Sorry, Mr Duggan, we'd reason to believe the person with you was... was needed for questioning.' Connolly stole a quick glance at Emma before addressing the young man. 'Are you Christopher White?'

'Yes, as a matter of fact, I am.'

'Fr O'Gorman's nephew?'

'Right again. Not that it's any business of yours.'

'We need to ask you some questions in connection with the deaths of Fr O'Gorman and Olive Moran.'

'Can't help you on that score,' White said, grinning smugly.

'And, why would that be?' Connolly asked.

'I've been in England for the past four months.'

'Whereabouts in England?'

'Been living in a commune in Penzance.'

'You never returned here during that period?'

'Not once. Didn't even get back for my beloved uncle's funeral.'

George Duggan squared up to Connolly. 'Now that that's all sorted out, would you and your associates kindly leave my study, get out of my house and go chase some real criminals.'

Thelma Duggan ushered the trio back to her kitchen. 'Don't mind George, he tries so hard to be a bully... there's no harm behind it. Can I make you a cup of tea; maybe something stronger?'

'Thank you, Mrs Duggan,' Connolly said, 'I'd love a coffee. I'm afraid the sergeant here has to get back to the station straight away.'

'Fine, I'll just show Ken out first. Be back in a tick.'

As soon as Thelma Duggan and McGettigan left the kitchen, Connolly turned to Emma. 'If the man with George Duggan is Christopher White, who did we see out at Tolka Demesne? What the hell's going on?'

'The whole thing is crazy. I was so sure...'

'Well, you were wrong, Emma.'

'We were *both* wrong.'

'The person we're chasing is not Christopher White.'

'I agree,' Emma said. 'White is not our murderer.'

Thelma returned to the kitchen and busied herself making coffee. Emma noticed how she surreptitiously poured a measure of cognac into her own coffee before joining them. Without going into fine detail, Connolly explained to Thelma how they had mistakenly assumed that their prime suspect for the recent murders was Christopher White. 'I'm telling you all this, Mrs Duggan, because I'm hoping you can help me with some new developments that have arisen.'

'If I can, I will,' she answered, sipping her laced coffee.

'We're holding a man in custody who is an accessory to the crime committed on Dallard Road. He was hired to engineer the crash. I've learned in the past hour that he was also hired to spy on the movements of your daughter, Yvonne, and her husband.

'What? What are you saying? Why would anyone want to… to…?'

'I was hoping you could tell me…'

'No, no, none of this is true. I talked to Yvonne before she left for work this morning. Everything was fine.'

'You've no idea why anyone would want to keep her under observation?'

'None whatsoever. I don't know what this is about. Maybe you should ask her yourself. It's after five now; she should be in from work. You want me to give her a call?'

'Good idea,' Connolly said. 'I'd like to ask her if she's noticed anything suspicious.'

Thelma picked the cordless phone off the kitchen table, punched some numbers, and held it to her ear. Nobody spoke while she waited for a response. 'She's not answering,' Thelma said, 'probably got delayed or went shopping.'

'What about her husband?'

'He doesn't get in from work until about seven most evenings.'

'Do you have Yvonne's work number?' Connolly asked.

'Yes, as a matter of fact I do. Hold on a second, it's written down in my little book of numbers.' Thelma went to the kitchen worktop and extracted a black plastic-covered notebook from beneath a pile of Farmer's Journals. She found the number, dialled and asked for Mr Johnston. Emma and Connolly could tell from the one-sided conversation that Yvonne had not reported for work that day. Thelma confirmed as much when she concluded the call.

'I don't want to scare you, Mrs Duggan,' Connolly said, 'but I think I'd like to have her house checked out, make sure that everything's in order. In the meantime, I'd like you to call her every ten minutes or so. There's probably no need for alarm but I'd like to be sure. I'll arrange to have someone from the local nick in Rathmines call to the house.'

Emma, who had remained quiet during the exchange, decided to ask the question that had been bothering her. 'Thelma, there's a sensitive subject I'd like to discuss with you. I wouldn't bring it up… only it might have something to do with this business of someone stalking Yvonne.'

'I'm not saying anything to you, young lady, not after the terrible things you wrote about me and my family in your newspaper.'

Emma had been expecting this reaction. 'I can understand that… and I apologise for any embarrassment caused, but I just want… what you want, what we all want… to get at the truth. And right now it's imperative, for Yvonne's sake, that you be honest with me.'

'What are you talking about?'

'There's no easy way to put this, Thelma, so I'll come right out and say it. I know that your husband George is not the biological father of your daughter, Yvonne.'

Thelma reacted as though someone had slapped her face. She opened her mouth, tried to speak, groped for words, staring at Emma, then at Connolly. 'How dare you! I want… I want both of you out of my house immediately,' she said with grim resolve, ushering them to the door.

'I'm sorry, Thelma,' Emma said, 'but this could be vital… If Yvonne is in any danger, we need to examine all possibilities. We need to know if there is someone out there with a motive to harm Yvonne.'

'How did you find out?' she asked, her voice little more than a whisper.

'That's not important,' Emma said. 'We need to establish whether a connection exists between Fr O'Gorman, Olive Moran and Yvonne.'

The colour drained from Thelma's face. She sat back down, said nothing, staring blankly at Emma.

'Was Fr O'Gorman the father? Was he Yvonne's father?' Emma asked.

'No, no, Fr O'Gorman was not Yvonne's father.'

Now it was Emma's turn to take a quick intake of breath. 'Well, if he wasn't,' she said, puzzlement in her voice, 'can you tell us who was?'

Thelma shook her head, despair in her eyes. Connolly interceded. 'It would help, Mrs Duggan, if you could tell us.'

'It was the cause of so much trouble and misery at the time,' Thelma said, her eyes misting. 'George knew Yvonne wasn't his daughter. He beat me black and blue until I confessed who the father was. In the end I had no choice but to tell him.'

'Can you tell me who that man was?' Connolly asked.

'I had hoped to take that information with me to the grave.'

'Please,' Connolly pleaded, 'it's very important you tell me.'

'Tom; it was Tom. Tom Moran is Yvonne's father.'

Emma and Connolly looked to each other.

Thelma hung her head, closed her eyes. 'Olive Moran and my Yvonne are sisters... well, half-sisters.'

Connolly reached out, took Thelma's hand in his. 'Tell me, Mrs Duggan, does your daughter know... does Yvonne know?'

'Yes, we told her when she got engaged.'

'How did she take it?'

'It was unpleasant... but we got over it.'

'Does her husband know?'

'I'm not sure. Yvonne said she told Alec... but I'm not sure.'

Unnoticed, George Duggan, followed by Christopher White, appeared in the kitchen. 'What the hell's going on here?' Duggan asked, subjecting Emma and Connolly in turn to a belligerent, eye-piercing stare.

Thelma looked up at her husband, tears in her eyes. 'Yvonne could be in trouble. These people are trying to help.'

'Huh? Like the way Ms Boylan helped with her scurrilous article?'

Emma attempted to speak. 'I'm sorry, Mr Duggan, I—'

'Sorry's not good enough,' Duggan cut in. 'You slandered my name; tried to drag me down to the gutter where you belong. I can do without that, thank you very much.' He turned his scorn on Connolly. 'And I don't need help from the law either; I just want you out of my house, right now.'

'And I think they should stay,' Thelma said with new-found authority. 'I think it's time some straight talking was done in this house. Our daughter's life may be in danger and for once, George, facing up to the truth might not be such a bad idea.'

George noted the determination in his wife's voice. 'I can't see how washing our dirty linen in public is going to help anyone.'

'George, George… please George,' she said sadly, 'the past has come back to haunt us. You know it, I know it. We can't run away from what's happening in front of our eyes. We've got to stop running away, we've got to face up to the truth. Lives may depend on it.'

Silent for a moment, George nodded his head gravely before moving to his wife's side and putting his arm around her shoulder. 'You're right, Thelma, you *are* right. The time has come to exorcise our demons.'

'I agree,' Thelma said nervously.

'But first, let me show my visitor, Mr White, to his car.'

Christopher White nodded his goodbye to Thelma, studiously ignoring Connolly and Emma, while following George to the door. Before leaving the room, George turned and took in Connolly and Emma with his gaze. 'I think you're going to need something a little stronger than coffee if you wish to revisit events from the darker side of Lonsdale's past.'

Chapter 39

The black-and-white photo of Nelly Joyce holding a blond-haired baby boy in her arms represented his most treasured possession.

He had been that baby. Nelly Joyce, his mother.

He wished fervently that he could recall even a single moment from the few days he'd remained with her before being handed up for adoption. Since receiving the picture five years earlier, he imagined those precious hours together but, as each year rolled by, the images became harder to conjure up. In marked contrast, his bitterness had grown over the same period. The bitterness was not aimed at his mother; he knew she loved him. The camera's lens had captured that love in her eyes. It had also captured the hurt and disillusionment in those beautiful eyes.

The reservoir of bitterness grew on a daily basis inside him, festering, waiting for release, waiting to destroy the man who had created Nelly Joyce's hell on earth. He smiled, returned the photograph to his wallet, and whispered aloud – It's all right, Mammy, they're paying now for what they did to you.

He thought about his adoptive parents, Frank and Síle Minogue, and his early days with them in London. They had christened him James, a name he hated. He had few memories of those first years of his life. They had come to live in Tipperary when he was five. It had not been a smooth transition. At school in the town of Clonmel, his teachers had a difficult time controlling his disruptive behaviour. He hated his teachers and loathed his adoptive parents. Every chance he got, he ran away from home.

Frank Minogue worked as a print rep and drank too much. His only passions, apart from booze, were listening to old rock 'n' roll records from the '50s and '60s, and taking the strap to his son. Sometimes, these two indulgences were practised simultaneously. As a child, having the crap knocked out of him by Frank

Minogue while Little Richard belted out lyrics that contained words like *a-wop-bam-a-luba-a-wop-bam-boom-tutti-frutti*, was not something he was likely to forget easily.

Síle Minogue, his adoptive mother, was a silly woman who spent her life trying to wangle her way on to every women's committee in the district. Frank Minogue, in a rare moment of sobriety, claimed she had developed welts on her hands from climbing the social ladder. Why she had ever bothered to adopt a son remained a mystery to him to this day.

His introduction to the world of computer games in his teens brought about a profound change in the way he viewed the world. Discovering that he had the ability to understand, create and design programs as good, if not better, than those already on the market gave him a kind of satisfaction he had never experienced before. Success came quickly. He sold his first world-wide game on his nineteenth birthday. After that he never had any financial worries. He immersed himself in the world of computer games and managed to infuse his own destructive urges into the virtual character he created.

A second profound change in his life occurred when his sister Ann-Marie first made contact with him. From the start, she insisted on calling him Séan, the name his real mother had given him. Her own name, she told him, had been changed from Ann-Marie to Caroline. They agreed to call each other by the name given them by Nelly Joyce. He got to meet Nelly before her death and had learned about her misfortunes from Caroline. She had shown him the diaries and, more importantly, she had tracked down and discovered the identity of the man their mother called Cherry Picker. Together they had formed a plan of revenge.

And now, sitting in the house owned by Yvonne Cobain and her husband Alec, he thought about what he would do next. He had spent most of the day with Yvonne, indulging his most outrageous fantasies, but he had kept her alive until now. It was important that she could hear him talk, important that she understood why all progeny from the loins of Cherry Picker must make retribution. The game was in its final stages, he had made it to the top level. Bringing Emma Boylan and her husband into the equation had been a ploy to give the opposition a stake in the contest. His heart hadn't really been in it, though. Too late, he realised it had been an unnecessary embellishment, an unsatisfactory distraction. But now he was back on track. Now he was doing what he and his sister had vowed to do.

Emma and Connolly did not take up George Duggan's offer of something stronger than coffee. Connolly, seeing Thelma's distressed state, made himself useful in the kitchen and produced fresh coffee all round. George returned five minutes later, poured a whiskey and a brandy. He removed the coffee cup from his wife's hand and replaced it with a glass of brandy. He then sat down beside her, held out his whiskey glass to her and said – cheers. She just nodded.

'Poor Thelma,' he said, 'she was beguiled by the bastard... a silver-tongued devil if ever there was one. I'd seen him sniffing around her from the first day he arrived in Lonsdale. You'd never think to look at Tom Moran these days but back then he was like a mongrel dog on heat, his nose forever in the air, sniffing every bitch's pooley in the neighbourhood. He took advantage of his looks, thought every woman was put on this earth just for his pleasure.

'When Thelma became pregnant I knew I couldn't be the father. I had suffered from mumps in my late teenage years. Tests carried out at the time showed I was infertile. I knew this when I married Thelma. I should have told her but I didn't. It was cowardly on my part, so maybe I deserved what happened. Anyway, when I discovered she was pregnant I went and had myself tested again. We were having an active sex life at the time so I thought maybe my condition had changed. Alas, the result was conclusive. I could not be the father. To my eternal shame and regret, I beat the name out of Thelma, something I have reproached myself with ever since. She put up a good show, swore there had been no one but me. I continued to slap her about until I got the name: Tom Moran.

'You must remember this was about twenty-seven years ago, different culture back then. I was a man in my prime who couldn't ever become a father. That was bad enough, but to discover my wife was pregnant by the local fancy man drove me over the edge.

It didn't help to know that Moran's own wife was also pregnant at the time. I'm not proud of how I reacted.

'Along with a friend of mine, Jimmy Looram – dead now, Lord have mercy on him – we fixed Tom Moran good and proper. Looram was a married man in his forties at the time, had an eighteen-year-old daughter. One night he caught her sneaking out of the house after midnight to see Moran. He put a stop to it before it started but he remained mad as hell with Moran. He was more than willing to fall in with my plans.

'It happened on a bright summer's evening. We were tanked to the gills on beer and whiskey. We bundled Moran into Looram's battered old Land Rover and brought him to a remote corner of the Looram farm. There was a cattle pen there. We stripped him, secured him to the bars of the pen and did a job on him. We got hold of the burdizzo pinchers we used for castrating young calves and threatened to snip him. He whimpered like a baby. We laughed. At first we clamped the instrument on to the base of his scrotum, not exerting too much pressure, promising to let him go if he told us everything. Scared out of his wits he confessed all, admitted he'd been poking Thelma.

'We asked him to tell us who else he had been having it off with. At first he wouldn't tell us, so we increased the pressure on his balls. He begged for mercy, screamed like a scalded pig, said he would tell us everything if we didn't harm him down there. He gave us the name of several girls from the town he'd been dicking, some of them happily married, or so we'd believed. Looram asked him about his daughter but Moran swore nothing had happened with her. And then, babbling, out of his mind with fear, he told us a very disturbing story about a girl he had being going out with before he got married.

'I still remember the girl's name to this day: Nelly Joyce.

'This affair took place sometime before Moran moved to the city and came to live here in Lonsdale. He had been a teacher in the same school as Nelly Joyce in Johnstown, a small town on the Dublin-Wicklow border. She became pregnant by him. To avoid a scandal she went to London. She told no one that he was the father so that he wouldn't lose his job. She loved him and believed he would marry her eventually. She was forced to give up the baby for adoption. She could not come back to this country to teach because the school authorities had blacklisted her name throughout the country.

'He visited her in London a few months after she had given up the baby. The poor deluded girl was still in love with him, believed he was going to marry her. It's hard to credit that anyone could be so bloody stupid, not see through the bastard, but you know what they say – love is blind. And nobody, it would appear, was more blind than Nelly Joyce. She took him into her bed and became pregnant by him for a second time. Later, she visited him in Johnstown and told him the news. He called her a slut, told her to go back to London, said he was getting engaged to a respectable girl in Lonsdale.

'At that point myself and Looram pressed home on the burdizzo.

'We castrated the bastard.

'He soiled himself. His legs went from under him, leaving him hanging from his wrists, screaming in agony. I wanted to finish off the job, wanted to kill him… and in a way, I suppose I did. He was never the same man after that. The spring went from his step, the gleam from his eye. He told his wife some cock-and-bull story about being mugged and kicked by drunken louts from the flats in the Setanta Mansions. Tom was, and still is, a master when it comes to selling the big lie. He never bothered anybody after that; devoted himself to his family and his job in the church. In the intervening years, we've kept our distance. He didn't report us. In return, we left him alone.'

'Do you know whatever became of Nelly Joyce?' Emma asked.

'You'd better ask Thelma about that,' Duggan suggested.

After a heavy silence, Thelma sipped her brandy and spoke. 'I've forgiven George for his act of barbarism and I've forgiven Tom, too. The only one I can't forgive is myself. As to Nelly Joyce, I just know she had a baby girl and a baby boy for Tom Moran. They were both given up for adoption in London. I know nothing else about them.'

'They're here,' Emma said, suddenly. 'Jesus Christ, that has to be it. Nelly Joyce's son and daughter have come back to Lonsdale.

The man we're looking for is Nelly Joyce's son... not Christopher White. It would explain what's been happening. It explains why Olive Moran was killed. He's come back to get revenge on Tom Moran.'

'You could be right, Emma,' Connolly said. 'It might explain the crash on the Dallard Road. But that still leaves me with a problem: if Tom Moran was the intended victim, why put Fr O'Gorman life on the line?'

'I don't know,' Emma said, 'I haven't figured that one out yet.'

'If the killer *is* Nelly Joyce's son, then I know who the daughter is,' Connolly said. 'The truck driver who pushed Tom Moran and the PP off the road informed me in custody that Caroline Blackman acted as the go-between.'

Emma tipped the heel of her hand against her forehead. 'Of course. It's Caroline Blackman. She's from London. She took on the job in the parochial house to get near Tom Moran and his family. She would — '

Connolly interrupted. 'If we're correct, then I think we need to establish straight away that Yvonne is OK. I have information to suggest she is being watched by the person we now think is Nelly Joyce's son.'

'You don't think he would go after...?' Thelma began to ask.

'I think it's important to check out her house in Rathmines,' Connolly said, already making a move to leave the house.

'What about Tom Moran?' Emma asked. 'If he was the intended victim of the crash, won't they try to get him again?'

'Yes, you could be right, Emma. If what we've surmised is correct, then Moran is still the main enemy in both their minds. I'll call hospital security, make sure they keep an eye on him until I get someone there.'

'And Brenda Moran,' Thelma added, 'she could be in danger, too.'

'I'll talk to her,' Connolly said.

'And I'll call at Yvonne's house in Rathmines,' Emma offered. 'I can pass that way on my way back to the apartment. I'll phone as soon as I get there, let you know if everything is all right.'

'Good,' Connolly said, 'but just to be on the safe side, I'll give the uniforms in Rathmines the address, have them check it out. Can't be too careful. There's been enough killing already.'

Brenda Moran felt tired after her trek to the hospital and back; tired but buoyed up by the substantial progress Tom had made. His voice had practically returned. It was little more than a whisper and he still had difficulty stringing words together but it was progress. The few words he had said, however, frightened her. He had held her hand, asked where Olive was. She had lied; told him Olive was on a special course in Belfast. He hadn't believed her. 'She's dead, isn't she?' he'd asked. She lied again. He would have to be told the truth eventually but she would put it off for as long as she could. She'd wait until he was stronger before confirming his worse fears.

Saying goodbye to him, he had become agitated. He took her two hands in his, surprising her with the pressure he asserted. 'Nelly Joyce killed Olive,' he said. 'She wants to kill us all… for what… what I did.'

'Don't be silly, Tom. Nelly Joyce is dead, you told me so yourself.'

'No, no, no, she'll never be dead… as long as…' That was all he said. There were tears running down his face, but no further words were spoken. She wiped the tears from his cheeks and kissed him goodbye.

And now, sitting in her own kitchen, she thought about his comments. She already knew about Nelly Joyce. Five years ago, when Caroline Blackman came to work in the parochial house, Tom told her about his past. Nelly Joyce, he informed her, was a young woman who had blighted his life. She was a teacher in the school where he worked. She had seduced him. He was young at the time, but even so he had tried to discourage her advances. Under the influence of alcohol he had allowed himself to be inveigled back to her flat. Once there she had behaved shamelessly and taken advantage of him.

According to Tom's story, Nelly Joyce tricked him into believing she was pregnant by him. He had agreed to stand by her; do the decent thing and marry her. But then he discovered she had been running around with several other men. When he confronted her with this, she fled to England, had her baby there and never returned home.

Brenda sighed. Dredging up details from the past was always painful but the images, once invoked, would not go away. She remembered her engagement to Tom, her wedding, her honeymoon and her homecoming to their first house. It had all been so blissfully happy. And then, three months into her pregnancy with Olive, Tom had been mugged. His injuries were serious enough to have him hospitalised for three days. At the time she knew nothing whatsoever about Nelly Joyce and presumed his attackers were hooligans who had randomly picked on him. He had always been a bit vague as to exactly what had happened.

Five years ago, after the appearance of Caroline Blackman had spooked him into telling her about his misadventure with Nelly Joyce, she remembered the mugging incident from that period of his life. She mentioned it to him at the time but he refused to discuss the subject or disclose who his attackers were. It had crossed her mind that perhaps Nelly Joyce had been the instigator behind the episode. Whether she was or was not, the unfortunate incident had lasting consequences; Tom had never been the same man after it happened.

Tom admitted to her that he had been badly shaken by Caroline Blackman's appearance. At first he thought he was seeing a ghost. According to him, Caroline resembled Nelly Joyce to an astonishing degree. He never mentioned anything to Caroline in this regard and Caroline never said anything to him. His initial fear that Caroline had come to Lonsdale to seek revenge on him gradually lessened as the weeks, months and years passed.

The story he told shocked her. She had been annoyed that he had kept such a secret from her for so many years. She demanded to know what other secrets he had kept hidden from her. He reacted badly, acted as though he were the injured party. They said unpleasant things to each other. In the end, though, she believed he had been the victim in the affair and forgave him.

And now, thinking about Tom's behaviour in the hospital, she realised that his fears in regard to the identity of Caroline Blackman were justified. The idea that Tom might have been economical with the truth in regard to events from that dark period in his life began to take shape in her mind.

The chimes from her front door gave her a start. Instinctively, she knew who the caller was.

She was right.

Caroline Blackman stood outside the door and asked if she could come in.

Chapter 40

It was 6.45pm by the time Alec Cobain got away from his desk, away from his demon terminal, the mouse and his overworked keyboard. It had been a volatile day on the world's monetary markets and, like the other traders in the Financial Centre, he had experienced something of a roller-coaster ride. His trading, though prolific, hadn't gained any extra revenue for his employers, but more importantly, his efforts ensured that no losses were incurred either. All in all, a frustrating day with nothing to show for his endeavours, a day he was glad to see the back of.

Striding towards his car, he called Yvonne on his mobile.

No reply.

Probably in the shower, he supposed, a smile breaking through on his face. She was, he had no doubt, in the throes of putting on the style. They had arranged to dine out with a few friends in one of the city's trendy Temple Bar restaurants later that evening. He knew what that meant: Yvonne would try on at least a dozen outfits. She would parade them, one by one, in front of the mirror – twirls and over-the-shoulder glances included – before satisfying herself that she had made the right choice. As soon as he got in from work she would seek his opinion. Always a tricky moment, that. He would be required to second-guess which ensemble she'd already settled for. Failure to choose correctly meant a continuance of the exercise until he got it right.

Evening traffic slowed to a crawl as he headed out from the city centre along the Grand Canal Way. It was 7.05pm by the time he turned off the Canal Road and entered Lower Rathmines Road. Since returning from the honeymoon, this was the place he called home. The house Yvonne and he had bought in Grove Park had been built back in the early 1950s and had at one stage been cannibalised and converted into flats. Its condition was deplorable when he made the purchase but he'd got it at a knock-down price. He redesigned its interior, refurbished it in contemporary style and turned it into something special. Even Yvonne, who had been pessimistic at first, had fallen in love with the house.

As he turned into Grove Park he saw Emma Boylan standing at his front door. He found a parking spot further down the street, and hurried back to her. 'Hello, Ms Boylan, what brings you here?'

'I'm glad to see you. Please, call me Emma,' she said, shaking his hand. 'There's been some developments and I just called to see that everything was all right with yourself and Yvonne.'

He stared at her, puzzlement in his eyes. 'She didn't answer the door?'

'Well, I've only got here this minute. I was about to ring the bell when I saw you coming along the street.'

'Well, you'd better come in,' he said putting his key in the door and pushing it open. 'We're going out tonight so Yvonne's probably busy sorting out her glad rags.'

Emma stood in the hallway while he shouted up the stairs.

'Yvonne, I'm home. We've got a visitor.'

No answer.

He pushed his way into the kitchen. 'Hi darling, I'm home.'

She wasn't there.

'Hold on a sec, Emma, I'll pop upstairs. She's probably having a bath. Make yourself at home. Plug in the kettle.'

Emma listened to him pound up the stairs, heard him call out his wife's name again. She was looking for the kettle when she heard his first scream, a terrifying high keening wail. She darted into the hallway and climbed the stairs two steps at a time, following sounds that led her to the master bedroom. The door to the en suite bathroom remained open. She could see Alec kneeling by the side of the bath, his back to her, his arms stretching ahead of him.

'Nooooooo!' he moaned. 'Noooooo.'

Emma moved behind him.

Now, she screamed.

In the bathtub, Yvonne Cobain's body, naked and streaked with blood, sat with her neck wedged between the hot and cold taps. One eye, still open, vacant, stared out in her direction, the other one swollen shut. Dried blood had caked beneath her nose and remained lodged at the corners of her mouth. The smell of death, unlike any other, clawed at her senses, a clammy pall, suffocating in its intensity. Blood splashes were smeared on the shower unit's glass panels. Blurred impressions of hands and sprayed fingers created overlapping bloodied patterns on the bathroom tiles, an indication of the desperate struggle for life Yvonne had waged against her attacker. Every inch of the room proclaimed the vicious conflict that had taken place. The toilet bowl, the wash-hand basin, the floor and the sides of the bath, all had been drenched red with blood.

Emma crouched to her knees beside Alec. She jammed the knuckles of her fist into her mouth to stifle the scream. Somewhere outside this crimson hell, a bell was ringing. It sounded like a door bell, insistently ringing and ringing and ringing. She ignored it, stunned into inaction by the vision confronting her. She had come face to face with death before in her line of work and believed her experience in reporting man's inhumanity to man had hardened her to the task. She was wrong. Nothing could have prepared her for this. It was horrible, too horrible.

Alec reached over to touch the lifeless face of his dead wife, his fingers pushing wet strands of hair back from the bruising and swelling that distorted her features, muttering the word '*no*' over and over again. The sound of the downstairs door being forced open barely registered with Emma. Her stomach constricted, her brain having difficulty accepting the grim reality in front of her.

Through sobs, she heard the sound of feet pounding up the stairs. Two uniformed officers entered the room. Alec, oblivious to their arrival, asked Emma to help him take his wife out of the bath. Emma was about to help but stopped suddenly. 'I'm so sorry, Alec, but the law has arrived. We'd better let them take charge of things...'

The two officers, both young men, pushed up to the bath. One of them, his face a combination of wonder and fear, backed out of the room, desperately trying not to retch. His companion stood gaping into the bath, all signs of blood drained from his face. 'Oh, sweet Jesus Christ,' he muttered, 'what the hell's happened here?'

'Help me, please,' Alec said, 'we've got to get her out of there.'

'I'm sorry, Sir,' the officer said, his voice shaking, 'we can't touch her. We've got to call the serious crime squad and forensic first. We can't touch anything until they arrive. I'll call Detective Inspector Connolly back, tell him what we've found.'

'No, I don't want anyone to see Yvonne like this. We have to—'

'I'm sorry, Sir, I know this is awful for you... and the lady with you, but you mustn't disturb the scene, you have to—'

'Damn you,' Alec shouted, pushing him to one side, 'that's my wife... *my wife*, d'you hear. I don't want the world to see her... not like this. Christ, not like this.' He stopped, turned his head away and began to cry. Emma put her arms around him, trying her best to comfort him. 'Come downstairs with me, Alec; we'll organise what has to be done from there.'

Alec Cobain stood without moving for several seconds before allowing himself to be ushered down the stairs. His eyes refused to let go of the image of Yvonne's butchered stomach. A long brutal gash extended from belly to ribs, exposing an aperture of dark crimson gore, intertwined with blue-veined intestines that pushed against the fingers of his wife's stilled hand, a hand that had, in those final moments of life, attempted to stall the extrusion. He could not blind himself to the horror that must have been evident to Yvonne in those last agonising seconds before death's merciful oblivion. Neither could he blind himself to the words written in blood on the inside of the bath's side panel:

END OF THE LINE.

Assuming there was nobody home, Connolly turned to walk away from Brenda Moran's door. Ringing the bell and banging on the knocker had failed to elicit a response. He was about to get into his car when he heard the sound of breaking glass. He swung about to where the sound came from and saw an object hit the ground outside the window of the house. He darted back to take a closer look. The remains of a jug lay among a pile of glass fragments. A jagged hole in the window pane suggested that someone from inside the house had thrown the jug. He put his face up to the broken window, held his hands above his eyes to cut out the reflected glare, and peered into the interior of the front room.

Everything looked peaceful. There was nobody there. He was about to try the door again when he saw a movement. From behind a couch he could see an arm moving. The limb was rising and falling, hitting the carpet. Squinting his eyes to see more clearly, he noticed the red stains on the arm. Whoever owned the arm was bleeding, and bleeding badly at that.

Connolly moved to the door, pushed at it with his full weight. It shot open after two heaves. He ran to the sitting room. Brenda Moran lay on the carpet behind the couch. Her eyes, wide open and terrified, stared up at him. 'Thank God,' she cried, 'oh, thank God.'

Connolly got down beside her. 'Mrs Moran, what happened?'

'Tried to kill me. She tried to kill me.'

'Who? Who tried to kill you?'

'Caroline Blackman came here… wanted to kill me.'

'How badly are you injured?'

'My leg is bleeding, my ankle is badly sprained.'

Connolly looked at the bloody cuts. They were deep gashes, ugly, and in need of immediate attention. He helped her off the floor and eased her into the couch. 'I'll ring for an ambulance,' he told her. 'Lucky I came by.'

'I know. I was out cold… don't know how long… the sound of the door bell must have brought me round. I was still in the pottery studio. I panicked. I knew I had to get to the door, get help, was afraid that whoever was there would go away and leave me. I gathered what little strength I'd left, forced myself to make it towards the door… legs went from under me on the spot where you found me, couldn't move another inch. Then I saw a jug that had fallen to the floor earlier.'

'Good thinking,' Connolly said, already dialling for help on his mobile. After he had contacted the emergency services, he asked Brenda where he could get some material to wrap around her leg. She gave him directions to the linen cupboard and allowed him to put temporary bandages over the deepest cuts. Throughout this ordeal he attempted to establish what had happened and how she managed to escape with her life.

'I let her in,' she told Connolly. 'I shouldn't have but I did. You see, Tom tried to warn me earlier. I wasn't surprised when she turned up.'

'What did she say... what did she do... where is she now?'

'I'll tell you all, detective, just give me a chance to catch my breath.'

'Sure, take you're time, no hurry.'

'Thanks. Well, first off, she told me *my* husband was her father. She told me a long, rambling tale about how Tom had mistreated her mother. I told her I didn't believe her. I said I knew from Tom all about Nelly Joyce, the trollop she called her mother. She got really mad and opened a small case she had with her. It was filled to the top with old copybooks. She began reading passages from the pages; said they were her mother's diaries. It was awful stuff. I shouted at her to stop and she became hysterical, hit me across the face. I was too shocked to hit back. She told me that she and her brother were going to destroy all fruits of Tom's loins.'

'Did she say who this brother was? Had she a name for him?'

'A name? Let me see, yeah. I think so, can't remember... Irish name; same as that Australian pop singer... what's her name?'

'Pop singer? Australian? Olivia Newton-John? Kylie Minogue?'

'Minogue, yeah, that's the one; that's her brother's name. James Minogue. She said her and her brother killed my Olive and were about to do the same to Yvonne Cobain. She claimed that Yvonne was Tom's child. She produced a knife, said she was going to kill me. I was paralysed with fear. Only at the last minute did my survival instincts kick in. It was when she told me that the two of them planned to meet in St Michael's Hospital to kill Tom. She said they wanted to look him in the eye when they did it. They would tell him first about the others who had died because of him and then they would cut his heart out. I snapped, attacked her.

'She wasn't expecting any fight from me so I managed to floor her. She recovered within seconds and came at me with the knife. I threw everything I could lay my hands on and ran. I ran into my pottery studio. She followed. We had a battle royal but she was too strong for me. She cut me every time she got near. I was drenched in my own blood, running out of things to throw at her. She pinned me to the floor and was about to drive the knife home when I found one last surge of energy. I wrestled her to the floor. She accidentally hit her head against the edge of a steel shelf, nearly split her head in two.

'I was sure she was dead but she wasn't, she was still alive. She kept moaning, stirring on the ground.

'I didn't know what to do. I was terrified that if she regained full consciousness, she'd kill me. I couldn't think what to do and then I looked around the studio and saw the kiln. I pulled the front open, removed the trays and somehow found the strength to push her inside. I closed the door, secured the clasps and left her there.

'By this stage my thinking was far from rational. I kept remembering Olive and thinking to myself, here is the person who helped kill her. I wanted to pull the lever switch on the power and fire up the kiln, turn her into toast, but I couldn't do it.'

'So, where is she?'

'She's still inside the kiln.'

Connolly made his way to the pottery studio. The place was like a mini-war zone, wreckage strewn everywhere, blood splattered all over the place. He saw the kiln in one corner of the studio. Its door remained locked. Before attempting to open it he made sure the power was turned off. He pulled the clasp that held the door shut. He found Caroline Blackman wedged inside the oven, her head pressed against her knees, blood dripping to the base of the oven.

She was dead.

Connolly called headquarters on his mobile. He told them what had happened, advised them to come and secure the place as soon as possible and have the appropriate personnel get to the scene. He had finished his series of calls and was making his way back to Brenda Moran when he heard the ambulance pull up outside her door. He directed the medical crew to where Brenda sat and watched as they dispatched her to the back of the ambulance.

He would have to stay until help arrived to secure the scene. Sergeant Gavin Duff from Rathmines station called his mobile number just as he was about to return to the pottery studio. Connolly listened, grave-faced, as the sergeant told him about the grim discovery in Grove Park. He sunk slowly down into the couch where Brenda had sat some minutes earlier, as though in a daze, hearing the grizzly details of what had happened. When Duff finished, Connolly called headquarters again. 'There's a second dead body to contend with,' he told them, scarcely believing the news himself.

Chapter 41

Over breakfast, Emma recounted most of what had happened the previous evening for Vinny's benefit. She hadn't come home to the apartment until after midnight but she had contacted him twice during the course of the evening to let him know about the tragic events that led to the deaths of Caroline Blackman and Yvonne Cobain.

Now she gave him a more comprehensive account.

She had remained in Grove Park with Alec Cobain until help arrived. The house had been sealed off to allow the forensic crew to secure the crime scene. Connolly could not be present because of the tragic developments that had taken place in Brenda Moran's house. He had put Detective Sergeant Gogan in charge of the Grove Park investigation until such time as he could get there himself. As far as Emma could tell, Gogan had done an efficient job.

She had waited in the Cobain household until George and Thelma Duggan arrived. Straight away she had taken them into the front sitting room where their son-in-law Alec sat, head in hands, inconsolable. Emma watched as they clung to each other, merged in unified grief, all three heaving bodily sighs, unable to come to grips with the enormity of what had happened. Feeling wretched herself, and excluded from the comforting loop of shared sorrow, Emma choked back the sighs struggling to escape from her constricted throat.

Gogan had asked her to help get George and Thelma Duggan away from the house without letting them see the horror inflicted on their daughter. Alec, with the grisly image of his wife's desecrated body so fresh in his mind, agreed with the detective. He wanted to spare his parents-in-law the sort of pain he was struggling to endure. He helped Emma persuade them to leave. The entreaties had worked up to a point, but just as the senior

Duggans were leaving, George bolted back inside. He rushed up the stairs, pushing aside those who tried to stop him. The sight of the mutilated body of his daughter brought a strangled scream from his throat. A strike from a sledgehammer could not have had a more startling effect had it struck him in the stomach. He bent in two, crashed to his knees and promptly threw up.

Three minutes later he emerged from the house looking old and spent, his face a greenish hue, his eyes red-rimmed and glazed, his lips trembling. He put his arms around Thelma and Alec. Misty-eyed, Emma watched this tableau of unbearable sorrow, wishing there was some way she could ease their pain. She was glad when Detective Gogan organised a car to take them home.

After that, Emma and Connolly had contacted each other via mobile phone and exchanged their tales of horror. Connolly, efficient as ever, had contacted security in St Michael's Hospital and arranged round-the-clock security for Tom Moran's room. Tom's wife, Brenda, had been taken to a different hospital. Her injuries, caused by Caroline Blackman's vicious attack, though serious, were not life-threatening. She would go to her husband's bedside in St Michael's as soon as she was discharged. The most chilling aspect of what Connolly told her concerned Caroline Blackman's assertion that she and her brother had planned to kill Tom Moran. Connolly had discovered from Brenda that the brother's name was James Minogue. Blackman and Minogue, it transpired, were prepared to cut Moran's heart out as retribution for the suffering he had inflicted on their mother, Nelly Joyce. As justification for this act, Caroline Blackman had shown Brenda some diaries written by Nelly Joyce.

Connolly was now in possession of these diaries. He had only had time to make a cursory examination of the writings but it was enough to give him an insight into all that had happened. What he told Emma was, he insisted, 'off the record'. He promised that, at the appropriate time, he would let her have sight of the diaries ahead of other media sources. There was, however, a condition. He demanded that she hold back the name Caroline Blackman when she filed her report to the *Post*. 'We don't want James Minogue to know his sister is dead. He will be waiting for her to join him in their plan to get to Tom Moran. This will buy us time to track him down.'

Emma had been as good as her word. In her reports, she withheld Caroline Blackman's name from her accounts of the fatal incident in Lonsdale. Her story about the killing in Grove Park was subject to no restraints and had taken up the front page of this morning's edition of the *Post*. An early morning edition had been sent to her apartment.

With breakfast over, Emma headed for St Michael's Hospital. She knew from Connolly that Tom Moran was subjected to strict security but she hoped to have a word with him. She wanted to write a piece that explained his central role in all that had happened. Her readers would want to know how so many deaths could follow on from actions taken by one individual three decades earlier.

St Michael's Hospital, a grey stone building, began life back in 1866 as a result of a severe epidemic of cholera in Dublin. It had, over a long period, developed and expanded to three times the size of its original structure. Situated on the western side of Dublin city, past the Strawberry Beds, overlooking the River Liffey, it was held in special affection by the capital's citizens.

Emma noted the heightened security in evidence as soon as she got to the barrier at the entrance gate. A security officer took her name, recorded her car's registration number, and enquired as to the nature of her business. The exercise was repeated in the front lobby of the hospital. After checking her credentials, a receptionist made a call to the ward where Tom Moran's private room was located. Several minutes later, the receptionist gave Emma a name badge and instructions on how to get there.

A uniformed guard sat outside the door of Tom Moran's room. He stood up as soon as Emma approached. 'Ms Boylan?' he said, eyeing her name tag.

'Yes, I'm here to see Tom Moran; may I go in?'

'Well, yes Ms Boylan, but you're going to have to wait.'

'Why do you mean?'

'Mr Moran is not in his room right now.'

'What? But...?'

'Relax, Ms Boylan, no need for alarm. He's been taken to the medical training unit here in the complex. There's a bunch of student doctors having a gawk at him... they do it with most of the patients on convalescence. He'll be back in twenty minutes. There's a guard with him as well as a nurse from the hospital. Everything's in order. He won't be out of our sight even for a second.'

'So what are you doing here? Shouldn't you be with him too?'

'I'm following orders, Ms Boylan. One of us has to be with him at all times and one of us has to check anyone who enters or leaves his room. That's what I'm doing.'

'Yes, I suppose that make's sense,' Emma conceded, less than satisfied with proceedings. 'Where is the medical training-unit section?'

'They'll give you directions at reception.'

'Can't you tell me? It's in this building, yes?'

'Well, no, it's not in this building exactly.'

'What? Where the hell is it?'

The young guard's face flushed. 'It's in the new training wing beside the nurses' quarters. Mr Moran was taken there in the ambulance. Oh, Christ, you don't think...?'

'I think we'd better get there quickly. You say a guard went with him and a nurse... a male nurse was it?'

'No, it was a female.'

'Good. And the guard? You know him?'

'Yeah, we qualified together. Danny Fitzgerald; know him well.'

'OK. Sounds all right. Still, I'd better double-check. I'll get reception to contact the training unit, make sure that Tom Moran is in safe hands.'

Emma hurried back to the reception area. She was about to seek information when she spotted Connolly pushing his way through the entrance doors. She told him straight away of her discoveries. His concern was immediate. He glanced around the reception area, spotted a young man in a slate-grey uniform talking to an elderly woman. An embossed emblem on the shoulder of the uniform had the words *DOVE SECURITY* highlighted in red lettering. Three long strides took Connolly to the man's side. The guard glanced at Connolly from behind pale-tinted spectacles, saw the expression on his face, and cut short his discussion with the woman. 'I'm Des Dillon, Security Officer,' he said, the smile on his handsome face as false as his tan. 'How may I help you, Sir?'

'I'm Detective Inspector Connolly. I'm enquiring about a patient, Tom Moran, who has been taken by ambulance to the medical training unit.'

'Yes, that's right, Detective Inspector. I personally escorted that patient to the ambulance about five... maybe ten minutes ago. We were told to keep a special eye on him and that's exactly what I did.'

'Would you check with the medical training unit for me,' Connolly asked, 'and confirm that Tom Moran got there?'

'Of course he got there,' Dillon said, an edge of annoyance creeping into his voice. 'Where else would he go?'

'Just check for me, would you. Quickly!'

Dillon resented Connolly's brusque manner and was about to say so, but the expression on the detective's face dissuaded him. Without protest, he contacted the training unit on his radio phone.

Seconds passed by in silence.

Dillon's eyebrows shot upward. 'What do you mean, they're not expecting him there?'

'What's the matter?' Connolly asked.

Dillon looked blankly at the detective. 'Tom Moran's not there.'

'So, where *is* he?'

'They don't know.'

'What? What do you mean, they—'

'They made no arrangements to have Tom Moran brought there.'

'Damn it,' Connolly swore. 'Quickly, check the hospital gates; find out if any ambulances have left in the last five minutes.'

A call to the gates established that no ambulances had left in that time span. 'Tell them to examine all outgoing ambulances,' Connolly instructed Dillon, 'and get them to make sure Tom Moran is not taken from the hospital grounds.'

Emma, fearing the worst, hurried towards the exit doors. 'I'm going to go to the training unit; see if the ambulance went there.'

'Fine, Emma,' Connolly said, 'but don't forget we're in a hospital complex; there's quite a few ambulances out there.' He turned to Dillon again. 'Can you get me the registration number of the ambulance that took Tom Moran?'

'Yes, sure. I have a list with me.' He opened a little notebook and read out the pertinent information.

Armed with the registration number. Connolly instructed Dillon to call for back-up. He hurried after Emma towards the central courtyard. Emma pointed to an arch that dissected the building's quadrangle layout. 'Look, there's the sign pointing to the training unit,' she shouted back to Connolly. 'We'll get there quicker on foot if we cut through the buildings.'

Nurses and other hospital personnel using the footpaths were startled to see Emma and Connolly dashing past them. Emma caught the enquiring glances coming her way but continued to run as fast as her legs would carry her. Connolly matched her stride for stride but his breath was sounding more laboured than hers. 'He's here,' Emma shouted, pointing to a building with a sign that said Training Unit. 'Look, his ambulance, outside the door.'

As she got closer, it was obvious that the registration number was not the one they were looking for. Connolly went to the back of the vehicle and opened the doors. It was empty. 'Had to check,' he said to Emma, a little out of breath.

Emma glanced nervously around the grounds. 'An ambulance can't disappear,' she said to Connolly. 'It's got to be here somewhere.'

'Where do you hide an ambulance?' Connolly asked.

'You hide it among other ambulances,' Emma said. 'There must be a parking bay somewhere on the complex.'

Connolly was considering this when Dillon came running towards them. The security guard explained that the papers giving permission to move Moran had been falsified. 'I've called for back-up and instructed security at the gates to detain all ambulances leaving the hospital. Is there anything else you'd like me to do?'

'Is there a place where the ambulances park when they're not on duty?'

'Yes, there's a refuelling depot and ambulance bay over behind the chapel and mortuary area.'

'Take us there,' Connolly ordered.'

'Sure, no sweat,' Dillon replied, pointing to a division between two tall buildings. 'It's just across this way.'

Emma and Connolly followed the security guard to a small courtyard with large oil tanks and several ambulances. Emma and Connolly scanned the registration numbers as they approached the area. None of the licence plates matched what they were looking for. Two of the stationary ambulances were parked broadside, their front and rear plates not visible from their vantage point. While closing in on the two vehicles to inspect the numbers, the back doors of one of them opened. A man wearing paramedical gear leaped from the ambulance and ran to the driver's door.

'It's him,' Emma shouted, 'it's James Minogue.'

'Damn it, he's spotted us,' Connolly cursed, racing towards the ambulance. He was about to pull the cab door open when the vehicle reversed swiftly, knocking him to the ground. Emma leaped out of the way just in time to save herself from a similar fate. With its engine roaring loudly, the ambulance backed away from them in an erratic arc before spinning its wheels and speeding away from them. A uniformed body lay on the ground behind where the vehicle had been. Connolly and Emma, shaken by events, moved to where the body lay. The guard was alive, moaning, feeling his head. 'What the hell happened?' they heard him ask.

'He's OK,' Connolly said before turning to Dillon, who seemed to have paled in the past few minutes. 'Get him some help.'

Emma heard a nearby ambulance engine start up. 'We can follow him,' she shouted to Connolly. 'We'll get him when he's stopped at the gate barrier.'

A mechanic sat in the driver's seat of the ambulance, gunning the engine, as Emma and Connolly approached. 'We want you to follow the ambulance that's just pulled out of here,' Connolly said.

'Sorry, no can do,' the man said belligerently. 'I'm a mechanic, not a bleedin' driver.'

Connolly forcibly pulled the mechanic from the seat and pushed him out of the way. 'Sorry about this,' the detective said. 'I've no time to explain but right now I'm commandeering this vehicle.' Connolly, ignoring the man's protestations, jumped into the ambulance and took his place behind the wheel. Emma got in on the passenger side. 'Hope you can drive this thing,' she said, listening to the engine scream in protest at his efforts to operate the gear stick. The vehicle bolted forward, stalled, shot forward again, gaining momentum in uneven jerking motions. Emma's head bobbed up and down involuntarily, like one of those spring-necked dogs you see in the back windows of cars. Connolly cursed but he appeared to be getting the hang of the thing, managing, with great difficulty, to crash and grind his way through the gears. 'Come on,' he screamed through clenched teeth, as the vehicle reluctantly responded to his efforts and grudgingly moved into top speed.

In the rear-view mirror Emma saw the mechanic wave his fists in the air, his mouth open in rage. Ahead, a winding perimeter road around the hospital complex led to the exit gates. They had raced on to a straight section of roadway on the approach to the gates when they caught sight of the fleeing ambulance ahead of them.

'We've got the bastard,' Connolly shouted. 'Let's just hope Tom Moran is still alive in the back.'

'There's a nurse with him,' Emma said. 'I hope she's OK.'

'Oh, shit!' Emma said, looking towards the gates. 'He's not slowing down, he's going to crash the barrier.'

They watched the ambulance plough through the barrier at top speed. The barrier splintered like so much matchwood, not impeding the ambulance in any way.

'What the hell do we do now?' Emma asked.

'We follow,' Connolly said, pressing down heavily on the accelerator pedal.

Chapter 42

For the most part, Dublin city and its immediate hinterland consisted of flat terrain, with few steep hills or valleys of consequence. An exception to the gently undulating landscape can be found on the western extremities of the city. The area stretches from Lucan's lower road and runs alongside the River Liffey, past a location known as the Strawberry Beds, before rising high to Knockmaroon Hill and then falling steeply into Martin's Row. The picturesque stretch, no more than five miles in length, ends when it connects with the Chapelizod Road junction.

It was this route, heading south towards the city centre, that James Minogue drove the ambulance he had stolen from St Michael's Hospital. Tom Moran and a dazed nurse remained trapped in the back of the vehicle. Minogue had little thought for their safety except that, in Moran's case, he would prefer that the patient remain alive so as not to deny him the pleasure of looking into his eyes when he killed him.

Right now, his priority was to get away from his pursuers – Connolly and the reporter.

Emma watched the ambulance ahead of her increase its speed to reckless proportions as it hurtled along the narrow roads, forcing other traffic to scramble out of the way. Sitting next to her, Connolly struggle to keep pace with Minogue, beads of sweat on his brow, a look of wild determination in his eyes. Both ambulances used their sirens, blaring full blast, to warn road users to move out of the way.

Climbing to the crest of Knockmaroon Hill, where the Phoenix Park's westernmost gate exit is located, James Minogue ignored the traffic signal ahead of him. The lights were on red. Motorists coming from the Park and the Mount Sackville Road junction, aware of the screaming sirens, attempted to pull to one side. Minogue made no effort to slow down. He clipped the side of a Ford Ka, sending it into a tailspin. He continued on his way, unabated. Connolly, seeing there was no serious injury, followed through. Passengers in the stalled cars stared in amazement as the two speeding ambulances ploughed through their midst.

Moving at full throttle down the steep, winding Knockmaroon road, Minogue grazed his vehicle off the side of a wall, where an overhead enclosed walkway stretches above the thoroughfare. He refused to apply the brakes. Connolly missed the same wall by a hair's-breadth. 'He's going to crash if he keeps this up,' Connolly shouted to Emma. 'This sort of speed is crazy.' As he spoke, two squad cars approached at speed from behind them. Connolly allowed them to pass. With their sirens wailing and blue strobes flashing, they were soon hanging on to the rear of Minogue's ambulance.

Martin's Row, a residential enclave sitting at the base of the hill, had a series of ramps constructed on the road to calm descending traffic. Minogue ignored the ramps. His ambulance hit the incline, bounced into the air, swerved wildly but somehow remained on course. He continued on his erratic way without let-up. 'Minogue's not going to allow anyone overtake him,' Emma said, watched the squad cars bob up and down over the ramps in a manner that would have been comical were the situation not so serious.

The chase came to an abrupt end at the junction of Martin's Row and Chapelizod Road, beside a pub named The Mullingar House. The sound of sirens brought the traffic on the busy inter-section to a halt, but a double-decker bus, unable to shift out of the way because of a congested tail-back, became the buffer that stopped Minogue's run.

His ambulance rammed the bus broadside.

Metal impacted on metal. The bus buckled and shifted with the force of the collision, its screaming passengers terrified. They were thrown about like ping-pong balls. James Minogue was catapulted through the windscreen of his ambulance. Jagged pieces of glass lacerated his face and body. He ended up wedged precariously, halfway between the two vehicles, his bloodied face hovering above the scattered passengers on the lower deck of the bus.

Emma and Connolly jumped from their ambulance and raced to the scene. Officers from the squad cars did likewise. Sirens continued to blare. Motorists got out of their stalled cars and stared open-mouthed at the two embedded vehicles. Screams came from inside the bus. The smell of spilt fuel was heavy on the air. 'Let's hope this doesn't go up in flames,' Connolly shouted to Emma.

'You check out Minogue,' Emma shouted back, 'I'll see how Tom Moran has fared. Uniformed officers attempted to stop Emma but Connolly flashed his badge and informed them she was with him. Emma approached the back of the ambulance and pulled open the doors. A uniformed nurse, on her knees, held her arms across the body of Tom Moran, her hands gripped tightly on the steel-frame bars of his stretcher. 'Thank God,' the nurse said, in a fear-filled voice, when she saw Emma. 'I couldn't have held on much longer.'

'Help will be here any minute,' Emma said, releasing the woman's clenched fingers from the steel frames. She could now see Tom Moran. His eyes appeared to flicker behind eyelids that were partially opened, his breathing irregular, coming in short little spasms. Emma returned her gaze to the nurse. 'You saved his life,' she said to the nurse, who had now slid to the floor of the ambulance in a state of exhaustion. 'What happened to our driver?' the nurse asked, groggily. 'He was hit on the head... back at the hospital.'

'He's being looked after,' Emma said, 'he'll be all right. What happened to you?'

'I got knocked out... a belt on the head. I remember nothing after that until the shaking woke me up. We were travelling at such speed, being thrown all over the place. It was terrible... the patient... his head-brace loosened, the spinal board shifted and I thought... I thought he was going to slip off... get himself killed. I managed to hold him there. I had no idea what was happening... I just held on for dear life.'

'You did well,' Emma said. 'I'm going to leave you now for a moment; get some assistance.'

The nurse tried to smile her thanks, unable to find the energy to utter another word. Before getting out of the ambulance,

Emma looked into the face of Tom Moran. His head, held between two polyfoam blocks, looked death-like, the eyes blinking. 'You, my friend,' she said to him, 'have caused a lot of people a great deal of grief.'

Tom Moran's eyelids flicked fully open. His hand reached out and clasped Emma's. She jumped with fright. He appeared to look directly into her eyes. 'I know... I know,' he said, and then let go of her hand and closed his eyes again.

Emma hadn't expected Moran to communicate with her, especially under such conditions, and was still recovering from the shock when Connolly arrived by her side. He looked at the nurse on the floor, at Tom Moran and then at Emma. She told him what the nurse had said and asked him to get some assistance quickly.

'Help is on its way... should be here any second,' Connolly said.

'What about Minogue... is he...?'

'Dead? No, he's not dead. He's in bad shape but he'll make it. Miracle no one got killed.'

Emma looked at Tom Moran and the nurse. 'Yes, it's a miracle.'

'Come on,' Connolly said, taking her by the arm, 'let's get out of here. I hear the other ambulances arriving.'

Extract from the diary of Nelly Joyce – aged 23
18th April 1975. Hammersmith London.

Dear Diary

Got a letter from Ireland today. Maura wrote me one of her newsy letters.

She's still living in the same flat in Johnstown. She asks all about Ann-Marie and Séan. Makes me cry. I miss my two babies so much.

But I believe in the goodness of God and pray that bitterness will not destroy my soul.

Maura told me about her visit to the school authorities in Johnstown.

She told the manager who the father of my two babies

was. She never forgave Cherry Picker for the day he met me in her flat, the day he told me he was getting engaged to a respectable woman.

The school manager forced Cherry Picker to give up his teaching post. He got him a job as a church sacristan in another parish, on condition that he kept quiet about his indiscretion and avoided all scandal.

Maura could not discover which parish Cherry Picker had gone to.

She went to the school manager a second time and asked to have my name removed from the blacklist. She threatened to talk to the media if he refused.

He agreed on condition that I delay 12 months before returning to Ireland. Maura accepted the terms on my behalf.

I'm already planning my return.

I pray to God that someday my two babies might look for me.

I would die happy if I could just have one look at both of them.

I ask God each night to look after them and protect them from all harm.

I hope they both enjoy better fortune in life than has been my lot.

Must write to Maura and thank her. She is such a good friend.

Goodnight Diary.

Chapter 43

It was the first time Connolly had ever set foot inside Emma's work cubicle at the *Post*. He had brought the Nelly Joyce diaries with him, as promised. As a favour to Emma, he allowed her to look at the battered volumes on the strict understanding that none of their contents would appear in print until he gave her the all clear. He had drawn her attention to several entries which helped clarify the strange relationship that existed between the diary's author, Nelly Joyce, her unfaithful lover, Tom Moran, and their two luckless offspring. Emma was saddened by what she read but she couldn't help notice that Connolly, who should have been pleased at having resolved the case, seemed burdened by a sadness that appeared to have little to do with the diaries.

'Jim, I don't mean to pry but I can't help noticing that something's bothering you... never seen you so glum. What's the matter?'

'Oh, it's nothing, Emma; at least nothing to do with this case.'

'Tell me about it. We've been through so much together, through thick and thin, as they say. You can talk to me. Maybe I can help.'

'Thanks, Emma, but I'm not sure anyone can help.'

'Try me.'

'Well, the truth is, myself and Iseult... we've split up. Things haven't been too good lately. She's seeking a divorce.'

'Oh, I'm sorry... that's awful, I'd no idea that you and—'

'No, of course not, you wouldn't. And I shouldn't really be talking... I normally don't but, well, this has taken the wind out of my sails. Two nights ago, I found myself locked out of my house. Iseult's had the locks changed, won't let me back until things are sorted out.'

Struggling to find words of comfort, Emma was glad when Bob Crosby appeared at the doorless opening to her cubicle.

'Quite a week,' he said, addressing both of them as he came into the work space and took a seat beside Emma.

'You got that right,' Connolly said, giving Emma a knowing look.

Emma returned the look before addressing Crosby. 'Yes, Bob, and it's not over yet. There are still five people, including James Minogue, in hospital. The casualties from the bus will all be discharged within the next day or so but it will be months before Minogue is fit enough to leave hospital.'

'And when he does,' Connolly said, regaining some of his old composure, 'his trial for multiple murder will swing into action.'

'Good,' Crosby beamed, 'that should give the story legs... keep the punters happy. Quite a few aspects of the case remain to be teased out.'

'Such as?' Connolly asked.

'Well, for one thing, we still don't know exactly *why* Fr O'Gorman had to die.'

Emma answered. 'To allow Caroline and her brother space and time to carry out their programme of killing. The death of Fr O'Gorman created a smoke screen that helped them throw people off their trail. But, interestingly, the initial car crash had been intended to kill Tom Moran.'

Crosby's pout let her know he wasn't convinced. 'Are you saying Fr O'Gorman was killed by accident?'

'Not exactly, Bob,' Emma said, defensively. 'I'm sure they knew that Fr O'Gorman could die or be injured in the crash. His death represented a bonus for them. It shifted attention away from their real target. When Moran survived and the parish priest died, they used this outcome to their advantage.'

'The cold-blooded devils.'

'That they were,' Connolly agreed. 'Seems clear to me now that James Minogue paid several visits to Donnie McCann's Arch Bar during this period. He ingratiated himself with a number of regulars there, suggesting at every opportunity that the Duggans were to blame for O'Gorman's death. He also infiltrated the animal-rights activists, again directing their attention towards Fr O'Gorman and the Duggans. Purely diversionary. The intention was to send the investigation in the wrong direction.'

'Well, it succeeded in that objective,' Crosby said, an impish glint in his expression. 'Had you both fooled.'

'True enough,' Connolly admitted.

'And the curate?' Crosby asked. 'Where does he fit into all this?'

'Fr Patterson was nothing more than a "patsy",' Connolly explained, 'Caroline Blackman used him to cloud the issue. I had the devil of a job trying to figure out how the curate's semen had found its way onto Olive Moran's corpse but, after some awkward questioning, I forced Fr Patterson to admit he had indulged in a little self-induced pleasure while alone in his bedroom. The fruits of his labour, he confirmed, were deposited in tissue paper. I figured that Caroline, in the process of cleaning his room, discovered the tissues in his wastebasket.'

Bob Crosby shook his head slowly, as though in wonderment. 'It's hard to credit that one man, this Tom Moran, could be responsible for all the mayhem that's gone down.'

A spark of anger reflected in Connolly's eyes. 'Makes you wonder about the notion of justice and fairness,' he said.

Emma suspected his comment had as much to do with his own marital situation as it had with the case in hand. A heartbeat of silence elapsed before Connolly continued. 'Tom Moran has survived but Nelly Joyce, Olive Moran and Yvonne Cobain, all innocent victims, have paid the ultimate price for his duplicity with their lives. How fair is that?'

'C'est la vie,' Emma said, with a degree of sympathy, 'but then you could also say that Caroline Blackman and James Minogue were victims, too. Their desperate acts were the product of Tom Moran's deceit.'

Crosby got out of the chair. 'Isn't it ironic,' he said, 'that James Minogue should have ended up in the same hospital where his estranged father, Tom Moran, remains a patient?'

'Yes, Bob, life has many cruel twists of fate,' Emma said.

'Amen to that,' Connolly added, failing to hide the edge of bitterness in his voice.

Crosby was about to say something when Emma's telephone rang. It was Vinny. She covered the mouthpiece and waved Connolly and Crosby out of the cubicle before talking to him. 'Hi Vinny, how are things?'

'Have you forgotten?'

'Forgotten what?'

'You were supposed to meet me for lunch. I've been waiting here for ten minutes.'

'I'm on my way, Vinny.'

Also published by The Do-Not Press

FICTION/BRITISH NOIR

Grief
John B Spencer

'GRIEF is a speed-freak's cocktail, one part Leonard and one part Ellroy, that goes right to the head.' George P Pelecanos

Simon likes to think of himself as a hard man and he's not about to stand by and watch his mum get ripped off by a smooth estate agent. Nor is he going to lose the love of his life – even if she happens to be his best mate's woman – without a fight.

The mate, Ollie, is too busy collecting debts and milking muddled old J W Morgan for money to 'dispose of' his ex-wife's new husband (a perverted German surveillance expert called Rolph) to notice.

And Lucy the journalist oscillates between a snide lesbian colleague, her evil junky brother and her married estate agent lover. Who, in turn, is trying to get Simon's mother to sell her house…

When these disparate individuals collide, it's Grief. John B Spencer died in 2002, aged just 57. This is his final and greatest novel.

'Spencer writes the tightest dialogue this side of Elmore Leonard, so bring on the blood, sweat and beers!' Ian Rankin

Casebound
ISBN 1-904316-11-5 £15
C-paperback
ISBN 1-904316-17-4 £7.99
Extent: 256 pages

Also published by The Do-Not Press

FICTION/CRIME & MYSTERY

No One Gets Hurt
Russell James

No One Gets Hurt is a hard-bitten, multi-layered underworld thriller of frightening intensity from 'the best of Britain's darker crime writers' (The Times).

When a young woman is gruesomely murdered, her friend and fellow reporter Kirsty Rice feels bound to investigate. Just as Kirsty enters the murky world of call-girls, porn and Internet sex, she discovers that she is pregnant. Despite his unconvincing denials, Kirsty is shocked to discover that the father of her unborn child is involved with the pornographers.
Did he know about the killing? And how far was he mixed up with London's infamous Miller family?
No One Gets Hurt is a tense and powerful thriller, hurtling from a truly shocking opening to an even more shattering climax.

'One of the UK's finest genre writers' – Booklist
BLOODLINES

Casebound edition
ISBN 1-904316-06-9 £15
B-paperback
ISBN 1-904316-07-7 £6.99
Extent: 402 pages

Also published by The Do-Not Press

LITERATURE

The Indispensable
Julian Rathbone

'Julian Rathbone's characters live; he writes with elegance, with wit and with conviction' Books & Bookmen

At last! The collected work of one of Britain's most successful and accomplished literarists, chosen by the author himself.' The Indispensable...' contains rare essays, shorts stories, reviews and even the complete novel, 'Lying In State'. Julian Rathbone has published over 30 novels in 16 languages, been shortlisted (twice) for the Booker, won a CWA dagger and his thrillers have won prestigious prizes in Germany and Denmark. Reviewers have compared him – to his advantage – with Graham Greene, Eric Ambler, John Updike, Charles Dickens, William Thackeray, John le Carré and William Burroughs. On top of that, he's an accomplished reviewer and essayist, has written successfully filmed screenplays, and much, much more.

'One of the best storytellers around' Daily Telegraph

With an introduction by Mike Phillips

Casebound   JULY
ISBN 1-904316-12-3 £17.99
C-paperback   JULY
ISBN 1-904316-13-1 £9.50
Extent: 468 pages
Rights: World